The Wedding Planners of
BUTTERNUT CREEK

Center Point
Large Print

Also by Jane Myers Perrine and available from Center Point Large Print

The Welcome Committee of Butternut Creek
The Matchmakers of Butternut Creek

**This Large Print Book carries the
Seal of Approval of N.A.V.H.**

The Wedding Planners of
BUTTERNUT CREEK

Jane Myers Perrine

CENTER POINT LARGE PRINT
THORNDIKE, MAINE

This Center Point Large Print edition is published
in the year 2013 by arrangement with FaithWords,
a division of Hachette Book Group, Inc.

This book is a work of fiction. Names,
characters, places, and incidents are the product
of the author's imagination or are used fictitiously.
Any resemblance to actual events, locales,
or persons, living or dead, is coincidental.

The text of this Large Print edition is unabridged.
In other aspects, this book may vary
from the original edition.
Printed in the United States of America
on permanent paper.
Set in 16-point Times New Roman type.

ISBN: 978-1-61173-882-7

Library of Congress Cataloging-in-Publication Data

Perrine, Jane Myers.
  The wedding planners of Butternut Creek / Jane Myers Perrine. —
  Center point large print edition.
  pages ; cm
  ISBN 978-1-61173-882-7 (library binding : alk. paper)
  1. Widows—Fiction. 2. Large type books. I. Title.
  PS3616.E79W43 2013b
  813´.6—dc23
                                                    2013026184

This book, as are all my books, is dedicated to my husband, with whom I spent nearly forty-seven years. Through his faith, intelligence, good humor, and example, he made me a better person.

Thank you, George, for sharing your stories. I love you and miss you more than I can ever say. You are still the joy of my life.

Acknowledgments

Many thanks to Kay Finch, who is always supportive and willing to answer questions. I appreciate input from my writing friends Pat Rosen O'Day, Mae Nunn, Ginni Farmer, Candis Terry, Linda Kearney, and Debbie Swanson as well as my brilliant sister-in-law, Diane Perrine Coon, for her insight and cheerfulness.

Extra treats go to my beloved cats for their willingness to nag me until I take a break to feed/scratch/spoil them. I always return to the keyboard refreshed, covered with black and white fur, and sneezing.

Also, deepest gratitude to Christina Boys, my editor, who makes me feel appreciated and talented, and to my agent, Pam Strickler, who inspired this series. Thanks to both of you for making Butternut Creek a wonderful place to visit and for allowing me to share the joys of small-town Central Texas with readers all over the world.

I also want to thank my teachers: my third-grade teacher at Border Star, who predicted I'd be a writer; those who taught me to be both logical and creative, especially Miss Atwood, my geometry teacher at Southwest High School; the many teachers who taught me to speak and write in both

English and Spanish; the dedicated teachers who sponsor clubs that allow students to try new experiences; and all who trained me in skills that have allowed me to earn a living and contribute to the lives of others at the same time.

Much appreciation goes to Margaret Beeson, my Spanish teacher at Kansas State University, in whose classes I learned to love the beautiful culture of the Spanish-speaking people, and to Frank Neussel at the University of Louisville, who introduced me to La Generación del '98 and the magic of words.

And to Paul Crow and William Barr at Lexington Theological Seminary, who both challenged me and taught me so much about faith.

Prologue

From the desk of
Adam Joseph Jordan, MDiv.

I'm fixin' to make Birdie MacDowell happy. Let me restate this: I hope I'm fixin' to make Miss Birdie happy.

I fell in love with Butternut Creek the first moment I arrived here nearly two years ago. In the center of the town square stands the courthouse, built in the Romanesque style and topped with a tower jutting into the clear blue Texas sky.

In this charming spot in the beautiful Hill Country of Texas, live oak trees trailing Spanish moss surround Victorian houses. Latticed gazebos sit proudly in front yards interspersed with a few pink flamingos. From the minute I entered town, Butternut Creek wrapped its charm around me. I felt truly blessed to be here, certain I'd find peace.

That was, of course, before I met Miss Birdie, a leader of the church forever—which is why I call her the pillar but never to her face. That first day in town, she strode into the parsonage and put me in my place without breaking a sweat.

Miss Birdie reminds me a little of the court-house. That building survived the tornadoes and wildfires that have battered Central Texas over the years and still stands. I've heard about rough times in Miss Birdie's life. Not that she's complained to me, but I know she lost her husband years ago and ended up raising her grand-daughters. Like the courthouse, she stands, bricks intact, proud, and strong.

Of course, she has no tower.

Another comparison: Just as the courthouse is at the center of Butternut Creek, Miss Birdie along with the three other women who call themselves the Widows function as the center of the Christian Church and most of the groups in town that do good works.

Unfortunately, in addition to their charitable tasks, all four of the Widows have chosen me as their major *project.*

Miss Birdie had studied me from head to toe the first time she marched into the parsonage and wondered if she could possibly accept this tall, skinny, young, and very inexperienced man as the minister of her church. With the support of Mercedes Rivera, Winnie Peterson, and Blossom Brown—the other Widows—a non-stop campaign has been waged, the first priority being to whip me into shape. The second, to find me a wife. Not easy in an area where all the young people head to Austin or

Dallas or Houston as soon as they graduate from high school.

The efforts of the Widows have led to mortification on my part and deep embarrassment for a few young women to whom the Widows attempted to marry me off.

As—or if ever—she reads this, pride will fill Miss Birdie at my use of to whom. Her minister's use of proper grammar is important to her. She once wanted to become an English teacher. However, she will shudder because I ended a sentence with off. I have no idea of a better way to write it but making Miss Birdie both proud and unhappy in one sentence feels like a remarkable accomplishment.

After nearly a year of endeavors to find me a wife, the Widows realized how perfect Gussie Milton was for me. One reason for this conclusion is that Gussie really is the perfect woman for me. The other advantage in the eyes of the Widows is that she's the only single woman within sixty miles. The acceptable distance for their search steadily increased the longer I remained single.

Although the Widows have little confidence in my ability to attract a woman without their assistance, Gussie's and my dating life has gone better than they or I had hoped. We aren't engaged, but everything is going well between us and we're quite happy together.

I've written these pages in the unrealistic belief that I have made Miss Birdie happy enough to leave me alone. I have no expectation that will ever happen.

Chapter One

"When are you getting married?" came a voice from the door to Adam Jordan's study in the Christian Church.

He didn't have to look up from his desk to know who spoke, but he did. The pillar expected and deserved that courtesy. "Good morning, Miss Birdie." He stood and smiled at her.

Birdie MacDowell didn't smile back. Because she looked like a complete professional in her pink waitress uniform, he almost expected to see a pencil stuck in her short white hair.

That moment of whimsy swiftly passed when she took several steps inside and headed toward her chair. The other Widows trailed in behind her: Mercedes, her dark gray-streaked hair in a tight French braid looking exactly like the librarian she was; Winnie, the recently married member of the foursome; and Blossom Brown, the newest and only divorced member of the group. All followed the pillar and settled in their places.

In his corner, Chewy, the enormous and curiously assembled dog Adam had taken in when Janey and Hector Firestone came to live in the parsonage, pulled his huge paws in toward his body hoping he'd escape the notice of Miss Birdie. The pillar did not approve of a dog in the church.

None of them returned his smile. Instead, they leaned forward and studied him in that uncomfortable way that made him feel as if they were determined to shove him in a direction he did *not* want to go. No, there was no "as if" about it. Their presence always intimidated him, and with good reason. From the beginning of his pastorate, he had a rule he followed when the Widows marched in: Never show fear.

"When are you getting married?" Winnie repeated.

"Ladies, Gussie and I decided to keep company only six or seven weeks ago. We aren't engaged."

"Not yet," Winnie said in a voice filled with both scorn and disappointment. She'd probably used exactly that tone to prod an unproductive employee back when she ran the asphalt plant.

"Hrrmph," Miss Birdie said. "We thought you'd finally gotten your mojo working . . ."

"I don't think *mojo* is the word you want," Mercedes said.

Miss Birdie silenced her with a glare. "Don't correct me. I know what I want to say. My granddaughters use that word." She turned back toward Adam. "With Gussie and her parents living in town . . ."

Adam held his hand up, a usually completely ineffectual gesture. However, this time, Miss Birdie, starved for information, stopped to listen.

"The Miltons are only renting Sam Peterson's

14

old house. Yvonne and Henry didn't expect to sell their house in Roundville the day it went on the market, right after New Year's," he said. "As soon as they decide where they want to live, they'll move, maybe back to Roundville."

"And Gussie? What about her?" Winnie asked.

"It really did work out for everyone. With the baby coming, Sam and Willow buying their new house, and Sam just starting teaching, the extra income from the rent is a blessing."

"Preacher, we know that. Everyone knows that. The question is, why did Gussie choose to live here?" The pillar jabbed the surface of the desk hard. "There are plenty of houses closer to Roundville. Why did she choose to live in Butternut Creek if you haven't even proposed yet?"

"Ladies," Blossom said in her gentle drawl. "Let's not interrogate the pastor about his private life."

A shush from the other Widows silenced Blossom, who didn't understand that interrogation was their middle name. Their first and last names as well. In her short time as a Widow, Blossom had yet to realize their true mission, or how effective they were at extracting information.

"Gussie's not living with her parents full-time," Adam said to distract the ladies from Blossom's comment.

He didn't utter another word, expecting his

silence to change the subject and focus on other areas in which he'd disappointed them. A foolish decision. Hadn't he learned by now that silence never worked with the Widows? No, they eyed him like cats with a moth. Their glare foretold his eventual doom. He had to either fly off or be devoured. If he—no, that metaphor was falling apart. With an inward sigh, he gave in and furnished the facts they wanted.

"She's staying with a friend in Austin during the week and with her parents in Sam's old house on weekends."

The Widows continued to stare but said nothing. He had no choice but to continue or sit in the silence until Mercedes or Miss Birdie had to get back to work.

"A long-distance courtship doesn't work well, we discovered," he said. "We want to get to know each other." Adam paused to consider how many details would satisfy the Widows without giving away more particulars than necessary.

Evidently he'd met their standard because the four grinned at him, delighted with the information he'd scattered before them.

Their satisfaction didn't last. He knew they'd either revisit the subject or move on to another item on their agenda.

"Blossom is a hand at planning events," Mercedes said.

"She did a lovely job with the spring bazaar and

always entertained for her husband," Winnie added. "Beautifully."

Blossom blushed, then immediately became a Widow focused on the next mission. "We must have the wedding date so I can get started," she said. "We'll have to rent the country club and talk to a florist. So much to do."

"Speaking of the florist," Winnie said, "you don't seem like a man who makes romantic gestures. Women love flowers. If you want a woman to marry you, you need to take action."

For less than a second, Adam considered telling the Widows that he had taken Gussie flowers, but he stopped himself. Giving the Widows additional data had never been a good idea. Instead, he waited for them to continue and watched them closely.

Lord, he loved these women. They did so much for the community and the church. If anyone needed help, they pitched in, usually led the effort. They'd furnished his house and had run the thrift shop from its inception as well as attempting to run or fix or even ruin his life, which they also considered one of their good works. They were meddlesome and terrifying and incredibly nosy, predictable and demanding but also very caring. Sometimes he didn't know whether to laugh or scream or run from them.

He usually chose to laugh. But only inside, because even a smile might insult them. He never ran. They'd find him.

"*If* I propose to Gussie and *if* she accepts, I'll tell you," Adam said. "You will not be the first to know, but I will tell you in plenty of time to plan a wedding. *If* Gussie . . ."

He'd known they wouldn't hear the *if*.

For a moment, as the women nodded and stood, Adam thought he was home free, fool that he was. Should've known better.

Birdie watched Winnie and Mercedes spring to their feet as they prepared to leave while Blossom took care to keep her feet together and lift herself out of the chair with a straight back. Probably learned that lady-like rubbish as a child. Of course, the preacher had stood as well. All four of them on their feet while she struggled to get out of the chair, to push herself up with the good arm. Goodness, her shoulder hurt. She'd worked an extra shift Friday. Her body always paid for days afterward. Made her feet hurt—exactly what she needed, another aching body part—but with Bree and Mac to raise, she could hardly become an invalid. And with those girls needing things for school and athletics and church, she didn't have money for new shoes. Not in the budget. Tonight she had to restart those physical therapy exercises the PT had sent home with her, then she'd elevate her feet. Pretty soon, she'd be good as new.

As she tried to stand, she noticed that the preacher and the other Widows pretended not to notice her struggle. Nice of them but embarrassing. Then her bad shoulder gave out and she plopped right back down in the chair.

To cover that awkward moment, she asked, "Pastor, have you ever proposed to a girl before?" She thought she'd used her sweet, gentle voice, but the way he started and the other Widows turned to look at her, she guessed she hadn't. She smiled. Sadly, she seldom looked jolly when she did.

"Not to a girl," he said.

"Humph." Birdie hadn't thought so.

"To a young woman, yes," he added.

The mouth of each woman dropped open, nearly simultaneously.

"You have proposed before?" Mercedes asked.

"To a woman?" Birdie shook her head. "Ladies"—she turned to the others—"why didn't we know that?" Then her gaze returned to the preacher. "How did we miss that?" she demanded.

"It wasn't on the ministerial information form. The only choices were single, married, and divorced. Nothing about 'once engaged.' "

"I bet none of the committee thought to ask," Winnie said with an expression of disappointment that echoed Birdie's dismay. "Men don't ask the important questions."

"What was her name?" Winnie asked.

"Her name was Laurel. Probably still is."

An enormous problem with a young minister

19

was he didn't know enough not to joke about serious subjects like engagements and marriage.

"Did she accept?" Blossom asked.

"Of course she didn't," Birdie snapped. Oh, dear. She hated it when pain made her short-tempered. Her irritability frightened Blossom, who hadn't learned to ignore it the way Mercedes and Winnie did.

"Your shoulder may hurt," Mercedes lectured. "But that doesn't give you the right to be rude."

That was the problem with a friend she'd known forever. Mercedes never minded pointing out her faults. This time Birdie deserved it. She should shut up now and let the others take over.

"I'm sorry, Blossom." Ashamed but undeterred, Birdie said, "Why'd she turn you down?"

"She didn't. She accepted."

Birdie gasped. "She accepted?"

"Ladies, I'm not as incompetent as you seem to believe."

"You're not?" Winnie asked, then hurried to add, "Of course you aren't. How nice that she accepted."

He nodded, which caused the three still-standing Widows to take a step forward until they had triangulated on him. For a moment he looked panicked.

Good.

"But she's not here." Winnie gestured in an arc that encompassed the entire town and perhaps all of Creek County. "What happened?"

"She broke the engagement."

"Oh, dear." Blossom reached out to pat his shoulder. "I'm so sorry." Her voice held a note of deep and genuine compassion.

Birdie needed to add that tone to her repertoire.

Blossom glanced at the other three. "We should leave him in peace. He faced a terrible disappointment. We shouldn't pry."

Blossom would never be a Widow, not completely. She was too sweet, too ready to let people off the hook. Did Birdie have to explain again that prying was at the top of the list of things the Widows did? How else could they fix people?

"What did you do that made her change her mind?" Winnie asked.

"Decided to become a minister."

"Oh, dear, dear, dear," Blossom comforted.

"She broke your engagement because she didn't want to marry a man of the cloth?" Mercedes asked, using that high-church language she seemed so fond of.

"I sprang it on her." He smiled sadly. "Laurel had no idea I was considering the ministry. She felt fine as the wife of a teacher but couldn't see herself making casseroles or leading the women's mission group."

"That's nearly unforgivable," Winnie said.

"You're better off without her," Mercedes

added. "No one should interfere with the call of God."

He gazed at the four women, one by one. They could read him so well. His posture and expression showed he hoped that pitiful story would make them forget their priorities. He should know good and well that although they might pity him, they weren't going to leave him alone.

"You do have experience in this area," Birdie said.

He nodded warily.

"Maybe we could give you some pointers, just in case you'd like to propose again," Blossom suggested sweetly.

"We could make some suggestions," Winnie added.

"Yes." Mercedes smiled. "For your edification."

"Ladies . . ."

"Won't hurt you to tell us about it," Birdie snapped. Honestly, someone had to push him or they'd never get the answers. Then she sat back in her chair and rotated her right shoulder. She had to stop barking at people.

"We might be able to help," Mercedes said quickly, as if to hide Birdie's harsh words.

"You know, Preacher," Winnie added, "we *could* help you. Think of it as a peer review."

Before he could respond to that, Blossom added, "We'd love to help you. We've all been proposed to. We know how a man acts to win his lady."

With that, the three remaining Widows returned to their chairs, sat, and watched him.

He struggled. Birdie could almost see his internal conflict, but she knew he'd give in. He couldn't hurt Blossom's feelings. The preacher had no compunction about standing up to any of the other Widows, but hurting Blossom was like swatting a butterfly.

He gave in. "There's a train, a dinner train, that goes from Louisville to Bardstown. I had a reservation for that."

"A lovely start," Blossom stated.

"When I bought the ticket, I asked them to play a special love song over the speaker, then to bring out the ring on a covered platter and set it down in front of her."

"What song?" Winnie asked.

" 'The Way You Look Tonight.' "

"An old song." Winnie wrote it in her notebook.

"But romantic," Blossom said. "Women like romance."

The Widows all nodded.

"Then I was going to ask her to marry me."

When he didn't continue, the pillar said, "How did that go?"

"After I bought the ring, I couldn't afford dinner. It cost over one hundred and fifty dollars and I needed new tires."

"So you didn't propose to this Laurel on that lovely train trip?" Mercedes asked.

"She didn't deserve it," Blossom said. "She must have broken your sweet heart."

"If you didn't propose to her on the train, where did you propose to her?" Birdie asked.

He didn't answer for several seconds.

"Well?" Birdie prompted.

"We have a sort of diner restaurant in Louisville. Has great hamburgers and a jukebox."

"You proposed at a hamburger place?" Blossom gasped, fell against the back of her chair, and placed her hand over her heart.

"At a diner?" Disappointment colored Winnie's voice.

"Not, of course, that there's anything wrong with a diner," Birdie stated clearly. "Not a thing wrong with a diner."

"Of course not," Winnie agreed. "But not a romantic place like that train."

"How could you possibly believe a diner would be the place to propose to a young woman?" Mercedes asked.

"It was the best I could afford." He shrugged. "She accepted."

Ooh, he looked so smug.

"Did you hide the ring anyplace?" Mercedes asked. "To add a little romance?"

"I've always thought that was silly and dangerous," Blossom said. "A person could swallow the ring and choke to death."

"Was there anything at all romantic about

your first proposal?" Mercedes persisted.

"I brought a roll of quarters and put them in the jukebox to play romantic songs."

"That's sweet," Blossom gushed.

Honestly, she was the gushiest woman Birdie had ever met.

"But there was only one love song, Dolly Parton's 'I Will Always Love You.' "

"Good choice. You did something right," Winnie said.

During all this, Birdie watched. She hated the fact she hurt so much, couldn't say a word without sounding cantankerous. Oh, my Lord, she hated this weakness.

"So I put in a whole bunch of quarters and punched it over and over. Unfortunately . . ."

"This isn't going to turn out well," Birdie muttered.

"Unfortunately, a lot of people before me had chosen songs."

"What *did* you propose to?" Mercedes asked.

"Something by Jay-Z."

"Who's Jay Zee?" Blossom asked.

"Some sort of rapper," Birdie explained. "Bree says he uses a lot of bad words."

"I don't know. I couldn't understand anything," Adam said.

"Doesn't sound very romantic," Mercedes said.

"No, it wasn't." He lifted both hands, palms up, as if he was saying *Go figure*. "But she did accept."

"Is that how you're planning to propose to Gussie?" Oh, Birdie had pushed too far. The preacher's bulldog expression underscored her error. She should shut up and allow the others to take over. They'd been doing fine on their own.

"Ladies." He paused. Looked like he was trying to think of a polite way to tell them to go away and leave him alone.

He didn't succeed.

"That's between Gussie and me." Although his voice sounded polite, the clipped words and his glower conveyed that this was none of their business, none of their business at all.

Words and facial expressions had never stopped Birdie. "But you are going to ask her?" As the head matchmaker she had a right to ask that, but she'd sounded mean.

When the words tumbled out, Mercedes stood, moved to Birdie's chair, took her good right arm, and said, "Time to go, Bird." She gently pulled Birdie to her feet and led her toward the door Winnie held open.

Birdie deserved a mutiny. She'd been rude and pushy. However, she still had to take charge of the insurrection. "Ladies, we have a lot of work ahead."

They all left with Blossom fluttering along behind them.

But that shoulder. No matter how often she

rotated it as she walked back to work—surreptitiously because she hated to show weakness—the movement didn't help. On top of that, her feet hurt.

"Dear Lord," she whispered, "please don't let me fall apart yet."

As the Widows left, Adam relaxed. He'd survived an interrogation by experts. If there'd been a bright light shining in his face, it would have looked like a scene from a police movie. Thank goodness for Blossom Brown. With her, he had the good cop on his side.

But he worried about the pillar. Not that she'd allow him to do anything for her, but he still worried about her pain, which made her extra surly.

He should have known better than to relax. At two thirty, the same time Adam stood to leave having completed his sermon preparation and, he knew, the time Miss Birdie finished her lunch shift, she knocked on the office door—which was not her usual MO—and came in without waiting for his answer, as usual.

"Nice sermon Sunday," she said. For a few seconds she stood in front of his desk.

When Miss Birdie harked back to a sermon preached nearly a week earlier, he knew it was an apology for her earlier behavior, as good a one as he'd ever get. "Thank you," he accepted graciously because he knew even this little bit of reconciliation was hard for the pillar. "How's that shoulder?"

"Fine." She nodded and turned to leave, mission accomplished, as if the only reason she'd dropped by was to compliment a sermon she probably didn't remember. No one remembered sermons. "Good-bye."

The pillar stopped at the door and turned back. "One more thing."

Every time he'd thought she had completed the meeting and he'd survived, she had one more question. Birdie MacDowell, the Columbo of Butternut Creek.

"What are you doing about the air-conditioning? Summer's not far away and you know how hot this place can get."

He sighed. "Miss Birdie, I don't know. I've talked to the property committee. They've seen Howard down at the bank, but we don't have the money for it and can't get a loan."

"We need it before it gets too hot here or everyone'll go to the Baptist Church," she said. "They've got a really good system."

"I know."

"When I go there, I have to take a sweater. Not that I go there often. Blossom takes a sweater when she goes to the Church of Christ because they have great air-conditioning." She nodded, her get-busy-on-this nod, before she turned and strode from his office.

"Thank you," he called after her. "I'll consider all you've said."

Her departure left him to ponder the terrible financial situation the church faced, which meant no raise for him and no air-conditioning this summer. No air-conditioning meant lower attendance.

With the increase in attendance and giving, the board had given him a one-hundred-dollar-per-month raise a few months ago, but that didn't go far. Not receiving more of a raise meant no new car, not even a less-than-ten-years-old one with a good paint job and an engine that didn't give up at the most inconvenient times. Hector had mentioned the kids called his poor old vehicle "the turtle" because it was old, slow, and ugly but usually got them where they were going. They were stuck with the turtle.

On top of that, how could he possibly afford a ring for Gussie when Janey had hit a growth spurt that meant her ankles showed when she wore last year's jeans?

Monday, Birdie had started out the door of her little house to work the lunch shift when the phone rang. Nowadays, with the possibility of a college scholarship, she didn't ignore a phone call. "Hello?"

"Good morning," the voice on the other end of the phone said. "This is Coach McGuffey from

Sunshine State College. May I speak to Bree MacDowell?"

"I'm sorry, she's not home." Why didn't these people realize a high school student would be at school on a weekday morning? But Birdie forced a pleasant response because, after all, these were people who wanted to pay for Bree's college education in exchange for her playing volleyball. Heaven knew, Birdie couldn't afford tuition, couldn't add much other than a tiny bit of spending money, and she didn't want Bree to acquire a huge debt.

"May I take a message?" she asked with a cheerfulness she seldom used. Took a lot of effort because today her feet ached like the dickens.

When she hung up after scribbling a note, Birdie reflected on the amazing fact that a college would offer scholarships because Bree could execute a perfect kill or Bobby could drop a ball into a hoop from twenty feet away or Hector could make a bounce pass through a zone defense.

Not that she minded. Bree would be the first MacDowell to go to college. Oh, Birdie had wanted to; then she'd fallen in love with Elmer when she was seventeen. Martha Patricia—their daughter and Mac and Bree's mother—had never shown a bit of interest in college or even high school. No, she'd been boy crazy. When she was sixteen, she ran off with that no-good man who got her pregnant twice. Birdie hadn't seen Martha

Patricia since the day she left Mac with her in Butternut Creek nearly two years after she'd left Bree here.

Not all bad, although she wouldn't have believed anything good could have come from Marty's partying her way out of school and leaving Butternut Creek with that man.

Goes to show what God could do with the tragedies and disasters of life. She had two marvelous granddaughters. They counted as the best thing that had ever happened to Birdie. Well, after Elmer. Not that she'd tell the girls, because it wasn't good for them to get swelled heads and she'd probably get all mushy and emotional. She had no desire for anyone to know what a softie she was about those two.

With a glance at the clock, she realized she'd better hustle, at least as much as she could. Lordy, she wished she could afford better shoes. The sole on the left one seemed to be pulling away a little. She opened the junk drawer, pulled out the glue, and dribbled a bit in the loose place. That should fix it. She hoped her foot wouldn't stick to the floor.

Then she hurried toward the door. Halfway there, Carlos the Cat darted out from behind the sofa and grabbed her ankle. Birdie nearly fell over, and he ran away.

Idiot cat. Didn't he know that if she fell, there'd be no more cat food for him? If the girls didn't love the sneaky creature so much, she'd give him away—but no one would want him.

Before she could make it out the door, the phone rang again. Torn about the need to get to work and the necessity of encouraging those recruiters, she chose the latter even if it meant dragging the cat a few feet.

"Mrs. MacDowell? This is Miss Phillips, the guidance counselor at the high school."

Guidance counselor. That meant Bree or Mac was okay. The principal had called a lot when Martha was in school. A call from the guidance counselor meant the girls weren't in trouble, not unless one of them had gone crazy and had been dragged to the counselor's office. Didn't sound likely.

"Yes?"

"I want to talk you about Mac. As you know, she's very bright in science."

"I know she likes science." Mac had a poster of Stephen Hawking over her bed, which had always seemed odd to Birdie. She noticed Carlos's paw reaching out from under the telephone table. She scooted her foot back before he could grab her shoelace.

"Her teachers tell me she's an outstanding student," the counselor said as Birdie fought the cat off. "They suggest she needs more of a challenge. We'd like to put her in a couple of science classes next year and prepare her for two or three AP exams when she's a senior."

"AP classes?" Birdie dropped into a chair. She hadn't realized her granddaughter was a genius. She struggled to get her mind around the concept. Where had her interest and ability and *brain* come from?

"Advanced placement. She can get college credit for high school classes."

"Yes, I know that. I didn't realize Mac . . ." Birdie stopped babbling to get to the point. "What do I need to do?"

"I'll send some information home with her. Please read it and get back to me if you have any questions."

Birdie clicked the phone off. Didn't that beat all. Oh, she knew Mac had won the science fair in seventh grade, but that was a small-town event with only three entries. Who knew it served as a sign of things to come? Mac's grades were A's, consistently. Birdie never had to force her to study.

Bree called her sister "Little Miss Perfect" for her fastidious ways. She said Mac wasn't merely tidy but *compulsively* neat. Yes, she was. Mac set everything parallel or at right angles with precision. Probably that scientific genius kicking in.

Birdie turned on the phone again to call Mercedes. All of Mercedes's children had gone to college, a couple to graduate school, and one had a PhD. Now Birdie had something to crow about. Then she'd call the preacher and tell him.

But first she had to get out the door before that stupid cat could attack again.

Friday afternoon, Chewy loped along next to Adam toward the parsonage. Some might consider Chewy ugly—well, Adam did, too—but because the dog had attached himself loyally to Adam, he couldn't hurt the creature's feelings. He allowed the dog to follow him around the parsonage and church except on Sundays.

Adam waved to his neighbor Ouida—a Southern name pronounced, strangely, *Weed-a*—Kowalski sitting on the front porch of her huge Victorian, the architectural twin of the parsonage. Her two daughters played on the lawn.

"Come on over and see Gussie later," he shouted.

"Thanks. We're going out to dinner when George gets home. Maybe tomorrow."

Sounded as if everything was going well in the Kowalski household. With Carol, the older daughter, in kindergarten and Gretchen in day care three mornings a week, Ouida had time to paint and sketch, at least until their third child arrived in late spring.

Fridays, Adam loved Fridays. He loved Saturday and Sunday even more since Gussie spent weekends in town. Although their courtship had been rocky, it had smoothed out. Maybe he could sneak a kiss or two. But he especially loved this Friday because Butternut Creek High School had a basketball game tonight.

By the time he reached the porch, Chewy had bounded ahead of him and sat by the door patiently, at least as patiently as Chewy ever waited. His tail beat out a steady tempo against the porch floor, his entire body wiggled, and he gave a demanding "Woof" all in the few seconds it took Adam to climb the porch steps.

"I'm home," Adam shouted as he opened the door and Chewy bounced inside ahead of him.

Home. He looked around at what had been an empty and echoing building when he first arrived, a huge parsonage built for a family with half a dozen children. Now Hector and Janey Firestone lived here and it had become home.

He started upstairs to change into a Butternut Creek Lions shirt. Gussie would meet them at the high school gym for what could be Hector's last high school basketball game, one of the regional games. Lose this and the Lions had completed the season. A win meant one game closer to the state title.

Catching him heading up, Gussie's mother, Yvonne Milton, said, "We're ready to go." She hustled down the hall toward him with Janey in tow.

Although the Miltons rented Sam's old house,

they spent much of their time in the parsonage, Yvonne cooking and cleaning—bless her—and Henry reading and napping, watching sports and walking Chewy. Both had practically adopted the Firestones.

Carrying a tote and a picnic basket, Henry came out of the kitchen behind his wife. "Aren't you ready for the game?"

"Let me change into my lucky shirt." He ran up the steps.

Even as early as they arrived, Adam had to park on the far end of the lot and hike toward the gym with the pack of fans. The green and gold of the Butternut Creek faithful mixed with the blue and white worn by the Bayou City crowd.

Inside, the bottleneck caused by fans attempting to buy tickets at a small table staffed by two outnumbered and overwhelmed teachers stopped them. Not that the numbers compared to the throngs in the huge high school field houses Adam had played in when he lived in Kentucky. In that state, basketball was more than king. It was president, prime minister, and senator.

In Texas, where football came close to being a religion, governors were known to drop into small towns by helicopter to recruit top athletes for their alma maters. On the other hand, a basketball game usually served only as a place for students to meet friends, get out of the house, maybe pick up a date, and for parents to spend a winter's evening cheering for their offspring in a mostly empty gym.

But tonight with the Butternut Creek faithful and fans from surrounding towns turning out, it would be standing room only. The noise and heat generated by all those bodies felt both suffocating and electrifying.

Once inside the gym, Adam searched the bleachers. His friend Sam Peterson stood and waved, then pointed toward the seats he and Willow had saved for them.

"Had to fight people off," Sam said when Adam got closer.

"Yeah, like anyone would mess with a marine," Willow said. She held her hands over her rounded stomach. Her pregnancy had begun to show more in the past month.

Adam sat next to Sam and saved a spot for Gussie on his right as Yvonne and Henry settled with Janey on a bleacher in front of them. "Where are the boys?" Adam searched the crowd for Leo and Nick until he spotted their red hair on the front row. "They don't want to sit with the old folks?"

"No, but I'm not sure it's wise to let them run around." Sam grinned. He'd adopted Willow's very active sons when they married. They would've driven Adam crazy but Sam loved them and they adored him. "Who knows what trouble they'll cause? The only way to keep them close is to rope them and tie them up." With a nod toward his wife, he added, "Their mother won't let me do that."

"I'm funny that way." Willow leaned forward to peer around Sam. "Is Gussie coming?"

He nodded, then glanced toward the door and she appeared. He watched her for a second as she looked around for them, her dark curls bouncing, her face glowing with the happiness that made everyone smile back.

As he gazed at her, he realized that home wasn't only the parsonage in Butternut Creek or the house in Kentucky where he'd grown up. Home was wherever Gussie and Hector and Janey were.

Now if he could just convince Gussie that her home was with him. He wouldn't have believed any chance of that existed a few months ago, but lately? She was here and the odds had improved greatly.

He stood and waved and shouted.

When she spied him, Gussie's smile widened. She loved him. He could see it on her face. Nothing in the world better than that—well, other than world peace and feeding the hungry. But knowing Gussie loved him came close to the top of his list.

She dodged other fans as she ran up the steps and slipped into the bleacher next to him. Adam put his arm around her shoulder, gave her a quick hug. "Game's about to begin. Did you get dinner on the way?"

"Didn't have time. Maybe we can grab something later." She laughed. "Anyplace in Butternut Creek that's still open after the game?"

"The parsonage. Your mother might rustle up something for you."

Janey turned around, pointed to the ceiling of the gym, and asked something Adam couldn't hear over all the noise.

But he didn't have to hear her, only look up at the thing on the ceiling, which looked like a large gold ball with green streamers. Definitely BCHS colors, but he had no idea what it was.

"It holds confetti," Willow shouted. "When I went to school here, we hung a huge bag of confetti up there to drop when we won a big game."

Cheers and clapping interrupted their speculation as the teams came onto the court, Bobby and Hector, the two seniors, leading the Lions across the floor toward the home team's bench as the band played the school fight song. He could see Mac with her trumpet and knew Miss Birdie had to be here somewhere.

Adam had known the game would be tough because the Bayou City Billy Goats had won the state 3A championship the last two years. The lead seesawed back and forth with the Lions leading by two at the half. After exciting third and fourth quarters, the game ended in a tie. Overtime.

Five more minutes and still a tie. By this time, both Bobby and the Lions' sophomore center had four fouls; the Billy Goats' big forward had fouled out.

At the end of the second overtime with two seconds left and the game knotted at seventy-two, Bobby stole the ball and passed it down the floor to Hector, who turned and tossed up a shot from the free-throw line.

The crowd erupted when the ball swished through the net. The band struck up again as the huge ball on the ceiling opened to dump an explosion of confetti. Within seconds, leaping athletes, screaming fans, and a layer of confetti scattered across the court.

Adam felt his hand being squeezed and looked down to see that Janey had moved next to him and was jumping up and down. "My brother won!"

Before he could respond, Adam noticed the refs standing in the middle of the floor. Although it looked as if they were blowing their whistles, the noise covered that, but they waved their hands wildly over their heads, looking like windmills caught in a tornado. Barely, through the noise of the crowd, he heard the insistent drone of the buzzer from the scorers' table.

He watched as Coach Borden stopped pounding his players on the back and turned toward the ref who'd put his hand on Gabe's shoulder. The official spoke directly into Gabe's ear. Coach's expression changed, first blank followed by disbelief. He pulled the players he could reach toward him, pointed at the clock, and said something. Confused, the athletes looked up. The eyes of all the fans followed their gaze. The scoreboard still showed a seventy-two to seventy-two tie with no time left. The celebration stopped. The teams headed toward the bench and sat: the Lions stunned and the Billy Goats elated.

"What happened?" Janey asked.

"I think Hector's shot didn't count," Adam answered. "Time ran out."

As the officials attempted to move the fans toward the seats, the announcer said, "Folks, that last shot came after time ran out. We have another overtime."

Moans came from the Lion fans while the Billy Goat faithful celebrated. Both teams headed back to the locker rooms.

With the departure of the teams, everyone looked at the court. The closest fans had a few scraps of paper in their hair—more covered the scorers' table—but the floor was heaped with drifts of multicolored paper scraps. It looked like a fanciful winter scene, the Hill Country covered with pink and blue and mint-green snow. Then two janitors stepped on the court, each with a trash barrel on wheels, push broom, and enormous dustpan.

"Folks, it's going to take a little while," the announcer said. "Just relax."

It might have, except the citizens of Butternut Creek surrounded the court, undaunted by the task ahead and the possible collateral damage to their clothing. With precision, they moved inward, picking up handfuls and armloads of paper and dumping them into the barrels. Wastebaskets and plastic bags were brought to the court. Others took the filled bags and containers outside and returned to pick up more.

In only minutes the fans had nearly cleared the floor; the custodians made quick work of sweeping up the last bit. With the court clear, both teams returned to cheers and hoopla.

Sadly, during that last overtime, both Bobby and the sophomore center fouled out. Bayou City won by five. While the Billy Goats celebrated the victory, the Lion players sat on the bench with towels over their heads until Coach Borden reminded them to congratulate the other team.

It's only a game played by high school kids, Adam told himself, but the words didn't make him feel any better and he knew how disappointed Hector would be.

Not that he had to worry about what to say to him right away. Bree and Hector and Bobby and whatever girl Bobby was dating would go someplace after they cleaned up. No reason to wait around.

Janey watched her brother, her chin quivering. He and Gussie held Janey's hands between them as they slowly made their way out of the stands, through the gym, and out to the parking lot. They walked Gussie to her car, which she'd had to park on the street about a block away.

"Hope you're still coming to the parsonage," Adam said.

"With all the overtime, it's late." Gussie glanced at Adam.

"I'd like to see you and you're hungry."

"Which one's more important?" She waved her hand. "You convinced me. Meet you there."

Janey dropped Adam's hand but kept hers in Gussie's. "Can I ride with Gussie?"

Good idea for them to go together, just the two of them. "I'll see you there." He watched two of the people he loved most get in the car and take off. Then he headed back to the parking lot to find the Miltons.

"Where to?" he asked Yvonne, who sat in the passenger seat.

"Let us off at our place," she said. "We old folks need our rest, and you need time alone with Gussie. If Hector hasn't polished them all off, there are plenty of leftovers in the fridge."

An hour later, after they'd eaten a few pieces of cold chicken and some biscuits and Janey had headed up to bed, Gussie leaned across the table. "Janey told me about her dyslexia."

"Oh? What did she say? She's very private."

"I know. That's why I felt honored. We just discussed what was going on. Was this the reason for the conference at school last week?"

"Sorry I couldn't tell you. Janey worried everyone would look down on her."

"She said it felt good to know what was wrong and that she wasn't alone or stupid." Gussie stood and began to clear the table. "My friend Clare is dyslexic so I know some of the issues."

"I wish I'd noticed earlier." Adam rinsed the plates and began to load the dishwasher.

"How would you have noticed? She's in third grade. Many trained professionals and teachers missed it."

"I know, but I should have known she had a problem. She always studied. I've never seen anyone study so hard except my sister." He shook his head. "But my sister got great grades and loved to study. Janey's grades are average, and I know she'd rather play than work so hard. I should have done better."

"Adam, give yourself a break. You found two kids sleeping in the park because their father had gone to prison and the landlord kicked them out. You took them home. You've given them security."

"But I always acted like a big brother not a father."

"Well, you weren't."

"I should have done more . . ."

"Oh, for heaven's sake." She put her hands on her hips and glared at him. "You've been great with them. You drive Hector to visit his father in prison. You've loved them and supported them and . . ."

"But if I'd . . ."

Before he could say more, Gussie took a few steps toward him, put her hands on his shoulders, and kissed him. A very nice, very unexpected action. After that, she leaned against Adam and put her arms around his waist.

"A great way to end an argument." He dropped his cheek onto the top of her head. "What do you want to fight about next?"

"Let's just finish up in the kitchen, then we'd better go outside. Preacher, being here alone with me is going to ruin your reputation."

"Okay, let's go on out. I'll finish up here later."

As they settled on the swing, Gussie took Adam's hand. "What's happening with Hannah? Where is she now? Is she still in London with your folks?"

"Haven't heard from my sister lately. I usually call on Sunday."

"Usually?"

"I'm not sure where she is. She hasn't answered an email for weeks."

"Do you worry?"

"No, Mom will tell me if I should worry. Hannah's not a touchy-feely stay-in-touch kind of person. I call her Gypsy because she's always wandering around and because she looks like a gypsy."

"When you were talking about Janey, you said Hannah studied a lot and liked it."

"Always. Never saw her without a book. Has an amazing brain, soaks up everything, always determined to know more, to do better than anyone, and to finish med school as soon as possible. She knew what she wanted to do, go to Africa and heal the entire continent."

They swung for a few minutes in contented silence. "I love this," he said. "I love everything about Butternut Creek. The people, the trees and houses, the church."

They waved as Tasha Ferguson, who lived across the street, headed out on her evening walk.

"But you and I are the very best part of Butternut Creek." It didn't make much sense but seemed to please Gussie.

She lifted her head and Adam placed his hand against her cheek.

"Definitely the best part," Gussie agreed.

Chapter Two

A few minutes later, Gussie reluctantly stood and got in her car to drive to Sam's old house. Adam waved, then went inside. He sat at the counter between the kitchen and family room where he often worked on a sermon or a Sunday school lesson. He could spread his books and notes out, and the hard stools kept him awake. For an hour, he turned the page of a Bible commentary and made notes on his tablet. The only sound came from Chewy, who snored on the dog bed next to the sofa.

He wished he had a computer in the parsonage. Why hadn't he bought a laptop back when he had the money? Didn't make much difference. He hadn't because the PC had cost almost nothing. He kept the computer at the office and toted it home when he needed it. Not the handiest plan.

For only a second, he dropped his head on his arms to think about finances. As well as a computer, he needed a new car. He trusted the old one around town, as long as he kept Rex the mechanic on speed dial. And, he hoped, a wedding was coming up.

How could he possibly afford all that?

"Pops!"

Adam blinked. Hector stood next to him, a hand grasping Adam's elbow.

"You don't have to wait up for me," Hector said. "How many times do I have to tell you? You were asleep and almost fell off your stool. Could've hurt yourself."

"Not asleep, meditating."

Hector snorted. "Guess the sound of snoring I heard came from Chewy."

"Probably. And I wasn't waiting up for you." Adam stretched. "Outlining sermons for the next few weeks. I'm doing a series based on the Psalms . . ."

"Uh-huh," Hector responded, then yawned so huge he nearly swallowed his hand.

Of course the kid wasn't all that interested in the series of sermons, so he said, "You have fun with Bree and Bobby and his date?"

"Didn't feel like having fun." Hector closed his eyes and shook his head, but he didn't say anything more, at least not with words.

Adam knew how he felt. He'd been through those big games and had come out on the losing end more often than winning, but he'd never had a college scholarship on the line. His parents paid for everything. He hadn't had to worry about the scouts in the stands—not that they'd ever been interested in him. Tall but way too skinny.

"Want to talk?"

Hector shook his head again. "No, I'll be okay. I know we did everything we could. I know it was only a game. I know"—he pointed at his head—"a lot of stuff but it still hurts to lose."

The kid walked into the kitchen, took down a glass, and opened the refrigerator to pour himself a glass of milk. Once he'd put the carton back and closed the fridge, he turned toward Adam. "We had fun in the other regional games. We played well and felt great when we won. But . . ." He paused to search for words. "That loss felt horrible, wiped out the good memories. The bad feels a lot worse than the good felt good."

Adam nodded. "Yeah, I know."

"I mean, it's not like when Mom passed or when our father went to prison. Not like that and I know it's not the end of the world but . . ."

Adam nodded again.

"Coach called a team meeting for tomorrow. We'll talk about it." Hector chugged his milk, then rinsed out the glass.

"Janey talked to Gussie about her dyslexia." Adam watched Hector place the glass in the dish-washer.

"She did?" Hector considered that. "Well, that's good. Pops, I think you'd better go ahead and marry Gussie. My sister needs a mother."

Adam laughed. "You sound just like Miss Birdie."

Hector looked embarrassed but the expression flickered past quickly. Adam would've missed it if he weren't familiar with Miss Birdie's tactic of bringing as many people as possible to her side and pushing them very hard to take action. He'd heard that Janey-needs-a-mother argument straight from the pillar's mouth.

Did he mind that the Widows had captured Hector and he'd become an additional nagging unit?

Not a bit. He remembered Sam's complete capitulation to the pillar and her cadre. In fact, Sam had welcomed anyone's efforts or input on his behalf to win Willow, even the Widows at their most officious and interfering. Like Sam, Adam would take any available help, but he felt maybe he could handle courting Gussie by himself from now on.

"Night. You need to go to bed, too. It's nearly one o'clock." Hector tiptoed up the back steps so he wouldn't awaken his sister. At least, he did what he thought was tiptoeing, but going up stairs quietly with feet as big as Hector's was impossible.

After the sermon and the offering Sunday morning, Adam gave the call to communion. "We meet here not because we are worthy but because we are called here," he said. "All believers are invited to gather around this table by our Savior. This is His table, not ours."

He loved to look out over the congregation when they celebrated communion every week. Gussie and Janey sat together with Yvonne, then

Hector, Bobby, and Henry nearly filling the third pew.

"Let us prepare ourselves for this meal by singing hymn number one fifteen." The elders and deacons came down the center aisle as the congregation sang.

In January, the worship committee—which was made up of the Widows and a few others who knew better than to oppose them—had decided to try a new method to celebrate the Eucharist. Though *Eucharist* was not the word they used because they considered that a high-church concept. They preferred the more informal terms of *Lord's Supper* and *Communion*.

With the old method, after the elders prayed, the deacons had one tray with wafers with the taste and consistency of Styrofoam in the middle and tiny, individual disposable plastic cups filled with grape juice in circles around them. However, the women had been to a retreat where the deacons used two trays and people broke off a piece of bread. Seemed a little unwieldy at first, but everyone had adjusted.

While they sang, Adam glanced down at the covered trays of bread in front of Ralph and the trays with juice in front of Pansy, the woman who did everything in the church that the Widows couldn't handle. She'd be a Widow, too, Miss Birdie had told Adam, if her husband would just go ahead and die.

For a second, Adam thought he saw something move, just a tiny jerk beneath the lid over one of the cups. He told himself not to allow his mind to wander and looked down at the hymnal.

When the congregation finished the hymn, Adam began the words of institution from First Corinthians, " 'For I received from the Lord . . .' " The scripture completed, Pansy said a prayer for the bread and wine.

As she said, "Amen," Pansy grasped the top of the communion cover and lifted it. Immediately a cloud of something leaped into the air from the tray. Although Ralph would always deny it later, both elders screamed, ran up the stairs to the chancel, and hid behind the organ.

Adam blinked several times. Not that he was made of stouter stuff than the elders, but he didn't run because he had no idea what made up this cloud. The deacons, two flanking each now-absent elder, hadn't immediately taken in either what had happened or why the elders had fled. When they did, they all leaped backward and began swatting at the cloud of what Adam suddenly recognized as crickets.

Crickets? Yes, masses of them, hordes leaping from the tray, across the table, and every which way. Mrs. Wade, one of the deacons, screamed and fell over a step as she attempted to escape while the other three ran toward the narthex and left her to fend for herself.

Before Adam could act, the throng of insects headed toward the front of the sanctuary. Many in the congregation who sat in the front rows leaped on their pews. That change of location didn't help much, because the crickets could hop farther and higher than Adam had realized. Finally he made the ineffectual response of slapping the cover back on the communion tray, then turning to help poor Mrs. Wade.

Fortunately, Mac, Bree, Bobby, and Hector ran forward. Bree opened the side door. They used that exit only in emergencies but if this didn't count as an emergency, Adam didn't know what did. Mac and Bobby attempted to herd the insects out that door by stomping and waving bulletins while Hector knelt next to the deacon who'd nearly passed out. He took her hand and said, "There, there, Mrs. Wade. You're going to be fine. You just take my hand and we'll get out of here."

Mrs. Wade grabbed his arm as if it were Moses's staff saving her from the plague of . . . well, crickets. Hector pulled her to her feet and out of the sanctuary into the office hallway.

Within a few minutes, the cricket population had been thinned and a tenuous order returned. Nearly immediately, all eyes turned to stare at Leo and Nick, easily located due to their red hair that shone like burning bushes in the light from the stained-glass windows.

Leo blurted out, "Don't look at me. I didn't do it. I don't know a thing about this."

Like the rest of the congregation, he looked at his brother.

Nick sat in the pew and lifted his eyes toward the stained-glass window of St. Cecilia over the organ, looking as innocent as a martyr.

As Sam fell back against the pew laughing so hard he couldn't sit up, Willow stood faster than Adam had thought a woman as pregnant as she could, glared at her husband, took Nick's hand, and dragged him down the aisle, around the side of the chancel, and toward the communion room.

The rest of the service was lost. Knowing there was no way he could get the congregation to focus and that no one really wanted to partake of grape juice crickets had romped through, Adam raised his hand, gave the benediction, and headed toward the doors to the highway to greet people as they left. Most of the worshippers seemed to have found the experience hilarious. One or two, including poor Pansy and Mrs. Wade, didn't. After comforting both women, Adam took off his robe, handed it to Gussie, and headed back to the communion room where the penitent and his family awaited him.

As he entered, Willow pointed at Sam, who still struggled not to laugh. "He's worse than either of the boys. Anytime the boys do something terrible, he thinks it's funny. It's as if I had three little boys."

Sam put his arm around her and hugged her. "Sorry. I love you. I love them, but they make me laugh. I'm doing the best I can." With great effort, he assumed a somber expression and, with a ferocious and fatherly glare, he turned to Nick. "Tell us what happened."

"Why does everyone assume I did this?" Nick asked in the quivering voice of the unjustly accused.

"Nicholas?" Sam said in that very marine voice.

"Yes, sir." Nick looked down at the floor. "I had to feed my lizard."

"Your what?" Willow demanded. "You have a lizard?"

Nick nodded.

"Did you know about this?" she asked Leo.

He nodded.

"Where is it?"

"Under my bed," Nick said.

"In my house?" Willow demanded. "You have a lizard under your bed in our house?"

Adam had not realized Willow could screech. Not that he blamed her. "Let's hear the story of the crickets, first," Adam suggested. "Then you can talk about the lizard as a family."

Willow nodded.

"Well," Nick started. "I found this lizard in the backyard of Sam's old house a few weeks ago."

He held his hands a foot or so apart. "He's about this big and boy does he eat a lot. I gave him lettuce and even bought some lizard food but I didn't have more money and I knew they liked crickets and I saw a bunch here last week." After he finished that long and complicated sentence, he took a deep breath. "During Sunday school this morning, I asked to go to the bathroom. Instead I went outside with a jar I hid back there and captured a whole bunch of crickets. Then I came into the communion room to give them a little water. I took the top of the jar off and dribbled some water in but . . ." He dropped his head.

"But?" Sam prodded.

"The glass was slippery from the water and I dropped the jar and it broke and all these crickets came out and jumped all over the place." He flapped his hands around to show the exodus of the insects. "Did you know crickets are really attracted to grape juice?" Nick shook his head. "I didn't."

"Interesting but not the reason we're here," Willow said. "Go on."

"Anyway, they all headed toward the communion tray like it was steak or something." He nodded. "Like, they attacked it. I tried to pick them off. I got a handful and took it outside, but when I came back all of them were swarming around the juice. I guess someone had forgotten to put the cover on."

"Our elders don't expect to have crickets in the communion room," Adam said.

"I know. I'm sorry." Nick looked around the group, at Sam, then Willow and Adam but skipping Leo. He was the picture of innocence, his skin pale as a martyr's, which made his freckles stand out while his eyes pled for understanding.

"You're not fooling us," Sam said. "Keep going."

Nick gulped. "I tried. I really tried. I kept taking handfuls of crickets out but it was like they were multiplying. I couldn't get them all." He shook his head. "And I'd taken so long and my Sunday school teacher was calling me so, finally, when there weren't as many crickets hopping around, I put the cover on the tray. I hoped they'd die before church, maybe drown or suffocate. I hoped no one would notice."

When Sam put his hand over his mouth to hide his grin, Willow glared at him.

"They didn't die," Leo said with big-brother superiority. "And people did notice."

"I know." Nick dropped his head and looked at the floor. Every inch of him from the top of his spiky red hair to the scuffed toes of his athletic shoes drooped in agony. "I'm so sorry."

No one could look as despondent, chastised, and thoroughly remorseful as Nick. Adam knew that because he'd been treated to the expressions of the repentant Nick on dozens of occasions. The depth of his contrition was always extraordinary. Every single time.

"Nick, communion is an important part of our service," Adam said in the serious, ministerial tones he used to preach. "It is a holy and sacred act. People meditate and pray. Do you know that?"

Nick nodded with what Adam felt could be true repentance.

"Do you remember the scripture I read before we share communion?" Adam said. "It invites people to the *Lord's Supper*. Having crickets in the communion tray is a very serious spiritual breach."

"Yes, sir." Nick gulped. "I'm so sorry."

"Preacher," Willow said. "How would you like to punish him?"

"First, I want you to go through the entire church and find every cricket—alive or dead—and dispose of them all. Start in the sanctuary with the communion trays."

"Yes, sir." Nick lifted his green eyes filled with deep remorse.

"After that, I'm going to turn you over to your mother to discipline."

"Not to Mom," Nick whispered. "Please not. She's tough."

All three adults nodded.

"Yes, sir."

"And Leo can help you," Willow said.

"Me?" Leo gasped. "I didn't . . ."

"But you knew about the lizard."

Leo nodded.

"Didn't you know that your little brother would do something like this to feed the creature?"

Leo nodded and followed his brother from the room.

"I'm sorry, Adam." Willow shook her head. "I never know what those boys are going to do. Leo's getting a little more mature, but crickets in the communion tray? And a lizard someplace in our home?"

"You might have Nick write an apology to the deacons and elders. They had quite a scare."

When Adam headed down the corridor to his office, he saw Miss Birdie waiting for him and tapping her foot. His first reaction was to turn and march the other way. When Miss Birdie looked like that, he always wanted to turn and march the other way.

"Preacher," she said.

Too late. "I took care of the crickets," he said. "The boys are cleaning the sanctuary and disposing of every insect, living or dead, at this moment."

"What about poor Pansy? And Mrs. Wade?"

"Nick will write them an apology."

She walked off, which made Adam feel great relief.

He found Gussie waiting in his church study. After a quick kiss on her cheek, he said, "Go on back to the parsonage. I'll be right over. I'm sure your mother has fixed a great Sunday dinner but I have to do something first. Won't take long."

As she left, he looked up and down the hall and in the reception room.

"Anyone here?" he shouted. No one answered. He was alone. He allowed himself to remember the moment Pansy had removed the top of the communion tray, the look on Mrs. Wade's face, and Ralph's escape to the chancel, and he burst out in laughter. A few minutes later, he attempted to stop, but the confusion and panic he recalled on the faces of the congregation members got him going again. He fell into one of the chairs and laughed so hard he could hardly breathe. Sometimes ministry was terribly difficult but at other times there was nothing like it.

After a snack supper Sunday evening, Gussie left town. She did that every weekend so she didn't have to get up early Monday morning to leave Butternut Creek and hit Austin traffic. They walked to Sam's house, and she went inside to grab her things.

As she stuffed a suitcase—which she refused to allow Adam to carry because she could handle it perfectly well, thank you—into the trunk, she turned to Adam. "Don't think I got a chance to tell you this, but Winnie asked me this morning if I preferred diamonds, emeralds, or another gem-stone."

"Why?"

"You know, for a ring."

He snorted. "I can't believe them." He paused. "Well, yes I can. Obviously attempting to push you into marriage." But he might as well find out. "How did you answer her?"

"Ask her. I'm sure she'll share it with you." She squeezed his hand and headed around the car and got inside.

She started the car and Adam said, "Be careful."

Why did people say that? *Be careful.*

Did he say those words because he worried Gussie would not be careful if he didn't warn her?

Did he fear she'd take off at eighty miles an hour and gather speed from there? Or that she'd run every red light between the parsonage and Austin? Had he told her to be careful because he thought Gussie would pay no attention to one-way streets and no-left-turn signs. Did he really think a gigantic game of bumper cars or a demolition derby awaited her on the highway?

He grinned. Of course not. He hadn't said *Be careful* to remind her not to drive like a crazy person, not completely.

No, those words were shorthand for *I love you.* Those words meant, *I care. Come back to me. Remember I'm waiting for you.* All that in two little words.

Gussie backed out of the drive.

"Be careful," Adam shouted.

Gussie waved. She knew what he meant.

Monday morning a week later, Adam looked up at a soft knock on the door of his church office.

"Preacher?" Blossom peeked inside.

"Come on in," Adam said. He stood and waited for the other Widows to follow her. None appeared. Actually, he should have guessed that, because Blossom had entered first and only the pillar was allowed to lead the group in.

"Please sit down." Once they'd both settled in chairs in front of his desk, Adam asked, "What can I do for you?"

"Well," she said, then paused with her gaze falling on her nicely manicured nails.

French tips, Adam thought. He'd learned that from his former fiancée many years earlier.

"Well." She glanced up at him. "It's about your reticence."

He blinked. "My reticence?"

"You know. Your stubbornness."

"Yes, I know what the word means, but I don't understand what you're talking about."

"The Widows asked me to talk to you about . . . you know."

Comprehension dawned in amazing clarity. Poor Blossom. The alien nature of the pillar had entered her body and taken over her sweet nature and she didn't feel a bit good about that.

"About your lack of action." Her cheeks turned scarlet. "You know. With Gussie Milton."

If it were any other Widow, he'd allow her to founder, but the pillar knew very well he would allow Blossom to badger him in her gentle way. It didn't seem like harassment when Blossom spoke softly and slipped into her best drawl, and he couldn't hurt her tender feelings.

On the other hand, he saw no need to help her interfere. "Could you be a little clearer?" he asked. "More specific?"

She opened a piece of paper she held in her palm and glanced at it before crumpling it. During all this, she didn't meet his gaze but addressed the comments to her fingernails. "We know you've proposed to a woman before but you're moseying along on this one. We've given you plenty of time to ask her."

"The last time you brought this up was only a few weeks ago."

"Plenty of time."

When he didn't answer, she closed her eyes for a moment, then opened them, looked into his face, and spoke. "Pastor, it is against my Southern upbringing to say this. I do not enjoy getting knee-deep and thigh-high into someone's business, but we *do* have a wedding to plan." She moved forward in her chair and placed her plump, dimpled hands on the desk. "We believe you may need a little help with this one." With a deep sigh, she sat back. Her posture said *I've done my duty.*

"I can't tell you how much I appreciate your concern," he said gently. "But I'll handle this when the time is right. Thank you for stopping by."

She didn't move. Instead of standing and toddling toward the door as he expected, she remained in the chair but relaxed.

"One more thing."

"Yes?" When she didn't answer, he sorted through his brain in an effort to figure out what in the world she would want to discuss besides his stubbornness in not following the Widows' time line.

"It's about the air-conditioning," she said. "The sanctuary gets really hot in the summer."

"Yes, I'm sorry. We got some fans—you know, the kind you hold—from the funeral home." They had a picture of Jesus in Gethsemane on one side and an ad for Sumner's Eternal Rest on the other.

"They don't help much."

"I know. We don't have the—"

"I'd like to contribute whatever is necessary to fix the air conditioner."

He blinked.

"The church has been very good to me, Preacher. I've found a place I belong." Tears formed in her eyes. "When my husband left me, I had no idea who I was or what I could do alone. Now I have purpose and an identity. I'm a Widow."

Adam handed her a tissue. "You don't have to do this."

Why did he say that? Why couldn't he have accepted graciously?

"I want to. In the last few months, I've learned to act when there is a need. I have the money for this project."

"Thank you. That's very generous."

"Not completely. It's for me, too. I don't like heat." She stood, and Adam did as well. "Please don't tell anyone," she whispered. "I want this to remain an anonymous gift."

"If that's what you want." As if no one could figure out that, unless someone had robbed a bank or set up a counterfeiting ring, the only person in the congregation with the resources to pay for the air-conditioning was Blossom.

"One more thing." She held her index finger up. "I want it to be a professional job." She leaned forward and whispered, "Pastor, you know how much I dislike to criticize other people, but if Ralph and the men try to do this, it will end up a disaster. We'd probably have heat during the summer and air-conditioning in December."

Didn't Adam know that. Ralph had worked on the phone system last year and even now it didn't work when it rained.

"I'll call Charley. He's a professional and will do a good job." If he didn't get stuck someplace.

"Have him send the bills to me."

"Thank you. I've been worried about warm weather and having that air conditioner sputtering." He walked around the desk and took Blossom's hand. "And I will keep your earlier advice about proposing in mind."

With a nod worthy of a true Southern belle, she turned and left the office.

As she left, Adam sat down. A catalog from a jewelry store lay open on his desk with a picture of a diamond ring circled and a note written in Blossom's flowing script, "I think she'd like this one," next to it.

When had she put that on his desk?

Blossom had become more of a Widow every day. He wasn't sure if that was a good thing or not.

"You've got to love them," he murmured. "And, Dear God, please help me do that." As the week went on, he repeated that prayer to himself several times, because they never gave up.

One morning, he found a rose on his desk with a list of addresses for florists in the area. When he opened the mail the next day, he found a two-for-one coupon for dinner at Red John's Country Barbeque and Used Car Mall—not an overly romantic spot, but five-star restaurants didn't sit on every street corner in Butternut Creek. He studied the envelope: plain white, address in block letters, and postmarked AUSTIN. The postmark meant nothing because all mail from small-town Central Texas went into Austin first to be sorted, then was shuffled back and delivered.

On Thursday, Maggie, the church receptionist, shouted from the front office, "Pastor, it's for you. Gussie's calling."

He grabbed the phone and turned it on. "Hey."

"Thank you," she said in a low voice that promised a number of pleasant actions would be forthcoming.

Problem was he didn't know what he'd done to deserve her gratitude and imagined the Widows had made a grand gesture on his behalf. He should probably ask Gussie what she believed he'd done and tell her he hadn't, but he felt the Widows would not appreciate that. They'd expect him to use Gussie's good mood for a purpose: to propose.

Sure. On the phone.

"You don't know what I'm talking about, do you?" She laughed. "I received a box of expensive chocolates from someone who signed himself as 'Snuggles.' "

Snuggles? "Do you think I'd identify myself as 'Snuggles'?"

"No, I didn't, but you're the only man I know who *might* send me a box of chocolates, well, other than the manager of the photo supply house I order from. I can't imagine Big Bobby would ever sign a card 'Snuggles.' " She paused. "Please thank the Widows for me."

Chapter Three

Wednesday morning, Adam stopped by the hospital to visit a few church members. Afterward, when he opened the door of his clunker of a car, there was an odd sound like a rasp, then a pop followed by the agonizing screech of a wounded creature. He'd learned to ignore those sounds in the hope that if he pretended he didn't hear them, the car would heal itself.

Besides, the noises that concerned him deeply came from the engine and usually required more money for repairs than he had. But a squeaking door did not foretell a crisis.

At least, that was his fervent hope. Until he got in the car and settled in the seat. He reached out to pull on the handle to shut the door.

The door didn't move at all. When he tugged harder, the handle came off. He let go of the handle but, still attached to the door by fabric, it hung uselessly. He sat there, looking at the door handle, then toward the door, still wide open.

After much consideration, he turned on the ignition, put the window down, then turned off the ignition. At least that worked, even if he had to be outside the car to pull the window back up. However, right now his greatest concern was how to shut the door. He'd face the other problems the car presented after he completed that.

With the window down, he grabbed the door with his left hand and pulled with gigantic efforts. Didn't move. Next, he faced the door, braced his feet on the floor, placed both hands on the door, and heaved. The hinge gave a soft pop and moved maybe an inch before an earsplitting shriek came from the mysterious nexus where the hinge disappeared into the car.

Using great effort to remember his high school physics, he realized pulling was not the best way to exert pressure. He slid out and considered how to exert irresistible force. No, that wasn't physics. Newton's Laws of Motion said something like he had to create a force or something to counteract . . . well, something. He didn't really remember it, but he felt sure pushing would create more force than pulling.

He planted his feet, put his hands below the window, and pushed.

Nothing.

"Need help?"

He turned to see Brother Swanson from the Church of Christ. "Yes, can you give me a hand? Or a shoulder? My door won't close."

With that, the two men stood a foot away from the car, Adam facing the center of the door and Brother Swanson on his right for optimal force.

"One, two, three," they counted together. On *three,* they leaned forward and heaved with every ounce of muscle as well as Brother Swanson's considerable mass.

When the door didn't move even a fraction of an inch, Adam thought the car must be snickering at him. After all the problems it had tossed at him, the car had finally outsmarted him.

He figured the mechanic who kept the car going could fix it, but he could hardly drive to the garage with the door sticking out.

"Think you're going to have to call the tow truck." Brother Swanson wiped his hands.

"Thanks."

As the vehicular good Samaritan strolled off, Adam decided to try one more thing. First Law of Physics: Every object in a state of uniform motion tends to remain in that state of motion unless an external force is applied to it. There, he'd thought of the entire law and realized he hadn't applied enough external force.

Filled with frustration and refusing to be defeated or to spend money on something he could fix, Adam stepped back six feet and hunkered down like a charging football lineman, right shoulder forward. He took a deep breath and charged.

By his second step, he realized the idiocy of this maneuver and attempted to stop. However, by then the law of momentum took over and kept him moving inexorably to meet the hulking turtle.

Pain exploded in his shoulder. After being

thrown backward in an arc, he fell on the ground moaning and holding his arm against him in an effort to relieve the pain shooting through him. Didn't work.

He'd forgotten Newton's Third Law of Motion: For every action there's an equal and opposite reaction. He lay there, a perfect example of that law.

Nevertheless, it seemed he'd exerted enough force to move the door because, when he glared at it, he realized it stood open only a couple of inches. Due to his own screams, he hadn't heard the shrieking of the metal.

Immediately he looked around in the hope no one had seen or heard this. For once, his idiocy had not been witnessed by a crowd. He attempted to leap to his feet before someone came by and asked him why he lay writhing on the asphalt. However, leaping to his feet was out of the question. He cradled his arm against his body and rolled up to a sitting position. Rear end firmly on the pavement and both feet flat on the ground, he glanced around again hoping no one could see his duck-like stance. Little by little and using his knees, he levered himself to his feet.

Once standing, he opened the back door to reach inside for the bag of athletic supplies he kept there, took out an instant cold pack, and attempted to break the seal with one hand. Impossible. He stuck it in his mouth, careful to keep his teeth on the flat edge, and pulled with the good hand. It popped and immediately cooled. He stuck that under his shirt, squarely on his right shoulder, and waited until the cold began to numb the pain.

He flexed his shoulder a little. Didn't kill him. Probably he was only bruised. No way he wanted to explain to anyone how this had happened. From the injury, it would be obvious he'd thrown himself against something and had lost.

He stared at the car, which still grinned at him although the vehicle would have to agree that Adam had done pretty well on that last battle.

If he'd dented the door, it wouldn't be obvious—a ding would blend in with the chipped paint, the other dents, and the overall sad appearance of the poor broken turtle.

Before he could decide what to do next, his cell rang. He awkwardly fished it out of his right pocket with his left hand.

"Preacher," Maggie said. "Abby Jenkins fell again."

"How is she?" He held on to his shoulder and hoped she was doing better than he was.

"Just bruised, but she'd like to see you at the nursing home."

"On my way."

He could, of course, leave the car here and walk to the nursing home. He did that often to visit Abby and the other church members who lived in town. Then what? Walk home and pick up the car here tomorrow? Darned if he'd send Hector after it because he'd have to explain. He didn't even want to contemplate the jostling a walk would do to his shoulder but, mostly, he didn't want to have to explain why he'd left the car in the hospital parking lot and wandered all over town on foot.

He knew he couldn't open the door on the driver's side again, both because he figured he physically couldn't and because then he'd have to close it again and he had only one healthy shoulder left, which he was *not* about to destroy. He walked around to the passenger side and opened the door wide. After inspecting the interior and planning the best entrance, he sat on the seat, pulled his legs inside, and turned, still protecting his shoulder from contact with the seat. Once settled, he turned, let go of his right elbow to reach his left hand across his body, and pulled the door shut. Then he slowly scooted across the seat and over the console—not as easy a maneuver as one might think—until he arrived in front of the steering wheel. He propped his right arm on the steering wheel and considered the situation.

How in the world was he going to keep the door from flying open? He didn't think it would, but it might could, as a final victory. If it did, it could cause an accident or hit someone. As a responsible driver, he couldn't risk that.

What had he done to deserve this? Well, he'd forced the turtle beyond its limits for years.

Poor old thing really was ready to give up.

The turtle was like an elderly horse who wanted to be left in the stable for the rest of its days. Sorry, he couldn't do that. He had no replacement and no choice but to just keep pushing it.

He glanced at the place where the door handle hung. Could he reattach it? He studied the handle and checked the mechanism. No, that was beyond him with only one usable hand.

As he reached for the seat belt, he realized he couldn't pull it down and buckle it. He'd have to hold the door shut through the window and drive with his right arm. That should work okay if he went very slowly and didn't have to make any fast turns. Probably not the best and safest method, but he had to move on. When he got home, he could work on a solution because he preferred not to call Rex and spend more money. He had higher priorities: He planned to feed the kids.

He couldn't put his key in the ignition with his right hand so he slid over the console, put the key in, and turned the engine on. Then he slid back behind the wheel and lifted his right arm on top of it before he realized he had to shift. Putting his foot on the brake, he reached the left hand way over and moved the gear into drive.

By this time, sweat was pouring down his face and entire body. Good thing the window was open to cool him down.

With that positive thought, he backed out of the

spot. Out on the highway and going five miles an hour, he could see that traffic had backed up behind him. The good thing about living in a small town? Everyone recognized his car and waved as they passed him, figuring the turtle had fallen apart again. No honking, no impatience, because the town folks enjoyed the eccentricities of the residents of Butternut Creek. The tale of the minister and his junker would be told and embellished for years.

That evening, Adam rested his arm at the dining room table as Janey worked on a math assignment. Hector had headed out to pick up Bree.

Only seconds after he left, Hector opened the front door and stuck his head inside. "Hey, Pops, did you know the door on the driver's side doesn't close?"

Friday evening, Gussie watched Adam and Janey head home. Janey had joined Adam to walk her home because Hector was out with friends. The two crossed the tiny porch of Sam's old house and leaped down the steps. When they reached the sidewalk, both turned to wave. She kept her eyes on them until they disappeared into the dark.

How could she have found a man so perfect for her? If this were a movie, she'd dance around the living room singing about his perfection and her adoration. If she still had the privacy of her upstairs room in the house her parents used to live in, she could have yodeled and no one would have heard her.

But three people lived in this house only a few square feet larger than her old bedroom, and she had to be sensitive. If she let loose of her joy, she'd wake up everyone on the block because Gussie could not sing quietly. And she was a terrible dancer. She approached the steps with great enthusiasm but little ability or grace.

Besides, her father was watching a game on television and probably wouldn't appreciate her boisterous expressions of love and joy. Her parents had their schedules and she had hers. When they didn't mesh, they tried to get along, but it did bring up conflict. Perhaps good practice for when she and Adam got married, except she'd move into that huge parsonage with two full bathrooms and two half-baths and lots of room in case she felt like yodeling or dancing or whooping.

She grinned inside, both amazed and delighted that marriage to Adam had become "when" not "if." Made her feel like whooping and dancing all over again, at least until her mother opened the bedroom door and leaned out.

"Did you and Adam have a nice evening?" she asked. "Never mind, I can tell that you did." She came out and hugged Gussie before she turned toward her husband. "Henry, are you coming to bed?"

Her father waved but didn't take his eyes from the screen. "Game's almost over. Just two minutes."

Of course, two minutes in a basketball game could last for hours.

Then he said, "Hey, Gus," but kept watching the game.

"I don't know why I even attempt to communicate with him during any type of televised game." Mom shook her head. "I should have learned over all these years." She kissed Gussie's cheek and headed back to the bedroom. "Good night, dear."

"Night, Mom." With the door closed, she asked her father, "Would you like a soda? I'm going to get something to drink."

"No, thanks. Game's almost over."

Her parents had put everything in storage in Austin, bringing just their clothing, books, and coffeemaker with them. After the move from a two-story house with four televisions to a house with one, Gussie and her mother had given all television rights to Henry.

If Gussie really wanted to watch something, she could fight for the set at the parsonage or visit Ouida or Mattie, the minister of the Presbyterian Church. Usually, it was easier to miss her programs and keep Dad happy. Less friction.

The hardest part of the arrangement was sharing a bathroom. The three of them were on top of each other all the time, and with her father's prostate problems . . . well, it was good she didn't live here all week.

"I'm going to bed, Dad." She picked up her glass and headed toward the smaller bedroom.

Chapter Four

The bump of the landing awakened Hannah Jordan. She'd slept during most of the flight from Nairobi to London, during the three days she spent with her parents in London, then the eight-hour flight to New York. The only thing that had awakened her from the trip on the red-eye between New York and Dallas was the change of planes in Atlanta.

She slept deeply, almost as if she were hibernating. She didn't merely doze off. As soon as she closed her eyes, it was as if she'd fallen into a deep pit and had to struggle to pull herself up and out when she woke up.

As a doctor, she knew her body was attempting to make up for the sleep deficit from the last few months of fighting off the effects of malaria and persistent insomnia—but she still hated it. Fatigue made her feel stupid and weak and altogether not like the Hannah Jordan who'd been the youngest person to receive the Gestner-Croft Fellowship in Epidemiology for study in Kenya. This noodle-like person bore no relationship to the young woman who, only two years before, had stood on the edge of her life, looking forward with excitement and joy and strength and enthusiasm and confidence.

Where had that Hannah gone?

Oh, she knew. A few months earlier, the young, optimistic Hannah who still had a functioning brain had expired in a refugee camp in Kenya, among the emaciated children and dying babies. This pathetic husk had been left behind.

"Ma'am, you'll need to collect your bags and deplane." A flight attendant stood beside the seat looking so perky and fresh and healthy, Hannah felt even more depressed.

She hadn't even noticed that the rest of the passengers had filed off the plane.

Putting her hand on the seat in front of her, Hannah pulled herself to her feet, grabbed her tote, wrenched her carry-on from the overhead compartment, and headed out.

When she arrived in the terminal, she considered flagging down one of the electrical carts that carried older and handicapped passengers between gates. Tempting, but she hated to confess to weakness and the constant beep-beeps would drive her nuts. Besides, the terminal had those moving sidewalks that made the trip easier.

Once she arrived at the baggage claim area and pulled her duffel bag from the carousel, she looked around. Her father had bought a car, which the dealer agreed to deliver to her at the airport as part of a plan her mother had come up with and her father had financed. She immediately saw a man holding a sign with her name on it.

"I'm Hannah," she said and handed him her passport for identification.

He studied it and passed it back. "My name is Eddie. I'll take your bags and meet you in the loading zone. I'll be driving your Escalade."

"My what?"

"Big black SUV. Lots of chrome," he explained. "I'll wave if you don't see me."

Considering her state of mind and the probable number of black SUVs, the wave sounded like a good idea. She watched him leave with her luggage and wondered if she should have asked him for ID. He could be headed off with her few possessions.

Why bother? Nothing she had was worth the effort.

Shoving that worry away, Hannah found a ladies' room and studiously avoided looking in a mirror. She knew she looked terrible. Had for months. But she didn't need to or want to or *have* to face that right now. Then she found a snack bar and grabbed a huge Coke and a protein bar. She paused to pull out her cell and called her parents. When the machine picked up, she said, "I'm here. Your plan is in place," and hung up. The message made her feel slightly like a character in a bad spy movie.

That accomplished, she headed toward passenger pickup. As she walked, she reminded herself that in the States, unlike London or Kenya, cars drove on the right. Then she told herself that again in an effort to reacclimate her porous brain to driving in the United States.

After she found Eddie and the car, and accepted and signed for the keys, she inspected the huge vehicle. She would have preferred something smaller and with better mileage. Her father had listened to her suggestions but chosen this enormous thing. She tossed her bag in the back and hauled herself into the front seat. What was the name of that place her brother lived now? Oh, yes—Butternut Stream or Buttercup Creek or Butter something else. By the time she'd consumed enough caffeine that she wouldn't be a hazard on the road and had headed south, she decided there couldn't be many places with such idyllic names in the state.

She also knew she'd hate anyplace with a name like Butter-whatever.

Adam wasn't expecting her. She hadn't told him she'd be coming. She'd ordered her parents not to tell him because she didn't know if she could actually go through with the visit, if she could face him. Adam exuded goodness and positiveness, traits she'd shed long ago and might nauseate her now. Could be she'd stop before she got to Butter-whatever, maybe head down to Houston and hide, like an injured lioness going into the bush to die. Where was the bush in Texas? The bush could cover the entire state, for all she knew, but she didn't see any around Dallas–Fort Worth.

Then the loud honking started. So much for not being a traffic hazard. The light must have turned green two seconds earlier and the cars behind her let her know. She reminded herself that in the United States, most people stopped at a light within a second of its turning red and started through the intersection when it turned green. In Nairobi, waves of drivers flowed through the intersection for seconds after the light changed and drove fast in the hope no other vehicle would hit their car. There, starting through an intersection at the exact time the light turned green was suicidal.

In an email, Adam once told her drivers in Texas believed yellow lights meant, *Speed up. You can make it through.* That constituted a problem for him. He'd never driven in Kenya.

Fifty miles south of DFW, she began to feel nostalgic. The landscape had become greener with more trees. The scenery of Texas, a state she'd always thought of as flat and barren, surprised her. It looked a little like Kentucky, a bit like parts of Africa.

But no matter how pretty, Texas wasn't Africa. The golden glow she associated with the continent didn't shimmer in the air or reflect against the brown fields. The trees looked like trees instead of the distinctive acacias she'd learned to love, as flat as if someone had squished the limbs down and parallel to the ground.

Seeing cattle grazing in a feedlot, the knowledge that she wouldn't gasp at the sight of a rhino or laugh at a curious monkey close to the camp hurt.

People had told her that Africa grabbed one's soul and squeezed it tight. At this moment, she knew that well. She almost couldn't breathe she missed Kenya so much, even more than she'd come to hate it.

Later that Saturday morning, when the phone in the parsonage rang again, Adam checked the calendar over the phone. He wanted to be sure he did nothing to mess up a scholarship opportunity for Hector. Right now, the college coaches were in an evaluation period. He knew a couple of scouts had attended the past few games but couldn't talk to him or Hector during that time frame. Still, college and juco coaches could email—Coach Borden dealt with those messages—and call. Adam answered the phone and took notes. Hector hadn't wanted to deal with them during the season and had asked Adam to continue fielding the calls.

After he hung up, Adam watched Janey and Yvonne. They sat at the dining room table, working on Janey's reading.

"You know," Yvonne said, "Janey's a really smart little girl."

Janey glowed with the praise.

He nodded. "People with dyslexia usually are. As the school counselor explained, that's how the problem is caught—when a bright student doesn't perform as well as expected."

"I found some fun ways to help with comprehension online," Yvonne said.

"Thanks. Hector and I really appreciate your help." Before he could say more the phone rang again.

He glanced at the messages in his hand, then at the clock. Ten o'clock Saturday morning and already eight calls from colleges recruiting Hector.

They started at nine, probably knowing that a kid wouldn't be up earlier and a parent wouldn't like being awakened early. On Saturdays—Adam's day to be with Gussie and the kids, an oasis of calm and quiet, a day to sleep a little late to recover from a basketball game, a day to tweak his sermon—he'd become an answering machine for calls from recruiters. In fact, every evening and all weekend he assumed that role.

He picked up the phone, chatted briefly with the assistant coach who called, wrote down the name of the college and of the coach, and thanked him.

As Adam promised to pass the message on, Gussie entered the front door. He quickly finished the telephone conversation, clicked the phone off, and headed toward her for a hug.

"Who was that?" she asked.

"Small college up close to Midland."

"Hector's a good player." She went into the kitchen and poured a cup of coffee. "A good player from a middle-size high school in a small town and you get lots of calls. How in the world do those top players from 5A high schools keep track of all this?"

"I had no idea the amount of time and organization it would take." He held up his hand. "Not that I mind. It's better for me to spend the time than take it from Hector's studies and basketball, but I'll be glad when the signing date arrives."

He grabbed a cup of coffee, left phone duty with Gussie, and headed for his study at the church. The house where Hector and Janey lived and where Gussie and her parents spent most of their time, a home filled with noise and activity, was great—but work there was impossible.

When he headed back to the parsonage for lunch, he waved at Hector, Bobby, and the other guys who were playing a pickup game in the parking lot.

For dinner that evening, five of them—all three Miltons, Janey, and Adam—sat around the table and lapped up Yvonne's homemade cream of broccoli soup. Hector was with his calculus study group and due to get in soon. In fact, those gathered at the table appreciated Hector's arriving a little late because they all got to fill their bowl and pick up a biscuit or two before the kid could eat everything.

"Has Hector come to a decision about school next year?" Henry asked.

"He and Coach are going to talk more and set up some visits." Adam reached for another biscuit. "Gabe's coming over later to share info from college scouts he's talked to."

Janey looked up, eyes wide. "I'm going to miss him."

"That's why we're looking for a school close by," Adam said. "So you can go to his games and he can come home."

"Okay." Janey nodded. "But I'm still going to miss him. I know it's good, but . . ."

Before she could finish the sentence, they heard the front door open.

"Hector?" Janey said.

"Gabe?" Adam shouted.

"You'd think someone in this town would know where Twelve Church Street is," a grumpy but definitely female voice grumbled loudly from the front hall.

Adam jumped to his feet and ran to the foyer. "Hannah? Is that you?" Of course it was. Who else but his sister would arrive unannounced and grouchy?

She looked terrible. Not that he'd tell her that and not that his parents hadn't warned him, but he hadn't expected her to look this bad. Pale, painfully thin, even for his family, and sagging against the doorjamb. Her short dark hair looked as if she had spikes sticking out all over her head. Not fashionable spikes, but spikes that looked as if she never combed it. Clean, of course, because Hannah was fastidious, but tangled and unruly and disheveled.

"Good to see you." Adam pulled his sister into his arms and hugged her.

Because she wasn't a particularly huggable person, Adam was surprised she didn't pull away immediately. No, she collapsed against him for nearly a second before she stiffened, then shoved him away weakly and took a stumbling step back. Was that a shimmer of tears in her eyes? Certainly not. Hannah never cried.

She blinked, and the impression disappeared. She repeated, "Why doesn't anyone in town know where Twelve Church Street is? That's the address Mom gave me." She pointed behind her. "The street sign says church street and the number by your front door says twelve but all anyone could tell me was to try behind the Christian Church. As if I knew where *that* was."

He heard Yvonne's footsteps in the hall.

"You must be Adam's sister," Yvonne said. "How good to see you."

Adam knew his sister, knew she wanted to answer with a snarky comment like, *Why* must *I be Adam's sister?* She had two ways of communicating: in scientific terms and in snark, the latter to protect herself. This time she didn't. She must be really sick.

Hannah sorted through the cotton candy her brain had become but couldn't come up with an answer. Instead, she gave Yvonne a quivery smile and said, "I'm Hannah. Are you Miss Birdie?"

"Oh, no, no. I'm Yvonne Milton." When that statement left Hannah confused and blinking, Yvonne added, "Gussie's mother."

"Oh, yes. Gussie's mother." Hannah nodded. *Who is Gussie?*

Yvonne must have read her expression because she said, "Gussie is Adam's young woman." She took Hannah's hand and patted it comfortingly. "You must be tired after that long trip."

Hannah felt her brain click onto "overload" again. Why couldn't she keep anything straight? Of course she knew who Gussie was, but she'd become so forgetful lately.

Even harder to understand that she'd allowed Adam to hug her and this woman she'd never met to grasp her hand and pat it. She'd never considered herself a person who liked to have her hand patted, but she did at this moment. Quickly Hannah snatched the patted body part back. Her plans did not include being happy and comfortable, although that soothing moment of compassion hadn't felt all that terrible.

"Dear, you look so tired," Yvonne said. "Why don't you join us for dinner, then we'll find you a bed and you can take a nice, long nap."

She didn't really feel like eating but it never worked to turn a meal down because no one ever listened to her when she said she wasn't hungry. Logically, if a person looked like a walking corpse, nice people assumed she should eat. Made sense, but she'd discovered that sitting down at a meal with others and stuffing food inside reminded her of starving refugees. Not the vision one wanted when gathered around a table of healthy people.

She followed her brother into the dining area as Yvonne went into the kitchen to get her a plate.

Adam waved around the table. "This is Henry, Gussie's father. That's Janey and here's Gussie."

As Adam held out a chair for her, a tall young man with dark skin thundered into the house. "Hey, Pops, come outside," he said in a voice that—along with the pounding of his huge feet—made her head hurt even more. "There's a really great car parked in front of the house."

"We'll look at it later." Adam motioned the kid to a seat. "Hannah, this is Hector."

They all smiled at Hannah. A huge smile covered Gussie's friendly face, her eyes shone brightly, and her dark curls bounced with vitality. Hannah could see why Adam loved Gussie, but the sight of all that energy absolutely exhausted her.

She nodded at everyone and attempted to think of something that sounded polite to respond to the welcome but nothing came to mind. "*Enchantée*," she whispered because she'd spoken French with the international medical personnel and seemed to have left her English-speaking mind in London. Fortunately, before Hannah felt the need to say more in a foreign language, Yvonne came from the kitchen with a bowl and a glass of something.

"Sweetened or unsweetened?" Gussie's mother asked.

What was she talking about?

"Your tea," the woman explained. "Sweetened or unsweetened?"

Hannah had never heard that question. Tea was tea. One added sugar or sweetener if one wanted it sweet. Why would anyone ask that?

"Unsweetened," Adam said for her. "Up north, we only have one choice. Tea, unsweetened."

"Well, don't that beat all," Yvonne said. "Customs are different all over." She placed the glass and bowl of soup in front of Hannah. "Try a few biscuits." She handed Hannah the basket.

"They're really good," said the little girl with a shy smile. "I like mine with lots of butter."

How sweet. For a moment Hannah considered smiling—until the faces of hungry children in Kenya surfaced in her mind. She swallowed hard and reminded herself of her decision not to allow those memories to haunt her. She had to learn how to live in *this* world, surrounded by healthy people who didn't have to cover their beds with mosquito netting to stay alive, by people who lived in houses with clean water and enough food and, oddly, a choice between sweetened and unsweetened tea.

Adam watched her, attempting to hide the expression of concern she'd seen on so many faces over the last months. When had she become an object of pity? Well, obviously during the last few months when she couldn't fight off the effects of malaria. Everyone else on the staff recovered from that disease quickly and easily. Not Hannah.

The soup looked delicious. As she reached for a spoon, the scent hit her and made her feel slightly nauseous. "I think I'll try a biscuit," she said, picking one from the basket. No butter. Her stomach didn't feel ready for that, but the biscuits tasted wonderful as they were.

"Yvonne," Janey said in a soft voice and with an expression of yearning in her dark eyes. "Could we bake brownies tonight? I really like brownies."

"Sis, you're shameless," Hector lectured before turning toward Yvonne. "Don't let her con you. She'll say anything to get brownies."

"How adorable." Yvonne leaned forward and took Janey's hand. "Of course I'll make you brownies. Let's do that tomorrow after church."

"Thank you, Yvonne." Janey grinned.

"Now, dear." Yvonne turned to Hannah. "If the soup doesn't look good to you, I could fix you some bouillon or a poached egg if you'd like. Maybe some toast?"

All this sweetness would raise Hannah's blood sugar to disastrous levels if she stuck around.

Adam had learned long ago not to push his sister for information or communication, and not to expect polite conversation, because Hannah considered it pointless. She believed anything that didn't relate to medicine or healing others to be useless chitchat. Unfortunately, he always forgot that until the next time her determination to do things her way slapped him in the face.

Sometimes he wondered where she'd come from. Like his mother, Adam was fairly laid-back. In grade school, he always received positive marks for "gets along well with others."

Their father was forceful, but Hannah had moved far beyond merely compelling. She radiated an intensity that scared all but the most confident of people. At least, she used to.

Nor did they look alike. Adam and his parents were fairly standard and boringly Scotch-Irish with a little German ancestry tossed in, but Hannah looked as if she'd been abducted from a band of wandering gypsies. Their mother had claimed Romany ancestry, and that heredity appeared undiluted in Hannah's dark eyes, olive skin, unruly hair, and wildly independent personality.

He also knew better than to tell her to go to bed. She'd stay up for hours or days to thwart him, but he hadn't been her little brother for all these years without learning a few tricks. She was immovable but not unmanipulatable. He'd stumbled on the method to induce her to do what he wanted when he discovered that if she thought he didn't care, she'd do whatever he wanted.

"How long are you staying?" he asked casually as he cleared the table.

"Don't know," Hannah answered after she swallowed the last of her second biscuit. "A few days? A month? A couple of hours?"

He placed the dishes in the sink and counted a few seconds before turning toward her. He leaned against the counter as if he didn't have a concern in the world. "Do you want to choose a bedroom?"

"All of these people are staying here and you have extra bedrooms?"

"Yvonne and Henry rent a house a few blocks away. Gussie stays with them on the weekends but spends weekdays in Austin." He gestured overhead. "Janey, Hector, and I each have bedrooms upstairs, which leaves two small, unoccupied ones on that floor." He shrugged indifferently. "Your choice."

Fortunately, as smart as Hannah was, she'd

never figured out his ploy of feigned indifference. His supervisor in clinical pastoral education would have said she had an oppositional personality. True, but not the whole story. She barreled straight through life without regard for anyone or anything that interfered with her goal of saving the world.

"Okay." She wiped her mouth with the napkin, tossed it on the table, and stood.

"Y'all go on," Henry said. "Janey and I'll bus the table."

"Hey, people." Bobby shoved through the front door and slammed it behind him.

Hannah cringed at the noise. She'd suffered from headaches as long as he could remember. All the pushing and stress and sheer stubbornness brought on headaches, and the trip probably hadn't helped.

"Hannah, this is Hector's friend, Bobby."

She nodded at him.

"Bobby and I are going to shoot some hoops," Hector said.

As the two young men headed outside, Adam shepherded his sister toward the back stairs, knowing that the less elegant flight would be more acceptable to Hannah than the beautifully carved and curved front steps. Besides, it was closer and he feared she couldn't walk any extra distance. Not that he'd ever say that.

Once on the second floor, he said, "Hector and

Janey share a bathroom between their rooms." He pointed down the hall to those two doors. "I have the big bedroom because, when I got here, no one else lived here." He pointed toward that door. "I have a bathroom that also opens to the hall."

"I'm not taking your bedroom," she stated.

He knew that. Without responding, Adam gestured to his left and right. "These two rooms at the back of the house are still up for grabs. They're quiet but a little smaller. You'd have to use the half-bath upstairs or share mine."

She shivered as if sharing a bathroom with her brother bothered her. Maybe as kids she'd had a reason, but he no longer left underwear or wet towels on the floor.

"What's upstairs?" She turned toward the narrow door next to the stairs.

"It's sort of a storage room or a play area." He opened that door, turned on the lights, and led her up the steep steps.

Running both the length and the breadth of the house, the area was huge and open, with storage built in to the eaves. At one end a window seat was built in the curve of the tower. A little dust covered the floor and surfaces because he never used it, but Janey often cleaned it because she loved to sit on the window seat and daydream.

"There's a half-bath in that corner."

Hannah nodded. "This will do."

"Hector and I'll bring up a bed and dresser."

"No, no. I'm fine. Just bring me a blanket. I'll sleep on the floor."

"You are so full of it." Adam shook his head. "I'm not going to allow you to sleep on the floor. Who are you attempting to be? Mother Teresa? Or one of those mystics who whip themselves and wear hair shirts?"

She glared at him, but he didn't budge.

"You're not going to repudiate all earthly comforts. We will bring up a bed," he stated in the tone he used to get Chewy to do everything the dog didn't want to. Never worked with Chewy.

"Oh, all right."

Surprisingly, it worked with his sister.

He called Hector and Bobby inside, and they disassembled the bed in one of the unused bedrooms. Adam joined them to navigate it up the staircase to the third floor. They found Hannah asleep on the window seat, her face peaceful and her breathing regular.

"Pops, let her sleep. We can finish this later. She looks so tired, I don't want to disturb her."

Adam didn't think a marching band could awaken his sister. "Let's set it up so she'll have a better place to sleep."

He was right. His sister didn't wake up even when Hector dropped one of the rails and Bobby whacked the wall with another. With the bed put together and made, he tucked a blanket around his sister and kissed her cheek, about the only time she allowed such displays of affection.

After they went downstairs, Hector looked outside. "Pops, you got the keys to that Escalade?"

"No, Hannah has them, but we can check it out even if we can't get inside."

Because the car doors were all locked—Hannah wasn't used to small towns—they had to enjoy it from outside. Hector rubbed his hand along the ebony surface of the car. "It's nice, Pops. Not a dent on it, no patches of peeling paint."

Bobby cupped his hands to look in a window. "No holes in the upholstery. No springs coming through."

"Bet the windows work." Hector looked at the SUV with longing.

"Do you think the doors open and close?" Bobby asked. "And maybe it doesn't stop in the middle of the highway and its parts don't fall off on the road."

"Might as well stop dreaming," Adam said. "Guys, I could never afford a car like this. Even paying the insurance would mean we couldn't eat again."

"Yeah, I know, but I didn't realize how horrible your car is until I saw this one." Hector walked around the Escalade, caressing it.

After a few minutes, Adam went back inside and left Bobby and Hector to admire the car, a doomed and one-sided attraction.

●●●

The next afternoon, Hannah glanced around the family room. After church and a quick lunch—of which she'd eaten much more than she'd expected—the men had cleaned the kitchen, then turned on the television to watch a college basketball game. On the other side of the high counter between this room and the kitchen, Janey and Yvonne stirred up a batch of brownies.

Hannah had curled up on the large comfortable chair, pulled the burnt orange throw she'd found on the back of the sofa over her, and now read a particularly interesting article on vector-borne diseases. She hated having to wrap up, hated huddling in a blanket, but—darn it!—she was cold. Had felt a chill even in the heat of Africa when she'd been sick, so why wouldn't she during a cooler Texas spring when she'd barely recovered? A shiver made her teeth chatter. Would she ever be warm again?

Henry watched her for a second before he stood, walked into the front parlor, and returned with a blanket. Without a word, he spread the cover over her and returned to the sofa.

How did he know he'd found the best way to handle her? Go ahead and do it, don't ask for permission, and ignore her protests. See a need, respond with an act of kindness, but don't mention it.

As Hector watched television, he surreptitiously

glanced toward her. From the thoroughness of his scrutiny, she felt like a recently cloned species, a rare specimen to welcome but not to understand.

Hannah had gotten to a particularly interesting section in her book on an experimental treatment for African trypanosomiasis when someone knocked on the front door.

"Hey, Coach," Hector yelled as he leaped to his feet—the young man always leaped and ran. Just watching him wore her out.

He reached the door and threw it open. "Come on in."

A perfect specimen of a man strode into the parlor. Taller than average, he possessed beautifully developed sets of biceps brachii and pectoralis major. He radiated such good health, it seemed as if a light glowed around him, as if sunlight constantly followed him and reflected from his blond hair.

The sight dazzled her. She closed her eyes for a second before she opened them because she wanted—almost needed—to study him. Only a slit, though, because she couldn't take much more. She drank in his splendor.

She bet he knew he was a special creation and had no desire to build his ego by allowing him to notice her scrutiny. With a tug, she pulled the blanket tighter around her and held the textbook closer to her face, making sure she could see over the top a smidge.

"Hey, everyone." The supernatural being smiled and waved.

Then, as she knew he would because guys like him believed everyone wanted to meet them, he shifted the folders he carried to his left hand, headed toward her, and held out his strong, tanned right hand. "I'm Gabe Borden."

She nodded without raising her eyes from the page.

"I'm Hector's basketball coach," he added.

"He used to play pro ball with the Rockets," Hector added. "Now he's my coach."

"Oh," she murmured because she had no idea what or who the Rockets were, but if he was Hector's coach, it must be a basketball team someplace. If he used to play pro ball and now coached high school, he must have fallen in the world. How had he lost all his money?

Adam leaped in, as she knew he would, because Adam was a nice guy and really hated when she behaved this way. "Gabe, this is my sister, Hannah."

She looked up, unwilling to be rude to her brother. For a moment, the guy's eyes studied her; then his glance jumped to the bookcase and the picture of her Adam kept there. She should have ripped the photo up the moment she arrived. It showed a healthy, optimistic, happy, sort of pretty, and maybe a little exotic Hannah only days before she'd left for Africa.

Now here she sat, the shattered shell she'd become. Even the most self-absorbed man would notice the difference between happy Hannah and shattered-shell Hannah.

She had to hand it to the guy. His expression didn't change when confronted with the wreckage of Hannah Jordan. He greeted her with a smile, white teeth shimmering. She could almost detect little stars glinting from their brilliance. In addition to the killer smile, he had a square chin with a tiny cleft and, for heaven's sake, gorgeous green eyes that must have enthralled hundreds, thousands, of women.

God must have felt generous when assembling Gabe Borden.

With iron will, she refused to allow her eyes to stray to his body—again. In her quick, surreptitious glance, she'd noted he was muscular and sculpted and cut. She had no desire to take in that glowing good health. Only made her depressed. Besides, she still needed to read about Crimean-Congo hemorrhagic fever.

Although this guy did look much more interesting than bleeding bowels, she had to prepare herself for if—no, when—she returned to the refugee camps to care for people who actually did suffer from this malady. She dropped her eyes to the article.

"Whose great car is that?" The supernatural being pointed a thumb toward the driveway.

Okay, so maybe she hadn't stopped peeking at him.

She raised her hand to claim ownership of the vehicle but continued to read. Well, to pretend to read.

"Great car, isn't it?" Hector said. "Can I drive it?"

What was it with men and cars? Well, maybe not with Adam because he drove that ugly clunker. All she cared about was that it got her where she wanted to go—which, from his emails, Adam's often didn't.

"Maybe later," she mumbled, because she found she couldn't treat Hector rudely, either.

When she didn't say more, Adam herded Hector away.

Gabe had trouble believing this malnourished waif hunched over a magazine was the same woman in the photo he'd occasionally glimpsed when he visited the parsonage. Occasionally glimpsed? He'd studied it every time he was alone in this room, halfway in love with the glowing creature standing next to her brother in the picture, laughing and filled with joy and vibrancy.

Somewhere under the wild hair and inside the cold eyes that had glared at him—what had he done to deserve that?—lived the woman in the photo. The woman he felt confident, after meeting her, would never fall in love with him. Doubted now she'd ever like him, maybe would never look at him or even say two or three words to him.

He studied the top of her head before saying, "Hector, let's look over these letters and emails and Adam's notes." He strode toward the counter between the kitchen and family room and began laying out file folders.

Adam handed the remote to Henry and joined them.

"Coach, you know I want to stay in Texas, close to here." Hector nodded toward Janey, who had placed the pan of brownies in the oven.

"That gets rid of these." Gabe picked up several thick folders. "You have lots of interest from out-of-state schools, good programs."

"I know."

"You've done a great job of converting to shooting guard, and that's the position they're scouting you for."

Hector nodded.

"This means we work on your outside shooting and look for a good small school here in Texas, four-year or juco, right?" Gabe said to make sure they all agreed.

"Right," Hector agreed.

"Seems like every town in Texas has a junior college or small college," Adam said.

"Seems like," Gabe agreed. "Here are the ones I think might fit you."

As Gabe listed colleges, Adam added information he'd picked up from the recruiting calls he'd fielded. They wrote all this down on the whiteboard they'd attached to the wall next to the counter.

"We need to set up your five visits," Gabe said. For another hour, they made lists and shared information, occasionally adding or crossing off a school. They ended up with a list of ten schools within one hundred miles of Butternut Creek that had shown interest. They worked just long enough for the brownies to bake and cool.

Finished, Gabe took one of the thick chocolate morsels from the plate Yvonne had set on the counter. For a moment as he chewed, Gabe allowed his eyes to drift toward Hannah. She occupied the same chair, but the book had fallen to the floor and she slept. In repose, her long, dark lashes curved against pale skin. Her closed eyes hid the glare she'd worn when she saw him. Soft snores came from a mouth that hadn't deigned to speak to him. Asleep, she looked calm, peaceful, and almost angelic.

"She's had a rough time," Adam said.

The dark smudges under the lashes and skin stretched across sharp cheekbones attested to Adam's observation. Yes, she look angelic, but not well. Not a bit. For a moment, he felt protective of her, as if a woman who'd survived the refugee camps of Kenya needed anyone to look after her, let alone him. She'd made it very clear that she didn't like him.

Why not? Women usually did. But her words and response made him realize he'd have to either develop a tough hide to get to know Hannah or forget that foolish attraction he'd felt for the woman she used to be.

"Thanks for the brownies," Gabe said to Yvonne. "Bye, y'all."

He left and headed toward his apartment. When he got inside, he realized he still thought about Hannah, still wondered. Should he forget her or attempt to win her with charm and persistence? Somehow he felt charm wouldn't sway her, especially since she'd given him little opportunity even to chat with her. As for persistence, he had no idea how long she'd be in town or if he'd ever exchange a word with her.

Instead of thinking about the impossibility of wooing Adam's sister, he turned on the television, took a brownie from the sack Yvonne had sent home with him, and watched an NBA game.

Birdie had heard that the preacher's sister had arrived in town a week earlier, but no one in her vast network of informants had reported a sighting. Well, Yvonne had talked to Hannah but refused to pass any information on. Family, she said, and confidential. Birdie had to admire that, darn it!

Her eyes moved around the sanctuary. The basketball coach sat next to Bobby and Hector. The Kowalskis sat in a pew near the back, all four of them. Good to see them. Birdie had never thought they'd come, but the girls loved Sunday school and the children's sermon. Adam had added that when they started having a few children in the service again.

Good crowd this morning. They were averaging seventy-five a Sunday, up from forty when the preacher first arrived. With her guidance, he'd done a good job building up the church. Now, if he'd get married and start producing children, he'd be as near perfect as she could stand.

Then her gaze returned to Coach Borden and she smiled, an expression she knew most of the men in Butternut Creek feared but the coach hadn't seen. He wouldn't run from her, not until he realized he was the Widows' next project.

After the service, Birdie hastened toward the door to the street as fast as her aching feet would allow.

"Where's your sister?" she asked Adam after she'd pushed through the crowd waiting to greet the preacher.

Adam blinked a few times when she spoke. Probably attempting to come down from the spiritual plane to the everyday, struggling with her demand for information that had nothing to do with the just-completed service.

"Nice sermon," she said to allow him a moment to switch his mind from unworldly to the important topics of the real world. "Where's your sister?"

"Resting. She had a long flight from London."

Birdie nodded. "But that was a week ago."

"Yes, she's still tired."

"When do we get to meet her? Will she be here next week?"

Adam shrugged. "Miss Birdie, I don't know. She needs rest and . . ." He paused.

"Poor dear," Birdie murmured.

He narrowed his eyes and scrutinized her. Too polite to insult her, his expression meant he didn't believe her sympathetic murmur. He knew very well what she wanted: information. He also knew she could outwit and outwait anyone.

"Miss Birdie, my sister's very independent. Usually refuses to do anything I suggest." He shrugged. "That *anyone* suggests."

"Aha," she said. Oh, she knew from his expression he wanted to take back those words. Too late. He'd issued a challenge to the Widows. Nothing they liked better than a challenge. They'd get his sister to church if they had to carry her.

"But don't worry," he hurried to say. "She'll come when she's able." He gulped and added, "Maybe."

The man couldn't lie. That's what made him so easy to read.

She smiled triumphantly. If he wasn't so distracted by the line of people behind her, he'd realize her questions had a goal other than his sister's church attendance. "How long is she staying?"

"I don't know."

She nodded. Probably plenty of time for their purposes.

"She's not interested in much of anything now. She has health issues and . . ."

Birdie tilted her head and stared at him in the way she knew he recognized. It meant, *You can't talk me out of this.*

"Miss Birdie, if you can get her here, great, but she's a really tough case, very strong-willed." He looked past her at the congregants attempting to pass by the two of them and get out the door.

No one had a stronger will than Birdie MacDowell. Squashing the desire to rejoice in her future victory of whatever kind presented itself, she headed toward the kitchen where she knew the other three Widows would be cleaning up.

From behind her, she heard the preacher say, "Do not try to . . . ," but his words tapered off as she moved farther away.

"Blossom says the wedding plans have hit a snag," Winnie said as she wiped down the counter.

"When the bride and groom aren't engaged, it

makes planning a lot harder." Blossom nodded morosely.

Birdie hadn't known Blossom could look morose.

"I'd like to use a theme." Blossom sounded even more miserable. "What colors should we use? We don't even know what season the wedding will be."

Birdie picked up the sleeve of coffee cups from next to the coffeepot and placed it on the shelf she'd reserved for it in the coffee-cup cupboard. She'd put a large sign there to remind people but they simply didn't pay attention.

"Sometimes we have no choice but to give in to the inevitable," Birdie stated.

"What?" Winnie asked. "You're giving in?"

"To the inevitable?" Mercedes said. "Birdie MacDowell, when have you ever given in to the inevitable? You fight the inevitable with every atom of your being."

"Perhaps we should take a break from planning a wedding." Birdie smiled at the women, who studied her as if a stranger had taken over her body. "Take on another project."

"What will we do if we don't plan that wedding?" Blossom asked in her soft voice, looking a little less sad in the hope, Birdie guessed, that their leader did have a new plan of action.

"Ladies, you forget. We have another purpose. Matchmaking."

"Oh, yes." Blossom clapped her hands.

The other two didn't look as pleased. No, they took a step closer and frowned.

"Who?" Winnie asked.

"The coach," Birdie responded.

"Well, of course, but we tried that," Winnie said. "We attempted to trick him into having breakfast with the clerk at the county court office."

"And with the new librarian I'm training and the math teacher at the middle school." Birdie paused. "Why didn't we try Reverend Patillo?"

"She talked to me at the diner and begged us to leave her alone. Said she couldn't face another breakfast with a new suitor after that last one was arrested."

"And we have, for a while," Winnie said. "Left her alone."

"We threw near every presently unmarried woman in the county at the coach, and none of them stuck," Winnie pointed out. "Who's left?"

"Oh, ladies, I can tell you have lost your edge," Birdie chortled.

"For heaven's sake, if you know something, tell us," Mercedes snapped.

"The preacher's sister arrived last week."

"Oh." The other three watched Birdie, their eyes sparkling with pleasure and anticipation.

"Why didn't we know that?" Winnie asked.

"She sneaked in quietly. No one knew except

111

the family and me." She glanced around the room triumphantly. "That big black car in the front of the parsonage belongs to her."

"How did you find out?" Winnie hated not knowing stuff before Birdie or anyone else.

"Hector told Bree. He says she's been sick and is sort of thin."

"We can fix that," Mercedes said. "Fatten her up. That's one of the things we do best. How old is she?"

"When he first got here, the preacher told me she was two years older than he is." Birdie shrugged. "Doesn't make much difference. They're close to the same age."

"And they're all we have to work with," Mercedes added, truthful as ever.

"Is she single?" Winnie asked.

Birdie blinked. She had no idea. Oh, dear, dear, dear. She *was* getting old if she'd forgotten to ask the most important question of all. Now she had to confess to these women who admired her matchmaking skill that she didn't know everything. She'd failed. Admitting to that distressed her deeply.

With nothing left to do but pull up her britches, accept defeat, and move on, Birdie said, "I don't know."

At those words, Blossom's eyes grew large and a hand flew to cover her mouth. Winnie glared at Birdie.

"What?" Mercedes said, her voice filled with shock. "You don't know?"

"No, but Hector says she arrived here alone. Surely a caring spouse would be with her when she's so sick." Birdie nodded, once, to make her point.

"But we have to be sure the people we match aren't married to someone else," Mercedes said. "Even if that person is elsewhere."

"Or separated," Blossom whispered, as if she didn't like to even approach that sad possibility. "Close to a divorce but still legally married."

"Guess we'll just have to find out." Winnie nodded emphatically. "Let's go."

They tracked down the preacher heading back to his office. Poor man cowered like a cornered gerbil.

"Is your sister married?" Birdie asked. The others probably thought she should have been more subtle, sneaked the question into a longer conversation, but they knew good and well that wasn't how Birdie MacDowell operated.

The preacher straightened and blinked. After a moment, after he cleared his head of all that churchy stuff that filled it after a service, he seemed to understand the reason for the question.

Of course he did.

He knew who the Widows were.

Because she knew him so well, she could tell he was attempting to come up with an answer that

113

would discourage them. She could read it in his eyes, because every one of his emotions ran through them like a slide show.

"My sister isn't interested in . . . ," he began.

"Simple question," Birdie said.

"Only for information," Winnie drawled.

"So we can serve her better," Mercedes added.

They all knew he wasn't buying a word of that explanation but, fortunately for them, he was far too polite to tell them to go away and leave him alone. "What does that mean?" He raised an eyebrow and studied them, almost as if he could read their minds—which, of course, he could after their two-year acquaintance. "Serve her better?"

"Is she married?" Blossom asked. Bless her. The preacher could never turn her down.

"No, she isn't married, but . . ."

They had the information they wanted. They turned to toddle back to the kitchen and make plans before he could say more.

Adam sat on the porch swing next to Gussie and put an arm around her, wishing he could kiss her. Not to be considered, of course. Well, that sentiment wasn't correct because he *was* considering it. Not to be done. The preacher kissing his girlfriend who was not yet his fiancée on the porch of the parsonage at four in the afternoon would start tongues wagging all over town.

"How do you think things are going?" Gussie asked, leaning her head on his shoulder. "Between you and me?"

"I like getting to know you better. Having you around all weekend, seeing you in church."

"And my parents? How are you guys getting along?"

"Great people. I love having them over here so much of the time. Your mother spoils us terribly and your father is a good guy. Janey likes having them around."

"Anything else?"

"Well, I'd like to kiss you." He paused to look down at her.

She laughed. "That wasn't exactly what I was asking."

"I don't care. That's what I'm usually thinking."

"There are always people around." Gussie glanced around the neighborhood. Ouida sat on the porch with George while the girls laughed and chased each other on the front lawn. The Fergusons across the street waved. He knew Tasha Ferguson—a good Baptist but a member of the Butternut Creek network that spread gossip through town faster than the Internet ever could —would rush inside and call Miss Birdie before they'd completed the kiss. It was hard for a man and a woman to get to know each other with the entire town watching and reporting.

"Why don't I come into Austin this week, take

you to dinner. Maybe we could be alone for a while, to see if the chemistry between us still exists."

"I'd love that. Let me assure you, the chemistry still exists on my part." She tilted her head with an implied question.

"And mine." He leaned forward and touched her cheek with his, but for only a second because he'd seen Tasha stroll with what he felt to be feigned casualness toward the mailbox. Checking her mail on Sunday?

"Good to hear." Gussie stood. "I've got to get going. You know I don't like to drive at night."

He held her hand as they strolled toward her car. Sure, he'd like to kiss her, but this touch would have to do. They were getting to know each other. That was the plan. That was happening. They were getting to know each other.

But he couldn't convince himself. Aware that Ouida and George and Tasha and probably her husband looked on, knowing Ouida would cheer for him and Tasha would pass the news to everyone, he leaned down and kissed Gussie. Not on the cheek, not a quick touch on her lips, but a nice, long kiss. If the neighbors were going to gossip, he might as well give them something to talk about.

"Wow." Gussie blinked. "Nice surprise. Now I don't want to leave."

• • •

That evening after a sandwich supper, Hector and Bree took Janey to an ice cream social at the Church of Christ, and the Miltons strolled home.

The absences left Adam on the long sofa watching a college basketball game and Hannah working on her laptop at the table.

He watched her for a few minutes. Once he saw a trace of a smile, a flicker of quickly suppressed pleasure. Had she read an email from a doctor in Kenya or a friend from med school? Did she keep up with anyone from either place?

When she closed the computer, she glanced up at him.

"Want to talk?" he asked.

"No." She dropped her eyes.

"I haven't seen you in two years, and the occasional emails don't make up for that. I'd like to know what you did, what Kenya was like."

"Don't you really mean, *Hey, Sis, what happened?* "

She spoke in a strangled voice, a voice so filled with pain he nearly stopped her. He didn't need to know that story if it hurt her so much. No, maybe he didn't have to know, but he felt she needed to tell him.

"You want to know how I screwed up so badly they sent me home?" she continued with an angry edge to her words. "Why I look like a refugee myself?"

117

"Well, actually, yeah, I'd like to know that, but I'm interested in other stuff, too, things you might feel better about sharing than that."

"Like?"

"Like what's Africa like? Who else worked there? Did you make any friends, visit any cities, learn anything new?"

"Africa is amazing; medical personnel and volunteers; yes, yes, and yes." She ticked the answers off on her fingers.

"Okay, here's another. I know you had malaria, but there are good treatments for that, and medication to avoid it. You're a doctor. You know that. So, how did you get so sick?"

"You used up your questions, little brother."

Those words constituted her attempt to put him in his place and usually worked. Her self-confidence had intimidated him when they were kids, but no longer. He'd faced down Miss Birdie and lived. His sister didn't scare him anymore.

"How did you feel about coming back?"

"Don't act like a minister."

"I'm not acting. I am a minister. I'm also your brother." He paused because, despite his bravado of twenty seconds earlier, she *did* intimidate him—but he refused to give in or give up. "I want to know more about your time in Africa, and I want to spend time with you before you flit off."

"Don't flit around much anymore," she sang.

Despite her pitiful effort to make a joke, she

didn't smile. His beautiful, brilliant sister who excelled at everything she did looked sad and sick. She played the violin well enough that she could have gone to Juilliard. She flew through every school she attended, driven to finish her education and begin saving the world. But in the end, after all that preparation and years of work, she hadn't. The world had broken her.

"I'm your brother. I love you," he said.

Before he realized she'd moved, Hannah stood and launched herself toward him. She threw herself on the sofa, leaned against him, and sobbed. Once he'd recovered from the shock, he put his arm around her and held her. She wept into his chest, the pitiable bawling of a calf that has lost its mother. He patted her back and said, "There, there," and "I love you." She'd never allowed that kind of contact before.

Finally she stopped crying and took a deep breath. "I am such a loser."

"Hannah, if there is anything you are *not* it's a loser."

"You don't know. Life hasn't turned out the way I hoped, the way I'd planned, the way I'd always expected." She pulled away and moved to the ottoman. "I'd always thought I'd be another Schweitzer or Livingstone." She held up her hand. "I know, I know. I don't play the organ and the only thing Livingstone and I have in common is malaria—although, of course, I didn't die." She looked up at him. "I thought I could save an entire continent."

What he saw in her eyes scared him. She looked hopeless, nearly doomed.

"Would you tell me about it?" He spoke casually, exerting no pressure on her, because pushing Hannah never worked.

"I've always done whatever I wanted." She glared at him. Daring him to disagree. "I've carried through on every decision I made, every one."

He knew that. High school in two and a half years with six AP courses, and she'd started college with eighteen hours of credit. She'd graduated from Harvard in two years with heavy class loads and dashed through medical school. The only thing that slowed her was the internship, because the hospital refused to allow her to take two rotations at the same time. Then, after a year of residency, she'd accepted the prestigious fellowship in Kenya.

"But I failed this one." She shook her head. "I realized the refugees in the camps were real people, not case studies in a book or a bunch of symptoms to study. But . . ." She stopped and swallowed hard. "The children." Her voice shook. "Oh, Adam, the children got to me. They were so thin and ill. They pulled at my heart." She shook her head. "They died. So many died, real people who depended on me but they still died. I could do nothing."

He listened silently, the only way, he'd learned, to deal with his sister. Listen the few times she shared.

"I couldn't eat. I worried about them. Then I got sick and I couldn't fight it." She gulped and shook her head. "I never get sick. I never stop fighting."

The realization of all she'd been through, her illness and mental state, hurt him. He wanted to say something comforting and deep and sensitive that would turn her life around.

"I love you," he said.

She nodded. He hoped his words had helped, but Hannah was hard to read at the best of times. Obviously, this was not even a *good* time for her.

"I love you," he repeated, because he wanted to emphasize that and to hear her speak, to know she had taken his words in.

"I know. Thank you." She reached across the gap between them to pat his hand. "All I heard from others was 'God talk,' those quotes that didn't help me but made me feel even more guilty."

"Like what?"

"Oh, the main one was, 'God doesn't give us more burdens than we can handle together.' " She swallowed hard. "I couldn't handle it all. I fell apart and that was all my fault because I didn't have enough faith. That's what everyone said."

For a moment, Adam felt the weight of ministry.

The counseling part had always frightened him. Who was he to have the wisdom to address his hurting sister? But if he didn't, who would?

"I don't like that quote," Adam said. "In the first place, I don't think God gave you the burdens." He paused, searching for words. "What you faced came from a lot of choices other people made. Deforestation, the lack of available medical care, drought, overuse of the land, greed. You didn't have a part in creating those."

"I know." She tapped her forehead. "Up here I know that but still, I couldn't handle it all. I got depressed and sick and didn't eat and didn't sleep. I broke and God wasn't there."

"Hannah, what do you know about sheep?"

"What . . ."

Before he could say anything more, laughter and the clomping of feet came from the front porch. Hector and Janey had arrived home and Hannah gathered her blanket around her, stood, and sprinted toward the back stairs.

"This isn't over," he shouted as she left.

"I don't care about sheep," she shouted back.

Then the front door opened and Hector galumphed through the foyer, his big feet pounding across the hardwood.

"God loves you even when you're stupid and smelly," Adam shouted to Hannah's disappearing back before he realized that didn't count as one of his best counseling efforts.

In addition, when he turned around, Hector and Janey were watching him from the doorway.

"That's from the Twenty-Third Psalm," he attempted to explain.

"Don't remember that part," Hector said after a few seconds of shocked silence.

"We brought everyone ice cream." Janey changed the subject. "Enough for everyone, for Gussie's mom and dad and your sister."

Chapter Five

With a glance around the sanctuary a few minutes into the service, Birdie couldn't spot the preacher's sister. Third Sunday she was in town, and still no show.

Gussie and Janey had just sung a wonderful anthem. Nice to have music, good music. Gussie even had the choir singing a prayer response. Not everyone in the choir liked that. Ralph complained he had to stay awake and Ethel Peavey hated to put down her crossword puzzle but Birdie thought it added to the service.

After another sweep of the sanctuary, Birdie couldn't help but think that the preacher's sister should attend to support and encourage her brother. But she didn't.

As the lay leader read the scripture, one Birdie knew well so she didn't have to pay attention, she stood and walked toward the outside door, not far because she usually chose one of the back rows to get a good view of the congregation, the choir, and the minister.

Outside, Birdie glanced at the parsonage in the hope that Adam's sister was running late. Seeing no one, she returned to the pew and settled next to Mercedes again.

"What were you doing?" her friend whispered.

"His sister hasn't left the parsonage yet. Not

coming. Again." Birdie hrrmphed. "Call the Widows together. We're going to have to come up with another plan to get her and the coach together."

That afternoon, Gabe considered going to the parsonage. Nothing better to do. He didn't care about today's televised games. Maybe he could find a pickup game in the church parking lot.

Why shouldn't he go? Why did he need a reason to visit Adam and Hector? They were close. He spent a lot of time at the parsonage, often played ball in the parking lot, and attended church. Besides, today he needed to talk to Hector about colleges, needed to set up a few visits. He'd be taking Hector on those visits because Adam's days were pretty full with church and Gussie.

Gabe had time on weekends with the basketball season over. He wasn't dating anyone steadily. The teacher in San Saba had begun to hint at spending more time together, which constituted a good reason to head out to small college towns Fridays and Saturdays. If she didn't like his absence, Gabe would find someone else to date, someone who didn't expect more of him than he wanted to give. He'd never had trouble finding a woman to keep him company. With little effort on his part, women wanted to spend time with him. Flirted and tossed their hair and let him know they were interested and available.

Except for Adam's sister.

Good Lord, she wasn't the reason he hesitated about going to the parsonage, was she? Okay, maybe a little. He'd never had a woman react to him like that: negatively. He had no idea how to respond to that, no experience in rejection. The lack made him feel inept and socially dysfunctional.

He felt like a high school girl with all the dithering. With a decisive stride, he headed over to the parsonage to talk to Adam and Hector, set up a game. Maybe he wouldn't see her. She could be someplace else, like upstairs.

But she wasn't. When he walked inside, Hannah huddled in the same chair reading, still wrapped in a blanket. Had she moved since the first time he'd seen her?

He had no more idea how to deal with her than a cat would know what to do with a grapefruit. Then his mouth opened on its own and said, "How ya doin'?" with absolutely no permission from his brain. He froze. He hadn't just used the pickup line from a sitcom character, had he? He'd entered a world of deep stupidity.

She glanced up. "Not original," she said before looking back at her magazine.

"What are you reading?" he asked, unable to move away from her and seemingly determined to sound like a geek attempting to pick up a woman and not doing it well—which was precisely why the guys were called "geeks."

This time she didn't glance up. "An article in *The Journal of Applied Helminthology.*"

What was she talking about?

"Helminthology is the study of parasitic worms," she explained.

"Oh," he said.

She looked up and smiled, not an actual smile, only a curving of the lips. No joy appeared in her eyes. "Have you read the article?"

"Umm, no." He sounded like an idiot. The woman could turn him inside out, make him feel stupid, then ignore him as she did now.

"I do know what a parasite is. I have been to college?" Why had he made that a question? He panicked around her. "University of Texas," he stated firmly.

She kept reading.

Fortunately, before he could say something that made him sound even more stupid, Hector said, "Coach, Pops and I have set up some college visits. They match up with the open dates on the calendar you gave us." Hector searched through the pile of papers and folders on the counter. "Think I left it upstairs. Be right back." He hurtled up the back steps.

As Gabe moved to the counter, Hannah glanced up at him for a second with a softer emotion in her eyes. Pity? Probably thought his entire calendar was empty, that the only thing he had to do was visit colleges with Hector.

Not true. He also planned to visit colleges with Bobby.

"You set up a visit at San Pablo College for April eighteenth." Adam tapped the list on the whiteboard and turned toward Gabe. "That still work for you?"

"I'm keeping my weekends free. Whatever you can set up."

Hannah mumbled something he didn't understand.

Gabe turned to look at her, but she'd buried her face in the magazine.

"Sis, play nice," Adam said. "Pretend you're an adult."

"What did she say?" Gabe asked.

"You don't want to know."

What had he done to hack her off so much? Had he said anything insulting? He didn't usually. Her prickly reactions reminded him of grade school when Linda Lockridge had shown her interest in him by kicking him in the shins during recess. The fact that Hannah had made a comment, even an unintelligible one, showed she hadn't really been reading but had listened to the conversation. Interesting. Could be she felt a little attraction, that a spark flared between them.

Then Adam whispered, "I think she likes you," before he burst out laughing. After that chortle, he became more solemn.

They'd looked through a few notes when Adam

spoke in a low voice. "What do you think about my sister?"

Why had Adam asked that? Had Gabe's interest and confusion been so obvious? Should've known he couldn't hide it from Adam. As a minister, Hannah's brother probably excelled at reading people and had extra sense about his sister. Wouldn't look kindly on Gabe's fiddling with her. Not that Gabe would ever fiddle with his friend's sister—or anyone's sister. He considered himself a gentleman. Okay, so why had he panicked at the question?

In an effort to dodge the query, because he did not want to discuss Adam's sister, Gabe looked up the back steps in the hope Hector had found the folder and was on his way down. He wasn't. Gabe would have to answer.

"Nothing. You know that. We've never had any contact when you haven't been around. She hasn't left this place, has she?" Probably way too much information, but Adam's query had rattled him. "Not with me. No, not with me. Never."

"What are you talking about?" Adam stared at him.

Gabe glanced at the stairs again, willing Hector to hurry back. "Why did you ask me that?"

"Looking for insight." Adam shook his head. "She doesn't listen to me. She opened up once, but she's closed the door." Adam looked at Gabe grimly. "What do you think about her? Any thoughts to help me? You know a lot more about women than I do. I could use any clues you've picked up on."

"No, none." Gabe attempted to back out of the conversation. "We need to check the calendar again . . ."

"Hey, I need input here, Coach," Adam said. "I'm not one of the Widows. I'm not attempting to fix you up with my sister."

"The Widows are trying to fix me up with your sister?"

Adam waved the question away. "Not important."

Gabe disagreed but kept his mouth shut.

"I'm worried," Adam said. "Because you're a friend and an outside observer, I need to know what you think about my sister."

What could he say to Hannah's brother? Acceptable words didn't come, so he shrugged.

Not satisfied with that, Adam kept watching him.

"Okay, I find her intimidating." Gabe moaned inside. Exactly what he did *not* want to do, insult both Adam and his sister.

Once, although it seemed in the far distant past, he'd been a cool guy, a man who could answer questions from friends and talk to women. That calm, composed communicator had disappeared when skinny, sickly, spiky-haired Hannah Jordan glared at him. He couldn't for the life of him understand why he couldn't speak lucidly or act normal around her.

Adam glanced at his sister and lowered his voice again. Probably not necessary because she didn't show the slightest interest in them or their conversation. "I wish you'd known her before she went to Africa."

Gabe did, too.

"I really need help on this," Adam continued. "I don't know who she is. I need reinforcements to reach her."

"I don't know how I could help you. She doesn't like me."

"Maybe because you're an athlete. The popular clique gave her a rough time." He gazed toward his sister. "She was two years younger than her classmates, skinny and intense. Wore thick glasses."

"Didn't you protect her?" That flash of anger surprised him.

Adam snorted. "If you think Hannah expected or wanted my interference, you don't know her well."

"I don't know her at all, Adam. Don't know how I could help. She isn't very chatty around me."

"Don't suppose you know anything about epidemiology?"

"No, not a lot of people do," he started, ready to take off on a rant that he did not consider himself to be a jock of very little brain only because he didn't know about epidemiology. Fortunately, before he could, Hector leaped down the stairs with a folder and tossed it on the counter.

Hannah enjoyed Coach Borden's visits. She could embarrass him with so little effort, almost too easily. That counted as a good thing, because with her brain fogged with exhaustion and depression she couldn't attempt anything more difficult than a short, snarky reply. Recently snark had come effortlessly to her. Although she had few social or personal communication skills, she'd learned to get along with people by swallowing sarcastic words, by acting polite and interested and friendly. Lately, however, cutting words seemed to tumble from her mouth with no effort and no filter.

She attempted to squelch her bottomless pit of snark, which the man did not deserve, really, and turned back to her medical journal. Aah, science. What a wonderful escape. Facts were either true or false and results could be duplicated or they weren't facts. People did not behave in a predictable way. Neither did life.

"Hannah."

She pulled her mind from the article and looked to see Janey in front of her. Hannah couldn't be snarky with Janey. She could imagine hurt in those dark eyes if Hannah ignored the child or used harsh words. Adam had told her about the Firestones in his emails, that they'd been homeless and living in the park by the basketball court before he moved them into the parsonage.

Besides, this was a child. Hannah had spent the last few years of her life attempting to save children. Could hardly hurt one now.

"Hey, Janey." She spoke in the liveliest voice she had. It didn't evoke rainbows or dancing unicorns but was the best she could muster. Then she attempted a sweet smile but discovered she no longer possessed that expression or anything close. "What do you need?"

"Miss Yvonne and I are gardening in the backyard." When Janey leaned forward, her floppy hat brushed Hannah's cheek as she whispered, "It's in really bad shape. The preacher hasn't done anything back there since he got here." Then she drew back and spoke in her normal soft voice. "Hector mows it but Yvonne says the soil isn't good."

Hannah nodded. What was the child saying? Did she expect Hannah to do something about the bad soil?

"It's hard work," Janey said. "We could really use your help."

Well, yes, Janey did expect her to do something about the bad soil. Mentally, she sorted through all her excuses: too tired, busy reading, hated gardens, and, the best one, the true reason: She really did not want to.

But she couldn't say any of those, not while looking into Janey's serious eyes. They showed a fear of rejection. Hannah could not do that.

Who knew Adam would unleash Janey, his secret weapon, on her?

"Let me get my shoes." Hannah unwound from the blanket and stood. "Do I need a jacket?" If she got really cold, she could come back inside right away using her recent bout with malaria to escape whatever Janey and Yvonne had in mind.

"I've got them." Janey held up Hannah's sneakers and hoodie.

Once shod and wrapped up against the cold of a Texas spring, Hannah followed Janey out the back door and into the yard.

"Welcome," Yvonne said heartily and waved with more energy in that gesture than Hannah had felt for months.

Stop being a whiner, she lectured herself. *You're out here. Get to work.*

In emails, Adam had told her about the charm and beauty of the Hill Country. She'd glimpsed it on her drive from the airport. For a moment, she stood in the sunlight and felt it settle in her bones and chase some of the chill away. She could see the glory he'd described in the huge sky that stretched around them, blue and clear. If she looked straight up, the vista looked so much like the big sky in Africa that she felt overwhelmed with homesickness for her people, her village, her camp.

In Africa, the clear, deep blueness stretched out all around her and went on forever and ever. Here, if she looked around her, the sky shrank. Trees defined the scope of the panorama, and houses limited the curve of the horizon.

"It's pretty in Butternut Creek, isn't it?" Janey said as she took Hannah's hand and pulled her toward Yvonne.

Yes, it was. Pretty but different. The fact hit her hard: She was in Texas. For a moment she prayed to herself. *Dear Lord, help me accept.*

She hadn't spoken to or even accepted God in months. Why had she breathed this prayer? Adam clearly exerted a terrible influence on her.

"Here's what we're doing, Hannah." Wearing a large-brimmed hat much like the one Janey had on, Yvonne waved toward the fence and the pile of dirt parallel to it with a gloved hand. "I want to plant flowers and rosebushes close to the fence and"—she gestured to a dug-up corner of the yard—"vegetables over there. We'll leave that area open." She pointed toward a section of fence between the parsonage and the parking lot split by a double gate. "Guess some previous minister had a camper and needed that entrance. Might could plant rosebushes to hide it, but not this summer."

Hannah nodded but wondered. Certainly it was

too early to plant, wasn't it? Of course, she'd never lived in Texas. In Kentucky, they didn't plant anything until after the Derby, the first Saturday in May, when the danger of a frost had passed.

"We can't plant until after Easter." Yvonne sighed. "This soil is Texas red clay."

Yes, Hannah reflected, it was red and they were in Texas, so that made sense. She'd accept Yvonne's statement about the texture of the soil.

"Hector tilled it this spring," Janey said proudly.

"Not optimal conditions. Tilling should be done in the fall, when the soil is dry, but in the fall, I didn't realize how serious Gussie and Adam were. Didn't have the slightest idea we'd sell the house and move to Butternut Creek." She smiled at Janey. "We're glad we did."

"A surprise to the entire family," Hannah said, the politest response she'd used in weeks.

"Will we get to meet your parents?" Yvonne spoke as if she didn't really care about that, but Hannah imagined she probably did.

"They're holding off to see if there's going to be a wedding," Hannah said. "They want to be here for that. Long trip to make two or three times a year." With that explained, and with the exertion of all this chatting and courtesy wearing her out, Hannah asked, "What do we have to do here?" Then she added, "In the garden," simply to make sure Yvonne didn't want to talk more about their family. Oh, Hannah loved them all, but she'd fled to Texas because her mother treated her like a rare and precious porcelain figurine with fragile parts that would break off at the slightest touch. Her father acted hearty and jolly as if Hannah's illness and expulsion from the refugee camp had never happened.

Yvonne nodded and began to point. "When he tilled, Hector worked in garden soil, but we're behind. No compost. Henry refused to allow me to move my compost pile here."

Sounded reasonable to Hannah. In her experience, compost was smelly, crawled with worms, and attracted vermin. Of course, she had limited experience, but Yvonne seemed to regret the lack of the odoriferous and pest-filled muck greatly.

"We have to work plant material in, let it sit until mid-April when we can plant. Still gets cold up here."

She handed Hannah gardening gloves and a trowel, then pointed at several bags scattered around the yard. "Garden soil is there. Work it in as deeply as you can." Yvonne glanced at Hannah. "You don't have anything to keep the sun off." She took her sun-repelling hat off and handed it to Hannah. "Wear mine."

Hannah waved it away. "I won't be out here all that long."

"All right, but I'll find you one for next time."

As if Hannah would come back to the garden again. Tomorrow Janey would be in school and couldn't make her feel guilty for five days. By next Saturday, she'd have come up with a good excuse.

"Any questions?" Yvonne asked. When Hannah couldn't come up with one, Yvonne and Janey took off to opposite corners of the fence and left Hannah to prepare her square for vegetables. She slipped on the gloves, opened the bag, dumped half of it on the garden, and knelt down.

Work it in deeply, Yvonne had said.

For ten minutes, Hannah was aware of the discomfort of kneeling, the itch on her nose she could only scratch with her forearm, and a trickle of sweat rolling down her neck. Then that changed. As she worked, the earth seemed to become a living, breathing organism filled with potential. The sun that warmed the earth felt like a partner in the miracle, part of the circle of growth and renewal. Here she worked in the midst of creation, no longer a co-worker of death. The dazzling revelation caused tears to roll down her cheeks, moisture she couldn't scrub because her sleeve had become so damp from perspiration. She allowed them to flow and mix with the sweat and trickle down her chin.

She could have taken the sweater off, but that would mean she'd have to stop and she didn't want to. She did put down the trowel and tug her gloves off, though, so that as she continued to dig and mix the soil, she could better feel and absorb the vital life-giving force bubbling up from the soil and roiling through her.

After an hour, Yvonne called a halt. Hannah turned around. Janey had disappeared, and Yvonne was pulling off her gloves.

"Probably enough for today," Yvonne said. "Don't want to wear you out." She walked toward Hannah's corner of the yard. "You've done a great job."

Satisfaction and a sense of accomplishment filled Hannah. What an idiot. She felt proud about mixing a few square feet of red clay with garden soil? Anyone could do that.

Yes, anyone could, but *she* had. It felt good. She had accomplished something positive and life affirming.

The euphoria didn't last. While she showered, most of it washed off with the soap, drained away with the water. She could feel herself rinsing off that last bit as she scrubbed away the dirt embedded in her nails and skin.

If Hannah had learned anything about feeling good, it was that it was fleeting.

But maybe it wouldn't be this time, here in Butternut Creek, the haven of hope and small-town happiness. If she gardened every day, maybe the feeling of harmony and joy would return.

• • •

Friday, the best evening of the week. His sermon almost finished except for a few hours tomorrow morning plus the late-Saturday-night and Sunday-morning repetitions, Adam had worry-free time to spend with Gussie.

He glanced down at her as they strolled from the parsonage to Sam's old house. Feeling his gaze on her, she looked up and smiled.

"I love Butternut Creek," she said. "The people, the houses, the breeze. It's a great place to be."

"Better than Roundville?"

"Based on name only, who wouldn't prefer to live in Butternut Creek than in Roundville? I love Sam's little house. It's cozy."

"Too cozy for three people?"

She grinned. "Maybe, but I'm not going to complain. I'm having too much fun here."

They turned up the sidewalk and onto the porch. A light shone from the living room and another from the front bedroom. He could hear the drone of a television.

"Have I told you about the first time I met Sam?" he asked. "It was on this swing." He held the swing for Gussie, then sat next to her.

"Don't think so." She pushed against the floor to move the swing back and forth. "Go ahead."

"You know Sam came home from Afghanistan as an amputee and suffering from PTSD."

She nodded. "It's no secret that he was depressed. Sam told me he'd become a hermit."

"He didn't like people, didn't want anyone intruding on him. Miss Birdie tried to talk to him, even invited him to church, but he didn't come. Didn't answer the phone or the door." Adam shook his head. "A tough case." He put his arm around Gussie. "I dropped by one afternoon and knocked for about a minute. No answer. So I sat here before I headed back to the church." He pointed toward the ceiling. "The whole thing came down, pulled right out of the ceiling. Huge crash. Dropped me on the floor."

"Oh," she responded.

He could tell Gussie was attempting to keep her face straight.

"Go ahead. Laugh. It was funny. It dumped me on the porch with my knees up to my chin and broken pieces of the swing all around me." He laughed with Gussie. "Sam opened the door and glared at me. He complained that we incredibly nosy church people would stop at nothing to get him to talk." He allowed the swing to go back and forth before he said, "Then he let me in. We had pizza and have been friends ever since."

Smiling, Gussie took his hand. "Wonderful story."

He pushed his feet on the floor to keep the swing going. "How's your parents' house hunt going?"

"Mom said she got a call from the Baptist

Retirement Center in Roundville. No opening in the foreseeable future."

"I like having them around," he said. "Your mom is great with Janey and they've teamed up on Hannah to go out to the garden. No one has ever forced my sister to do anything, but your mother and Janey can."

"And Mom's a great cook."

"Always a plus." He took Gussie's hand. "Your father's a good guy. He watches basketball with Hector and me and walks Chewy. Hope they stay in town for a long time."

"They said they're waiting to know what my plans are before they make a decision. They may return to Roundville or move into Austin or San Antonio. They love the River Walk and Austin is close to friends, but it depends on my future."

"They're putting off a decision based on you? Where you're going to live?"

She nodded. "They've grown fond of me over the years."

For a moment, they swung while Adam thought.

"Then why don't all of you stay here?" The words had popped out without thought, but they sounded good so he repeated them. "Why don't you stay here? In Butternut Creek?"

"Stay here?" She waved around her.

"Yes, here in Butternut Creek?"

Gussie tilted her head, a sure sign of confusion. Wasn't a difficult concept, but Gussie seemed to have a great deal of trouble grasping his suggestion, so he said, "Why don't you marry me and stay here?"

Her reaction was not an expression of undying love or a quick acceptance. No, she blinked. Then she put her feet firmly on the floor, stopped the swing, and studied the far railing of the porch as if letting the words sink in, as if attempting to understand them. Finally, she turned toward him and said, "What?"

"You can't be surprised. Didn't we both think your move here meant marriage was a fairly obvious possibility?"

"I . . . I . . . I . . ." She swallowed and started over. "I didn't expect a proposal tonight."

"I didn't expect to ask." Adam realized immediately he hadn't made the situation any better but, nonetheless, he continued a few words farther down the path to destruction. "I didn't *want* to propose."

"You didn't?" She frowned, then studied his face, possibly in an effort to figure out his meaning.

She leaned forward. Her proximity only rattled him more.

"I don't want you to marry me," he said. What an idiot. "I mean, I do, but not if you feel pushed or overwhelmed or confused."

"Confused," she answered, as if this were a multiple choice question.

He felt the same but he shouldn't. He was the one proposing. "I thought it would be handy, you know. For us to get married."

"Handy?"

He couldn't seem to stop the stupid words and suggestions pouring from his mouth. "You said your parents were waiting until they knew where you'd be before they bought a house. I thought, maybe, if we got married, you know, they could make that decision more easily. With more information."

When comprehension showed in her eyes, she began to laugh until she had to hold on to the arm of the swing to steady herself. He loved her laugh, joyful and free and filled with delight, but Adam had never had a woman laugh at his marriage proposal before. Oh, he'd only proposed to one other woman, but Laurel had smiled and accepted his proposal demurely and with a kiss.

Didn't look as if Gussie would react like that. In fact, for nearly a minute, he didn't think she'd answer at all.

When she could finally speak, Gussie said, "You're asking me to marry you because it's handy? Because that would make my parents' choice of a place to live easier?" She shook her head but still smiled. "I'd always dreamed of something a little more romantic when a man asked me to marry him. Maybe a mention of eternal, undying love."

"It should be more romantic," he agreed. "But the words just popped out."

Gussie leaned away from him. Not a good sign. She coolly raised her right eyebrow. "Oh?"

"That's . . . that's not what I meant. Not at all," he sputtered. "I've wanted to ask you to marry me for a long time."

She nodded encouragingly.

"But I wanted to give you time. You know, to get to know me. To feel comfortable here." There, that sounded good, and she'd stopped glaring.

"How long do you think I need?"

Her voice was steady and emotionless. He could not interpret it. "A few months?" he asked.

"Is that a question?"

Not going well. He preferred her laughter to the frigid thud of her last words. Couldn't blame her. She'd like a romantic proposal. She deserved one. The Widows were right. He was hopeless. He needed direction. He had botched up asking Gussie to marry him.

Only one way to rectify those mistakes. With his future riding on this, Adam stood, turned, and dropped to one knee in front of Gussie.

Her eyes widened and she put a hand over her mouth.

He took the other hand and held it. "Gussie Milton, I pledge my undying and eternal love to you. I want to spend the rest of my life with you. Will you marry me?"

For a moment, she froze, eyes still huge, right hand in his. Then she dropped her left hand and grasped his and smiled, the brilliant, beautiful, adorable, joyful expression he loved.

"Yes." She nodded. "Yes, Adam. I will marry you."

With that, Adam stood and tugged her to her feet. Then he put his arm around her shoulder to pull her close. "When?"

"I don't know. I feel a little overwhelmed at the moment."

He dropped a kiss on her forehead.

"I don't know." She didn't speak for a few seconds. "Don't tell anyone, not yet. I know what's going to happen when Miss Birdie finds out, and my mother will be nearly as bad. Right now I want to hug my happiness close."

"Don't tell anyone?" He turned her so they faced the other side of the street. As they watched, a light flickered on in the house immediately across from the porch of Sam's house.

Then a light came on in the house two doors to the left, and a few seconds later light flickered through blinds on a house down the street. Little by little, lights twinkled on in most of the houses in the neighborhood.

"If you don't think that lots of people saw me get on one knee in front of you and haven't called the Widows yet, you don't know Butternut Creek very well."

"Of course. I should have remembered that about small towns. In a few minutes, everyone will know." She nodded. "And probably most of Roundville."

"You've made me very happy, Gussie." He brushed a light kiss across her lips. "You've made the Widows happy, too."

Then they heard the sound of a phone ringing inside the house. Gussie pulled on Adam's hand. "Guess we'd better go inside and tell your folks before Miss Birdie and everyone else in town does."

"I think there's one more thing the community would like."

He pulled her close and kissed her deeply and with every bit of his love.

Aah, the joy of being engaged.

"I'll meet you in Austin next week and we'll shop for a ring," he said as they stood with their foreheads touching.

"Adam." She stepped back and looked into his eyes. "I don't want a ring. You can't afford one, not with two children to raise."

"I'll work it out."

"But I don't want one. Really." She held her hand up when he started to argue. "I don't want to insult you about your finances or ability to work things out, but I don't want an engagement ring. Have you noticed Mom and Dad's rings?"

He shook his head. He wasn't very observant about jewelry.

"They have plain gold bands. They've been married for nearly fifty years and those rings symbolize their love and commitment. All I want is a plain gold wedding band like theirs."

What a relief.

"Gussie?" Yvonne's voice interrupted the delightful experience. "What's happening?"

Adam lifted his head to see Gussie's mother standing in the doorway in her robe.

"We're engaged, Mom." Gussie, her face shining with joy, turned toward her mother.

"Oh, my." Yvonne took a quick step back and crashed into Henry, lurking behind her. She ignored his "whoof" and said, "Have you set a date? Come in and tell us all about it." She reached forward to take Gussie's hand. "No ring yet?"

"He didn't buy one because he didn't plan to ask me." With a grin at Adam, she followed her mother into the house. "And I don't really want one."

"Did you hear?" Mercedes asked Birdie.

Birdie held the phone and struggled to wake up. Why did people call this late at night? She glanced at the clock. Ten fifteen.

Okay, not all that late. Not dark thirty yet, but still—she was a working woman. Had to open the diner tomorrow morning.

"Bird? You there?"

"Mrph."

"Have you heard? I tried to call a few minutes ago but no one answered," Mercedes continued.

One of the girls must have been on the phone and ignored the incoming call. They weren't supposed to be on the phone that late, but it happened. Birdie rolled to the side of the bed and pushed herself up, exactly as the physical therapist had told her, to keep the pressure off that bad shoulder. "What happened?" she asked, still groggy.

"The preacher and Gussie are engaged."

Birdie dropped the phone. For a moment, she stared at it. The preacher and Gussie were engaged and she'd slept through the excitement? Probably the last to know. When she reached down to pick up the receiver, she heard, "Bird? Bird? Are you there?" softly echoing.

"Yes, I'm here. Just surprised. When did this happen?"

"About twenty minutes ago. Everyone knows."

Everyone knew but Birdie. Mortifying. "Did you talk to Blossom?"

"Called her when I couldn't get you. She'd already heard."

Even Blossom knew before she did. The fabric of the universe was unraveling.

"And Winnie?"

"She called me. Bet she's been trying to call you, too."

Birdie heard the buzzing tone of an incoming call and ignored it.

"Everybody knows," Mercedes repeated.

All right, she had to accept everyone knew before she did, but she didn't have to broadcast her failure. Nothing to do but pick up and move on. That had always been her motto. Just do it. That darned company had stolen the words from her.

"Bird?"

"Sorry. I'm thinking this all through. Do you know anything more?"

"No. He proposed on the porch of Sam Peterson's old house. Got down on one knee according to Marcella Perry."

"Marcella's a strong Episcopalian. Lives right across from that house." Birdie nodded decisively. A reliable source of gossip counted as extremely important, a necessity. "We can believe her."

"Then the preacher kissed her . . ."

"Oh, my. Right there on the porch in front of God and everyone, he kissed her?"

"Then they went inside. Must be talking to her parents."

"Mercedes, you realize what this means? We succeeded."

"And it means babies," Mercedes added. "Babies to fill the parsonage, babies to grow up and fill the Sunday school classes."

"How long should we give them before we start mentioning that it's about time they get busy procreating?"

"I don't know." Mercedes paused. "You know, Gussie's not young. What is she? Thirty? Thirty-one? Might be hard for her to get pregnant. Old eggs, you know, and fewer."

"All they need are a couple of good eggs. Half a dozen or so." She considered the idea. "But you're right. We don't want to butt into their private lives yet. We'll give them six months after the wedding before we start encouraging them."

"Yes, encouraging them, not nagging. But I'd really like to see a few babies before I pass on."

Birdie blinked. "Before you pass on? Is there something I should know? Are you sick?"

"No, nothing, only becoming aware of my mortality." Mercedes sighed.

"Well, we're all mortal. When did you think you weren't?"

"Bird, we're nearly seventy."

"Mercedes, we *are* seventy. We've been seventy for a while. Why do you sound so gloomy when the preacher just got engaged?" She yawned. "Let's meet tomorrow at the diner. You call the others." With that, she switched off the phone and set it on the nightstand.

She'd never get back to sleep. The Widows had a wedding to plan, whether the preacher wanted it or not. Probably wouldn't want their input. Too bad. He'd have to accept their suggestions, give in to their instructions. Surely he knew that.

Between the wedding and the additional task of finding a wife for the coach, they had their hands full. Maybe they needed to split into two groups: She and Mercedes could work on matchmaking and Winnie and Blossom could handle the wedding.

No, Birdie had worked and pushed and prodded and planned too hard and too long to get the preacher married. She had to savor the victory by being part of the wedding. She'd have to schedule her time.

With that, she got up, went to her tiny desk in the corner, picked up a couple of sheets of paper and a pen, and began to make notes.

Chapter Six

Gussie watched her parents, her mother fussing in the kitchen, determined to celebrate the proposal with food while her father just dithered. First he'd grabbed Adam's hand and shaken it, then he'd gone to her mother and hugged her, then hugged Gussie before he shook Adam's hand again. She hadn't seen either of them this excited in a long time.

Happy didn't begin to describe how she felt. The reason for her happiness and the excitement of her parents had his arm around her shoulder.

Was she crazy to trust this man? To share the rest of her life with him?

No, not a bit. She'd allowed Lennie's actions to live inside her, chipping away at her life. She shouldn't have let that one act of violence control her for all these years.

She knew she could trust Adam. She leaned against him and could feel his strength. This was a good man, and she loved him deeply.

"Now, let's go into the dining room and you tell us everything," Mom said. "Henry, you bring the cake."

Before they even sat down, the music of "Ode to Joy" sounded from her mother's cell on the kitchen counter. She looked at the ID, then said, "I need to take this," and turned away.

"Can't talk now, Birdie," Mom whispered.

The area was very small. Even if she went into the living room or the kitchen, they could hear her end of the conversation.

In an effort to give her privacy, Adam said with a glance into the living room, "The place hasn't changed much since I used to visit Sam."

"Lots of pink," Gussie added.

"Odd color for a marine," Henry said.

They all nodded at each other as bits of words reached them from the phone. Not that the subject or words mattered much. They all knew exactly what she was talking about.

"His aunt chose the colors when she lived here," Adam said.

They all nodded.

"I'll come to the diner tomorrow afternoon." With that, Mom shut off the phone and dropped it into her pocket.

Always the perfect hostess, even dressed for bed, she calmly and carefully placed each piece of cake on a plate and handed them around with napkins and forks. "Wait for them to thaw. They just came out of the freezer."

After she saw everyone had a plate and a napkin and a fork, Mom said, "Now, what are your plans?"

"We don't have any yet. We've only been engaged five minutes."

"We're getting married," Adam added. "Some-time."

"Oh, oh," Yvonne cooed. "Henry, what do you think."

"Young man, she's a great girl but"—he spoke directly to Adam—"she can be stubborn."

"Dad," Gussie gasped.

"Henry," her mother chimed in.

"I know." Adam nodded. "That's one of the things I love about Gussie." He took her hand and held on to it when she attempted to pull it away after that remark.

Her father shook his head. "Then you must really love her because she can be a real . . ." He stopped and smiled at them.

"Yes, I love her very much," Adam said, answering Henry's question.

"We expect you to take good care of her."

Before Gussie could say she could take care of herself, Adam said, "Yes, sir."

With those words, her father leaned back in the chair, closed his eyes for a moment, and whispered, "Thank you, Lord."

Until she saw that, Gussie hadn't realized how deeply her father had worried about her.

His prayer finished, Dad opened his eyes and smiled at Adam. "Let loose of her for a few seconds, Adam. This is Yvonne's Chocolate Guilt Cake, best chocolate cake you've ever had. Eat up."

155

"We're looking forward to meeting your parents," Mom said.

"Gussie tells us your father's name is Clive and they live in London," Henry said between bites. "Why London? Will they be able to come to the wedding?"

"Dad grew up in London. Graduated from Cambridge. Came to Philadelphia to work on a master's and met my mother there, at Wharton. Her name is Lily. She grew up in Kentucky. When they got married, Dad started a business in Cincinnati but we lived in a little town in Kentucky. He got rich but always wanted to retire to London, so they did."

"So you're marrying into money, Gus. That's good news," Henry said.

"Shush, Henry," her mother said, as Gussie knew she would.

Saturday noon, Birdie leaned against a counter and closed her eyes. *Lord, give me strength,* she prayed.

You know I've got this bad shoulder and a wedding to plan but my feet are killing me and I've got those two girls to raise so I took the Saturday shift. Dear Lord, help me remember never to work six days a week again.

For a few seconds, she lifted her right foot and squinched her toes up inside the old shoes. She really needed a new pair, but where would that money come from?

"Birdie."

Farley Masterson's voice cut across her moment of meditation. The man ate breakfast and now had returned for lunch, still trying to flirt with her. How did he get his lovely wife—may she rest in peace—when he had no idea how to talk to a woman?

Not that she had a bit of interest in him. As the former sheriff of Creek County, he'd picked up her prodigal daughter and brought her home under the influence of something illegal more times than Birdie wanted to remember. Oh, Birdie hated to admit it but she'd almost felt relief when Martha had taken off and, after that, Birdie didn't need to see Farley standing on her porch in the middle of the night.

Birdie put her foot down, took a deep breath, and picked up the fresh carafe of coffee. "Here you go." She filled his cup, then looked around at her other tables. All needed something. Lunchtime on Saturday had been a bad time for Birdie to stop and meditate on her life and health and aching feet. She needed a quiet moment, but she needed tips more.

Before she could take a step away from his table, Farley said, "Birdie?" in an unusually uncertain voice for the former chief of police.

"Got to check on my other customers." She headed toward the tables and filled cups, then set the coffeepot on the burner to remove dishes, bring more condiments, and take orders for dessert.

Surely after all that time, Farley had left. With a lightning-fast glance over her shoulder, she saw he still sat at his table. He'd piled his dishes up —to make them easier for her to bus?—and held his coffee cup up.

The old coot must have the biggest bladder in town. All he did was sit there and drink coffee. They should charge him extra but she couldn't ignore him. Farley was a good tipper.

"Here you go." She filled his cup again and picked up a few dishes with her other hand. Not the entire stack. Her shoulder wouldn't handle that, but a couple of small plates felt okay.

"Birdie," he repeated, still in that odd and almost vulnerable tone of voice. He looked up at her. She guessed he could see her fatigue because he said, "You work too hard."

She snorted.

"I mean, you're too old to . . ."

"Farley, don't you tell me what I can do and what I shouldn't do." She turned away and dropped the dishes in the plastic bin.

"Birdie," he called after her. "Shouldn't have said that. Sorry."

She looked back at him. He did look contrite.

He'd aged well. Handsome man. Didn't look older than her although she knew he was. Four or five years. Nice head of thick, white hair and dressed nicely.

"Birdie, would you just come here and talk to me for a minute?"

He used the voice of a cop telling a criminal to come out with his hands up. Everyone in the diner turned in their direction. She had to scuttle over there or gossip would spread around town.

"What is it?" she said as softly as she could, which she knew was only a mini decibel lower than Farley's voice.

"You know there's a new James Bond movie playing in Marble Falls."

She shook her head. "Didn't know that." Why did the man think that bit of information would interest her? She took a step away.

"Want to see it with me next week?"

All the customers heard those words loud and clear. The men who liked to think of themselves as the town movers and shakers and who met here every day for lunch stopped their discussion and turned to watch. So did the ranchers sitting at the counter sucking down coffee and the group of women from the Presbyterian Church who met for lunch on Saturday. Even the two or three families of tourists who must have gotten lost to end up in Butternut Creek studied her and that old coot.

She moved back toward him and leaned down close to his ear. "What's the matter with you?"

She lifted her eyes to see if everyone was still watching them. They were. "Why did you ask that? And why here?" she whispered.

"Birdie, you have the loudest whisper in the world." He shook his head. "If you don't want everyone to know our business, then hush."

"How can I tell you *no* if I can't talk?"

"You're turning me down?"

For a second, he looked wounded. She almost felt sorry for him. Had no idea she could break a man's heart. Hadn't at sixteen and she was a lot skinnier and grumpier now, but the look on his face made her feel bad, almost sorry for her harsh words.

Then his hurt expression disappeared. "Have it your way." His voice sounded hard and chilled. "Thought we could keep each other company."

Didn't that beat all? Birdie MacDowell had become a vamp at seventy.

He stood, tossed some bills on the table, and stalked out. She watched him go.

The memory of his uncertain voice when he asked her and the stricken look forced her to realize she'd behaved badly. Surprise and that darned shoulder pain had forced a grouchy answer.

No, she couldn't blame pain for those harsh words. She had to admit she'd behaved poorly, almost cruelly. She could have handled it better. Should have handled his request better. From the way he stomped out of here, she knew he wouldn't be asking her out again, knew he might even stop sitting at her tables, which meant no more nice tips. But that wasn't the worst part. She hadn't behaved like a Christian.

And maybe she'd miss him.

"You could be nicer to the man," Mercedes told her as the Widows gathered at their usual table after the lunch crowd had left.

Obviously the story had already spread through the entire town, as she'd known it would.

"Wouldn't hurt to accept his invitation. It's nice to have someone to go to dinner or a movie with. You know Bill Jones down at the bank and I have been keeping company for years."

"That's not what we're here to discuss," Birdie said clearly.

Usually, the Widows came together after a crisis or to head one off. Today they met to discuss the preacher's recent engagement and his future wedding. Before this she'd had little confidence in Adam's ability to hold on to a woman like Gussie, not that he'd gotten her to the altar yet. A huge chore faced them. For that reason, they'd added a guest, the mother of the bride.

"You could have . . . ," Mercedes began.

"What do you know so far?" Birdie asked Yvonne, effectively cutting off her friend's words.

"Nothing." Gussie's mother looked back and

161

forth between Birdie and Mercedes apprehensively. "They just got engaged." She held out her hand. "Gussie didn't want an engagement ring, only a gold band like mine."

Good thing because he can't afford a fancy ring, Birdie thought, but even she wasn't rude enough to mention the preacher's financial situation or the inability of the church to give him much of a raise.

"Perhaps there's more information you can share with us," Blossom said.

As a Southerner, she always phrased her questions so much better than Birdie. Blossom spoke so softly and gently, no one ever noticed that she demanded information, too, in her own very effective way.

"For example, what are Gussie's favorite colors?" Blossom asked.

"She hates pink," Yvonne said.

Blossom looked disappointed. "Pink is such a pretty color for a spring wedding."

"Doubt if it will be a spring wedding," Winnie said. "Not enough time to plan that unless we wait a year."

"They aren't planning to wait that long, are they?" Birdie asked.

Yvonne shrugged.

"Maybe a summer wedding?" Mercedes asked.

"Still cutting it close," Winnie said.

"Or late this year or next year," Blossom said.

"We have a lot of planning to do but we could put together a lovely wedding for Christmas."

"Busy time for a minister," Winnie said. "Let's go ahead and plan for this autumn. We can always reconsider."

All five women nodded.

"We'll tell them September or October." Winnie wrote that down.

Blossom looked around the group. "What are good colors for a fall wedding?"

"Gussie loves orange," Yvonne said.

For a moment they all considered that. "No, I don't believe orange is a good color," Blossom said. "Maybe a very pale orange, a pastel. Maybe peach."

"Gussie doesn't like pastels," Yvonne said.

"Doesn't really matter," Birdie said dismissively.

"Peach would be pretty. Maybe even a pale blue or an apple green," Blossom mused.

"Pastels. Nice colors for spring," Mercedes said. "But would they work in October?"

"But Gussie doesn't really like . . . ," Yvonne attempted to explain.

Rushing right past that bit of information, the Widows began brainstorming while Winnie took notes. After twenty minutes and lots of ideas, Birdie turned to Yvonne. "You can go now. We have other things to discuss."

Startled for a moment, Yvonne stood.

As she watched Gussie's mother walk away,

Mercedes said, "That wasn't very polite, Bird. Couldn't you think of another way to say that?"

"We've known each other for years. Yvonne's used to me. Besides, we need to discuss the coach and she barely knows him." She paused to look around at the three remaining women. "Any ideas for getting the coach and the preacher's sister together?"

"Do you think we might be taking on too much?" Mercedes said. "Shouldn't we wait until after the wedding?"

Birdie snorted. "Who knows what women will be around in September?"

"New teachers will be coming in," Winnie said. "And I hear the Episcopalians have called an associate, a young woman."

"But the preacher's sister will probably leave after the wedding and we'd have to start all over," Birdie stated. Honestly, these women should understand the theory of matchmaking by now. A single woman in town now was worth any number of teachers or ministers who might show up in August.

"Do you have any plans to meet the preacher's sister?" Winnie said. "She hasn't been to church. Has she left the parsonage yet?"

The Widows shook their heads.

"That makes it hard to plan," Blossom agreed.

"She could be really ugly. I believe the coach likes pretty women," Mercedes said.

"Now, now, ladies. The preacher's a nice-looking man, even if he is still too skinny." Birdie tapped her coffee cup as she considered her words. "She's not going to be ugly. Skinny for a woman is fashionable."

"How will we find out?" Blossom asked softly.

They all thought.

"You know," Winnie said, "Yvonne's in and out of the parsonage all the time. She could tell us a lot."

"She won't. Says it's family and personal," Blossom said. "But maybe she could suggest how we could get inside."

For a moment Birdie regretted her hasty decision to dismiss Gussie's mother. "I'm sorry, ladies. I shouldn't have sent Yvonne away." She looked around the group. "Blossom, you two are friends. Why don't you see what the two of you can work out about getting into the parsonage unobtrusively, maybe setting up a private moment between our future lovebirds."

Blossom smiled and clapped her plump little hands together. "Of course. We'll have fun planning that."

The same afternoon, Gussie sat on the sofa in the living room of the parsonage as her mother bustled around the kitchen. Gussie had no idea what her mother was doing, because bustling around the kitchen was one of Yvonne's favorite activities and filled much of the day. Smelled as if she'd put cookies in the oven. Snickerdoodles, Gussie guessed from the cinnamon aroma.

A diabetic, Yvonne figured if she couldn't eat them, she could make cookies for others. She had a great deal more self-control than Gussie.

Adam had left the parsonage at nine to make a hospital call, then spent the morning at the church working on his sermon before he came home for lunch. Gussie had several books but couldn't concentrate on any of them. She considered taking a walk or weeding the garden but knew those actions only put off what she did not want to do.

She had to call her best friend, the one who'd supported her during the hardest weeks and months of her life, who'd always encouraged and loved her. She hoped Clare would be happy about the engagement, but a tiny part of her feared the reaction.

She flipped her phone open and pressed Clare's number.

"I'm getting married," Gussie said when Clare answered.

On the other end of the phone, silence.

"Did you hear me?" she asked. "Adam and I are engaged."

"Are you sure, Gussie?" Clare laced the words with concern. "Are you rushing into this?"

"Adam and I started seeing each other six or seven months ago." She really should know the exact number. Didn't women usually remember how long they'd been dating a man? Have monthly anniversaries?

"You can't say you've been dating for that long because you haven't. Sure, you started going out with him last summer, but you broke up with him because you weren't ready. You've only been together again for two or three months."

Gussie blinked and attempted to answer but the words piled up in her throat as she pondered what her friend had said. She'd held her feelings and hurts inside for so long, she struggled to find a way to describe the joy that had taken over her life.

"Gus? Are you there? I love you. I want you to be sure, very sure."

"I am sure, very sure. Be happy for me."

"All right!" Clare squealed. "Do I get to be in the wedding?"

"We haven't set a date."

They chatted for a few more minutes, tossing about ideas for the wedding until, as usual, the discussion turned to news about Clare's children and Gussie's parents. Finally, Clare said, "Gotta go. Suspicious noises coming from the kitchen."

With that, Gussie turned off the phone, leaned back in the sofa, and closed her eyes, the better to savor her happiness. A few minutes of savoring later, she felt a weight—a slight weight—settle on the other end of the couch. She opened her eyes and glanced over. Hannah sat a foot away, studying her.

Gussie didn't know how to react to Adam's sister. Her fiancé—oh, she loved the sound of that word and rolled it around in her brain for a moment—her fiancé had told her about Hannah's drive and her life of achievement as well as what Hannah perceived as her ignominious return to the States.

Right now, Hannah glared at her. What had Gussie done to deserve that? She stopped herself from scurrying away from her future sister-in-law. Warily, she smiled.

Hannah didn't.

For nearly a minute, Hannah kept her gaze on Gussie while Gussie attempted to figure out the problem and how she could react. She became more uncomfortable with every second that ticked by.

Finally Hannah spoke in a low, almost menacing voice. "I love my little brother. He's one of the best people on the earth."

Gussie nodded.

"I don't want him hurt." After several seconds passed, Hannah said, "Do you love him?"

Gussie nodded again.

"Are you going to make him happy?"

"I'm going to try." Obviously not the right response. For a second, she thought Hannah would quote Yoda: "There is no try . . ." Well,

Gussie could never remember exactly how that went. So she smiled again. "Of course I will."

That didn't seem to satisfy Hannah, either. Adam had said she was tough, and now Gussie understood what he meant. No one survived what his sister had faced without being tough. However, Gussie hadn't realized how focused Hannah was until those dark eyes were fixed on her. She could almost feel them drilling a hole through bone and inside her head straight into the brain. Not a pleasant image but true.

After a moment of deep, focused scrutiny, Hannah nodded and stood. In anyone else, Gussie would have thought that action showed satisfaction. With Hannah, she couldn't be sure. At this moment, Adam's sister seemed to have only two expressions: intense and more intense.

As Gussie watched, Hannah pulled out her phone, punched a button, and waited. After several seconds, she said, "Adam, I need to see you." Then she snapped the phone off and stuck it in her pocket.

Only moments later, Adam sprinted in. He looked first at Gussie, then his sister. Obviously pleased neither was in pain or bleeding, he lifted his eyes toward the kitchen. "Yvonne, are you okay?"

"Of course. Do you want a cookie?"

He stared at his sister. "Why did you call? I thought someone was close to dying." He turned toward Gussie. "You don't know this yet, but a

169

call from Hannah usually means death, destruction, and possibly the end of the world."

Instead of answering, Hannah held out her hand. A set of keys dangled from her fingers. "The SUV outside? That's yours. Dad bought it for you as a wedding present."

"What?"

Hannah closed her eyes and sighed before she opened them. "Dad . . . bought . . . it . . . for . . ."

"I heard you." He shoved her hand away. "I don't need a new car."

"Yes, you do," both women said in unison.

"I can take care of myself. I don't need my parents to bail me out."

"Don't be a jerk," Hannah said. "Accept it—graciously if possible."

Before Adam could respond with what Gussie feared might lead to a huge argument, she stood and took his arm. " 'The fruit of the spirit is love, joy, peace, patience, kindness, generosity, faithfulness, gentleness, and self-control.' "

Both Jordans turned to look at her.

"What does that mean?" Adam said.

"Your father cares, he's being generous. Can't you accept his gift with equal generosity plus some kindness and gentleness?"

Although those words got his attention, Hannah cut to the core. "The car you have is going to kill you someday, and maybe Gussie and Janey and who knows who else."

"I . . . I . . ." Adam started a sentence that he didn't complete because Yvonne came into the room and took the arm Gussie hadn't captured.

"Parents worry. We know you want to support yourself, be independent, but sometimes you have to accept. Your father loves you and . . ."

Before Yvonne could finish, Hannah, not the most patient of people, broke in. "It's a wedding present, jerk," she said, again hitting the center of the controversy.

"But how did he know we were going to get married?"

"He didn't. Mom did. She guessed that as soon as Gussie moved to Butternut Creek. If it didn't happen, I could return it to the dealer. That's the deal he set up."

"I can't accept," Adam began to protest again.

"Be grateful. I talked him out of giving you a gas-guzzling sports car." She held up the keys again. "This car is big enough to hold a bunch of kids, has pretty good gas mileage and high safety ratings, and is in ministerial black."

Adam mulled over his sister's words and Yvonne's. Stubbornness, pride, and longing warred inside.

"It's a pretty car," Gussie said. "Practical and safe."

Adam had to concede, inside and only to himself, that it did seem like a perfect vehicle, but he wasn't ready to stop protesting. He had his pride. "I don't want to depend on my father for a new car."

Everyone watched him but didn't say a word. He studied each woman. Yvonne looked hopeful, Gussie smiled, and Hannah dared him to turn it down. He knew the expression well from the Hannah-controls-her-little-brother game. He hated her gloating look of triumph; he'd endured it through his childhood and youth and, actually, through his entire life up to this moment. For that reason, he drew the moment out to deny her that victory for as long as possible.

"Be nice," Hannah said. "Take the SUV and tell Dad thank you." She tossed the keys.

He watched their arc through the air. He had no choice but to catch them. To protest more would sound churlish, immature. Besides, if he didn't catch them, they could crash into something fragile and break it, if he possessed anything fragile and valuable.

As he grabbed the keys, he admitted he really wanted to accept it. He'd admired the SUV. Actually, he coveted it, which made him feel really guilty.

Adam looked at the women again. Gussie and her mother stood on each side of him while Hannah leaned back, crossed her arms in front of her, and clearly challenged him to turn the gift down.

"I can't afford the insurance," he said. "That's

probably hundreds of dollars more than I pay now."

"Part of the gift," Hannah said. "He'll pay your insurance for five years and he'll pay for your mechanic to fix your old car so Hector can drive it. Safely. Since he's paying, you might as well get a paint job for it."

They'd thought of everything. He shrugged and attempted to hide a smile at the thought of having a safe car, a car that didn't break down every week or so, a car with air-conditioning that didn't involve shoving a broken window down. A slick, sleek, gorgeous new vehicle. Although his pride warred with the idea of how much Hector needed transportation, he wasn't ready to give in yet. "I don't know," he said.

"You are so full of crap." Hannah shook her head. "I could always read you. You want that car but you have to protest."

Problem with his sister. She knew him too well. He glanced at Gussie, who just smiled. She was on to him, too.

"Just accept it," Yvonne said. "Accept it for me, for an old lady who prefers my grandchildren, God willing they come soon, to ride in a car that won't endanger their lives."

"If you all insist . . ." He drew the words out and stood still because he didn't want to show how excited the thought of driving this vehicle made him.

"If our insisting means you'll graciously accept

the gift," Gussie said, "then yes, we insist."

She'd make a perfect wife, nagging him to do exactly what he wanted to do.

"Okay." He tossed the keys up in the air and caught them. "Let's go for a ride."

The vehicle seemed perfect. No, it *was* perfect, as he'd noticed before. The dark, shiny surface had no nicks or scratches, and paint smoothly covered every inch of the exterior. He rubbed his hands over it. Oh, he'd done the same before, but the car didn't belong to him when he had. With a click, he unlocked all of the doors and climbed inside to settle on the leather-covered seat.

"It has a heater in the seat," Hannah said.

Not really necessary in Texas, but his father always wanted every accessory a dealer offered.

He put the key in the ignition and turned it on. A soft purr came from the engine immediately with no grinding. The clock showed the correct time, and he bet the radio worked. It also had a slot for a CD and a plug for an iPod. Those would make Hector happy. Adam couldn't wait for him to find out they owned it. He'd want to drive it around town, pick up Bobby and Bree.

After he looked around at the gleaming array of dials and buttons, Adam hit the knob to put down the driver's-side window. It slowly descended, then closed again with a simple touch. After that, merely because he could, he put all the windows down and laughed.

"Seems to have all the fenders and bumpers," Gussie noted as she circled the SUV. "Mom, why don't you get in the front with Adam." She opened the passenger door.

"Oh, no, he's your fiancé," Yvonne protested until Gussie had shoved her in place and got in the back with Hannah.

While he adjusted the rearview mirror, he glanced at his sister. She looked smug, savoring her victory. Okay, he didn't mind that this time.

As he put the car in gear and pulled out of the drive, Adam felt a twinge of guilt, exactly like the one he'd felt when the truck had delivered the new sofa and tables and all the furniture the Widows had rounded up after he arrived in Butternut Creek without even a bed. He shouldn't like material possessions so much. For a second, he understood why his father enjoyed the luxuries his money provided. Adam had promised himself he'd never feel that way about earthly possessions.

But he did love this vehicle.

He smoothly turned onto the highway and touched the accelerator. The car took off without his having to pray or pedal madly. He flipped on the radio to hear music coming from behind him and next to him. With a touch, he put the windows up and flicked on the air conditioner.

Dear God, he prayed. *I really love this car. Please forgive me.*

Chapter Seven

Saturday evening with the sun heading toward the horizon and casting shadows from the live oak trees across the lawn of the parsonage, Gussie stood on the porch and breathed in the scented air of a warm summer's dusk.

When Hector mowed the last few times, he'd left a broad strip of wildflowers on the north side of the parsonage. The bluebonnets were past their prime and had gotten a little straggly, but even a straggly bluebonnet beat out any flower anywhere for beauty. Indian paintbrush took up nearly half of the space, their brilliant orange bracts poking up higher than the bluebonnets. A few purple wine cups showed here and there, fragile and not nearly as showy as the other wildflowers but so lovely.

Some might prefer orchids or other hothouse plants, but they didn't compare to the brilliant spring beauty before her.

From the porch, Gussie saw the Widows park in the church lot, pull their various canvas totes and quilted casserole carriers from Blossom's car, and head, each in her own gait, toward the parsonage.

Miss Birdie always strode, certain of her destination and determined to arrive first. Winnie, in deference to Miss Birdie's leadership and seniority, followed behind her, only a step, and marched with equal resolve. Mercedes carefully balanced her load and moved like a graceful steamer across a calm sea. With tiny steps, Blossom flounced across the narrow path Hector had cut through the wildflowers.

For a moment, Gussie watched as they approached. The Widows were the bountiful fauna of Butternut Creek making their way through the profuse flora of the Hill Country.

"Hector," Gussie called as she descended the porch steps and hurried toward the Widows.

"Now, don't be pushy," Gussie heard Mercedes warn the others, glaring at Miss Birdie. "I hear this Hannah is skittish."

"Let me help, ladies." Gussie took a tote from Winnie and a dish from Blossom before she headed back toward the parsonage. She could still hear them talking, because three of the Widows had no idea what "talk softly" meant.

"I'm not going to push," Birdie said to the other Widows as they headed toward the parsonage. "You know I'm not pushy." She paused to consider that statement. No one on earth would believe that. "Not all the time."

"Birdie MacDowell, I've known you for seventy years," Mercedes said. "Even in the church nursery, you were pushy."

"Now, now," Winnie said. "Let's not scare the young woman by bickering. None of us should try to push her."

Hrmph, Birdie thought. Like Winnie had anything to talk about. Bossiest woman Birdie had ever known.

When they reached the parsonage, Birdie followed by the other Widows entered through the door Gussie held for them and shouted, "Dinner's here?"

She heard Hector walking down the upstairs hall. The boy had the biggest feet she'd ever seen and had never learned to move quietly. He bounded down the stairs, two or three at a time.

"Ladies, let me help you." He took the totes Birdie carried. "I would have brought them in. Miss Birdie, you know carrying all this can't be good for your shoulder." With the other hand, he took a casserole dish from Mercedes. "Ladies, you leave the rest of that food on the hall table. I'll carry it to the kitchen."

"Nice young man," Winnie said as he left for the kitchen.

"He and Bree still keeping company?" Mercedes asked.

Birdie nodded. "He's a good kid but they're so young."

After placing most of the bags on the hall table, the Widows hurried back to the kitchen and dining room. Blossom pulled a lace tablecloth from her bag and shook it out over the dining table. "If one of you would place the napkins." She motioned toward another bag.

"What is this for?" Hector asked, carrying the totes and a long box. "Looks like flowers."

"I have a lovely cut-crystal vase in that bag." Blossom pointed as she spoke to Hector. "I'll arrange the roses while you ladies get the food ready."

Birdie couldn't complain when Blossom took over. The newest Widow knew how to entertain and decorate in a way Birdie could never approach.

At seven, Gabe knocked on the front door of the parsonage before opening it and shouting inside, "Can I come in?"

To his amazement, those ladies from the church hustled toward him.

He wanted to take a step back but one of them, the lead woman, the white-haired lady—what was her name? Oh, yes, Miss Birdie, the one Adam and Sam had warned him about. Anyway, she grabbed his arm and heaved him inside while another closed the front door behind him. For a moment, he feared she was going to lock it in an effort to imprison him.

Surely, if the need arose, he could shove aside one of these ladies to escape, right? But at six-five and weighing at least a hundred pounds more than any of them—except maybe the fluttery one with the blond hair—he'd look like a bully.

"Hello, ladies." He forced a smile and shoved back that first reaction to escape.

"We're so glad to see you," Miss Birdie, the obvious leader, gushed. She didn't act or sound like a woman who usually gushed.

Could be she was trying to put him at ease, but her powerful-for-an-elderly-lady hold on his arm didn't help him relax. In fact, her intense interest scared him a little.

"I'm Birdie MacDowell." She pointed at herself. "This is Mercedes Rivera." She waved toward the pretty Latina woman standing with her back against the door. "Winnie Peterson and Blossom Brown."

The women smiled. Why did he feel so uncomfortable? They looked like perfectly nice women, welcoming and friendly.

With that, Miss Birdie—Adam had warned him to call her that, not just plain Birdie, which might seem too familiar to her, or Mrs. MacDowell because that would sound too formal—grasped his arm even more tightly.

"We are the Widows," she said.

The words struck fear in him. Instantly, Gabe remembered more about these women. Sam Peterson had told him about the Widows and their matchmaking. Adam had warned him.

Now three of them surrounded Gabe, and Mercedes blocked his escape route.

With their alarming and predatory presence, he

recalled the odd incident that had happened a few months earlier at church. Miss Birdie had put exactly the same hold on him as she'd dragged him out of the building. She had looked all around the sidewalk, then, still hauling him along, searched the parking lot.

After a sigh of disappointment, Miss Birdie had explained that she'd wanted to introduce him to the new dental hygienist down at Dr. Winder's office. She'd scrutinized him for a moment with particular attention to his mouth before she asked, "Having any problems with your teeth?" For a moment he feared she'd pry his lips open and check but she hadn't. He'd run toward his truck and driven away.

The memory of that episode returned in great detail tinged with fear. Surely these women weren't going to try to get *him* married, were they? At some point, he might reach a time in his life when he did want to find the perfect woman, fall in love, and get married, but he'd always considered *he'd* make the choice of who and when. He refused to allow the Widows to take over, to push him toward something he didn't want. Could he stop them? Sam and Adam hadn't succeeded, and they seemed happy about that failure and their futures.

Then the woman called Blossom stepped forward and took his other arm. Together they towed him into the living room. He didn't resist because he refused to hurt them. After all, if the moment arrived when he did need to flee, he could—Mercedes had moved away from the door.

They led him toward the ottoman and, with one final Amazonian effort, heaved him toward it.

Unfortunately, Hannah's feet already occupied the footstool. As he began to plummet and before gravity dragged him down on her, the two Widows did an amazing deke with his body. He landed on the corner of the stool. They steadied him for a few seconds before moving away, chuckling.

Hannah glanced up from the *Journal of the Institute of Theoretical Pathogenics* to see the Widows hurrying toward the kitchen and the basketball coach sitting only inches from her toes. She dropped her feet to the floor and straightened.

"What are you doing here?" she asked.

For a man who must have excited great interest in millions of women, he looked painfully awkward. His lips curved into an artificial smile with more than a bit of embarrassment. In addition, the footstool was so low his knees almost touched his chin. Not an attractive position.

"I have no idea." He shrugged.

She lifted her eyes toward the sofa, where her brother had been watching some sports show with Gussie. Probably basketball because he lived for that. Maybe some running thing. When the word *deuce* came from the television, she realized it was tennis.

Not that she cared.

What did grab her attention was that Adam had stopped watching the program. So had Gussie. They both observed her and Gabe with a great deal more interest than they'd shown in the match.

Why?

In fact, she noticed, both sat forward, elbows on their knees, their eyes flipping back and forth between Gabe and her as if they were still watching tennis.

Why?

With the sound of retreating footsteps tapping across the hardwood floor, she turned toward the kitchen to study the Widows. Blossom hastened toward the dining room carrying a tray while the other three had begun shoving pans into the microwave and ladling food into serving bowls, all those movements done with great energy and focus. None would meet her gaze.

Very suspicious.

Closing her eyes to a slit, she studied Gabe. Really good looking, almost perfection. Most women would consider him yummy. Actually, she did, too, in a watching-from-afar-and-pretending-I'm-not way. Very pleasing, aesthetically. Who wouldn't appreciate those shoulders and that smile? Although the expression did seem a little forced at the moment.

Adam and Gussie turned their gazes back to the television. Gabe leaned forward and twisted his neck so he could watch with them, too polite to move or perhaps still intimidated by the women who'd abandoned him there. Hannah alternated between reading her journal and admiring the amazing morsel of masculinity. Finally, she completely stopped reading and watched Gabe, who'd turned away from her. She enjoyed the view of the muscles on his arms and neck, the great haircut, how his shirt stretched across his back. She didn't feel a bit guilty for allowing herself those few seconds of visual pleasure, suddenly understanding what *eye candy* meant.

Having fulfilled her aesthetic quota, she turned her interest back to an article on exposure assessment modeling.

After about fifteen minutes, Winnie called, "Dinner's ready," from the arch into the dining room. At the same time Henry Milton shouted out the back door, "Hector, Janey, dinner."

Janey must be playing on the swing set and Hector, as usual, shooting buckets in the church parking lot. Adam would probably be with him if Gussie wasn't leaving after dinner.

After Hector clomped inside and Janey came in from the backyard, both washed their hands. The Widows waited in the kitchen to serve while the families gathered to stand at the table and took each other's hands around the circle.

"Tonight, let's sing the Doxology for grace," Gussie said. They joined their voices.

Hannah would really prefer if Janey and Gussie sang a duet. Adam's voice wavered, the Miltons only listened, and Hannah's voice, although steady and usually on key, couldn't compare to Janey's and Gussie's. Next to her, she heard a clear tenor. She didn't turn to see who it was, because it had to be Gabe. How had he ended up next to her? When she'd first arrived at the table, her brother had stood to her right. Sometime in the nanosecond between arriving at the table and stretching her hand out, the men had switched places.

When they sang, "Amen," the Widows sprang into action, hurrying back and forth between the kitchen and the dining room carrying steaming bowls and heavy platters.

"My cook makes these." Blossom spooned something orange and runny on Hannah's plate. "You'll love them."

Every time the Widows passed in and out, they smiled smugly at Hannah and Gabe.

Okay, what was going on?

Then she leaned back in the chair and closed her eyes to sort this out.

It only took a few seconds. Only someone illogical and incompetent could miss it, and she was neither. What an idiot she was not to have recognized the Widows' stratagem much earlier.

All the clues had been in front of her but she'd gone blithely skipping by them, ignoring them until this very moment. She so seldom blithely skipped by anything, she could only blame the lingering effects of malaria for the sludge her brain had become. Also, she found it difficult to imagine that anyone would have the slightest bit of interest in her love life. She didn't.

Now she understood.

Matchmaking. She could have hit herself in the forehead at the revelation but didn't want to attract even more attention. Oh, she'd heard about *the Widows* aka *the Matchmakers*. Adam had emailed her at least weekly to cheer her up and often included stories about the women. Her favorite had been when they trapped him and Gussie on a sofa during a youth rally at church. But she also remembered—although with a lot less detail—what Adam had written about the Widows setting up a romantic dinner for Sam and Willow early in their courtship. Widows + dinner + hunky coach + pitiful and needy girl = something she did not want to face.

This meal resembled those efforts far too much for Hannah to feel in the least bit comfortable. She opened her eyes again to meet three pairs of eyes—Gabe's wary stare and the fascinated gaze of Adam and Gussie—while the rest served themselves and started to eat.

She couldn't force herself to look at the four women standing in the corners of the dining room. She bet they'd all have their eyes on her. She felt like an exotic animal, hunted down, trapped, and caged.

"Coach, here are some of my special yams with butter-coconut sauce." Mercedes stood on the other side of Gabe and gave his chair a shove toward Hannah with more strength than Hannah would have thought a woman her age could exert. The coach wasn't a lightweight.

As his chair flew across the narrow space and bounced against hers, Gabe glanced at Hannah. He looked as if this counted as the worst moment of his life.

She felt absolutely and appallingly humiliated, emotionally naked. She had not felt this terrible since Doug Cater had rubbed black chalk on the eyepiece of her microscope in college. Back then, everyone laughed.

She couldn't face that again.

If she'd felt better, stronger, more Hannah-ish, she would have joked, said something snarky, stared them down, told them to leave her alone, or shoved the coach away, but she couldn't. She hadn't fully recovered her brain or her personality.

Before she started to blubber in front of all these people, Hannah stood, shoved her chair back until it hit the wall, and ran.

The sound of Hannah's chair banging against the wall echoed, and Adam heard her footsteps pounding up the back stairs. Beside him, Gabe froze with the bowl of yams in his hand, passing it toward an empty space and staring at the spot where Hannah had been. Yvonne clenched her hands in front of her while Henry blinked.

"Oh, dear," Blossom murmured, her eyes on that vacant chair.

"What happened?" Miss Birdie demanded.

"I feel terrible," Gussie whispered. "At first I thought it was funny, like what they did to you and me." She shook her head. "But it was terrible. I should have remembered that, at the time it happened to us, it was really embarrassing."

Gabe put the bowl down. "Did I do something wrong?" He shook his head. "I don't think I said anything to upset her."

"Oh, oh, oh," Blossom murmured, her pink mouth round. "We really upset her."

"I should've stopped you," Adam said to the Widows who'd frozen in place, their expressions stunned, even Miss Birdie's. He glanced around the room at the stricken faces.

"You didn't know what they would do." Henry glared at each Widow to define the antecedent of the pronoun *they*.

"I should have realized. These are, after all, the Widows. They cannot leave a single man or woman unmarried. Matchmaking is an addiction for them." Adam shook his head.

"What did we do wrong, Pastor?" Winnie asked in a worried voice.

"Our matchmaking efforts have always been successful," Mercedes said.

"Sooner or later," Miss Birdie said.

"I really should have foreseen this, both your efforts"—Adam nodded toward the Widows—"and Hannah's reaction. It's my fault."

"And mine," Gussie added.

"Mine, too," Blossom said.

Before anyone else could enter the orgy of guilt, Adam said, "Hannah's never been very sociable. Now, because she's sick and had to leave Kenya, she's more sensitive than usual." As he spoke, Janey quietly pushed her chair back and left the room.

"We probably shouldn't try to find her a husband right away," Winnie stated.

"How long will she be here?" Miss Birdie asked. "Maybe we struck too soon."

"We could put this off a little," Mercedes agreed.

"Ladies, I suggest—" Adam began.

He should have known better than to suggest an action to the Widows. They hustled into the kitchen and toward the back door where they couldn't be seen from the dining room and began to chatter. With everyone else distracted, Hector helped himself to another piece of chicken and a huge helping of yams.

Hannah sat on the window seat and looked out at the street in front of the parsonage. Across the street stood several nearly identical Victorian houses painted in different hues. She felt as if she were in a tree house, surrounded by huge live oaks, and wished she could stay here. But she couldn't. She wasn't a quitter or a weakling.

What had she done?

She knew good and well what she'd done. She'd behaved like an idiot, embarrassed herself and run away. Her reaction had been immature and spineless. She'd never been a quitter or a runner. When had she become a coward? A baby who couldn't handle life. When they were kids, Adam would have called her a scaredy-cat—and he'd be right, at least today.

Even worse, she'd embarrassed her little brother. The women of the church had prepared a lovely meal, invited Adam's friend and Hector's coach to share it, and she'd run away. If she didn't care what an idiot she must have appeared, rude and not well bred, she had to care about how her behavior reflected on Adam.

She loved Adam. Even though he was two years younger, Adam had always supported her, stood up for her. He'd been like a big brother, protecting and encouraging her. When she'd locked herself in her room for hours to study, her parents had attempted to lure her out, nagged her to be more sociable. Adam told them to let her decide what to do with her life.

When she'd wanted to head off to Africa and her parents had been appalled, he'd interceded.

How had she repaid him? She'd embarrassed him in front of people in the church he served. She should go back downstairs, apologize, and join the others for dinner. The first problem with that action: She didn't apologize well.

Second, she followed an important rule in her life: Never return to the site of earlier humiliation. After the many mortifications she'd suffered being a brilliant nerd in a world of older, less intelligent beings, she'd learned avoidance and denial very well.

Third: She wasn't hungry.

But none of those points mattered.

What should she do?

To her left, although she couldn't see it from here, stood the church Adam served. Her little brother, a minister. The thought awed her.

In this situation a few years ago, Hannah would've prayed for guidance. But she'd lost the God of her youth in Kenya. Actually, she believed God had deserted her and all those suffering people and starving children. Certainly the Creator of the universe could do better than to allow such horror to exist.

She hadn't prayed in a year, except for that odd time in the garden that she still didn't understand.

That left prayer out. The only alternative to sitting up here like a spoiled baby was penance and apology. Her brother deserved it. She couldn't ruin what made him happy because she was such a blockhead.

"Hannah?"

On top of that, she'd behaved so poorly in front of sweet Janey, the only person in the world who accepted her unconditionally—well, except her brother and maybe Yvonne and Gussie and Henry and Hector.

"I'm sorry, Janey."

What relation was Janey? Her brother's almost foster daughter made her Hannah's sort of niece?

"Why are you sorry?" Janey asked. "You're unhappy. When I'm sad, chocolate helps." She held out her hand with something wrapped in a napkin. "Blossom's cook makes the best chocolate chip cookies. They look really good."

"Oh?" Hannah reached for the cookie, took a bite, chewed, and swallowed. "I do feel better. Thank you." She wrapped the cookie up and put it on the window ledge.

"I need to go back. Will you come with me?" With that, Hannah took a deep breath and stood to take Janey's hand. The connection gave Hannah strength. They went down the steps and into the kitchen.

"I'm sorry," Hannah said to the Widows. Okay, that hadn't hurt too much. "I'm sorry for running off."

The women watched her with compassionate gazes, which almost forced her back upstairs.

Then Blossom patted her shoulder. "We're sorry we upset you. Don't you worry."

"Thank you." Hannah allowed Janey to pull her into the dining room where the others looked up and gave her broad and totally fake smiles, then took a bite of food. To give them something to do, Hannah guessed. The sound of chewing replaced conversation as if mastication were the most important action in their lives. None of them watched her, maybe showing her they hadn't noticed her disappearance.

"Hello," Hannah said to everyone as she slipped into her chair. Henry winked at her and her brother smiled but Gabe moved his chair a little to the right so they weren't slammed up next to each other.

"I'm sorry," she mumbled.

"That's all right" and "We love you" and other encouraging words and phrases mingled together. They all looked at her and nodded and smiled.

Still a little overcome and nervous, Hannah took a forkful of something on her plate. She didn't realize until she had it in her mouth that it was cheese grits. She didn't like grits. Not even butter or onions or hot sauce or cheese could turn those gritty molecules into tasty treats. However, having embarrassed herself and her brother once, she swallowed the unpleasant mouthful and smiled.

Gabe glanced at Hannah from the corner of his eye. He admired the fact that she'd come back. Couldn't have been easy.

But why had she run? Did the idea of being matched with him sound so terrible, she fled? That was an ego buster.

He looked up at Blossom, who was placing a piece of cake in front of Yvonne.

"It's a hummingbird cake," Yvonne said. "My favorite."

"It has pineapple and bananas." Blossom placed the second plate in front of Hannah. "All good for you. We'll leave the rest of the cake here for you, Hannah. Fatten you up."

"Fattening people up is a favorite activity of the Widows," Adam said jovially. He'd never heard Adam sound jovial before.

Everyone smiled, still artificially. Even *he* recognized the efforts to cheer Hannah up, and he was probably one of the worst readers of body language ever. She probably recognized that as well.

Then Gabe looked at Hector. The kid showed that even he could tell everything was phony, and he *never* recognized nuance. What high school kid did? What male did more than once or twice a year?

Later, as he helped clear the table, Gabe studied the Widows. Why had they chosen to put him together with Hannah? He noted that he, Hannah, Hector, and Janey were the only single people under the age of sixty, maybe seventy, and he and Hannah were the only single adults over twenty in the room. Those factors pretty much narrowed the demographic of those the Widows had available to match.

Could be they hadn't made an effort to set him and Hannah up. After all, he visited the parsonage often. He was Hector's coach and spent most Sunday evenings with him lining up colleges and scheduling visits. Maybe he wasn't the target.

But if he wasn't, why had they forced him to sit on her footstool and next to her at dinner? Why the bump to shove his chair closer to—on top of, really—Hannah? He placed his stack of plates in the sink and turned around to study the other room. The Firestones seemed completely out of the loop, he thought.

But when he came back into the dining room, the Widows sized him up and smiles flickered around the lips of three of them. Miss Birdie just observed him carefully. Finally she smiled as well and turned toward Hannah, who had just finished her second or third piece of cake. At that moment, he knew he'd been drawn into the trap along with Hannah and, in no time, no matter what Adam said or how he warned the Widows off, they were not going to leave them alone. Someday, they'd ignore Adam's opposition and Gabe's objections and Hannah's obstinacy and he and Hannah'd end up married, too.

He didn't want to get married, not yet. He still had a lot of living and partying to do.

But if that was true, why had he come to Butternut Creek? Hardly the number one party spot in the world. Butternut Creek was the biggest get-married-and-settle-down-for-the-rest-of-your-life place he'd ever lived. Look at Sam and Willow and Gussie and Adam. Those four made love and marriage sound good. Almost.

Then he glanced at Hannah. For a moment, she lifted eyes toward him. Not a flicker of interest showed in the calm and cold depths.

In that moment, he realized that no matter what or how hard the Widows tried and no matter that he'd fallen a little in love with her when he first saw her photo, Hannah was not the woman he'd spend the rest of his life with. Not even the next week or two. He didn't attract her, and she'd lost the appeal that had fascinated him.

Then Janey approached and put her arm around Hannah's shoulders and the woman changed. For a second, when she looked at Janey, she glowed. Didn't last long but he'd seen it and it nearly blinded him. In that second, he saw her spirit that had attracted him in the photo. He saw the woman Adam had called "Gypsy." In that second, he realized two women lived in that skinny body. Unfortunately, neither one of them seemed to like him very much.

Adam opened the car door for Gussie. "You know they won't leave us alone until we set a date, right?" he said.

Once settled in the car, Gussie asked, "Do you really think they'll leave us alone even after we decide on a date?"

"No, they won't."

"If they ask you my favorite colors, say red or orange or ultraviolet. Do not let this be a pink wedding!" She started the engine.

"Be careful." With those words, he watched her back down the drive and pull into the street.

"She's getting off a little late," Hannah said from the porch swing.

He glanced at the darkening sky. "She'll call when she gets back to her apartment."

"Have you talked to Mom and Dad about your engagement?"

"I emailed them. They're happy."

"Come sit with me." She took his hand and tugged. "You really love her, don't you?"

"Yes, I do." Adam joined her. They sat for a moment, silent, enjoying the breeze and the swaying of the swing and the comfort of being together.

"What's it like?" Hannah asked. "What's it like to care for someone enough to want to spend your life with her?"

He couldn't read her expression. Usually couldn't unless she allowed him inside. "You've been in love, haven't you?"

"Despite the fact that I'm your older sister and you think of me as worldly and glamorous, no, I haven't."

"Oh." He considered those words. "Mom told me about guys you dated in college and med school."

"I lied. I made most of them up. Made her happy and she left me alone."

"Oh."

"Didn't you ever notice I never brought any guys home? I always told Mom we broke up just before the holidays." She grinned slightly. "I think she caught on after a few years and gave up."

"Don't understand why you didn't date. You're attractive."

"I intimidate men. I can't understand why I have to pretend I'm not who I am to attract them." She shrugged. "And I've always been a geek."

"Have not. You were cool in college."

She chuckled. "No, I was such a geek I frightened other geeks away." She shoved the swing back and forth with her feet. "In college, I was younger and smarter than anyone, which did not make me popular." She shrugged. "Not that I cared. You may have noticed I don't have really good people skills."

"Oh?"

She laughed. "Of course you have. I shoved people away because I really did not know how to act. I still have no idea how to carry on a normal conversation with anyone outside the family or science, although I'm good with children. Over the years, I've found it's easier to be alone than make the effort to figure out relationships."

"Maybe you could learn?"

"Don't know if I want to and I'm pretty old to change. Besides, guys never seemed more important to me than parasitology. A few broke up with me because I was smarter than they were. The rest did because they expected me to spend time with them." She sounded truly amazed. "Can you believe that? They wanted me to go to a movie with lots of explosions and breaking glass instead of working in the lab or reading journals."

"Yeah, men are like that."

"I know." She shook her head. "If I were a normal person and really wanted a relationship, I'd recognize it's necessary to spend time together, but I don't want to."

"Being normal is overrated."

"Spoken by someone who never had to worry

about fitting in." She closed her eyes. "I'm a geek and a loner. I've accepted that."

"You get along with Gussie and the Miltons, Janey and Hector."

"Everyone gets along with them."

They swung in silence and enjoyed the coolness of the evening until Adam said, "Look what you've accomplished."

"Look where I am now." She made a sweeping motion with her hand that ended up pointing at herself. "The motivating goal of my life is gone. My dreams have crumbled and my health is shot."

"You've just returned from serving a refugee camp in Kenya. That's pretty good."

She shook her head. "You're so full of crap, little brother. I'm a colossal failure."

"Do you want to talk about it?"

"Heavens, no," she responded. "They set me up with counselors in Kenya, then in Germany, and finally in London. I've talked for hours and hours, confessed my weaknesses, listed my strengths. I tried to accept my fears and express the horrors of the camp." Her voice broke and she took a deep breath before finishing. "None of that helped."

He considered her words. "Okay."

"Don't start with the God talk," Hannah warned. "I've heard it and I know it's your job, but don't." She held up her hand. "I'm sick and miserable and a failure. I lost my faith after seeing a few hundred children starve. God didn't help then. God won't help now."

He pushed against the porch to increase the motion of the swing. "What do you know about sheep?"

Her eyes flew to his face. "That again? I don't want to talk about sheep." She put her feet on the floor of the porch to stop the swing and stood.

"Psalm Twenty-Three," he said.

She turned and ran into the house.

A crestfallen and completely disheartened crew of Widows gathered at the diner on Monday afternoon. Each sipped her coffee and broke off tiny pieces of blueberry muffins left over from Saturday to pop in their mouths.

"I'm sorry, ladies, and I'm ashamed." Winnie shook her head.

"Hannah looked stunned and so unhappy when she realized what we were doing." At the memory, tears gathered in Mercedes's eyes. "She ran away from us."

The Widows had become maudlin.

"Yes, it's a mess," Birdie said, "but nothing to cry over, not yet. There's no crying in match-making."

"I felt ashamed to be part of it." Winnie flipped her notebook open and clicked the pen. "She looked so little and thin and vulnerable."

Blossom pursed her pink lips and cooed softly.

Birdie had no idea what that sound meant but felt sure it didn't count as a vote of confidence in the matchmaking skills of their leader.

"On top of that, the coach didn't seem interested," Birdie observed.

"Not a bit," Mercedes agreed. "Seemed a little frightened."

"Do we agree that the method that worked so well with dozens of couples did not work with these two?"

"We should probably study our failure," Winnie said.

"Study our failure?" Mercedes asked.

"Yes," Winnie stated firmly. "What have we learned from our failure?"

Birdie nodded. As much as she hated to admit it, they had cluster-failed.

"We've learned we can't use the same strategy for everyone," Mercedes said.

Winnie added, "And that both of the people we choose should be in good physical and mental health."

"Sam wasn't," Birdie pointed out.

"But Hannah's not ready," Mercedes said.

Birdie glanced around the group and saw resolve in those three faces, even Blossom's soft, pudgy features. They refused to follow her here, at least in their efforts to match Gabe and Hannah. Looked like she had a rebellion on her hands—except she agreed with them, all three of them, even the cooing Blossom. They had failed. "But if we give up on matchmaking, what do we do?" She turned to Blossom. "What about wedding plans."

"I've tried." Blossom's chin quivered.

Mercedes patted Blossom's hand. "It's not your fault they haven't made any plans yet," she murmured.

Whole place felt soggy with all the mushy sentiment.

"No, it's not." Blossom straightened and smiled. "They're not a bit cooperative. The preacher and Gussie seem perfectly happy to be engaged."

"Maybe we need to stop pushing so hard," Mercedes said. "I'm fine with those two being happy. After all, we never thought the preacher would get married. Now he's engaged. We did a good job with him."

"That's right." Winnie nodded. "We should leave them alone. No need to meddle simply because we need something to do."

When had Birdie lost control of the group? Winnie should know that meddling was precisely what they did very well, and as often as possible.

"But, ladies, if the wedding planning isn't going well and the matchmaking has failed, what is our purpose?" Birdie looked around the group again, studying each face.

"I thought our purpose was to go around doing good." Blossom smiled beatifically. "We could just do good deeds."

All four considered that.

"Sounds good, but what does that mean?" Winnie asked, always methodical. "What else can we do?"

"Suggestions for good deeds?" Birdie asked in what she considered her most encouraging and least aggressive tone.

"The thrift shop is running well," Winnie said. "We all take our shifts."

"The emergency food pantry is well stocked." Mercedes finished off the last bit of muffin. "No need for a food drive."

"Looks like our good works are up-to-date," Birdie said.

"Does anyone have a suggestion for another project?" Winnie asked.

Three of them shook their heads, but Blossom lifted hers.

"I have a vision," she said in a more determined voice than Birdie had ever heard her use before. She even stood. "I have a goal for the future. I want to turn that old gym into a community center. To sand down that floor or replace it, to redo the plumbing and electrical, to put up a new scoreboard and bleachers." She lifted her hand in a dramatic gesture that encircled all of Creek County. "I see this as a place where all our people can come together—Baptists, and Episcopalians, and Methodists, and Catholics." She paused. "Do we have any Jewish people in the community?

Doesn't matter." She waved her hand. "A place where *all* people gather, where children can be tutored and the older youth can have an indoor recreation site, where old men can play checkers when it's raining and women can quilt and make clothes for poor children."

Birdie, Mercedes, and Winnie watched her in amazement, eyes wide and mouths open, at least until Winnie snapped her notebook shut and said, "That's a lovely vision but that's not one of the choices. We have to decide between match-making and wedding planning."

"Oh," Blossom said and dropped back on her chair.

Mercedes patted Blossom's hand. "That's a wonderful vision. Keep that in mind. Maybe someday."

As Birdie considered the blighted future of the Widows, she looked around the diner. Her eyes stopped at the big corner booth. A glimmer of a new mission began to form, not Blossom's but a more practical one. "I have an idea. Winnie, take notes."

They'd let Reverend Patillo off the hook for months, but they had to do something or give up their reputation as matchmakers. And her plan was too good to waste.

Chapter Eight

"Do you want me to go to church with you?" Janey asked from the top of the staircase.

Hannah gave her hair one more rub with the towel and hung it on the rack. "No, thanks. I'll be fine. You go on. Meet me in the sanctuary after Sunday school."

"You will come?"

Hannah studied Janey's concerned expression. "Don't trust me, huh?" The knowledge that Janey had been let down by adults prompted her to add, "I'll be there. I promise."

"Okay." She turned and Hannah heard her feet echoing on the staircase.

Janey had no cause to worry. Hannah had left the house so seldom since she arrived. She gardened and ran and that wrapped up her activities. Not that she felt safe inside the parsonage, not after the Widows ambushed her with Gabe, but she owed it to her brother to go to church and support him. She hadn't been to a service since she left Kenya. No matter how often her mother had invited her, then nagged her, Hannah had refused to go. But Adam served this church and she'd like to watch him lead the service, preach a sermon.

Besides, Gabe wouldn't be there this morning. She'd heard—because she shamelessly listened to any conversation that included or mentioned him—that he was visiting his family in someplace called Big Spring. Texans certainly liked to name towns after bodies of water.

Not that his absence mattered, of course, not to her.

She had nothing, not a thing, not a blessed thing, in common with the man.

Unfortunately, she possessed a previously unrecognized yearning and a well-hidden weakness for gorgeous men, at least this particular one. Her interest in him could constitute a much delayed stirring, perhaps her womanhood awakening from years of hibernation within the logical lair of science.

In the rare moments she'd felt this way before, she usually ignored the spasm of womanliness, shoved it away and picked up an article on vectors of duplication in a water-borne virus. However, with Gabe she couldn't disregard the attraction. Fortunately, she wouldn't see him so she didn't have to worry about anything that might lead to a messy or emotional relationship. The awareness curiously depressed her.

"Bye," Janey called from the hallway. "See you in church."

Plus, she'd promised Janey, a commitment she'd never go back on.

Didn't take long to get ready. She fluffed up her hair, squinched it a little, brushed her teeth, and smoothed on a tiny bit of lip gloss because she was, after all, going to church. After slipping on a neat white shirt and dark blue slacks, she stuck her feet in sandals—and there she was. Clean, neat, and professional. Ready with almost an hour to spare.

Ten minutes before the service began, she put down her book, fluffed her hair a little more, and headed out. Most of the people entering the church or standing outside chatting smiled or waved at her. Janey ran from the steps to the sanctuary to greet her.

"I'm here," Hannah said, but before she could do anything or say another word, the Widows swept out of the church like vultures gliding off a telephone wire after spying a particularly tasty bit of roadkill.

Oh, yes, roadkill. That's what she suddenly felt like. She wanted to escape but couldn't move. Janey held her hand on the left while the Widows fanned out to surround her in front, in back, and two on the right. For a moment, she wondered if the Widows hovered by that door to leap on unsuspecting visitors. Actually, in her case, she had not been unsuspecting but had underestimated the speed and accuracy of the four women.

"Hello, ladies." Hannah forced a friendly greeting and a smile.

"We're so glad to see you," Miss Birdie said.

The other three murmured agreement.

"Let's introduce her to everyone."

And they did. Herding her—now her metaphor broke down because the Widows could not be both vultures and Border collies—they steered her into the yard and began introducing so many people whose names she either would never remember or didn't hear, because they dashed around the yard so fast. Within two minutes, she'd met twenty people. Then the Widows ushered her into the church.

"Isn't this lovely?" Blossom said. "We've recovered the cushions and replaced the curtain in front of the baptistry."

"Very pretty."

"A generous donor," Winnie said as she, Mercedes, and Miss Birdie subtly nodded toward Blossom, "donated to have the air-conditioning fixed so we'll all be comfortable this summer."

"How lovely."

As Hannah spoke, Janey tugged on her hand. "Let's find a place to sit."

The service reminded Hannah of the church in Maysville she'd grown up in, without a great deal of liturgy but friendly.

With a glance at the bulletin, Hannah realized the service was heavy on songs about sheep and shepherds, probably because the scripture for the day was the Twenty-Third Psalm. The mention of sheep made her suspicious.

After the worship leader read the Psalm, Adam stood from behind the pulpit.

"The Lord is my Shepherd," he repeated as he stepped from the chancel and walked across the front of the church, the section between the chancel and the pews. "What do you know about sheep?" Adam looked around. "Anyone?"

The familiar question made Hannah even more apprehensive.

"They smell bad," Ralph answered.

"Exactly. What else?"

"They wander off," Winnie said. "We had some when I was a child."

"They follow any sheep wherever he goes," someone else shouted.

"Stupid creatures," another added.

"They get lost," Gussie said. "Easily."

"Absolutely right," Adam said. "Shepherds have to go out and find them."

Adam really had people taking part in the sermon. A great preacher, but she didn't trust him. She knew this was the sermon he'd wanted to preach to her. If she could have left now, she would have, but she couldn't embarrass him that way. Besides, Janey held her hand tightly.

He turned and slowly walked up the steps to stand behind the pulpit but didn't say anything, only moved his gaze around the sanctuary. "And yet, the writer of Psalms compares us, you and me, to those smelly, stupid, easily led astray sheep."

A few laughs came from the sanctuary.

"Did you pick that up in this morning's scripture? 'The Lord is my Shepherd.' That Psalm is talking about us, folks, comparing us to sheep. But in a good way.

" 'The Lord is my Shepherd.' " He leaned toward them. "What does that mean to you? To me, those words mean that even when we go astray, mess up, get lost, even when we smell bad, God loves us, God is with us."

God is with us, Hannah repeated silently.

"During the hardest of times, God never leaves us lost and alone," Adam said. "God doesn't leave us stranded on a mountainside. God loves us and cares for us even and most especially when we feel farthest from Him. When we are lost, God seeks us out. When we are alone, God finds us and tenderly lifts us into those strong and gentle arms."

Hannah took a deep breath and held it. He was talking to her. Not that she'd doubted that from the beginning of the service. Everyone needed a sermon, a promise like this, but Adam had known she really did. She'd refused to listen to him because she could be a stubborn jerk at times. For that reason, he'd given it to them all.

"God carries us to green pasture." Adam came down from the chancel and into the front of the sanctuary again. "When we thirst, God leads us to still waters. In the midst of the storms and crises of life, when we are abandoned by friends, when we are lost, God restores our souls. And surely, with the Lord as our shepherd, 'goodness and mercy shall follow us all the days of our lives, and we shall dwell in the house of the Lord our whole lives long.' " He paused and looked around the sanctuary until his gaze found Hannah. "Amen and amen."

Hannah let the breath out and pondered his words. "Thank you," she whispered. Peace filled her as his words soaked into her injured soul.

Gabe entered the diner at seven o'clock on Monday morning, a week after what he mentally called the fiasco with Hannah.

Not that he'd hidden from her or the shared embarrassment. He'd dropped by the parsonage several times since—had to discuss recruiting with Hector, and Adam was his friend. When he was there, Hannah wandered in and out on the way to the kitchen or out to the backyard to garden with Janey, but she ignored him completely.

This morning, he'd come to the diner for breakfast, at Miss Birdie's request. Before he could even look around for an empty spot, Miss Birdie shoved him ahead of the dozen others waiting for a table by holding his arm tightly with the arm that didn't hold the coffeepot. For a moment, he resisted, but that hot coffeepot so close to his body concerned him.

Might as well give in. As she dragged him along, he realized she had a great deal of strength in her skinny arm. Probably from lifting all those trays.

"Nice of you to invite me to breakfast."

"Just a welcome to town."

He didn't mention he'd been in town for months, since the beginning of the school year, both because that would be rude and because she was pulling him so fast toward a booth that he didn't have time to consider a suitable answer. His only focus became not to run into a chair or to trip over people's feet as she dragged him inexorably behind her.

"Miss Birdie." He pointed to a group of men, fathers of players on the basketball team, at one of the tables. He attempted to tell her he'd sit with them, but by the time he'd formed the words, she'd stopped before a large booth in the corner of the diner, secluded and certainly too big for only one person.

Besides, there was another person already there reading a newspaper. He recognized Mattie Patillo, the minister of the Presbyterian Church.

"Hello, Gabe." The minister put her *Austin American-Statesman* on the table. "Might as well join me." She waved toward the other side of the booth, and he slipped in.

With a nod, Miss Birdie said, "I'll bring you coffee and breakfast. I'm giving you a senior citizens' discount."

Hadn't she invited him to breakfast? Never mind. He could afford it.

"I see Miss Birdie has trapped you." Mattie spread jelly on her toast before she looked up at him and smiled.

Nice smile. Dimples, even. Gabe had never noticed that. Well, he hadn't seen her very often, just at community events where she looked very ministerial. Still did, actually. She wore her dark hair pulled back in a braid of some kind. Sweet, round face, but the smile and the dimple turned her into a real person. Not, of course, that ministers weren't real people. He knew that from Adam, but, okay, she looked like an attractive woman, if he could forget she was a minister.

Before he could respond to her remark, Miss Birdie approached with a cup of coffee and placed it in front of him. "Isn't she the prettiest thing you've ever seen?" She glanced at the minister, then back to him. A triumphant smile stretched across her face. He'd already learned not to trust that. She turned to serve other tables, still wearing that look of victory.

"If you haven't guessed, we've been set up." Mattie chuckled, a warm, friendly sound. "I'm surprised this hasn't happened earlier."

"Set up?" As she spoke, he realized that Miss Birdie had fooled him again. He struggled to accept it, to admit that these ladies could be so sneaky. Yes, they'd tried it at the parsonage. If they were attempting to fix him up with Mattie, they must have given up on forcing him and Hannah to be a loving couple. Guess they realized starting over presented a better option than to push him toward a woman he repulsed.

He'd hoped they'd have more persistence. From what his friends told him, the Widows had pushed Sam together with Willow and paired Adam and Gussie for months, but they'd given up on Gabe and Hannah after an hour.

When he realized Mattie expected him to say more, he added, "Looks like we have. Do you mind?"

Waiting for her answer, he glanced around to see the eyes of every person in the diner watching the booth, their gazes quickly sliding away when he looked.

Seemed he was the last to realize why he and Mattie were here. They all lived in Butternut Creek or the surrounding territory, where everyone knew everyone else's business—or if they didn't, the Widows would tell them.

Mattie waved her hand dismissively. "I'm used to it. Miss Birdie and her cohorts believe they are called to marry off all single people. In fact, people have nicknamed this particular table 'the courting booth.' " She paused and counted on her fingers. "You're the sixth possibility they've tried for me."

"Oh?" He took a gulp of coffee. "Six men?"

"First was Adam." She touched her index finger. "You know, ministers have so much in common. The Widows thought we should get married and raise holy, reverent, well-behaved children."

"Didn't work?"

"Obviously not. We're good friends but there was no attraction. After he met Gussie, the Widows recognized we were a lost cause." She touched the next finger. "Then there was the Catholic priest who'd left the church only a month earlier. Not quite ready for marriage. And the really good-looking insurance salesman who's now serving time for fraud. Actually, those are the best ones. The rest I've attempted to forget."

"Here's your breakfast." In front of him, Miss Birdie set down a platter covered with huge mounds of scrambled eggs, hash browns, and grits bordered with sausage and bacon. A plate of waffles covered with fruit and whipped cream followed. "Be right back." She hurried away.

His first thought was that he couldn't possibly eat all that food, but he knew he could. He picked up the jar of salsa and poured it on about everything on the platter as Miss Birdie set butter, syrup, and an enormous glass of orange juice on the table and moved away. Still grinning.

"All those calories," Mattie said with yearning and a little anger in her voice. "I envy you." Then she pulled over her grapefruit half and picked up the spoon.

After a few bites, she asked, "Don't you have to teach today? What time does school start?"

He glanced at the clock over the door. "I've got plenty of time. Classes start at eight but coaches don't have to show up before . . . oh, noon. If at all."

"You don't?" She paused, digging out a piece of grapefruit. "When I was in school, coaches taught health or PE."

"You didn't grow up in Texas, did you?"

She shook her head.

"Here assistant coaches teach a couple of classes, but head football and basketball coaches only coach." He held up his hand. "Not that that doesn't take a great deal of time. During the season, it's pretty much seventy or eighty hours a week, maybe more. But now, with the season over, I don't have to keep regular hours as long as I have my cell on."

Having finished the waffles and sausage, he moved on to the hill of eggs. "I do know about the deviousness of the Widows. They already tried to set me up once. Didn't work."

"Really? With whom?"

He paused, not sure if he wanted to say, but he had brought this up. "Adam's sister, Hannah."

"You're kidding, right?" She tilted her head as she thought about that. "Even I know she came home exhausted and mentally . . . I don't know.

Stressed? Fragile? Probably not ready to even think about marriage."

"We discovered that. Hannah ran off rather than sit next to me."

"Ouch." Mattie's voice held deep sympathy.

"Yeah." He took another bite and swallowed. "Want to go to Austin with me Friday? Maybe dinner and a movie?"

"You mean it? You're not just saying that to make the Widows happy?"

"Exactly the reason I asked. I live to make Miss Birdie happy."

"I'd like to go to Austin with you." She scrutinized him for a moment.

What had he done or said to require that?

"But I have a question or two first." She leaned forward. The smile had disappeared.

Uh-oh. Maybe Mattie wasn't as easy to get along with as Gabe thought. Adam had told him she had a strong personality, but she didn't look tough.

She started that counting-on-her-fingers thing again. "First." She touched her index finger. "What happened to that college student you were dating a while back?"

"You know about her?"

She nodded. "Everyone does. You live in Butternut Creek."

"I thought if I went into Austin . . ."

"No, people from here go to Austin, too. Saw you with a blonde, a very young blonde."

"No secrets here, huh?" He shrugged. "I discovered I'm too old to date a college student. She didn't know anything about the world and had atrocious taste in music."

"Even gorgeous can't make up for that?"

He nodded again. "Must be getting old. I'd always thought gorgeous made up for almost anything."

"Okay, that third-grade teacher from San Saba." She counted on her next finger.

"We're no longer dating."

"Everyone said she was getting too serious." She grinned at his look of consternation. "No secrets here."

"Why all the questions?"

She sighed. "I'm a minister. An unmarried woman minister. That makes dating hard. I have to be careful. There are people who will use anything to get rid of me because they cannot believe God called me."

"How would they know? Wasn't that conversation between you and God?"

"I'd thought so but evidently not, because those people say God doesn't call women." She took another sip of coffee. "Second"—she held up two fingers—"there are guys who think seducing a minister would be fun. I really have to be careful about my reputation."

"I'm not dating anyone now. Will knowing that you aren't a scarlet woman luring me away from other females satisfy the gossips in Butternut Creek?"

"I'm not sure they're ever satisfied, but this should help. Churches prefer their ministers to be boringly and unrealistically pure, especially the women."

After spending a few more minutes eating and chatting, Gabe stood, tossing a few bills on the table that would easily pay for the meal without a senior discount and leave a nice tip for Miss Birdie. "I'll pick you up at six."

As he left, he could actually feel Miss Birdie's eyes on his back. He didn't give anything away. Let her and the other Widows find out about that date. They would, soon enough. He didn't have to help.

When he got to the door, he glanced back to see Miss Birdie heading toward the booth where he'd left Mattie alone. Didn't feel a bit guilty. With the woman Adam called "the pillar," it was every man for himself or woman for herself, whichever applied.

Adam woke up at two a.m. Why?

The phone hadn't awakened him, thank goodness. Calls in the middle of the night didn't bode well, meant a health problem, usually a severe one.

No, not the phone but something had interrupted his sleep. Maybe the unusual experience of not having the enormous dog attempting to shove him out of the bed had awakened him. Adam rolled over and stretched out in the warm and slightly canine-scented space Chewy had vacated.

Had the dog heard something? Had Adam? He listened. No noise came from the hallway or from outside the parsonage, but Chewy whimpered a few feet away. When Adam ignored the sounds, the dog scratched the bedroom door.

"Chewy, stop," he mumbled.

As usual, the dog ignored his master's suggestion and kept scratching. Someday Adam was going to have to teach him to open the door for himself.

"What is it, buddy?" he asked, although he didn't really expect a reply. "Have to go out?"

Chewy kept scratching. Answer enough.

Adam rolled over and stood, slipped on jeans, and pushed his feet into flip-flops.

"Okay, let's go," he said to Chewy.

The dog ran through the open door ahead of Adam and hurled himself down the back steps. By the time Adam reached the first floor, Chewy stood by the back door and whimpered, his body shaking with excitement like the most eager of guard dogs.

"Something out there? What do you think it is, buddy?" he asked. Still no verbal answer.

The light on the back porch illuminated the area around the stoop but left the rest of the yard in darkness. Had he left it on?

Then Adam opened the door. Chewy zoomed past him, baying, and bounded down the back steps. The dog disappeared into the shadows but, from the panting and woofing, Adam knew where he was: in the corner of the yard that contained the recently planted vegetable garden. Then the creature howled.

Had Chewy caught something? A rabbit or a mole or some other creature? Had someone climbed over the fence? Should he call the police? Probably not a good idea—he'd have to wake up the patrolman who, everyone knew, grabbed a nap in the grade school parking lot at this time. If criminals took out the sleeping cop, they'd open the entire town to anarchy until the chief arrived at the police station the next morning.

Knowing he was delaying his investigation, Adam shoved the thought of criminals and anarchists aside, stepped outside, and said, "Hello?"

No answer.

"Hello?" Still no one answered, and he didn't want to shout and awaken his neighbors. Adam glanced around at the houses close to the parsonage. No lights showed yet.

Squinting, he tried to penetrate the darkness beyond the circle of illumination from the porch light but couldn't. Was there a movement in the corner of the vegetable garden? Other than Chewy's wiggling? With a final glance around, he called, "Chewy." The silly dog didn't come but had stopped howling.

Might as well give up. He'd leave Chewy outside until he started barking. Once he was back inside, Adam closed and locked the door so anyone skulking back there couldn't get inside and turned the porch light off.

"Hey!" came a voice from the outside.

From that one word, he couldn't recognize who spoke, but he knew someone actually did lurk out there. He didn't believe a murderer or thief would call *Hey,* but he could be mistaken. He opened the junk drawer in the kitchen and took out a flashlight before flipping the outside light back on. Cautiously, he opened the door an inch as if the narrow gap would deter anyone with a nefarious plot in mind.

"Who is it?" He pitched his voice low, in a menacing tone he hoped made him sound big and tough and mean.

"For heaven's sake, speak like yourself," Hannah said. "You sound ridiculous."

Yes, obviously his sister. With that assurance, he opened the door and stepped out to shine the flashlight toward the vegetable garden. At first he didn't see anything.

He descended the steps. When he strode closer he could make out Hannah crouching on the ground and attempting to fight off the excited Chewy and his enormous, friendly tongue.

Adam stopped and watched her in the weak glow of the flashlight, which really needed new batteries. "What are you doing?"

"N-nothing." Her voice shook a little.

Hannah never sounded uncertain, even during arguments when everyone knew she was wrong and seven reference books didn't back her assertions. So why did she sound timid now?

"Meditating," she suggested and pushed Chewy away.

He took another step toward her. "Why are you out here?" he demanded. "You scared me." He picked up a rock and tossed it toward the middle of the yard. Chewy took off after it.

"Oh, for heaven's sake," Hannah said in a voice dripping with scorn. "There's nothing to be afraid of in Butternut Creek. Ax murderers seldom creep around in the backyard of the parsonage."

Deflect, don't answer the question, that had always been Hannah's strategy. Usually successful with people who didn't know her well but never with him.

He asked for a third time, "What are you doing out here?" and took several more steps toward her, entering murky darkness as the flashlight died. The glow from the porch didn't reach this far.

"Gardening," she said in a soft voice and gestured toward what he thought was a flat of tomatoes.

"You're gardening in the middle of the night, in the dark?"

"Not that dark. Moon's out."

"Not that dark?" he asked. "It's the middle of the night."

"You've said that. Let your eyes get used to the dark."

"Hannah." He took another step, hunkered next to her, and gazed at the pale oval of her face. "What's going on? Why are you out here? Why are you gardening?"

"I like to dig in the dirt."

Partial answer, another of his sister's favorite defenses. In the futile hope he could intimidate her, he stood, crossed his arms, and tapped his toe to show his annoyance. Unfortunately, tapping one's flip-flops on the dirt of a garden made very little sound. "Well?"

"Your sermon helped me a lot. Thank you. But even with that, I was feeling a little . . . nervous. You know, anxious."

"I know what *nervous* means, thank you. That still doesn't explain why you're here." He pointed to the ground as if she could see that. "In the backyard in the middle of the night."

"Gardening calms me. It makes me think of growth and life. When I bury my hands in the soil, I feel at peace."

He knelt next to her. "Okay, if sitting in the garden helps, I'm all for it, but could you do it when the sun's out?"

"I'm anxious now."

"Could you . . ."

Before he could finish the question, the back light at the home of his next-door neighbors flashed on and George stuck his head outside.

"Everything okay over there?" George asked.

"We're fine," Adam yelled back, a soft shout so he wouldn't awaken more of the neighbors.

"Chewy sick?" George asked. "One of the kids?"

"No, we . . ."

"Praying?" he asked.

Sounded like as good a reason as any to be kneeling here after midnight but before he could agree to undertaking this odd mystical practice, his truthfulness gene kicked in. Instead he said, "No, chatting with my sister."

"Outside?"

"Right."

"In the middle of the night?"

"Yup."

Fortunately, George had learned to accept odd behavior from the inhabitants of the parsonage and didn't pry. Good old George waved and said, "Let me know if you need anything." With that, he backed inside, shut the door, and turned off the light.

"Why would your neighbors come out and check just because we're in your backyard at night? Seems really nosey." Hannah deflected again.

"That's how small towns are. Neighbors care."

He paused then, to pull her back on track, asked, "Do you want to talk?"

"I want to plant tomatoes."

"All right." Before he could stand, he heard a siren and saw a flashing blue light in the parking lot that separated the church and the parsonage, then a faint blip, like a siren dying. Adam realized the patrolman didn't spend every night sleeping in the elementary school parking lot because he was right here.

Had someone broken into the church?

He wanted to leap to his feet and stride to the fence but next to him, Hannah shivered. She'd wrapped herself in a heavy sweat suit, so she couldn't be cold. Maybe she was, but the quaking felt more like fear. Was she experiencing a flashback to something that had happened in a refugee camp? He slipped his arm around his sister and pulled her against him.

The spotlight on the side of the patrol car went on but only illuminated the second and third stories of the parsonage. The section of the backyard that the high fence cut off remained pretty dark.

"Sir, I'm Patrolman Oglethorpe," the cop called from the other side of the barrier. Then he shone the brilliance of his huge flashlight over the fence and into the yard where Hannah and Adam crouched in the deep shadows. "Got a report of suspicious behavior here," Oglethorpe continued.

"Sir, who are you and why are you lurking out here in the dark? Would you explain that?"

"Yes, sir," Adam started. Before he could, a light from the second story of the house that backed up to the parsonage went on and Philemon Roberts, a deacon at AME Church, leaned out.

"What's going on here, Brother Adam?" Philemon boomed. The man sounded exactly the way Adam thought God did, if God spoke from a second-story window. "You need help?"

The booming voice woke up the neighborhood. Windows lit up in two houses to the south, but it didn't faze the patrolman.

"What are you doing out here, sir?" Oglethorpe asked, completely ignoring the deacon but turning his Maglite on the yard.

Adam searched for a reasonable, believable answer but came up only with, "Gardening."

In the firm voice of a man determined to get to the bottom of the disturbance and refusing to be sidetracked by absurd statements, the officer asked, "Are you alone out here in the dark . . . umm, gardening?" He snickered.

Of course the cop couldn't see Hannah, so very small, and leaning against her brother. Probably looked more like a shadow than a person.

"No, sir," Hannah answered. "He's not alone."

"You have a woman out here, sir?" Condemnation hardened the patrolman's voice. "Ma'am, are you being held against your will?"

Against his side, he felt Hannah's quivering change. No longer terrified, she doubled over with laughter.

"No, sir," she said, but her voice shook with amusement. If he hadn't known better, Adam would have heard that as a frightened, shaky plea for rescue.

Must have sounded as if she were in peril to Oglethorpe as well, because the patrolman said, "Hold on, ma'am. I'm coming in there. You'll be fine."

Immediately, Adam heard the sound of feet scrambling against the wooden fence, then a muffled curse. He couldn't help but admire the man's persistence and his protective instinct. At the same time, he wondered how Oglethorpe thought he could climb over a five-foot wooden fence holding a flashlight.

"The police? Really?" Hannah asked. "Don't they have bigger crimes to investigate?"

"Not in Butternut Creek." Adam stood and pulled Hannah up with him. By that time not only were heads popping out of back windows up and down the fence line but both George and Ouida had come outside and stood next to the fence as backup.

"Folks, move back." The patrolman waved toward the Kowalskis before he addressed Adam. "Sir, step away from her and put your hands up." He continued to struggle to get a foothold in the wooden fence.

"Officer, it's fine," Hannah said. "He's not hurting me. He's my brother."

Oglethorpe turned the light directly on Adam. "You're attacking your sister?" he asked, his voice heavy with revulsion.

"No, sir," Adam said. "We're gardening. Like I said."

A few seconds of silence followed until the deacon stated, "It's late to be gardening."

"Dark, too," the patrolman added suspiciously, and he began anew his effort to climb the fence.

For a heartbeat Adam thought about opening one side of the huge double gate for Oglethorpe, but he remembered the warning about stepping away from Hannah and putting his hands up. Adam had no idea if members of the Butternut Creek Police Department packed heat but he didn't want to find out. He stood very still.

"Sir, these are good people," Ouida shouted across the yard.

With that, several more lights went on down the street, south of the deacon's house.

"I'm the minister at the Christian Church," Adam stated.

"He is," Ouida shouted. "He lives in the parsonage."

"I know this man. He's an upstanding citizen," Philemon said. His words were followed by words of agreement from houses to the south.

"A good neighbor," George added.

"Officer," Hannah said and took a step toward the fence and into the bright beam of the megalight. "I find working in the garden soothing." She shrugged. "I know it sounds odd, but I woke up and couldn't get back to sleep. I came down here to dig for a few minutes. Reverend Jordan is my brother. He found me and tried to get me to go inside." She took another step. "I'm fine, I really am."

After a few more seconds of silence, she added, "Thank you for your concern about my well-being. I appreciate it."

Sounds of agreement came from all over the neighborhood.

"You have a lot of character witnesses," Oglethorpe said. "I'm new to town and don't know the preachers here, but I still find this situation strange and perplexing."

"Thank you, sir. Sorry for the disturbance," Adam said. "We feel safe with you on the job."

Oglethorpe turned off his Maglite. "Glad to be of service," he said before turning away.

"If you don't have a church home," Adam said, "we'd love to see you here on Sunday."

"Thank you." With that, the patrolman got into his car, turned off the flashing light, and drove away. Windows slammed shut down the fence line.

"Good night, folks." Adam waved and dragged

Hannah toward the house. "Thanks, George and Ouida," he said as his neighbors strolled back toward their house.

"I can't believe you did that. You invited him to church." Stubborn as ever, Hannah stopped and pulled against his hand. "The man thought you were a sex fiend and pervert. He nearly arrested you, and you invited him to church."

"It was the right thing to do and don't change the topic. This would never have happened if you hadn't gone outside to garden in the middle of the night." He dropped her hand and glared at her, but that didn't intimidate her. Nothing he did ever had.

"You've already said that but if you'd stayed inside, nothing would have happened." She leaned forward and met his glare with her glower. "I can't believe people in small towns act like this."

"You grew up in Maysville, Kentucky, Sis. You know what small towns are like."

"I . . . I . . ." She searched for a retort.

"Let's not bicker, children."

They looked up to see Hector at the door.

"I was very young at the time." Hannah stalked inside and up the stairs.

"You almost got arrested, Pops." Hector studied him with a mix of amazement and what Adam feared was admiration.

"What could have been worse than to have the

minister of the Christian Church nearly handcuffed and taken to jail?" Adam asked.

"Yeah, sure, but almost getting arrested's not the only thing you need to worry about." Hector paused to drag out the suspense. "Pretty soon, if not already, Miss Birdie's going to find out a cop showed up at the parsonage." He grinned as Adam came inside. "You can expect an early visit from her."

Adam breathed a prayer of thanksgiving that he had a few hours left before the wrath of the pillar fell upon him.

Could be she'd get a laugh out of the situation, but he didn't think so. The police car investigating a disturbance at the parsonage didn't seem like anything she'd find funny. He headed toward the stairs.

"Going to talk to Hannah about what happened? The cop and everything?" Hector asked before he could move farther. "About causing such a ruckus? Waking the neighbors?"

Adam didn't know.

"Pops, you aren't afraid of her, are you?"

"You don't have an older sister you haven't mentioned, do you?" Adam asked.

"No. Why?"

"If you've never had an older sister, you don't have the right to judge the fear one engenders."

"She's a little bitty thing. She couldn't hurt you."

"When we were kids, she was two years older

and bigger than me. When we walked to school, she put her hand on the back of my neck and squeezed if I didn't go in the direction she wanted. She took away all my toy guns and GI figures because she was a pacifist even back then, except with her brother. She . . ." He stopped and smiled at the memories. "She was a terror, even as a little girl, and my parents told me I couldn't hit her because she was a girl."

"That's got to be twenty years ago."

"Old fears never go away. Besides, she's my sister and she's struggling. I don't want to upset her more."

"Maybe you could get a big box of dirt for her to dig in at night."

"Or a flower box." Adam snapped his fingers. "Not a bad idea at all."

The next morning, Hannah pulled on her running shoes and Velcroed them shut. Unzipping the pocket in her shoe, she stuffed her ID and a couple of dollars inside. She considered sticking her phone in the slit of a pocket on her shorts, but who needed a phone in Butternut Creek? In case of emergency, just shout. Someone would come to help.

With that, she grabbed her sunglasses, slipped them on, and headed downstairs. How far should she go this morning? Probably should start slow. She hadn't run for three months and had lost a lot of strength.

She hadn't jogged in London because her mother got so anxious about Hannah's health, certain her daughter would have a heart attack or a stroke or relapse, maybe get lost or be hit by a car, and she couldn't allow Mom to worry any more about her. Besides, for months she'd felt noodleishly weak from the malaria. But here in Butternut Creek, she'd regained some strength. The weather and the town were beautiful. She hoped this would help her recover from her stress and anxiety. If so, maybe she wouldn't have to go outside at night to work the soil, wake the neighbors, and cause a cop to drop by. Living in a small town certainly cut down on privacy.

She made it five blocks before she was sucking wind and her legs wobbled. A start. She could go a block farther every morning. Soon she'd be running to Marble Falls and back.

On Friday night, Gussie glanced around the family room. Everyone had settled in their normal places. She and Adam and her parents had pushed together on the sofa that really needed to be just a few inches longer. Not that she minded being curled up next to Adam.

Hannah sat in what they now considered her chair, a medical magazine on the floor next to her. Janey had shoved Hannah's feet from the ottoman and sat there. All watched *Singing in the Rain*, one of her old favorites. A nice family evening.

But wouldn't it be nice if she and Adam could be alone for a minute? Not only to smooch, although she'd like that, but to talk. Maybe even to set a wedding date. The way their lives were now, they emailed and chatted on the phone or sat around with her parents, alone only during the time Adam walked her back to Sam's old house or when he came into Austin.

"What are you thinking?" With his arm around her, Adam squeezed her shoulder.

"This is nice." Gussie leaned back a little so she could see him better, then lay her head on his shoulder.

They'd arrived at her favorite part of the movie, "Make Them Laugh," when Hector came down the back stairs. He clattered across the kitchen and into the family room. "I'm going out now. Meeting Bobby and some of the guys at the Burger Barn." He hugged his sister and headed toward the door.

"Where's your coach?" Hannah asked.

Because Mom had paused the movie, Hannah's words sounded loud in the silence. Everyone turned toward her.

"I mean," Hannah explained, "isn't he usually part of your gang?"

"Not always." He shrugged. "Not usually. Besides, Coach has a date tonight." He took off.

When Hector said the words. Hannah blinked twice and said, "Oh? How nice." Her voice sounded surprised and, maybe, a little disappointed.

Gussie thought only she had noticed the reaction because the others had turned to wave at Hector, focused on Hector's departure and not Hannah's expression or tone. She continued to study her future sister-in-law. Hannah had slid down in the chair and tucked her chin into her chest to present the top of her head to the group.

Interesting. Should she tell Adam what she'd observed? No, Hannah deserved privacy. Goodness how Gussie had hated it when the Widows had attempted to force her and Adam together.

Besides, the Widows had already made that disastrous and horribly embarrassing effort to match Hannah and Gabe. Could be Gussie's observation was wrong, that Hannah didn't have feelings for the coach, only asked for information from politeness, to have a friendly conversation with Hector.

But no. Gussie had recognized that hastily hidden emotion. She knew far too well the difficulty of living a normal life when the Widows were around to embarrass. No one could protect another person from the Widows, but she could be Hannah's friend and attempt to shield her from the worst of the pillar's machinations.

Chapter Nine

After Hector left, Adam glanced at his watch. Nearly eight. The kid should be home in four or five hours. He still worried after the time a year ago when Hector had been so drunk that he'd called Adam to pick him up. He was glad he called but hated teenage drinking. They were going to drink. Teenagers thought they were indestructible. Others might die but not them, and no adult could change their minds.

Adam had to trust Hector. Not to have faith in him would weaken their relationship. Trust was the only answer. He settled back on the sofa and put his arm around Gussie before glancing at his sister. She didn't seem to care about the movie. She sat in the huge chair that made her look even thinner and more miserable, the blanket pulled nearly to her nose.

What could he do to help her? Then Yvonne took his hand and squeezed it lightly. "It'll work out," she whispered.

Adam didn't feel nearly as confident. He'd prayed about his sister but knew that praying for *other* people to change seldom worked. Instead, he'd prayed for her to heal and for him to be patient. Neither prayer seemed to be working, but God seldom worked on Adam's schedule.

"Preacher?" Charley Parsons's voice came from

the front porch at the same time he knocked.

"I completely forgot." Adam got to his feet reluctantly. "I was supposed to meet Charley in the sanctuary at eight to . . ." He stopped talking as he remembered he wasn't supposed to say anything about the air-conditioning until the anonymous donor gave the okay. "To meet Charley."

"Is he all right?" Yvonne asked. "Are you going to pray with him?"

"No. Charley's a good Presbyterian."

"Why isn't he meeting with his minister instead of you?" Hannah asked.

"Don't they pray the same way we do?" Janey asked.

"It's not a spiritual thing." He glanced at Gussie, blinked and grimaced in the hope she could read his silent signal to stop the questions.

"That's nice." Gussie stood. "Charley's a good man." She followed him toward the door. "How long will this take?" she asked.

"An hour, maybe?"

"Fine. Hurry back so you can walk me home." She opened the door and shoved him outside, then waved at Charley. "Nice to see you."

"Sorry I interrupted," Charley said.

The plumber was, to speak kindly, a large man: six-three and over three hundred pounds. Shortly after Adam's arrival in town, Charley had gotten stuck in a parsonage bathroom. At least there shouldn't be any tight spaces in putting in air-conditioning. Wasn't the ductwork already there?

"Sorry I wasn't ready." Adam pulled his keys out.

"Thanks for meeting me so late. This has been a real busy week, but I want to work on the air conditioner as soon as I can."

When they reached the front entrance, Adam unlocked the door. Even in Butternut Creek, he locked things up at night, a habit that displayed he was an outlander. "Hate to take you away from Rita Mae and the kids."

"She took them to a movie. I'll be home before they are. Only need to take measurements and look at the wiring and a few other things so I can give you a bid."

It took nearly an hour for Charley to inspect the system and make notes. Part of the unit was under the floor in the narthex, which worried Adam. When Charley got in and out of that pit without too much trouble, Adam relaxed. The plumber checked the fuse box and the outdoor unit, measuring everything and taking precise notes. Each place looked large enough that Charley wouldn't get stuck. Until they came to the fellowship hall.

"You know, Preacher." Charley pointed toward the ceiling. "It wouldn't cost much more to check out the ductwork and mechanics all over the church. They used to install ductwork with more bends than we do today. A redo could lower your utility bill." Charley kept his gaze up, inspecting the area. "We'll have to get up there and check. Might should replace those stained ceiling tiles, too."

Adam froze. The idea of Charley crawling through the ceiling made him shudder. The entire structure could fall down if Charley got stuck up there.

"Don't worry. I'm not climbing up there." He grinned. "Have a young, skinny apprentice to do that kind of thing."

From the porch late Friday afternoon, Adam watched Hector stuff his duffel bag in the backseat of Gabe's truck in preparation for their overnight visit to San Pablo.

Nice truck. Four doors with lots of chrome and a perfectly tailored cover snapped over the bed. Although he must have earned a lot of money in the pros, Gabe never showed off except with this vehicle. Must have cost more than Adam could even conceive. Yeah, nice truck, but not as nice as Adam's new car. Adam didn't even attempt to squash that non-ministerial quiver of pride.

He stepped into the yard to study the sky. The dark clouds worried him. The forecast for Saturday wasn't good, but *bad weather* pretty much described Texas during the spring. Months of drought alternated with weeks of torrential rain and storm warnings, and high winds and the possibility of tornadoes usually accompanied those storms.

As Hector got into the front seat, Adam waved and headed inside.

Hannah stood beside the window in the front hall and watched the truck back out. She started when she saw him and looked a little embarrassed. Why?

"Want to go out and wave?" he asked.

"No, that's okay. Having his elderly aunt hover over him would embarrass Hector." She looked out the window. "What do you think about the sky?" she asked.

"I have to admit I'm worried," he said.

"Me, too." She headed into the family room.

Why had Hannah been standing at the front window? She liked Hector but had never felt the need to fawn all over him. Other than that, she could only be studying the sky or watching Gabe. The window in the front was under the roof of the porch; very little sky was visible from there. He didn't ask because by the time he'd followed her, she'd curled up in her chair. She looked the same as she had since her arrival except now she read books about gardening.

No, that was wrong. She did look better. During her nearly two months here, she'd put on about ten pounds but still needed to gain more. Although still spiky and uneven, her hair had regained its shine, and the dark circles around her eyes no longer looked as if someone had broken her nose. Even her color had improved. She looked pasty but no longer deathly gray, and she'd started running again.

"Did you know lantana and Mexican bush sage attract butterflies?" She glanced up from her book. "We need to plant some and create a container of water for them. Butterflies don't drink from birdbaths or ponds."

"Hate to have thirsty butterflies." Then he heard the sound of a car in the drive. "Must be Gussie," he said and hurried to the front door and outside.

"I'm so glad you're here," he told Gussie, taking her hand as they walked inside. Once in the front hall, he kissed her.

"I can't take all the lovey-doveyness," Hannah shouted. "There are other people who live in this house."

"She's feeling a little grumpy today," Adam said. "Maybe you could draw her out. If you can talk about communicable diseases, Hannah's really an interesting person."

"I'm sure she is." Gussie kissed his cheek before she headed into the family room and settled on the ottoman Adam still associated with Gabe. "Okay, no more mushy stuff. So, tell me, what do you want to talk about?"

"Didn't particularly want to talk. Just didn't want to be bombarded with all that *love*." Hannah imbued the last word with such scorn, Gussie laughed.

"If you talk to me, I can't possibly kiss your brother. What are you reading?"

As the sound of rain began to patter steadily on the roof, they chatted about planting vegetables. Although Gussie knew little about diseases, she'd learned about gardens from her parents. After about fifteen minutes, she stood. "I've got to drop off my bags and pick up my parents. Mom fixed something special for dinner."

"I don't like you driving in this weather," Adam said.

"It's a short drive. We'll be okay." She hugged him before dashing through the rain to her car.

"Okay, hurry back."

He didn't like anyone out in this weather, but no one listened to him.

After Gabe drove for ten minutes, rain began to fall. Every few minutes, the amount increased, which challenged the windshield wipers to keep up. With defrost on the highest setting, the cab was hot, but they couldn't open the windows without sheets of rain blowing inside. By the time it was bad enough that he considered turning back to Butternut Creek, they were over halfway to San Pablo. He kept going.

Twenty miles outside San Pablo, the driving rain smashed against the windshield with such a force

Gabe struggled to control the truck, amazed the wind could shove the heavy vehicle around so easily. If he'd seen a motel, he would have pulled over and spent the night, but he didn't see any along this section of highway.

"*Llueve a cántaros*," Hector said. "That means 'it's raining from large pitchers' in Spanish, like our expression it's raining cats and dogs."

"Certainly coming down hard." Gabe peered through the windshield that the wipers struggled to clear. "I'm impressed you can talk about the weather in two languages."

For the rest of the drive, Gabe concentrated hard, focusing on peering through the downpour until he saw the city limits sign and entered San Pablo.

Thank goodness.

Hector pointed a few blocks ahead. "There's the motel."

Gabe pulled the truck under the covered entrance in front of the office. "I'll check us in," he shouted as he got out, the wind whipping his words away.

"Two rooms on the ground floor," he said to the clerk. Due to recruiting rules, he couldn't pay for Hector's room and neither could the junior college so they'd picked a fairly cheap place. As the wind whipped around outside, he hoped the building could withstand the storm. That was why he'd asked for rooms on the ground floor. Less likely to be swept away, although more chance of being crushed.

He should probably stop thinking about that last part.

Once outside, he studied the sky. It had turned the greenish color he associated with tornadoes. Not much he could do now. Thoroughly drenched, he got in the truck, pulled it around the building, and parked. "You get the bags. I'll go ahead of you and open the door."

They dashed inside one of the rooms, arriving safe and fairly dry.

"Okay, you take this one. I'll go next door." Gabe handed Hector the key card. "You stay here and I'll get us Cokes and ice."

Hector said, "Do you think the wind's going to blow me away?" and went out for ice and drinks, returning soggy and with shoes that squished from the deep puddles and the blowing downpour.

By that time, Gabe had come back from dropping his bags in his room and turned on the television to watch the weather warnings. Nothing they could do now but wait and listen to the news. The maps showed storm warnings all across Central Texas. No one knew where a tornado might drop from the sky. They could be in as much danger in Butternut Creek as they were here.

Because Yvonne had packed their dinner, they spread out the dishes and kept the television on.

. . .

Adam and Gussie sat on the sofa and watched the ten o'clock news, which focused on the weather.

"You know your sister's determined to go wherever there's an emergency, don't you?"

He nodded. "Don't think I can stop her." He shook his head. "We are so different."

"No, you're not. You're determined to go, too."

"Oh, yes, we are different. She's really driven. Mom and Dad had high expectations for both of us," Adam said. "Especially for Hannah because she was the oldest and smarter than me. She could never please Dad, not even graduating early from high school as valedictorian."

Gussie blinked. "What could be better than that?"

"She had to become a doctor, the best doctor in the world." He put his arm around Gussie. "I think they meant well. I know they did. They wanted to challenge us to do our best. I couldn't live up to that. I tuned them out when I was twelve, lived my life the way I wanted to."

Gussie squeezed his hand. "Must have been tough."

"Not for me. But for Hannah?" He shrugged.

Before he could say more, the warning sirens blasted. Yvonne and Henry rushed in from the porch where they'd been watching the sky. He'd asked all three Miltons to spend the night because the parsonage had an old storm cellar and Sam's old house was built on a slab. Houses in Texas seldom—actually, almost never—had basements, but his did. Years earlier, it had been closed from the outside and turned into a laundry and storage area, but it was still the safest place on the block.

He ran upstairs, shouted up to Hannah, then ran into Janey's room, wrapped her in her blanket, and hurried back down with his sister right behind them. The Miltons had already turned on the dim basement light and started downstairs. When a knock sounded, he gave Janey to Hannah and headed to the front door.

The Kowalskis stood on the porch, completely drenched. George carried Carol and Ouida had Gretchen while torrents of water streamed off their slickers. "Come on in." Adam waved toward the kitchen. "You know the way. I have a couple of folding chairs next to the dryer."

"Thanks, Adam, for sharing your shelter," Ouida said as she and George ran into the kitchen and put the girls down. Once they'd shrugged off their wet rain gear, they draped it all across the kitchen counter to dry.

"Oh, sure, I'd allow my neighbors to blow away." Adam waved them toward the steps. "Where would I get my morning scones if that happened?" They headed down, the very pregnant Ouida holding on to the rail.

Before Adam could follow, another knock came.

248

Standing on the porch were the deacon and his wife and the Ferguson family from across the street. Seven more people.

Adam had never considered how many people could fit in the small space, but fifteen seemed half a dozen too many. Fortunately, the children and Hannah took up little space, and he wasn't about to kick anyone out.

In the middle of the ceiling hung a bare lightbulb, which cast shadows in the corners. He and a few of the weather refugees stood around the walls, leaning against shelving or the appliances. Ouida and Yvonne had the chairs while the rest sat on rag rugs he'd tossed across the dirt floor. They all listened to the weather radio Adam had brought down. Gussie sat close to Adam's feet with Janey in her lap.

"This hazardous weather warning is for Central Texas in Creek, San Pablo, Mason, Kimble, and Kerr Counties and moving northwest toward Llano, Burnet, Williamson, and Travis Counties tonight and early tomorrow."

Not just Creek County but San Pablo, where Hector was. He should never have allowed him to go west with the forecast for bad weather. Yeah, like that made any sense. Any tornado was as likely to hit Butternut Creek as San Pablo. But if it hit here, Hector would be down in the storm cellar and safe. He trusted Gabe to watch out for Hector.

"Severe thunderstorms likely across most of the state of Texas. A weather front is approaching from the west, bringing showers and thunderstorms as it moves through."

It would hit San Pablo first. The weather broadcast would report if Gabe and Hector had driven into a tornado. The thought almost made him want to turn the radio off.

He leaned forward and dropped his hand on Gussie's shoulder, then gently touched Janey's head as he straightened.

"Severe weather will be most probable in the central part of the state, roughly ten miles south of Mason and west of Fallen Oak in Fell County. Temperatures will create an unstable air mass, increasing the chances of heavy precipitation. Damaging winds, tornadoes, and large hail will all be possible."

The adults started, then glanced at each other when the gale drove rain against the windows. Ouida held Carol more securely as if, with the protection of her body, the storm couldn't injure her child. George stood by the weather radio holding Gretchen. Thank goodness all the children dozed, probably exhausted by being out so late.

Until the storm hit. Twenty minutes after they'd gathered, the winds had picked up more and swept around the house, battering it. Hail pounded against the windows and drowned out the radio.

Not that they needed more information to know that gale-force winds had hit and that, perhaps, a tornado would follow. Downed branches hurled around by powerful winds struck the house, banging. It sounded as if someone were bombarding it with rocks or firing bullets toward the walls and windows.

The thunder and howling tumult startled the children awake. They all clung to whoever held them and sobbed in fear, even the two boys from across the street. Adam felt like doing the same. Oh, not clinging, but that hard sobbing would probably relieve a lot of tension.

Instead of crying, he began to sing. He didn't know why. He wasn't a singer by any means. And as for choice of a song? The only one that came to mind was a really old one, "The Battle of New Orleans." The deacon and Gussie began to sing with him. Thank goodness, because he couldn't carry the tune. Little by little, all the adults joined in and added whatever words they could think of, but for the most part they sang "We dum-de-de dum and we . . ." When they got to "We fired our guns . . ." all the adults knew the words. Fortunately, the kids were so distracted by their parents' singing, the deacon's rich bass, and Gussie's lovely and loud voice, they calmed down as the sound covered much of the resounding chaos outside.

After the adults mumbled their way through a

couple of verses, Janey said, "Sing something I know."

"Maybe a prayer first, Brother Adam," the deacon said. With a voice louder than the thunder he began, "For those who are out in this storm, dear Lord, we just pray for Your protection." His gigantic voice drowned out the frightening sounds outside and calmed the fear inside. Afterward he said, "We just hope all your children find safe harbor. Amen." Then he began to sing "Amazing Grace."

A much better choice.

After eating, Gabe and Hector watched the weather reports on television. Weather forecasters with Doppler radar had replaced all regular programming on local channels.

"Could we watch some baseball?" Hector asked. "The Astros are playing out west tonight and I bet they'll have a crawl about the weather."

Gabe shook his head. "I have to make sure you're okay. I want to know what's headed toward us." As he read that a tornado had been sighted in a town to the west, the siren blared outside. "Come on, Hector. Help me with this." He stood, strode toward the bed, flung the covers off, and tugged on the mattress.

"What are you doing, man? Are we going to sleep on the floor?"

"Help me pull this into the bathroom."

"We're going to sleep on the bathroom floor?" He took the other end of the mattress and followed Gabe.

Once inside the bathroom, Gabe said, "Okay, get in the tub."

"What . . . ?"

"Don't argue. Do what I say."

Hector slid into the tub and Gabe flipped the mattress on top of him.

"Stay there until I come back."

"Like I could move."

Gabe ran out of the bathroom, headed for his room and tub. Outside, the wind slapped his face, rain soaked him, and hail battered against his back and arms. In the short distance between Hector's door and his, the wind had increased to such a level that he had to grasp the door handle to steady himself enough to insert the key card. Once open, the door flew against the wall with a crash. He struggled to close it against the force, then ran toward the bathroom. Before he could reach it, something crashed through the big window facing the parking lot. Automatically, he looked toward the sound as glass exploded throughout the room.

By instinct, he closed his eyes and put his hands over them as he fell on the floor between the bed and the back wall. He hoped the narrow space provided enough cover, because he wasn't about to stand up again to reach a safer place.

He lay on the carpet in the darkness and listened

as the chaos outside increased. He'd heard that a tornado sounded like a train. It did, but louder, as if it were in the room with him, deafening and so powerful the room vibrated. The whooshing roar of the tornado, the crash of debris against the building, and the buffeting of the rain and hail and wind outside underscored how finite and vulnerable his body was against the force of the storm. Scared him to death.

He wished he could get at least part of himself under the bed, but it had a solid platform. Nothing to hold on to, nothing to slide under as he huddled there. He breathed a prayer more heartfelt than any he'd ever said before. "Dear God, please . . . please . . . ," he repeated, sure God would understand because his brain seemed incapable of deciding what, exactly, to ask for.

How was Hector? He should have stayed there. He could have huddled beside the bed in the other room as well as he did here. "God, please watch over Hector." There, a real, solid prayer.

The noise and terror lasted forever. He shook and the bed shook and, he imagined, everything in town shook.

But it didn't last forever. Felt like it, but it didn't. After a period of time—hours, minutes, seconds, or years—the level of noise decreased. Although the rain still fell, it no longer hammered. He pressed the button on his watch that illuminated the dial. Didn't help, because he hadn't checked before the tornado had hit. Twenty seconds, probably.

Then he pulled himself to his knees and looked toward the window. The curtains still blew straight in but fluttered a bit. The sound of debris crashing into cars and windows had stopped. On the wall, a weak light came from the security system.

He slowly stood. Once on his feet, he rubbed his hands over his face. They came away wet, from the rain, he guessed, but sticky. When he wiped them on his jeans, glass embedded there scraped his hands. He shook his legs to get rid of whatever had accumulated on top of him. Then he walked slowly to the door, mentally checking his body for damage. He could walk fine. His hands were sticky. His face and back burned and his feet squished on carpet soaked from rain blown inside. Something—hail and glass, he guessed—crunched under his shoes.

He opened the door, took a step outside, and stood for a moment, in the pouring rain. He was alive. He lifted his hands and turned his face up to wash them off before he inspected the exterior damage. His truck had a broken window and probably more damage from the chunks of rubble that covered it. A couple of trees were blown down, and the roof on the other end of the motel had been torn off.

He'd always thought of nature as being a gentle

breeze or the sound of a peaceful brook gurgling across rocks or a sunrise. Now he truly understood nature, both sides. He glanced up. On the top floor, parts of the roof had been peeled back and chunks of walls were missing, but this floor looked stable.

As other guests had begun to look out doors, he turned toward Hector's room and was at the door before he realized he didn't have a key. Fear for the kid's safety hit him, but he attempted to push it aside. Hector was safe, he told himself, safe in the tub covered with a mattress.

Of course, he could also be covered by piles of debris from damage to the second floor.

Like the other windows he could see, those on Hector's room had been smashed. He could climb inside, but jagged pieces of glass stuck up from the bottom sill. He should check with the office about a key—if the office still existed—before he climbed inside. He'd turned that way and had taken several steps in that direction when he saw the manager.

"Can you get me in here?" Gabe shouted. "I need to check on my friend."

Without a word, the woman slipped a card in the lock and shoved the door open before she headed to the other rooms.

"Hector!" Gabe ran into the bathroom. "Hector."

"I'm fine," the kid shouted.

Before he attempted to move the mattress, Gabe

tossed off several chunks of the ceiling that had landed on it. "Give me a little help."

With that, they shoved the mattress aside. Hector stood, placed his hand on the towel rack, and stepped out. "That was wild, wasn't it?" Then he looked at Gabe in the eerie light from the window and the faint light of the security system. "What happened to you?"

"What do you mean? We just survived a tornado."

"You're covered with blood." Hector pointed. "On your face and your shirt."

Gabe held his hands out. Now that he could see cuts on the back of his hand he realized why they'd felt sticky. Glass, the glass from the shattered window, had hit him, Gabe guessed. He hadn't noticed, probably because of the adrenaline that had flowed through him and the sharpness of the shards.

"It's nothing." He pulled out his phone. "I'm going to call Adam. See what's going on there, let him know we're okay." He let the phone ring but it went to voice mail so he left a message. "We're okay."

With that, he clicked off the phone and moved toward the parking lot, Hector behind him. "Let's see how we can help."

Adam could feel his phone vibrating in his pocket. He couldn't answer because smiling, singing, and attempting to look relaxed and calm kept him busy enough. Besides, he didn't think he could hear the person on the other end. He pulled it out to see Gabe's number and grinned.

During the next song as the noise outside lessened, George turned around and waved. "All clear," he said. They all shouted and clapped with relief. "Everyone can go back home. A weak tornado came down in San Pablo but missed us."

With those words, he and the Miltons froze. Janey pulled away from Gussie and stood next to Adam, her hands over her mouth and eyes wide. "Is that where my brother is?" she asked.

Adam pulled out his phone and listened to the message. "They're okay," he told the group. He hit REDIAL and waited. When Gabe answered, he put the phone on speaker.

"We're okay. Hector and I are fine," Gabe said without waiting for a greeting or question. "But we've got a lot of destruction here. The town really needs help. They'll need generators, water, clothes, medical help. You name it. They'll need it."

"I'll call Sam. We'll get there as soon as possible."

"Meet you at the high school."

Adam clicked off the call, then clicked the phone on again. Before he could hit Sam's number, Gussie said, loudly and forcefully, "I want to get married."

His gaze flew toward her, as did the eyes of everyone else in the storm cellar. "Right now?"

"I want to set the date." She leaped to her feet, put her arms around Adam's neck, and leaned against him.

"Yes. Of course," he said because he desperately wanted to marry Gussie, tomorrow or sooner if possible.

"I know this is crazy but I thought . . . I was so afraid." Gussie stepped to look directly at Adam. "I've been so wishy-washy but *now* I know what I really want. I love you. I want to get married. Soon."

Henry stood. "Great idea. You and Adam discuss this. We'll get Janey to bed."

With that, most of the crowd hustled out except Gussie and Adam. Hannah stood with her arms folded, and George monitored the radio.

"I know this is crazy but as the wind whipped by, I was so scared." Gussie's voice was deeply emotional. "I thought, *Gussie, you're an idiot to have put off marrying Adam for this long. It could be too late. We could all die.*"

Adam leaned forward to take Gussie's hand but before he could, Hannah spoke.

"Okay," she said. "Cut the lovey stuff. You can do that later. Now we need to move. They need doctors." Hannah stepped in the narrow space between the two and faced Adam. She would have grabbed his arm to hurry him along, but Adam glared at her. Most unlike Hannah, she recognized the warning and moved to the right. "Okay." Hannah sighed. "I'll get packed while you guys waste time." She stomped up the steps.

"June?" he suggested. "July? I'll have to check on Hector's schedule."

"We've decided." She nodded. "We're getting married in the very near future. This summer."

He nodded, then leaned down to kiss her.

"That's a relief." Henry came back down the stairs and picked up Janey's blanket. "I was afraid Gussie'd be living with us in that little house forever. Not sure if we'd survive that much longer." He headed back up the steps.

Adam turned to George. "Once we get packed up, I'm taking Hannah to San Pablo. Can we take that generator in your garage?"

At George's nod, he and Gussie headed upstairs. When they got to the kitchen, Adam called Sam and asked him to pick up whatever they could pack at the thrift shop and carry it to San Pablo.

That completed, he turned to Yvonne. "Would you call Miss Birdie and get the Widows moving? Tell them what we need?"

Then he turned to see Hannah with her bulging duffel and a bag that looked like one of those black valises country doctors used to carry. Wisely, she didn't say anything, only put down her luggage and stood, tapping a toe.

Adam's first reaction was to tell her she couldn't

go. Oh, sure, that would work. Hannah was still weak and the toll of this emergency might cause her to relapse but he knew better than to suggest she stay here. She'd walk to San Pablo if she had to. Besides, he saw more focus and intense emotion than he had since she'd showed up. An emergency was exactly what Hannah needed to get her up and going again.

"Give me your keys." George came upstairs and held out a hand. "I'll load the generator in the back of your SUV. We have a pantry full of food and Ouida probably has some diapers stored away we won't need for a while. I'll put those in, too."

Adam and Gussie followed George outside to look around. Not a lot of destruction here. A tree lay in the church parking lot and several limbs littered the lawn but Butternut Creek, at least this part, looked pretty good. Although rain still dripped from the trees, the storm had passed, headed east.

After arranging for the Miltons to stay and care for Janey, Gussie said, "I'm going to run home and pack a bag, get some of our food ready to go. Pick me up there."

Adam went back in the house to see Hannah still standing by her duffel bag, nearly quivering with excitement and impatience.

"Sis, if you need something to do, look around the parsonage and see what you can find that people might need. Get those jugs of water from the basement. Do something useful while I get my stuff."

"Okay," Hannah said. "Henry, let's bring up the water jugs from the basement." She waved him toward the stairs. "I'll check the shed in the back. Probably some tools there, maybe a shovel we could use." She headed toward the yard. "Yvonne, put together some bags with emergency essentials in them."

Even upstairs, Adam could hear his sister barking out orders. He grinned. She seemed back to her normal self, in full doctor mode—which resembled her big-sister mode a great deal.

Chapter Ten

In half an hour, the SUV was packed with gallons of water, cans, clothing, and tools from the neighbors. Much to Hannah's relief and the joy of those she'd ordered around, they took off, picked Gussie up, and headed out of town.

With downed limbs and power lines, detours and blocked lanes, the trip took longer than the usual hour. Not a lot of traffic. The wise and cautious population probably still hunkered down or surveyed damage while he and Gussie and his single-minded sister pressed on against a still-high wind and around abandoned cars and the other, miscellaneous obstacles littering the two-lane highway.

"Can't you go any faster?" Hannah asked again from the backseat, where she was crowded between bags of clothing and supplies.

The first time she'd asked that, he'd said, "Not in these conditions."

The second time, he'd responded, "Only if you run ahead and clear the highway."

He no longer answered that question.

"Are you sure you know where the high school is?" she asked.

The first time he'd replied, "Yes, I've been there."

When she asked again ten minutes later, he said, "No, I'm driving off into unmapped space and hope we find it the next time we circle the earth."

While Gussie tried unsuccessfully not to laugh, Hannah had scowled at both of them. But she didn't ask that question again.

As much as Hannah was duplicating the constant questions she'd asked years ago when they went on trips with their parents, Adam knew why she asked. Hannah had never counted patience as one of her virtues. She wanted to leap into healing immediately; any delay drove her nuts.

He began several conversations with Gussie, but every time they started, his sister interrupted with a question.

Instead of ordering her out of the car, he ignored her until, pushed to the end of his tolerance, he said, "Hannah, be quiet. Gussie and I want to talk about our wedding."

She must have realized wedding discussion trumped her topics and was quiet.

"We don't want it too early in July, with the Fourth and all." Gussie pulled out her cell and opened the calendar. "June might work better for Hector. Who knows what might be expected of him for basketball?"

"I don't know. Do they have weight lifting we'd need to work around?"

"Maybe June seventh or fourteenth. We can

check with friends and family to see which is better." She continued to study the calendar. "Camp starts June twenty-ninth."

"You're planning your wedding around Hector's school schedule and camp?" Hannah asked.

"That's what ministers do," he said. "Early June sounds good." He grinned at Gussie and reached for her hand. "Sounds great. Ask Maggie to put those dates on the calendar. Do you think that gives the Widows enough time to plan?"

"Why don't you just elope, not worry about the fuss of a wedding?" Hannah asked.

"That would break the Widows' hearts," Gussie said. "We couldn't do that to them."

"But they'll make your lives crazy and try to take over."

"Making the Widows happy is one of the priorities of a minister in Butternut Creek," Adam explained. "And in a small town, the entire community celebrates the marriage of a minister."

"It will be the social event of the year."

By this time, they'd entered an area where more obstacles littered the highway. At a few places, they had to drive on the shoulder—on one side or the other—in an effort to avoid entire trees and large parts of roofs.

As they entered San Pablo ten minutes later, Gussie and Hannah leaned forward to study the destruction while Adam attempted to avoid it.

Rubble stretched down Main Street farther than

he could see and looked six or seven blocks wide. In front of him, he could see that the tornado had skipped through downtown. He doubted any loss of life or many injuries here, because most small towns in central Texas had long since lost their downtown businesses to discount stores outside the city limits.

The tornado had churned up the ground of a park and torn asphalt up in a parking lot. The worst damage seemed to be around the motel where Hector and Gabe had stayed.

"There's Gabe's truck." Hannah pointed at the formerly sleek vehicle now covered in debris. Could have been anyone's, but it looked like Gabe's.

Two women in neon orange vests stood at a sawhorse across the highway. Farther down, Adam could glimpse a couple of groups of people. He cautiously maneuvered the SUV toward the women at the makeshift checkpoint.

Relief filled Hannah. They'd finally arrived. She could get to performing her life's work.

Sitting in that storm cellar and listening to the news about destruction from the tornado, the realization that people were hurt and needed her skills had filled her with focus and purpose. She felt more energetic than she had for a long time and, at the same time, guilty that the suffering of others made her feel alive. Yes, it was horrifying that a crisis, that people she didn't know losing their houses and getting injured or even killed, filled her with excitement.

She shouldn't have given Adam the keys to the Escalade. If she'd kept them, she could have jumped in and driven off instead of waiting for him, for supplies, for Gussie. No matter how much she organized and pleaded and pushed, no one else seemed to feel the same deep need to respond immediately to the disaster that she could feel throbbing in the air and vibrating through her body.

She'd always worked in hospitals and camps with the victims of destruction. Most often she'd witnessed not destroyed villages but the terrible damage and pain people inflicted on each other, the scars that hate and war and greed left on human bodies. Here in San Pablo the destruction was impersonal, a force of nature that showed no bias in its action. The good and the bad, rich and poor, different races—everyone in the area was impacted by the amazing force of nature.

As her gaze scanned the area, the sight of Gabe's truck produced both an unexpected spasm and an illogical sense of panic. He was here, he was safe, she reminded herself. Inside she felt relief as well as a mixture of other emotions.

Hannah scrutinized the damage. In the middle of a debris-covered lot, Gabe's truck had escaped lightly. The tornado had dumped trees and roofs and signs and other wreckage she couldn't recognize for blocks and blocks, as far as she could see west of here and south. She struggled to take in the damage as Adam stopped in front of a barricade.

"Can't come through here," said a woman in an orange vest who stood in front of a flashing arrow as she waved them toward the north.

"Do you know how to get to the high school from here?" Hannah asked Adam. "Maybe you should ask this lady."

Without a word, Adam pointed toward a large sign on slightly bent poles with an arrow pointing north and SAN PABLO HIGH SCHOOL in huge letters.

She didn't speak, merely studied the destruction as they drove. The power of nature in a civilized world, a world humans thought they controlled until wind, water, fire, or the movement of tectonic plates took over—well, it astounded her.

They passed the hospital just before the turn into the high school. Cars were scattered across the lot and people moved in and out while several ambulances and a few police cars waited at the emergency entrance.

When they arrived at the school, about twenty trucks sat in the parking lot. Close to the front entrance, she saw Hector help a woman from a vehicle. Adam immediately headed in that direction and pulled up a few feet away. But instead of getting out, he turned toward Hannah. "You've been sick, Sis."

Not wanting to hear this, she unfastened her seat belt and attempted to open the door but bags of supplies hemmed her in. As much as she wished she could put her hands over her ears and sing, *La-la-la-la-la,* that was immature. He had her trapped.

"Please take it easy," he said.

She nodded. He didn't believe her. After more than twenty-five years as siblings, he knew that once she got going, she didn't, couldn't, and wouldn't stop, not while people needed her, not while there were injuries and sick children.

"Please," he said. "Just rest every now and then. Eat. Try to be normal."

"Thanks," she growled.

Before he could say more, Gussie got out and started moving bundles to release Hannah.

"Hey, Pops and Pops's sister and Pops's girl," Hector shouted as he settled the woman into a wheelchair. "Let me push Mrs. Everley inside, then I'll be right back."

"Let me check her over." Hannah leaped from the SUV as the supplies she'd been supporting with her body collapsed into her vacated space.

"Doc, there's medical staff inside. Let's get her out of the heat." With that, he pushed ahead and through the doors.

When Hannah would have followed, a man stepped forward. "Only medical and approved personnel inside," he said. "Are you a doctor?"

"Yes, I'm an epidemiologist."

"Sorry." The man blocked the entrance. "We're only admitting medical doctors."

She reached in her pocket, pulled out a laminated identification tag from Kenya, and handed it to the man. "I am a doctor. A medical doctor."

He studied the tag, compared her with the picture, then handed it back. "Okay, take it to that desk and check in with the lady up there."

As she glanced toward that desk, Hector returned.

"Where's Gabe?" she heard Adam ask him.

Although Hannah had taken a step toward the desk, she stopped to listen. It would seem churlish not to show interest in Hector's coach and Adam's friend. Amazing how she could lie to herself.

"He's still around the motel helping sift through the rubble. I hitched a ride here to meet you. He said for you to take me back to the motel, but I'm going to stay here. Bunch of guys from the college basketball team volunteering here. Want to get to know them."

"Sounds good." Adam nodded. "Sis, you'll be okay here?"

She waved and headed toward the desk again. "Of course. This is what I do." Energy filled her.

Time to focus, save lives, and maybe make contact with the doctor and person she used to be.

Once her credentials had been recorded and accepted, the woman said, "The hospital is overwhelmed so we turned the cafeteria into a hospital annex and the gym into triage. They really need help in triage."

She felt like a horse returning to the barn, like Br'er Rabbit tossed into the briar patch. Actually like Hannah Jordan, MD, back home. She grabbed a clipboard, strode toward the line of people awaiting service, and started asking questions and taking histories.

In the middle of the destruction, Adam didn't immediately rise to the challenge as his sister had. In fact, he felt overwhelmed with no idea where to start. Rubble covered every inch; blocks and blocks of ruined buildings surrounded Gussie and him and the few other volunteers.

"Hey, guys. Good to see you," Gabe shouted when he saw them and crossed the parking lot. Large floodlights powered by generators partially illuminated the area but left a lot in deep shadows. "Let me explain what we're doing. This was a skipping tornado, which means three different tornadoes hopped across the town. We have damage here and farther west, then southwest. We'll start with the basics of search and clear."

Everyone nodded.

"That"—Gabe pointed toward what must have been a strip mall yesterday—"contained a video game gallery, one of the few places open when the tornado hit. Fortunately, only a few injuries and no fatalities." He pointed toward the southwest. "Some volunteers have branched out to survey damage in the neighborhoods, searching for the wounded and transporting them to the high school."

"What can we do?" Adam asked.

"What did you bring with you?"

"We have a generator in the back of the SUV." Gussie waved toward where they'd parked.

"Have a chain saw?" Gabe asked.

"Sam's bringing one," Adam said.

"Great. First, we'll clear what we can on the street. Once the heavy equipment gets here from construction sites, we'll start clearing downed trees in the residential sections. The sun will be up soon, so it'll be easier."

"You sound like an old hand," Adam said.

Gabe nodded. "Not my first rodeo. The 'dozers should arrive in a couple of hours. We'll clear what we can, but in the meantime we need to scout the area and listen. If you hear someone buried, don't take chances. If you can't safely dig them out, let them know help's coming and they aren't alone."

Adam and Gussie chose an area no one else had

covered. Walking in different directions, they shouted and listened. Neither heard anything and didn't know if that counted as good news—no one buried there—or bad news if someone couldn't respond.

Within an hour, Adam spotted Sam and George making their way through the debris. "Did Ouida make you come?" he asked George.

"No," George replied. "She suggested it but I made the decision."

Even wearing jeans, athletic shoes, and a T-shirt covered with a hoodie, George looked like the best-dressed emergency responder ever.

"You guys have a chain saw?" At Sam's nod, Gabe added, "Take the generator and drive to the residential area behind the motel. Get started clearing that."

Then Gabe glanced into the rising sun. Adam nearly gasped at the sight of the cuts and darkening bruises. "What happened to your face?"

"Nothing." Gabe turned away. "We need to get going. Grab a . . ."

"You have to have someone check that out. May need stitches." When Gabe didn't answer, he said, "Don't be macho."

Gabe turned to glare at Adam. "I'm here to work."

"You know, there are diseases in a place like this that can get into an untreated wound and cause you a lot of trouble. Etiologic agents of zygomycosis can cause serious wound infections. It has high mortality rates. It's often found in rubble and disaster sites."

"How do you . . ." Gabe shook his head. "Just my luck. My friend's sister is an epidemiologist. Do you guys talk about infections a lot?"

"I used to quiz her in a few subjects. She's up at the high school. You should have her look you over."

For a moment Gabe said nothing. Looked as if a huge piece of rubble had whomped him in the head. "Your sister's at the high school? But she's too weak and sick to work here, right?"

"She demanded to come with me." He shook his head. "No one messes with Hannah once she's made up her mind." He paused. "I hate to ask you, but I really worry about my sister. Would you check on her while you're up there? See how she's doing?"

Gabe looked around. He didn't want to leave. He loved this kind of work but the thought of a serious infection with high mortality rates motivated him. With a nod, he automatically headed toward his truck, saw he'd never get it out of the lot even if it still started, then turned toward the highway headed for the high school.

The run took him nearly ten minutes. For the first few minutes, the sun rose behind him and he felt its warmth on his back. After a few blocks, he turned to watch it. He'd seen sunrises all over the world, but they seemed different in each place. Here, little by little, fingers of light spread across destroyed houses and buildings to color the piles of rubble with a gentle yellow touch. With the passing seconds, the illumination added a softness not seen in the glare of the emergency lights and made the chaos less stark, as if it all were part of the cycle of nature.

As the sun painted vacant streets with light and shadows, he began to run again, feeling warmth from a sun-kissed breeze on his back. During the next eight minutes, Gabe realized he wasn't in as good a shape as he'd thought. He gasped for air the last few blocks.

He had to admit he wanted to see Hannah, see what she looked like in her natural element. The thought of her made his heart beat faster. Of course, that could just be another sign that he was really out of shape.

By the time he arrived at the parking lot, Gabe had to lean over and gulp in air. His breathing slowed; he entered the building, and walked toward a table with a handwritten sign taped to it: ADMISSIONS AND INFO. Three women sat there: two tiny and one who looked like she could've played on the line at UT. The large woman wore a badge that said DESDEMONA.

"I'd like to see Dr. Jordan, please."

Desdemona glanced at him. "Ouch. I can see why." She spoke in a soft voice. Despite the gentle tones, he bet she could keep order if someone tried to make a break for the gym. "Why don't you go in the restroom," she added, pointing, "and clean yourself up a little? Then come back and do some paperwork. When you finish, we'll get you in to see someone as soon as possible."

When Gabe looked at himself in the mirror, he understood all the gasps. His face was smeared with dried blood; a little still leaked from cuts. He rinsed off as much as he could without opening up any lacerations. He looked slightly less hideous. He washed his hands and used a towel to scrub lightly around his neck.

Finished, he returned to the hallway, picked up the clipboard of paperwork, and flipped through the five pages. Probably impossible to get inside without that. He glanced at Desdemona, who kept her eyes on him. He filled them in, then pulled out his driver's license and insurance card and handed them to the women.

"I'd like to see Dr. Jordan, please."

"She's busy now."

"Her brother told me to ask for her. He's working downtown. Said she had the background I needed, knows about cuts and infections and stuff." When the women continued to stare at him, he added, "She's an epidemiologist, you know."

"Oh." The small woman named Marcella

studied him with an eyebrow lifted. "You think that laceration requires an epidemiologist?"

"Her brother said so. I'd hate to die." That statement probably laid it on a little thick.

Marcella nodded, added several numbers to an index card, and handed it to him.

"Go inside and hand this to Abraham, the man standing by the door. He'll get you settled in the right place."

Before Birdie arrived at the thrift shop, bedlam had filled the parking lot. Within minutes, she'd taken charge and organized everything. Now cars pulled in on the north driveway to leave food, clothing, and bottles of water as well as bags of groceries and piles of blankets. Volunteers carted all donations inside to separate and organize, then carried boxes of the sorted goods out the south door to load into a caravan of vehicles leaving for San Pablo. Birdie stood in the center of the movement, pointing and shouting and making order from chaos—exactly what she loved most.

Once traffic was moving well, she handed the duty over to Ralph and went inside. Winnie had done a good job of assigning jobs to volunteers. Ouida and her girls sorted toys. Mercedes and a group from the Methodist Church packed paperback books in small boxes. In the grocery area, several from the primitive Baptist Church out on the highway put together meals and stuffed them into sacks. At a back table, Bree separated clothing into boxes by age and gender with several of her friends. Mac toted stacks of jeans and shirts to the table from shelves and racks.

Blossom, sweet but completely ineffectual here, fluttered around, making every effort to help with little success. She didn't completely understand what people in an emergency needed. This morning she'd showed up with several bags of groceries, which included artichoke hearts and a tin of anchovy paste. Birdie wanted to ask her why she thought anyone in an emergency situation needed them but didn't. She hated it when Blossom's soft eyes filled with tears.

Instead, Birdie said, "Blossom, take that carton of canned fruit out to Ralph's pickup."

With a smile, Blossom followed orders.

"How are you doing, Ouida?" Birdie asked. "Where's your husband? Working in Austin today?"

Ouida shook her head and grinned. "No, he went with Sam to San Pablo. Guess church is good for him. I'd never have thought he'd rush into a messy emergency like this but as soon as we got home from the storm cellar, he called Sam and set it up."

"Have any more boxes, Miss Birdie?" Father Joe said from the door to the parking lot. "We need some of those little ones."

"I'll bring 'em right out." With a nod, Birdie headed into the storeroom. She pulled a dozen broken-down boxes from behind the shelf and picked up a pair of scissors and a roll of tape from a basket. As she turned to leave, she heard voices at the table where the girls worked.

"So how are you and Hector doing?" Birdie identified the voice of Angela, the tall spiker on the volleyball team. "Sweet, sweet Hector."

"We're fine."

Birdie recognized Bree's I-don't-want-to-discuss-this voice. Angela obviously didn't.

"Tommy John Schmidt told me he saw you two kissing in that deserted hallway behind the gym. Is that true?" Angela said.

"Tommy John should keep his mouth shut," Bree stated.

"Were you?" Angela pushed.

"Shh, Angela. Don't say anything. Yes, I kissed him, but that's all. You know I wouldn't do more than that. Hector doesn't expect it. He's a good guy."

Birdie let out the breath she'd been holding.

"Why not? He's hot." That sounded like Becky, the girl with the killer serve.

"Because I won't. I'll never get pregnant before marriage because I don't believe in fooling around." After a pause, she added, "Don't tease me. I know I'm a goody-goody and I accept that. Besides, if that happened—" Bree's voice broke.

279

"If I got pregnant, it would mess up our lives and break my grandmother's heart. I couldn't do that to her. Now," she continued, "I have a box of clothes for boy sizes seven to twenty. Anyone have something to put in here?"

Birdie leaned against the wall and felt like crying. Oh, she was so proud of Bree. At the same time, she felt bad. She hadn't realized how much she must have harped on their mother for Bree to say those words. No, she didn't want either sister to end up pregnant too soon or unmarried, but she hadn't ever wanted to put their mother down.

"Hey," a man shouted. "We need blankets, quilts, whatever you have. We're going to pack a truck with ice."

She didn't have time to even think about anything Bree had said, not now. Birdie had a town to rescue. She gripped the boxes, grabbed an armful of blankets, and headed outside to hand it all to Father Joe. In the parking lot, she checked on all the activity. Winnie made lists of what volunteers had loaded into each truck as Ralph guided vehicles in and out of the driveways. Mercedes stood by the front door to direct the volunteers.

And Blossom smiled sweetly and waved her pretty plump hands at everyone.

Hannah paused for a moment and took a deep breath. Energy filled her, but how long would it last? No sleep, working for hours, but she still felt good and would push until she didn't.

"Hey, sweetheart." She knelt in front of a girl about five or six years old with wide, frightened eyes. Lacerations covered her arms, face, and legs.

"Did the nurse clean up all those cuts?" Hannah asked in the gentle, soft voice she used for the frightened and suffering and the very young.

The child nodded.

"I see your name is Yolanda." Hannah checked the chart in her hand before she studied the cuts on the girl's face and legs. "Yolanda's a pretty name." She looked around. No parent close by. With another glance at the chart, she saw that Yolanda's father had been admitted to the hospital a few hours earlier.

"How did you get here?" Hannah asked. "Where's your mom?"

"She's with my little brother," Yolanda explained in a whisper so soft Hannah had to lean way over to hear her. "My aunt Melanie brought me in. She's sitting with a friend now."

Hannah glanced around, searching for someone who might be Yolanda's aunt, when her eyes found . . . oh, dear, no . . . Gabe, sitting in the line waiting to see a doctor, his face crusty with blood.

She hadn't expected to see him *here,* on her turf, where she felt comfortable and secure. Adam had said both he and Hector were fine.

Why should the presence of her brother's friend make her feel unsafe?

Stupid question. She knew. The man made her breathless with absolutely no scientific basis for her reaction. If she wasn't careful, she'd start hyperventilating. Hard to take care of patients after passing out.

She dropped her gaze back to Yolanda and modulated her breathing. "Can you show me where she is?"

Yolanda waved, and a heavyset woman with dark braids left a chair and came toward them.

For the next five minutes, Hannah concentrated on Yolanda and asked her aunt a few questions about the girl's health.

"Yolanda, I need to check your blood pressure," Hannah said as she wrapped the cuff around the girl's upper arm. After watching the gauge, Hannah said, "Very good. One twenty over seventy-five." Moving her stethoscope, she said, "Now. I need to listen to your heart and lungs. Take a deep breath, please."

After listening, she tapped on Yolanda's chest, palpated her abdomen, and peered down her throat. "Sounds good, Miss Yolanda."

The little girl giggled. "I'm not 'Miss' Yolanda."

Hannah smiled. "Well, whoever you are, almost everything looks fine, but I'm hearing a little wheezing." She looked at the aunt. "Has she ever had trouble with asthma?"

"Don't believe so," Aunt Melanie said, and Yolanda shook her head.

"I'd like to keep you here for a few hours. First, we'll draw your blood for some tests, and clean and dress out your cuts. While you're here, we'll take your temperature and listen to your lungs every hour. You might have inhaled something, so I want to monitor you."

"All right," Aunt Melanie said. "Her daddy got her into a closet and shielded her, but he got a couple of broken bones when the ceiling fell in. When she's ready, we'll visit him, then I'll take her to my house."

"And her mother and brother?"

"They were at the grocery store. Whole thing fell in on them. They're in X-ray over at the hospital. They think everything's okay, but they hurt. Lots of bruises."

When Yolanda left her area, Hannah glanced at the waiting area surreptitiously, or so she thought. Gabe waved.

Surely he wasn't waiting for her, was he?

Chapter Eleven

Lips pursed, Hannah looked as if she'd swallowed a pickle when she saw him. As Gabe watched her watching him, her eyes became slits.

If he didn't know better, he'd think she wasn't happy to see him. Actually, he knew she wasn't happy to see him. Her consistency constituted a challenge. Why did this woman dislike him?

He enjoyed the fact that at least she'd displayed some kind of emotion when she'd seen him. A negative reaction, sure, but she had noticed him. She also had an interesting expression in her eyes. Even if it looked like the glare she might give to the gangrenous toe of a diabetic, at least she didn't completely ignore him. Yeah, that felt like real progress. Maybe in a year or two she would only snarl when he approached.

"You're next for Dr. Jordan," Abraham said, after the medical staff had seen a dozen more patients.

He ushered Gabe toward her station.

Gabe could almost hear the gears turning in Hannah's head and her heels digging in, but he knew she couldn't come up with a reason not to treat him. She was a doctor, sworn to do no harm and to help all people, even those she didn't particularly like.

Then Abraham took a good look at him. "Hey, aren't you Flash Borden. Played for UT and the Rockets?"

He nodded and smiled even though he hated that nickname.

"Never forgot the three-point shot you hit to win the championship. Had to be fifty feet away." The man shook his head in wonder.

"Sit down," Hannah said with her back toward him, pretending, he thought, to straighten her tools. But when she glanced at him and studied his face, Hannah Jordan, MD, took over. She took a couple of steps toward him, put her fingers on his chin, gently turned his face toward the light to scrutinize it. "What happened?"

He shrugged because he hated to discuss injuries. "Window broke."

"What did you do? Bury your face in the shards?"

"When the tornado hit, the window broke before I found cover."

She lifted one of his eyelids and shone a penlight into it. With a nod, she studied the other. "You covered your eyes. They look fine."

"Yeah," he said, showing his brilliant conversational skills.

"But the part you couldn't cover—your forehead, your chin, your ears and neck . . ." She studied each as she talked. "They have deep cuts. You should've come in hours ago." She lifted his chin carefully and touched his cheek lightly. "Several of these are going to need stitches."

He refused to pull away but that last contact hurt.

"I'm going to have to clean all the lacerations. It's going to hurt because there's so much dried blood."

She wasn't kidding. It felt like sandpaper scrubbing at his wounds, but he would not react to the anguish. He refused to emasculate himself as he usually did with Hannah.

After five minutes of torment, she stopped and said, "Take your shirt off."

"Hardly the place, Doc." He grinned at the same time he knew he sounded corny and desperate and not a bit amusing to a medical professional.

"Very funny." She hadn't laughed. No, she folded her arms. "You've got blood on the back of your shirt."

"I probably . . ."

"Take your shirt off," she said in a tone that probably made everybody she dealt with do exactly what she said.

He bet everyone in the gym—staff and patients and volunteers alike—had started to unbutton their shirts when they heard her command.

So, of course, he took his shirt off. He didn't want to, but, in this situation, she was the boss. Besides, his back did feel scratchy and painful.

He tried to wiggle free of the shirt but

couldn't. He guessed dried blood held it in place because it hurt to pull it away.

"I'm going to have to cut it off," she said.

Might as well. He couldn't wear it again anyway.

He watched as she took blunt-ended scissors and disappeared behind him. When she'd finished cutting, he heard a ripping sound and pain exploded across the right side of his back, where she'd ripped it off. Fortunately, as much as he screamed inside, it came out more like a whimper. Not a macho whimper. He didn't think those existed. More like a little boy who'd watched his mother walk away. That had hurt.

"Sorry," she said in a voice that held not one note of apology. "I've learned that quick and unexpected usually is less painful."

At the moment he opened his mouth to disagree, she ripped the shirt off the left side of his back. "Ouch," he shouted. Better than a whimper except that everyone who wasn't comatose turned to stare at him.

"Okay, let's wiggle your arms out of the sleeves," she threatened him.

Oh, he didn't believe she *meant* it as a threat, but she wasn't the one who'd nearly had the top three layers of skin pulled off.

"No," he said quickly before she could even lay a finger on his sleeves. "I'll do it."

While he slowly removed the remains of his

shirt, she stood behind him and leaned across the examining table to scrutinize the wounds. She punched him and rubbed her fingers across his back, very pleasant if not for the excruciating pain he refused to acknowledge. Then she began cleaning the wounds, and he had to bite his lip to stop himself from sniveling.

"I know this must hurt like crazy," she said. "But the blood has dried and I almost have to chip it off."

"Does hurt a bit," he said through his clenched jaw.

Finally finished with inflicting torture, she said, "Okay, lie down on your stomach."

When he did, with a gentle touch this time, she slid her hands across his back. "Don't think you'll need stitches on any of these. I can close them with butterfly bandages." She took a step back. "After that, I want you to take off your jeans. I'll put up a privacy screen, then ask Dr. Fritz to—"

"No." Hard to be tough when lying flat on his stomach, his face in the pillow and his words garbled, but he made the effort. "My legs are fine and so is everything else down there. I know. Nothing hurts. No blood on the jeans. Do what you need to do so I can get back to work."

"You really should . . ."

He pushed himself up, turned, and sat on the side of the table. "Hannah, you can be tough and stubborn but no one in the world can outstubborn me when I'm determined. No one," he added to spell this out clearly to her.

"Coach . . ."

"Doc, I'm the patient. I'll sign a release if you need it, but all I want done is a couple of bandages and a few stitches."

Her chin lifted a little as she watched him through narrowed eyes. "As a doctor . . ." When he didn't say anything, she said, "Okay, but I'm not going to clear you to work in the rubble." She tapped her finger on his chest, and her gaze didn't waver. "You have far too many open wounds to allow you to immerse yourself in that pit of infection."

When she described it that way, he realized he no longer wanted to return. "Okay." He lay on his stomach. "Just take care of my back and my face."

"I need an assistant and a dressing tray," she called. After she cleaned his back again, Hannah pressed on several dressings. Then she said, "I'm going to find a surgeon to do the stitches on your face."

"I don't want a surgeon," he sat up and stated clearly and forcefully. "I want you to do that."

"Don't be an idiot. I know how to do sutures but not like a surgeon. I could stitch up a cut in your arm, but not on your face. I don't do that well enough for it to heal invisibly." She held her hand up. "I'm not being snarky when I say what I'm going to say." She paused and tilted her head. "Okay, maybe I'm being a little snarky but you really don't want me to do this. It'd be a shame to mar all that beauty."

"No, not snarky at all and I don't care. I'm not as wrapped up in my amazing good looks as you think I am."

She opened her mouth to protest but nothing came out. Finally, she snapped, "Okay. You win." With that, she waved toward an attendant and said, "I need a nurse, lidocaine, and a suture kit."

"I don't need lidocaine."

"Let's pretend I'm the doctor here. Are you with me on that?"

He nodded.

"You can be brave and manly if you want, but I'm still going to deaden the area before I start. Shrieks of pain distract me and scare the other patients." She took the syringe from the nurse, filled it, and began injecting the lidocaine around each cut.

It wasn't pretty and he felt deep gratitude that she had ignored him when he'd requested not to have painkiller. He didn't want to repeat stitching up the cut next to his lip ever again. Or the one over his eyebrow.

"I'm going to give you a shot of antibiotics as well as a tetanus shot. Don't suppose you know when you had your last one."

He shook his head. "Probably while I was playing ball."

"You are not to be around patients until I clear you, either. Too easy to pass on an infection or pick one up."

An hour later, Gabe sat at a table in the middle of the library, now being used as a makeshift cafeteria after the real cafeteria had been turned into the hospital overflow. He picked up the sack of peanuts he'd bought at the vending machine and poured it into his Pepsi. He preferred Royal Crown Cola but that was hard to find. He jiggled the bottle, only a little to mix the flavors, then took a long, crunchy drink.

On restricted duty, he repeated to himself. No contact with patients until cleared. No working in rubble until cleared.

He took another drink and looked around. Plenty of books, but he'd come here to work.

Couldn't leave with his truck in bad shape. He'd have to find something to keep busy and feel as if he were helping. He stood, finished off the Pepsi, and tossed the bottle into the trash. He bet he could talk Desdemona into giving him something to do.

After spending the morning doing office work and entering information on computers, he wandered into the library again and grabbed a few sandwiches. As volunteers entered for lunch, each grabbed a bottle of water from an ice chest and gulped half of it down immediately. Within a few minutes, a few of the Butternut Creek group wandered in. Gussie dragged her arm over her forehead while Sam's and Adam's shirts were wet with sweat and plastered against their bodies. Only George looked as if he hadn't done a lick of work.

"Take another." A volunteer shoved a plastic bottle of lukewarm water at Gussie. "Don't want to get dehydrated."

Once they were through the line, Gabe waved for them to join him.

"Why didn't you come back to work?" After he set his tray down, Adam scrutinized Gabe's face.

"They have me shuffling papers here because your sister won't let me near patients or rubble. Too many open cuts." Gabe shook his head. "I'm afraid to cross her."

"Me, too," Gussie said. George nodded agreement. "I bet Dr. Hannah Jordan is a very tough lady."

"She actually mentioned that fungus you warned me about," Gabe said.

Adam nodded. "I know my zygomycosis."

"And she said I'd scare people looking like this."

"My sister has a great sense of humor."

"Yeah, she's a laugh riot." Gabe shook his head.

"Anyway, I'm not doing anything worthwhile yet, not until she clears me."

Adam glanced around. "Where is my sister?"

"Still seeing patients, I guess. Hector's around someplace. He and his new basketball buddies have been transferring patients." Gabe picked up a fork and started on the huge piece of pecan pie.

"Good." Adam attacked his spaghetti. "If you see him, tell him I'll pick him up about five to head home."

"He won't want to come," Gabe said.

"He's got school on Monday."

They ate in silence for nearly a minute before Gussie asked, "How long are you staying, Gabe? Maybe you could bring him tomorrow."

Gabe shook his head. "I already called the superintendent, told him I'm staying all week or as long as they need me here. And I don't have transportation because my truck doesn't run." He studied the gang from Butternut Creek. "Y'all look like you worked hard."

"After all those hours of work, I looked around. Rubble still covered every inch. Didn't seem as if we'd accomplished a thing," Gussie said. "There's so much devastation."

"You know who's a great worker?" Adam asked. "George. He doesn't look like it and I have no idea how he keeps his jeans clean, but he's amazing."

George reacted to the praise with a quick grin.

"We moved to a residential area to clean up

downed trees and limbs after the heavy equipment came," Gussie said. "George used the chain saw to cut up the big pieces."

"I've never seen anything like it," Sam said. "George sliced them into the most precise pieces I've ever seen. Every branch cut to the exact same length."

"George cut while we stacked pieces along the curb for pickup," Gussie said.

"Where's Hannah working?" Adam asked.

"Triage in the gym. They're pretty busy there. People keep coming in as emergency workers make it farther out in the county and find more damage and injured people."

Finished with her lunch, Gussie said, "I'm going to throw some water on my face and wash up a little." She stood, picked up her tray, and headed off.

"Me, too." George moved toward the men's restroom.

Before Gabe could stand, Adam said, "Don't leave. I really need your help. How long has Hannah been working?"

"You know. You dropped her off here before you came to where I was." He glanced at his watch. "So about nine hours?"

"Nine hours straight? No break?"

Gabe nodded.

"She has no idea how to take care of herself." Adam leaned forward on his elbows and dropped his forehead on his hands. "I'm going to have to leave in a couple of hours. She has no idea how to slow down. I know she's going to wear out if someone doesn't step in."

Adam looked up at him with such an earnest expression that Gabe knew exactly what his friend wanted. Instinct made him want to leap to his feet and run as fast as he could. Friendship kept him in the chair.

"While you're here, would you watch over my sister?"

Gabe cursed, inside. Even though he'd known Adam was going to ask this, he'd hoped he'd been mistaken. "You've got to be kidding. She'd no more allow me to tell her what to do than . . . than . . ." He had no idea how to complete that comparison.

"Than she'd let me tell her what to do," Adam finished. "But you're not her brother. I really need you to help."

"You're asking me to watch over a woman that hates me."

"Doesn't hate you, exactly."

"She has a deep abiding love for me that she shows by not talking to me?"

"Just take care of her, okay? I really need this. She does, too. Besides, you have a way with women. Maybe you can get her to listen, force her to rest and eat or at least suggest that. Tell her she needs sleep to be sharp. You know. Whatever works. I really need this. I worry about her. She could have a relapse."

Gabe still stared. "I think you overestimate my way with women. My amazing charm hasn't exactly swept your sister away."

"Please. When she's wrapped up in a project, she pushes herself into exhaustion and beyond. That's what happened in Kenya. For being such a smart person, she has little common sense and few survival skills."

Gabe considered the plea. He didn't want to agree because he didn't know if he could carry through. Hannah would fight him every minute and for every inch of control. It would be horrible and messy and not a bit of fun . . .

Okay, it might be fun. It might lighten life around here to spar with Hannah, might give a little interest to the day since he couldn't be out helping others and searching.

He pretended to consider Adam's request because he hated to give in too quickly. Someday he might need a favor from him. Finally, he shrugged and said, "Okay, I'll try to watch over her, keep her from wearing herself out. I'll bring her home when this is under control. I'll have to get my truck fixed or rent something, but I'll take care of it. And her." He cringed. "If I can."

"Don't let her know," Adam warned. "Whatever you do, don't let her know I asked you to do this."

"You're a real profile in courage."

"I know my sister. This isn't only to cover my involvement. You don't want her to know you're watching out for her, either. She'll be furious with everyone involved."

"I'm pretty sure your sister will figure this out. She's pretty smart, you know."

Actually, she might be grateful and consider Gabe's efforts a sign of his deep devotion—although he had yet to show any. More likely, she'd see them as a suggestion from her brother or even stalking on Gabe's part. None seemed likely to end happily ever after. He wasn't looking for that ever-after thing but he really hated her you're-such-an-idiot point of view. Maybe he could convince her he wasn't a stupid jock but a good guy with a brain that, if not as huge as hers, did have a few functioning cells.

Making certain Hannah didn't wear herself out counted as a humanitarian effort. Maybe, in addition, Gabe could undertake an investigation to find the woman in the photo. He'd caught a flash of her when she took care of that little girl, even a bit of gentleness when she'd swabbed his face.

If following Adam's orders gave him an excuse to find her, he would. If necessary, he'd even toss Adam to the lions—in this case, to his sister whom they all feared more—and tell Hannah the whole thing was not Gabe's idea. He'd only done it as a favor to a friend.

Having accepted the challenge and after everyone finished lunch and left to clear rubble, Gabe meandered back to the converted gym and strolled to the line of waiting patients.

"How's Dr. Jordan doing? Can you set her up for a lunch break?"

"Sure," Abraham said. "Won't send anyone to her after she finishes with this patient."

Gabe settled on a chair and prepared to watch and wait. He knew good and well she wouldn't leave on her own.

Hannah handed a prescription to her patient, then turned toward the chair where the next one waited.

Gabe. Terrific. She closed her eyes, then opened them. He'd stood and now walked closer. "You're still here," she said, hoping her voice sounded less pleased about his reappearance than she felt. "Need your bandages checked?"

"Sure," he said.

As he closed the distance between them, she wanted to close her eyes again, to shield herself from all that perfection in motion. She couldn't. "Actually," she said in her best professional voice, "it's too early to recheck them." She studied the gauze covering his wounds. "I don't notice any obvious draining on the gauze or redness around the site."

"Okay. How long before I can do real work?"

"I'll check you over tomorrow morning. If everything's healing well, I'll approve you for contact with patients but not work in the disaster area yet."

At his disappointed expression, she said, "Gabe, it's too dangerous for you. Far too great a chance of infection unless we covered your lacerations with polyurethane."

She glanced toward the chair. Empty.

"Where's my next patient?" she called to Abraham.

"He's not going to send one. It's your lunch break."

"I don't . . . ," she began.

"Might as well give up. I'm not going away and Abraham's not going to send you another patient until you get something to eat."

"Did you bribe him?"

"No, I told him he'd be helping the cause of young love."

She snorted. "We're hardly young and we certainly aren't in love."

"He liked being in on the secret romance."

It hurt to admit it, but he was right. Oh, not about the secret romance but about her needing a break. This is how she'd started her downward spiral in Africa. She hadn't eaten enough, hadn't rested. She'd carried the entire country on her shoulders in an attempt to save it, her health had failed, and she'd had to leave. Shouldn't she have learned something from that? Obviously, she hadn't.

"All right." She strode ahead of Gabe across the

gym and into the hallway before she realized she had no idea where the food might be located.

"This way."

Before he could reach out to take her arm, she headed that way. She knew she could be a jerk but today—well, today she was really tired and couldn't seem to stop herself. She did need to eat.

Why was she such a grumpus she couldn't accept support or care or even kindness? A character defect. Adam had told her that often. But did she have to wear it like a badge only because she always had?

Gabe never minded an extra meal. As he finished a sandwich and started on a piece of pie—apple this time—he watched Hannah. She didn't speak but shoved down more food than he'd thought she'd ever be able to.

Then, when she finished her sandwich, she smiled at him.

Wow. That was a surprise.

"Thank you. I needed to eat. I appreciate your bringing me here." With those words, she stood, bused the tray, and headed back toward the gym, leaving him amazed and confused. She'd been nice. She'd expressed gratitude. He'd never understand Hannah. Maybe that was the reason she interested him.

He dumped the paper plates and napkins in the

trash before he headed across the parking lot and the grassy area that separated the high school from the middle school gym. Once inside, he looked around. Cots covered most of the area, some pulled into square formations where evacuated families rested while others marched in precise rows across the floor, sheets folded on them and awaiting occupants. A curtain divided the gym in half.

"Where do volunteers sleep?" he asked a woman at the table.

"On the other side of the curtain."

"Do we need to sign in or show ID?"

"Show your ID when you come in, that's it."

"Can I reserve a place?"

"First come, first served. Should be plenty."

"Thanks." He headed around the curtain to find, not surprisingly, more cots lined up.

At four, after Hannah had worked twelve hours with only the lunch break, Gabe carried a tray of cookies and juice boxes into triage. "Break time," he shouted.

The doctors, nurses, and orderlies converged on him, grabbed cookies and cartons, saying "Thank you" before leaning against a wall to drink, crunch, and rest.

Of course, the woman he'd brought this offering to hadn't appeared. She stood next to the little girl he'd seen her with before.

"Gabe," she called. "Can you bring me some juice?"

He grabbed a couple of cartons and picked up the plate of cookies.

When he arrived, she took the proffered juice box and stuck the straw in. "Here you go," she said to the girl. "Don't drink it too fast."

"I brought one for you, too."

"Thanks. Don't need one." She smiled at him for a nanosecond. "I had a huge lunch."

"Yes, Doctor, you do. All the others are taking a break. Your turn." With that, he put the cookies and carton on a small table. "Dr. Jordan, you have to take care of yourself," he commanded.

"You sound exactly like my brother," she said.

"Believe me, if there's anything I don't want to be, it's your brother."

As he spoke those words, her glance flew to his face, this time searching for clues to his meaning. He kept his features expressionless and wondered why he'd spoken so honestly.

"Okay, okay. I can see you won't go away." She took the snickerdoodle he held out.

"Right, and if you don't take a drink, I'll follow you all over carrying a carton and embarrassing you."

She laughed. "You are such a jerk," she said, but not in a snarky way.

She also sat and reached for the juice. After finishing the snack, she tossed the carton and napkin in the trash, leaned her head back, and within seconds seemed to have dozed off.

Mission accomplished. For a moment, he watched her. She looked young and vulnerable and deceptively sweet in her sleep.

Hannah noticed that Adam's friend had left her alone for two hours. She'd awakened from her quick nap in ten minutes. The juice, cookie, and sleep had revived her.

She glanced around. All the patients were resting comfortably. Two doctors and several nurses wandered around the gym. Most of the professionals would leave tomorrow or Monday. Several volunteers had come from New Mexico, others from Oklahoma and Arizona.

Whether she wanted to admit it or not, her gaze continued to search for Adam's friend. She called him "Adam's friend" in her mind to distance herself from him, to build a barrier between them, as if he didn't mean anything to her in any other role. Didn't work. Neither did "Hector's coach." That shouldn't surprise her because the idea had not an iota of scientific evidence to support it. She might as well recognize that no barrier—visible, invisible, or logical—existed.

When she located Gabe, he was chatting with an elderly Hispanic man about five rows away, a patient who didn't speak English.

"You speak Spanish?" she asked Gabe after the conversation ended.

"Surprised? I grew up in Texas, spent a lot of

time with my aunt on the border. Know a lot of words I refuse to repeat. Played with Ginobili a couple of years."

What was a Ginobili?

"No," she said. "I'm not surprised you speak another language."

"Really?" He shook his head, calling her bluff.

"No." She paused to consider her exact opinion. "I'm impressed." Admitting that didn't hurt as much as she'd thought. "Most people don't speak two languages."

"Also picked up some French from Tony Parker, a little German from Nowitzki."

"Who are they?"

"You don't know?" He sounded incredulous. Those two people seemed important to him. "Ginobili and Parker and Nowitzki played in the NBA at the same time I did," he explained.

She had no idea what he'd just said. Oh, she'd heard the words, but the meaning escaped her.

"You can't tell me you have no idea what the NBA is."

"Not the slightest." She hated, absolutely hated, to admit lack of knowledge. Well, no she didn't, not at this moment. Admitting ignorance didn't feel nearly as bad or as humiliating as she'd always believed it would, possibly because she did it so seldom. Maybe never.

"The National Basketball Association, professional basketball in the United States."

"Oh." The explanation clicked into the part of her brain where she stored facts she'd never access again. "You played basketball *and* learned other languages in this association."

"Yes! Pro ball isn't all orgies with nubile young women." After the words left his mouth, he thunked his hand on his forehead and said, "I don't mean we have orgies in pro ball. I don't."

She immediately and oddly discovered she had much more interest in his relationships with nubile young women than she dared to consider. How interesting. She should have known from the perfection of Gabe that he had a past that included women so gorgeous she could never compete. Why try? Why should she even consider opening herself to heartbreak?

She had to face facts. They'd been thrown together by this emergency. He was her brother's friend and behaved nicely to her. He'd forget her as soon as he returned to Butternut Creek unless he remembered her as Adam's pitiful sister. She'd forget him when she returned to . . . to wherever she went from here. Her uncertain future shouldn't be complicated by attraction to this man. Well, to *any* man, but particularly this one.

And yet his statement had opened up an amazing new world to her. Always curious and willing to expand her limited knowledge of certain aspects of the rest of the world, she asked,

"What sort of things go on at these orgies?"

"You don't want to know. Besides, I didn't go to them. I only heard about them from other players. I'm not really an orgy man."

"I like to learn about stuff," she said seriously.

Gabe stood and held out his hand. "Time for dinner. Let's go."

Although she'd never read people well, Hannah did recognize an effort to change the subject. People behaved that way around her often.

"I'm not hungry," she said before she realized she was and she could use a rest, too. She nearly quivered with exhaustion and had only overcome it by sheer willpower. What had happened to her? She used to be able to work around the clock and still feel great. Unlike other interns, she hadn't depended on vast infusions of caffeine to stay awake and keep going.

"You need to eat. You're just getting over malaria," he said. "And you're not as young as you used to be."

"Did you say I'm getting old?" She bit the words off.

He grinned. For a second and before she— foolish, foolish woman—could stop the reaction, her heart began to beat faster.

"You don't tell a lady that," she said after a deep but not-in-the-least-bit-calming breath.

His grin deepened, and his eyes had a great

squinched look. She not only couldn't take a deep breath, she couldn't breathe. What was happening to her? Levelheaded, that's what she'd always called herself. Focused—actually much too narrowly focused—had been the description even her friends had used. Hard to get along with and not at all likely to forget who she was for a man. Her few former and short-term boyfriends had called her a sarcastic witch.

But at this moment with this man standing in front of her, she was tongue-tied. Sarcasm was the last thing she had on her mind.

The first and most important thing she had on her mind was unthinkable and yet she *was* thinking it.

She was falling. Oh, not in love, of course. She wasn't the kind of woman who was ruled by fickle and frivolous emotions. However, she had to recognize that, as she got to know him, she'd moved past her initial bedazzled attraction and the internal paean she'd written to his beauty. She was maybe falling in lust or, perhaps, in deep infatuation with this man who was completely, absolutely, and recklessly the wrong person for her. Even if she wasn't the kind of woman who did that, either.

"So," she said in a voice carefully modulated to show no emotion other than hunger—for food —"thanks. I'll go grab a tray. I can do this by myself. I know the way. You don't have to come with me," she babbled, but at least managed an unemotional tone.

"I know I don't," he said. "But I promised your brother I'd look out for you and I can hardly allow you to get lost in San Pablo High School or pass out on the way to dinner."

Oh, he'd promised her brother? Anger at herself for thinking this guy was interested in her and fury with her brother collided.

"Wh . . . wh . . . who? What?" She turned toward Gabe, sputtering in rage. Then she made a huge mistake. Fists on her hips and fuming, she glared at him.

She should never have looked directly at him.

Unfair that a man should look like Gabe. Created to lead women away from their goals and concerns and their chosen work, endowed with so much of everything. Not even the injuries to his face seemed to dim that aura. " 'To whom much is given, much shall be required,' " she said.

Oh, she hadn't really said that out loud, had she? His presence and that smile had destroyed every bit of the logic she'd always prided herself on and left quoting the Bible as her only means of communication.

" 'From the one to whom much has been entrusted, even more will be demanded.' "

Not fair. He even knew the Bible. He seemed almost as smart as she. Of course, he knew nothing about quantitative parasitology. The realization rebuilt a little of her ego.

"Don't be impressed," Gabe said. "Your brother has said that before, I picked it up from him."

"Well, in all fairness, I know nothing about basketball," she blurted. Why? She'd seldom considered fairness an important attribute. It was one of those nebulous concepts that couldn't be scientifically proven.

She realized, as he nodded, that something was going on between the two of them and *both* of them felt it.

"That's okay," he said in a voice low and intimate, as if sharing a wonderful secret. "I can teach you."

She felt her defenses slip even more. Regardless of what he'd said, from the tone of his voice he didn't consider her an assignment from her brother. Something was happening between the two of them, but only he seemed to know exactly what.

For the first time in her life, she was bumfuzzled.

Chapter Twelve

Adam left San Pablo late Saturday afternoon in the hope he'd have time to rest a little and work on his sermon. He knew the congregation would understand what he'd been doing instead of sermon preparation. Despite fatigue and a sore body, he still felt the need to feed the flock.

Due to that exhaustion, he'd headed home while he could still stay awake. Hector snored behind him, sprawled out all over the backseat. Beside him, Gussie's eyes looked as if they'd begun to close.

"What do you want to talk about?" he said.

When her head dropped onto the back of the seat, he gave her a gentle shove. "Come on, Gussie, you need to talk to me and keep me awake."

"Okay." She straightened, shook her head, and blinked. "Let's talk about our wedding. What do you think?" She reached in her fanny pack and pulled out her cell. "Still okay with those weekends?"

"Hey, I'm okay with tomorrow." Adam gave her a quick smile before he turned his eyes toward the road. "Those dates sound good. I'll email my friends and family. But, if this is too much trouble, as Hannah said, we could run off."

"You can't do that to Miss Birdie," Hector said

from the backseat. "That would hurt her and the other ladies."

"You're awake." Gussie twisted to look back at him. "We wouldn't do that. They need a wedding to plan and to invite the entire town to attend." She waited for an answer but none came so she turned forward again. "I think he's already back to sleep."

She put her hand on Adam's shoulder. "We'll need to discuss the dates with the Widows."

Adam groaned. "I know we have to, of course. If we allow them a say in a few little details, maybe we can develop enough good will that you'll get one or two of your choices."

"My thoughts exactly. I refuse to have a pink wedding. Anything other than that is negotiable. We'll start with the dates we chose, check with the church calendar . . ."

He laughed. "In case someone else is getting married in the church on those weekends?"

"We don't want to leave this to chance. You know how I like to plan and make lists so I'm sure about everything."

He didn't say it but he believed Winnie could beat her in list making.

"Okay." She squeezed his shoulder, which put pressure on muscles that were sore from the rescue work. Still, he didn't mind—not when Gussie did the squeezing and not when they were discussing their wedding.

He grinned. This was going to happen. He and Gussie were going to get married soon. Life was good, unless, of course, one's home had been leveled by a tornado. As much as Adam worried about those people, he still rejoiced that he and Gussie had set a date—or two—for the wedding.

Gabe attempted to pull Hannah away from triage at eight thirty. By the time he succeeded, thirty minutes had passed. "You haven't slept for hours. Days, maybe."

"I took a nap. I don't need . . ."

"You took a very short nap and yes, you do. We all do."

"Just because I gave in and ate dinner and took a break doesn't mean you can tell me what to do."

"I'd never dare."

He could see she didn't believe him.

"Please listen to me for a minute, Dr. Jordan."

She nodded.

"The staff has set up a rotation chart. You're off until eight in the morning. Might as well get some sleep."

"Did you . . ."

"Didn't have anything to do with it." He held his hands in front of himself palms forward. "To provide coverage, the staff set up a schedule: twelve hours on, twelve hours off. Some of the volunteers have to go home tomorrow evening. One of the doctors in town had a heart attack when the winds hit so he's out of commission. Another doctor's house blew away so she's gone. You're still needed until things get sorted out, but a rested doctor is a better doctor." Was that stupid slogan the best he could come up with?

"You're right." She nodded. "Or the staff is right. Whatever." She glanced around triage. All looked calm. "Okay." When she pulled her duffel from under the exam table, he took it from her.

Must be really tired. She didn't protest.

In San Pablo and other towns in the far west of the central time zone, darkness arrived late. As they left the building, the sun still shone but headed toward the horizon.

The wind had increased a little. Not nearly tornado velocity but strong gusts. In the heat of July when daytime high temperatures averaged over one hundred degrees, any breeze felt hot and dry, as if someone had opened a gigantic celestial oven and the hot air rushed out.

But tonight felt like a cool spring evening. In a few hours, the temperature would drop into the sixties, the plains would cool off, and they could sleep.

He glanced at Hannah. The brisk breeze couldn't mess up her spiky hair but it cooled the dusky skin of her cheeks and flapped at her boxy scrubs. Then he pointed toward the middle school. "They set up cots for volunteers over there."

She stopped and looked around. "Peaceful," she said in a soft voice missing the edge of stress he'd heard earlier. "Can we sit here for a bit?" She pointed toward a bench on the edge of a grove of live oak trees. "I'd like to be outside awhile before I go into another building." She lifted her head into the breeze and looked around the area.

"This reminds me of Africa a little." She swept her hand above her. "The vastness of the sky here. The horizon's bigger in Kenya because there's nothing around the refugee camp, not for miles and miles. Deforestation's a huge problem. Without trees, the sky in Africa stretches forever."

Because emotion colored her voice, he didn't say anything, only listened to her.

"There are sounds around the camp all night. You can hear lions roaring and elephants trumpeting. But there are also the sounds of people in pain and mothers sobbing.

"I miss it," she said. "It's the most beautiful place in the world and the hardest. The saying is that once you fall in love with Africa, she will never let you go." She closed her eyes for a moment, then opened them and turned away.

He watched her walk to the bench, sit, take a deep breath, and lean against a tree. Even as he started toward the bench, she fell asleep. Just like that. He dropped the duffel and settled next to her, putting his arm around her to keep him from falling off, to give her a pillow. Only, of course, because he'd promised Adam he'd watch out for her.

When he sat, she changed positions, still asleep, and cradled her head against his shoulder. She obviously thought of him not as a man but a large, warm, and hard pillow that she hit several times to make more comfortable.

An hour later, she woke up and yawned.

"How do you feel?"

"Great." Noticing his arm around her and her head snuggled against him, Hannah leaned forward and away to stretch, covering her yawn with one hand.

When she moved, he shook his cramped arm. His hand had fallen asleep holding her and his muscles had tightened, but he still wished she'd lean against him again.

Night had completely fallen a few minutes earlier. In the heaven that surrounded San Pablo, a thick stream of stars flowed across the sky in a radiance Gabe had never seen until he came to small-town Texas. No lights from the city intruded here to obscure the stars, just the dim illumination from the hospital a block behind them. With only a few trees silhouetted against the flat horizon, a depth and width of sky appeared, a vision no one could see through the buildings of town, even in Butternut Creek.

●●●

It had taken great effort for Hannah to straighten and lean away from Gabe. His arm around her shoulders had felt nice, warm. And his chest, well, it was a great chest. Although a little hard for comfort, she'd slept against it contentedly. She'd probably drooled and snored and knew she'd hit him several times, thinking as exhaustion overcame her that he was a pillow. When she woke up again, she realized she hadn't been sleeping against a pillow because, when she thumped it again, it whoofed. She felt awkward and embarrassed. After a few words and some time breathing in the beauty of the nighttime sky, she made that same terrible mistake. She looked into his eyes. As if they were alone in the world, the two of them, as if an unknown power directed her actions, she raised her hand and put it on his cheek.

Why?

To thank him, she reasoned, although she knew that wasn't true.

He'd taken the gesture as an invitation—why wouldn't he? He leaned toward her. Slowly, little by little dropping his head, giving her the opportunity to pull away, even to hit him with a hard right cross if she wanted.

Not that she wanted to. In fact, she wanted to stay right there, even to lean into the kiss.

But she couldn't. Even during this magical

moment, her mind kept churning out rational thoughts. She couldn't forget who she was and who he was and that this was not logical behavior. No, this was a capricious coming together, and Hannah never did anything on a whim. Despite the longing, despite the wish to act without thinking, she couldn't cross that barrier.

With great but reasoned regret, she put her hand on his chest to stop him at the same time she kept her gaze on his face. "Why do you want to kiss me?" she whispered.

"What?" He straightened.

"Why . . . do . . . you . . ."

"No, I heard you," he said, his voice colored with confusion. "I just didn't understand." When she started to explain, he held a hand up. "Okay." He took a deep breath. "Why did I want to kiss you?" He waved toward the sky. "Moon." Then he pointed at himself, then at her. "Man, woman, romantic night."

She considered his words. "You mean you'd kiss any woman who was sitting here? You don't necessarily want to kiss *me,* right?"

"Well, yes, I wanted to kiss you."

"Why me?"

"I don't know." He shook his head, bewildered. "No one's ever asked that. I guess they wanted to kiss me as well."

"*That* I can understand." She nodded her head vigorously in complete agreement. "You are very charming and I bet you're a terrific kisser. Any woman would want to kiss you, but I don't understand . . ."

He didn't say a word. She wished she could see his face. As poorly as she read people, expressions did help. Here trees filtered out most of the light and hid those details.

"What I don't understand is why me? I'm coming off a long shift, probably smell like a hospital or worse, and, on my best days, I could only be considered somewhat attractive."

"So?"

"Well, I'd think you'd prefer tall blondes. Beautiful women." She paused to consider her next words. "Of course, there isn't much choice here. Am I the best alternative?"

He still didn't speak. When he leaned back and away from her, the hand Hannah had placed on his chest slipped into her lap.

"You think I'm really shallow," he said.

"Oh, no. I didn't mean to insult you, but I'm a scientist. I like—no, I need to know reasons, motivation. I'm expecting you to be truthful."

"Am I a rare virus you're studying?" With those words, he started to laugh. For a while Hannah thought he'd never quit. She feared that in the morning, they'd find them here, Gabe still laughing while Hannah slept.

But he did stop. Then he took her hand and stood, pulling her to her feet. "We'd better go inside. You need to go to bed. You're worn out and I'm completely baffled." He picked up the duffel bag and, still holding her hand, tugged her toward the dorm space.

At that moment she realized with deep disappointment that Gabe didn't want to kiss her anymore.

"Is it okay if I hold your hand?" he asked as they neared the gym. "I have to tell you I cannot explain scientifically or logically *why* I want to hold your hand."

She did that to people, bewildered them. She didn't know why. She didn't speak in difficult words or convoluted arguments because she'd learned long ago that people didn't understand them. Even with her effort to express herself more clearly it often seemed as if she and the person she conversed with spoke completely different languages.

"The truth is that I want to make sure you're heading in the right direction and won't fall down because the ground is uneven."

Ouch. That hurt. She realized he could be as snarky as she—which she admired in an odd way.

When they entered the middle school gym, he dropped her hand. They both showed their IDs to the man on duty, then she followed him around a curtain. Almost half of the cots were empty. He stopped at one, dropped the duffel, and helped her stretch a sheet across the bed before he said, "Good night."

She slipped off her shoes, lay down, and remembered no more.

Gabe couldn't sleep. The cot was too narrow and too short for him. His shoulders hit the hard sides and either his head or his feet had to hang off. He chose his feet.

His face hurt, especially the cut close to his lip. If he slept on his back, the cuts on his back hurt. If he slept on his stomach, curved like a big bowl, the cuts on his face hurt. When he slept on his side, he had an irrational fear the cot would tip over.

But his whirring brain was the main reason for his insomnia. It kept playing that scene with Hannah. What was he thinking? Adam had asked him to look out for his sister and he'd hit on her. She'd been right about the tall blondes he usually dated. He hadn't made a move on her, at least not like he would have with those experienced and sophisticated women who knew exactly what his words and actions meant, who interpreted his move and responded without asking for a reason. But she *had* put her hand on his cheek.

He felt no attraction toward Hannah. Too skinny, too bossy, and too not his type of woman.

He shifted on the cot. It almost tipped over. Once he steadied it with a hand on the floor, he had to admit it. He was full of baloney. Oh, sure, he could *tell* himself he didn't find her attractive but he'd be lying. He'd really wanted to kiss her and not only because he was a man and she was a woman and the moon shone above them.

Yes, he was shallow. Yes, he pretty much wanted to kiss any woman—young and attractive—who cuddled against him.

However, the desire to kiss Hannah had been a mind-numbing and obviously ethics-flauting combination of moon and her warmth against him as she slept and, okay, attraction. Her uniqueness drew him, the fact that she didn't fall unquestioningly at his feet, that she was completely honest and brutally frank. He even found her occasionally prickly personality, if not charming, at least cute. Okay, he found it charming and funny and completely Hannah.

However, although he could be shallow and Hannah attracted him, usually he wasn't suicidal. He knew Adam would kill him if he took advantage of his sister. She truly was an innocent. Not that he'd take advantage of Hannah, but he might hurt her.

His entire body aching from the odd position on the cot and his cuts and his brain's refusal to shut off, he glared at the ceiling. Didn't help a bit, because Gabe still wanted to kiss Hannah— only he didn't want her to ask why. Her scientific analysis of his desire made him feel like a womanizer who went after anyone in a skirt. Not that Hannah wore a skirt, but he knew what he meant and what she'd implied.

He turned over and stared at the wall.

When Hannah woke up, the rising sun filtered through the high, wire-covered windows of the gym and sketched a diamond pattern across the ceiling. She stretched and smiled. The first night of really good sleep she'd had in a year.

She rolled out of bed and pulled her running clothes and shoes from the duffel, then hurried into the shower room to change. That done, she moved silently across the gym to the door and slipped outside.

Taking a deep breath of Texas air tinged with the scent of plants she couldn't yet identify, she began to jog. With each stride, she remembered those runs across the treeless plains of Kenya with whichever member of the medical staff wanted some exercise. Even more precious were the early mornings spent with Munira or Basma. The girls could run faster and longer than she because running was what they did, nearly who they were. During those times, the girls talked excitedly about Kip Keino and the other great distance runners from Kenya and how someday they, too, would compete in the Olympics. And how, someday, they'd come back and help the orphans in their country.

Back then, after two or three miles, with the children loping along so easily, Hannah stopped to watch the girls and waved as they kept going, beautiful and joyful, so filled with hope. Then she turned back to the camp.

As she remembered that scene from what seemed like hundreds of years earlier as well as only yesterday, Hannah stopped jogging and lowered her head to whisper a prayer. She asked God to watch over all of her children in Kenya but especially Munira and Basma. *Dear Lord, if they are still alive, watch over them, keep them healthy, still running and smiling.*

How odd that this moment had come. She so seldom prayed, but recently prayers seemed to burst from her at the oddest times. Back when she did pray, people had come to the refugee camp sick and exhausted with dying children. The stream of patients never stopped or lessened, no matter what she did or how fervently she prayed. It seemed as if God had turned away from the struggle of the Kenyan people, and her anger about the desertion had eaten her inside. Probably the reason she'd become so worn down with her efforts to stave off the tide of death, her futile attempts to save a few of those lives. Not that she had. All she'd accomplished was to end up here, in the middle of Texas, sent home for her failures physical, mental, and professional.

Dear God, how did I end up here?

This morning, the idea of talking with God made her feel as if she were still in touch with the children who had run free and happily, who had such big dreams for the future.

Feeling the joy of running and the peace of prayer flood her body, she realized she'd started healing. In fact, it had started weeks ago with gardening and being surrounded by people who cared about her. A sense of mission and a need to serve rushed through her body as she turned back toward the high school.

The goodness of her brother and the love and trust from Janey and gardening and being here had all helped her. Gabe had, too. He'd given her something else to think about and ponder. Not that she could figure out why she felt that odd spark of interest. No, she had to be honest with herself. Her feeling toward Gabe did not qualify as a spark; it was a fire raging illogically out of control.

Perhaps that night of sleep had put out the flame. She stopped and pictured Gabe in her mind and when the image of him appeared—all six-feet plus with the blond hair and all those other great parts that came together in the stunning package labeled "Gabe"—she nearly could not breathe.

That fact proved she was, deep down and as much as she had always refused to face it, a woman. On a dark, starry night with a gorgeous man, what woman wouldn't be swept away? She imagined few had resisted this man. Probably none. Depressing to realize she'd wanted to join the long line of kiss-ees reaching back through Gabe's past. At the same time, it felt good that he'd wanted to add her to that group, sort of like a secret handshake, an entry to a selective club.

Although she, of course, hadn't allowed the kiss. Now she couldn't figure out how she could have been touching him and yet acted like a scientist instead of the woman she realized she was. Probably because the metamorphosis had blossomed so slowly. The mixed thinking—that a metamorphosis could blossom—only showed how unscientific her thinking had become.

"Idiot," she shouted at herself in frustration. Why hadn't she recognized her womanhood a few seconds earlier last night, before she'd shoved that luscious man away?

Back in the gym, she hurried to take a shower, towel-dried her hair, then looked in the mirror. The Hannah she'd always been looked back at her.

Feeling particularly girly, she wondered if she should put on makeup. A moot question. She hadn't brought any with her. And, besides, no amount of makeup could change her into a tall, blond beauty, not with her short legs, nearly black hair, and coppery skin. With a last rumple of her hair—which had grown so long the spikes had become little curls—she dressed and headed over for breakfast.

When she reached the library, she looked around. No tall, blond man. Despite her earlier thoughts, it felt odd to be disappointed because Gabe wasn't there. Then she felt a hand on her shoulder and looked behind her.

"Good morning," he said, the most normal greeting ever, nothing suggestive or seductive in the words, but the sight of all that Gabeness caused every inch of her to feel, well, seduced.

Maybe they *could* spend a few days or a couple of evenings together, enjoy several kisses out here where no one knew her. She could be a different and new Hannah Jordan. She could think of no reason why she should not enjoy this man in this place at this time.

"I've already had breakfast and have been working for about an hour."

"Oh." How disappointing.

"But I had a lookout tell me so I could join you for coffee."

"'Kay." Gabe had made her monosyllabic. No one—no one!—had ever done that.

As she worked through the day, Hannah tamped down the excitement that kept rising back up when she thought of Gabe. A good thing because she barely saw him that evening. When she got off at nearly eight thirty, he'd headed into Fredericksburg with some young doctor he'd been playing basketball with.

She'd hoped to have dinner with him. Instead,

she picked up a tray and sat at a table with the last group to eat. When he came back with a pile of pizza boxes, everyone grabbed a few slices and pulled up chairs around a table to talk sports.

However, he did pull her chair to the table and hand her a slice of vegetarian pizza. As she ate, she realized how tired she was. She thought of asking Gabe to walk her to the middle school gym but he looked busy and boisterous, slapping back insults about UT basketball.

Filled with an unwelcome twinge of disappointment, she stood and headed toward the door and outside. After she'd taken a few steps, she heard the door open. Gabe called, "Wait for me."

With a grin, she did.

"Why'd you take off?" he asked once he'd reached her.

"You looked busy with your friends."

"I'll go back but I don't want you walking out here alone. Who knows what could be lurking?"

"In the dangerous wilds of West Texas? Not likely."

"After a tornado when the law is absent, who knows what horror we might face? Who can guess the mutations that may lurk in the dark . . ."

She punched his arm. "Don't try to scare me."

It took such a short time to reach the middle school gym. Only minutes. When they arrived, he whispered, "Sleep tight," turned, and headed back to the high school.

She watched as he walked off; then he stopped and returned to stand next to her. She grinned.

"Don't worry," he whispered. "I'm not going to try to kiss you."

Leaving her with her mouth open, he turned back again toward the high school. She watched until he reached the lights around the high school and went inside. No scientific explanation existed for the emptiness she felt after his departure.

Gussie put off leaving Butternut Creek until Monday morning. She'd stayed in town after Adam set off back to San Pablo with an SUV filled with supplies. Her purpose? She'd promised him she'd go to the church this morning and check the calendar for the wedding date.

The poor man had looked so worried, as if he feared she'd back out of this. Silly Adam, didn't he realize how much she adored him? Guess not. She'd have to think of ways to reassure him.

She arrived in the office soon after Maggie, who'd just unlocked the door.

"I need to check with you about our wedding date," Gussie said.

Maggie dropped her keys on the floor and gasped. "You've set a date? I wonder who won?"

"Who won what?"

"Nothing." Maggie picked up her keys and headed into the office. "Nothing at all."

"Maggie?" Gussie said in her toughest voice.

Maggie caved. "I shouldn't have said a word but you startled me." She turned on the coffeemaker before turning toward Gussie. "You know how small towns are."

Gussie nodded.

"There's a betting pool on when or if you'll get married."

Of course the citizens of Butternut Creek would do that. She imagined the people in Roundville had one as well. "Who's ahead? What date did you choose?"

"Can't say. We have to wait until you actually do walk down the aisle before the winner is announced." Maggie zipped her lips.

"There are people betting against our ever getting married?"

"Some. I can't say more." She zipped her lips again but kept talking. "Wouldn't be fair but I can tell you this. The odds favor next summer."

"Well, get the church calendar out and I'll tell you."

Maggie sat at her desk, flipped on the computer to bring up the calendar, and sat poised to click on the month. "Okay, when?"

"June."

Maggie began scrolling to the following year.

"No, this June."

"What?" Maggie looked up. "That's barely two months away. Who would've thunk?" She scrolled back up. "What date?"

"June seventh or fourteenth, I think. I'm not sure."

"Oh, Gussie, be sure. Be very, very sure." Maggie spoke in the worried tone of a divorcée.

"Oh, I'm very sure about getting married. The date is the question. We need to make sure these are open, then check with friends and family."

"All right." She looked at the first date. "The seventh is free all day. I'll put you down with the rehearsal the evening before."

"Great."

"And the next weekend as well." Maggie smiled. "The Widows will be so happy. Everyone will, but the Widows especially." She sighed. "They've been so worried."

"Oh?"

"Miss Birdie said you and the preacher were the hardest couple they've ever tried to get together. Took forever. She even said she might have to cut back because the matchmaking wore her out." She grinned. "When are you going to tell them?"

"After we talk to our families, I'll call Blossom." She considered adding, *Please don't tell anyone,* but worried the words could insult the secretary.

"Don't worry. I've been secretary here long enough that I don't tell anyone anything." She paused. "Where are you going to live after you get married? Still going to be running back and forth?"

Oh, my goodness. She'd never even thought about that. "We still have to discuss that," Gussie said. With that, she left, got in her car, and drove off to Austin. As she drove, she mulled over where she'd live after the wedding. Adam couldn't leave the parsonage and she'd sort of assumed she'd live with him.

Farley Masterson sat in Birdie's section again. She'd changed sections with Maybelle last week, but he'd caught on and moved when the other waitress had attempted to take his order. Maybelle, the traitor, had pointed him toward one of Birdie's tables.

She blinked. Her eyes had been foggy all morning. Hated to think about the expense, but she should go to Marble Falls and get her vision checked. Wouldn't do if she fell over a table or a customer.

After she topped off everyone's coffee, she couldn't ignore Farley anymore. Since he'd said her smile looked like her teeth hurt, she no longer made the effort to look happy to see him.

"How's your morning going, Birdie?" he asked.

He'd used a nice voice, a pleasant voice, which made her wonder if she should revise her opinion of the old coot. No, she wouldn't. No matter how friendly he seemed, she had no interest in the man and knew he'd never ask her out again.

"Just fine. What can I get you for breakfast?"

"I'll have number four with extra jelly and eggs over easy."

"The usual." Birdie nodded and moved toward the kitchen to slip the order onto a clip.

She served several breakfasts and filled numerous cups before Farley's order was called. She picked up the plate and headed toward his table. Then something happened. She guessed she'd tripped because suddenly her feet lost contact with the floor and she shot forward. Time seemed to slow down as she watched the plate sail through the air, land on the floor next to Farley, and break. At the same time, in an effort to cushion her fall, Birdie reached out her right hand. When her hand hit the floor, pain exploded up her arm.

She lay there, holding her arm and groaning. Darn, that hurt!

In no time Farley jumped to his feet and ran to where she lay. "Birdie? You okay? What happened?"

She nodded toward her arm. "Broke something."

Farley's gaze became concerned. "You're okay, old girl." He pulled out his phone. "We'll take care of you."

• • •

That morning, they closed down triage because the mob had slowed to one or two injured an hour and those injuries were fairly minor. The plan was to sanitize the gym and move the hospital annex there, returning the cafeteria to food preparation and service.

Earlier, Gabe had walked over to the downtown parking lot. With the rubble mostly cleared, he opened the door of his truck and leaned inside to turn on the ignition. The engine caught and started immediately, but he still couldn't drive it until the rubble inside was cleared and the windows were replaced. He called Rex in Butternut Creek, who promised to get a guy he knew in the area to take care of it.

With that, he headed back to the high school. Once he was inside the triage area, Hannah grabbed his arm.

"I need to check your face and back." She dragged him to her examining table, still there although most of the others had been collapsed and moved out so the area could be disinfected. "Want to do it while I still can before they pack my station and supplies."

She pulled off his bandages, which hurt, but he machoed up and didn't flinch.

After that, she cleaned off his entire face slowly and inspected each wound. "Most look good," she said. "Healing well, but I still want to keep an eye on the one by your mouth. If your back looks this good, you can work in the rubble if they need you or keep working with patients here. Just make sure we clean you up every evening."

Before he could move, she added, "Take off your shirt." After swabbing that area and sticking on a few bandages, she nodded. "Okay. You're released."

When he got off the table, a crew broke it down and hauled it off. Then Desdemona entered triage and said, "Listen up. We're closing this place down now. Need everyone to move so we can disinfect it. Take a rest. Relax because there are some injured folks from close to Mason arriving in about thirty minutes. You'll be plenty busy then." She strode off.

The few workers from triage ended up in the area between the middle school and high school. Gabe sat on the bench in the grove of trees.

"Come sit with me," he said. "Enjoy the shade."

When she joined him, he asked, "Where do you go next?"

"To the gym when it's cleaned up and the injured from Mason arrive."

He took her hand. "Don't know where they'll assign me. If I'm not around, will you promise me you'll eat and rest?"

She smiled at him. "Of course."

Like he believed that.

Chapter Thirteen

"Hannah! Gabe!" Adam shouted when he saw them. He'd been searching for them inside when someone had told him triage was closing and pointed him toward the green space outside.

As soon as he shouted, he slapped his lips together. Only after he spoke had he realized they were holding hands and leaning toward each other as he'd seen Sam and Willow do, as he and Gussie did. Something had happened between them and he'd interrupted, but his shout broke the silence and the moment. Both jumped to their feet.

"Hey, Sis," Adam shouted, although a million questions buzzed around his brain.

Hannah ran to hug him. Adam waved toward Gabe.

"Hey." Adam put his arms around his sister, then stepped back to study her. "You look great. Can't believe working twenty hours a day agrees with you so much."

"I'm fine. Gabe only allows me to work twelve hours a day," she said.

He glanced up at his friend, whose expression remained neutral while his body language looked casual.

"What are you doing here?" Hannah asked.

"Brought a load of emergency supplies. After

we unloaded the SUV downtown, they told me to come up here and help clear out triage."

Gabe wandered over. "Good to see you," he said and almost sounded convincing.

Over his years—okay, relatively few—in the ministry, Adam had learned to read people a bit. Gabe seemed comfortable. He met Adam's eyes and smiled, looked normal, but there was something going on. Adam had seen that moment between his friend and his sister.

Then Gabe glanced at his sister and quickly back toward Adam. In that second, Adam read a tinge of something. Guilt? If so, why? Hannah looked fine, like herself with the usual edge of intensity, but also happy.

Quickly she glanced at Gabe. Lot of gazing and glancing going on. For a moment, she smiled at Gabe, an expression most unlike Hannah.

Didn't take a great detective to figure out something was going on.

Or at least something had started to be going on, which was one of the most convoluted sentences he'd ever put together but he knew what he meant. Maybe a tentative budding of attraction that neither seemed to have acknowledged to the other and certainly didn't plan to share with him.

Why did Gabe feel uneasy about that? Must be, Adam guessed, because Hannah was his sister and he'd asked his friend to take care of her.

Certainly Adam knew that if a man existed whom he could trust with his sister, it was Gabe.

Not that he could say that because they clearly hadn't admitted anything to each other. Adam grinned, but not outside. He couldn't tease Hannah and didn't want to embarrass either of them so he simply said, "Hannah, go on inside. I need to talk to Gabe a minute about some . . . stuff. See if you can find out where they can use me."

He watched her move out of earshot before he asked, "Okay, what's going on, buddy?"

Gabe held his hands up. "Nothing. You know me. Nothing."

Like all good interrogators who know that if they don't say a word, a confession might tumble out, Adam didn't say a word. Unfortunately, before a confession tumbled out, his cell rang. He looked at the number. "Have to take this."

"Adam Jordan," he answered.

"Preacher, this is Farley Masterson. Birdie fell this morning. Probably broke her arm. She's in the hospital."

"In Butternut Creek? Should she be in Austin?"

"No, she's fine here. Good orthopedic surgeon on call. She's in X-ray now and they want to do a few other checks. Heart, blood pressure, the sort of stuff they do to elderly people."

"Okay, I'll head back now." He flipped the

phone closed. "Miss Birdie fell. Got to go home. Tell Hannah, please." He left with a wave toward Gabe.

He wondered about them as he pulled out of town. Despite the way Hannah had been looking out the window the other day, he'd never have thought of the two of them together. Could be the proximity and forced familiarity of working together, but a less compatible couple—at least in his estimation—he'd never seen. As the miles passed, he attempted to figure out a scenario in which Gabe and his sister came together and lived happily but couldn't come up with one.

The highway had been almost completely cleared although, here and there, flaggers waved him down because one or the other lane was blocked. However, the waits were short and he arrived at the hospital in a little over an hour.

When he walked up to the information desk, the volunteer said, "She's in room A-215, Brother Jordan, and there's a crowd over there." She gestured across the hall.

Church people and members of the community filled the chairs in the waiting room. They all stood when he came in. Winnie and Blossom hurried over to him.

"What do you know?" Adam asked.

"She won't let us see her," Blossom said, her voice filled with regret.

"Mercedes is in her room and Farley refused to

leave but she won't admit anyone else," Winnie added.

"I'll check and be back." Adam headed toward A-215.

For a moment he stood at the door. Farley sat next to the bed and read the newspaper while Mercedes stood by the window. He walked into the room and stood by the side of the bed. Birdie looked more fragile than he'd ever seen her, tiny and frail. When she strode around the church and the town, the force of her personality made her seem taller and stronger. Now, as she dozed, she looked like a seventy-year-old woman who'd fallen and was in pain.

"Hello, Preacher," both Farley and Mercedes said.

Mercedes gestured toward the bed. "She'll be glad to see you when she wakes up."

"I'm awake." Miss Birdie opened one eye to stare at him.

Her voice quivered but he could hear the steel as well. Knowing better than to take her hand, Adam said, "Lots of people waiting outside to see you."

She closed her eyes.

"I came in with her, Preacher," Farley said. "She's tried to throw me out but I'm not leaving."

"What happened?" Adam asked.

"She fell." He shrugged. "Don't know why. Didn't seem to trip on anything."

"Hrmph." She opened her eyes and raised her head. "Fell over my shoe. The sole came loose."

"I could tell she hurt because she could barely talk. You know Birdie's in bad shape when she can't talk."

"I was in pain."

"But they think she might have had a slight stroke," Mercedes said. "That may be the reason she fell and couldn't speak."

"Didn't have anything to say," Birdie said.

"Blood pressure's sky-high." Farley put the newspaper down and folded it neatly. "They're going to do the test for a stroke."

"Only stress and those stupid shoes," Birdie argued. "Nothing to worry about. Being in the hospital makes anyone's blood pressure go up."

"Of course." Mercedes took Miss Birdie's hand and patted it.

Miss Birdie snorted.

"Why no visitors?" Adam asked.

"She doesn't want anyone to see her like this," Farley said. "At least that's what I think. She doesn't say." He turned toward the bed. "Is that right, old girl?"

"I'm weak and pitiful," Birdie said in a quavering voice. Then she stated forcefully, "But I'm not an old girl."

"What's the diagnosis? Has the doctor been in?" Adam asked.

"Broken ulna." Farley put his index finger on

his wrist. "About an inch above the wrist. Says that's normal with the fall. She tripped, put her arm out to catch herself, and snap."

"She has an ice pack for the swelling and medication for pain." Mercedes picked up a cup of water and put the straw between Miss Birdie's lips. "The doctor will be in later, once he's studied the X-ray and the test results."

"If she needs surgery, he wants to let the swelling go down and has to make sure that old heart can stand up to surgery."

Miss Birdie spit out the straw and said, "Don't have an old heart, just old shoes."

For nearly a minute, no one said a word. Mercedes put the cup on the bed table, Farley ruminated, and Adam watched the pillar's pale face. He had to say something pastoral. Since the day he arrived, she'd ordered him around and never been afraid to speak her mind. She'd criticized him and attempted to control every facet of his life but she'd always accepted him as her minister and he'd had to step up.

"Miss Birdie," Adam said. "You are the toughest woman I've ever met." He thought he caught a little curve of her lips. "Problem is, you're also human. We all fall down. We break bones. Everyone does."

She didn't answer. Her silence worried him greatly. Miss Birdie, the iron Widow, never backed down, never didn't answer. He couldn't express his concern because she'd get mad both for his judging her and for his use of a double negative.

"Where are the girls?" Adam asked.

"At school," Farley answered when Birdie didn't.

"Birdie didn't want to upset them. Won't let me call them. But I'm going to pick them up because I'm on the approved list," Mercedes said. "In fact, I should go now so I'll be there when school lets out." She strode toward the door and out with her keys jangling.

Still he hadn't said anything to comfort or anger or uplift Miss Birdie. He had to.

Dear Lord, please fill me with words, the right words.

After that fervent prayer, he pulled up a chair on the side Miss Birdie faced, sat, and leaned forward. She didn't meet his eyes. He didn't remember a time she didn't at least glare at him.

Undaunted, Adam began, "Miss Birdie, you are loved in this town."

"Hrmph."

"Do not disagree with me." He mimicked the tone she used with him so often. "You know you are. You've been serving the folks in Butternut Creek for fifty or sixty years."

"Fifty," she muttered.

Heaven forbid he should make her older than she was.

"Do you know how many people are out there

to pay tribute to you because they love you?"

"I told her," Farley said. "But you know how stubborn she can be."

"I bet you've helped every person out there in some way, probably all of them more than once, over and over." Adam paused to search for words. "They want to show their gratitude. They want to support you, to bring you meals so the girls don't have to cook, and keep you company."

"You're going to need that, Birdie," Farley said. "You and the girls."

"They want to give you what you've given them for years. It's time for you to receive what they are offering generously because they love you."

Nothing. No reaction. Then he realized a tear had trickled down her cheek.

Okay, he'd reached her a little, but she still looked despondent. Time for the big guns.

If this didn't beat all. Birdie flopped on her back and stared at the ceiling tiles, counting them compulsively.

The old coot sat on one side of the bed. The preacher sat on the other.

No escape. The railings seemed more like fences. With this stupid arm and the IV dripping into her and those monitors attached, she couldn't escape even if another tornado hit.

No matter what the preacher said—and his

words had been nice and inspiring—she still felt like a weak old woman.

"Preacher," she said. "I can't see them now. I can't. I hurt and my brain's fuzzy from the pain medication."

She cleared her throat because her voice sounded rusty. Adam picked up a cup of water and stuck the straw in her mouth. She took a deep gulp. Tasted good. Then she turned to Farley and said, "Would you go out and tell everyone thank you, that I don't feel like seeing them but I really appreciate them coming by?"

He nodded and left.

Then the preacher spoke.

"And the wedding." He shook his head and sighed. "I don't know what Gussie will do without you."

The wedding. Those two words echoed in her brain. Blood roared through her veins, bringing strength and focus. She attempted to sit up but, with all the tubes and lines that connected her to machines, she failed.

"Of course, the wedding. We have to make plans."

"Miss Birdie, are you strong enough? Do you think . . ."

Oh, that preacher. He knew good and well what to say to her to break through her self-pity. She knew he'd manipulated her but didn't care. She'd needed that shove like Popeye needed spinach, like . . . well, like the Widows needed to plan a wedding. "Ask Blossom and Winnie to come in. We need to get to work."

He nodded and left the room.

When he returned with Winnie and Blossom, Farley following them, she waved the men away. "We've got to get busy and we don't need you here. Farley, you get some lunch and go on home. We need that chair."

Dismissed, both left obediently.

"Someone call Yvonne," the pillar continued. "Get her over here right away. Blossom, hand me the control so I can raise the head of the bed. Winnie, you ready to take notes? Mercedes will be back with the girls in no time, but we'll start without her."

She'd show everyone she wasn't over the hill, not yet.

Could be she'd accept some of that help the preacher had mentioned. Not because she'd become so pitiful she needed it. She just shouldn't be so prideful she couldn't allow people to grow spiritually by helping her.

But she'd be goldurned if she'd give up this wedding. She'd worked too hard to get these two together to sit it out. They'd tell the bride about the plans later, when they had the details all tied up.

"Oh, Preacher." Winnie ran out of the room and pulled Adam back inside. "Have you set a date for the wedding yet?"

He shook his head and lowered his eyes. Looked so uncomfortable Birdie knew they had. "You'll need to take that up with Gussie. We still need to confirm the date with our families," he hedged.

"Please tell us, Adam," Blossom said in the pleading note he hated to turn down. "So we can plan, set a schedule."

He sighed.

"June. The fourteenth. Probably."

"Oh, dear." Blossom's mouth formed the little pink circle. "That's not far away."

"September or October would be better for us," Birdie said.

"More convenient," Winnie agreed.

Adam laughed. "Ladies, you've been after me to get married since I drove into town. You should be happy we've set a date."

"Yes, we should," Winnie said. "The sooner they get married, the less likely Gussie is to get cold feet."

"We don't know exactly when our friends and families can come. Maggie put the dates on the church schedule," Adam said.

"We're up to the challenge," Winnie said. "Might not be quite as fancy as Blossom would like."

"It will be lovely," Blossom said in her honey-sweet voice. "Thank you, Preacher, for letting us know."

With her good arm, Birdie waved him away as Winnie flipped to her calendar and Blossom smiled.

"I'll just go back to the parsonage and get a little work done," he said. "If you don't need any input from me about the wedding."

Of course they didn't. What would the groom have to say about his own wedding? "Just show up in a nice suit and with a haircut," Birdie said.

When Blossom began to talk about flowers, he hightailed it out.

After dinner Monday evening as the light was disappearing, Gabe and Hannah wandered around the area north of the high school, an open spot with downed trees, scattered limbs, and miscellaneous debris, probably the last area to be cleared.

Gabe was acting like . . . well, like her brother, for goodness' sake. He'd teased her, and he was walking nearly a foot away. Didn't touch her. Didn't even take her hand when she tripped over a root. She guessed he allowed her to tag along because of his promise to Adam.

When they reached the middle of the damage, Gabe said, "I want to set your mind at ease. I'm not going to try to kiss you."

Which, of course, did not set her mind at ease and only made her think about kissing him. Just like when he'd said the same thing last night. In the vanishing light, she could see a slight grin and that dimple that she found so attractive, and she knew he was laughing at her. An odd situation. Few people found her in the least bit amusing.

After nearly fifty yards, a fallen tree blocked the way. He stepped on it and dropped to the other side before he held out his hand. "I want you to know," he said, "that I'm not attempting to seduce you. I'm giving you my hand to help you over the barrier and promise that I will not try to kiss you because my kissing you makes no logical sense. Don't worry. I will let go of your hand as soon as you are safe on this side."

Which made her want to throw herself at him or hit him. Of course, she did neither.

Within a few minutes, they'd reached a county road and stopped. Ahead of them lay a field with several downed trees. It looked exactly like the one they'd just crossed, although with fewer trees. Hannah wouldn't have minded walking farther with him.

"Guess we'd better head back." He pointed down the path next to the road that must lead to the high school, turned, and walked off.

"Wait for me," Hannah said and ran along behind him. How had he gotten so far ahead of her? Probably because she hadn't been paying a bit of attention. Standing behind him, she'd been so distracted by the glory of the back of his neck, which tucked right into those broad shoulders, that she hadn't moved. And probably because his legs were at least a foot longer than hers so his stride covered a lot of ground.

In fact, she had to jog to keep up with him until they got back to the middle school. He waited for her when she arrived a few steps behind him. Before he could say anything about *not* kissing her, again, she flung the door open and strode inside ahead of him.

She did not want to hear it.

After a hard day of work Tuesday, a mechanic delivered Gabe's truck to the high school.

"Let's see how my truck runs," he said to Hannah when he dropped by the cafeteria at six. "Go get some dinner."

Because she knew he was about to say, *If you come, I promise not to kiss you,* she held her hand up. "Don't," she said with the note of warning in her voice that terrified anyone else she used it with.

He smiled. The dimple deepened, and his eyes twinkled. Darn the man.

They headed to Llano for Cooper's Barbeque. After she'd devoured most of a huge pork chop and a cup of apple cobbler, they drove back to San Pablo. They'd chatted during dinner—not that chatting counted as one of Hannah's strong points, but Gabe was very good at it. Left on her own, she'd ask questions and wait for answers, then debate. Gabe introduced relevant topics for discussion. Interesting style. She might work on conversation instead of interrogation. The trip back seemed much too short.

Once he'd parked, Gabe got out of his side of the truck, walked around it, and opened her door. As he reached out his hand to help her down, he said, "I just want to tell you that you don't have to worry about . . ."

A red haze obscured her vision. She'd never been so incredibly angry or so extremely attracted in her life. Acting purely from frustration, she leaped down from the truck, grabbed the back of Gabe's neck, and, not a bit gently and making no effort to avoid any of his cuts, hauled his head toward her. Then she plastered her lips on his in the most passionate kiss she'd ever given. When she could no longer breathe, she shoved him away and glared at him.

Gabe didn't move for a long time.

Good.

Finally, he shut her door and looked at Hannah. "What was that about?" But before she could answer, he pulled her into his arms and responded with great enthusiasm.

Just before she lost all rational thought, the idea that logic was greatly overrated struck Hannah hard.

By Wednesday, few patients remained in the gym as hospital beds emptied and patients were sent home. By Thursday, they wouldn't need her.

With Gabe helping transport released patients home in his truck, she didn't see him during the day.

She missed him.

Tonight? Well, tonight would be the last night here. Time to return to reality. Time to wonder what would happen when they got back to Butternut Creek.

"Doctor, we need you at bed seven," one of the volunteers said.

Time to take care of her patients.

After she'd checked a couple of new patients and prepared several others for the move, she sat down.

Also time to think about her future. Not, of course, that Gabe had ever indicated a future between them, although he participated enthusiastically in more kisses when they returned to San Pablo. Also and strangely, he teased her and kissed her. No one ever teased her, and not many had kissed her.

Gabe watched Hannah from the side of the gym as she cared for the few patients who hadn't been dismissed or found a bed in the hospital.

He had fun with her. Her quick brain and intelligence delighted him, and she was so funny. Not that she realized that and he'd never mention it. As frustrated and embarrassed as he'd been by her question about why he wanted to kiss her, she made him laugh. She was different from any woman he'd ever met. Not a flirtatious move or a compliment about his shoulders, although he'd seen her studying them. If she liked him—and from those kisses he felt sure she did—she liked him as Gabe Borden, her brother's friend and Hector's coach. She behaved like herself, not really a normal person but a completely natural one and not a woman with her eye out for a rich jock. He liked that. He liked her.

"Preacher, I'm here to start work on the air-conditioning ducts in the fellowship hall."

Adam looked up from his computer to see Charley Parsons—all three-hundred-plus pounds of him—standing at the door to the minister's study. He stood and moved around the desk. "Charley, great to see you. Even though it wasn't hot out, we tried the air-conditioning in the sanctuary the other day and it worked great. Thanks."

"Good." After the two men shook hands, Charley said, "Got to get going. I want to finish it before your wedding." He moved across the outer office and toward the fellowship hall.

After the plumber left, Adam heard a ladder bumping down the hall and into the fellowship hall followed by thuds as Charley began to pull the tiles from the suspended ceiling and throw them on the floor. Involuntarily, Adam flinched every time a tile hit the floor. With all the noise, he'd never get any work done. He left his office, picked up the list of calls Maggie had left for him, and walked out of the church.

A few hours later, he'd finished up his last visit at the nursing home when his cell rang.

"Rita Mae Parsons called me on my cell," Maggie said. "Charley didn't come home for lunch. She expected him an hour ago. Do you know where he is?"

A tremor of dread hit Adam. "I'll check and get back to her," he told Maggie. After clicking off the phone, he jumped into the SUV and headed back to the church, rejoicing he had a vehicle that sped up and didn't make suspicious grinding sounds.

He pulled into the parking lot five minutes later. When he ran through the door into the fellowship hall, he almost fell over a pile of the old ductwork and a heap of ceiling tiles. After he steadied himself, he looked around for Charley, then looked up to see two thick legs encased in overalls dangling from the ceiling. On the floor beneath them lay a collapsed ladder.

"Charley?" he shouted. "Charley, are you okay?"

"Hello, Preacher. You may have noticed I'm stuck."

Adam swallowed a sarcastic response because Charley was such a nice guy. Instead he said, "You told me you had a little skinny guy to climb up there."

"I did, two of them, but they both went to San Pablo to help and I wanted to get this done."

Adam walked around under Charley to study the situation. With most of the tiles gone, he could see the rest of Charley clearly. "What's holding you up there? Why haven't you fallen on the floor?"

"Well, I'm pretty well jammed in here. I grabbed one of the joists when the ladder fell over so I feel pretty safe. Unless I move or my arms start to hurt."

"Then don't move," Adam said.

"Not planning to for a while. I've got to tell you, from this view I can see this church was well built. A really strong structure."

"Good to know," Adam said although the construction of the building wasn't his first concern. As he further studied Charley's position, Adam realized the plumber lay partially on one beam and held a transecting support with both hands.

"My arms are getting sore," Charley said.

How to get the man down? Adam couldn't think of a way to do that alone.

"Let me call a few men. Howard'll come up from the bank and . . . ," Adam began.

"No, Preacher, please don't," Charley exclaimed before Adam could pull out his cell. "Everyone would laugh at me. The entire town would gossip and laugh at me. Even worse, Rita Mae'd put me on a grapefruit and egg-white diet for the rest of my life. Can we work together and try to get me down first? If that doesn't work . . ." The ceiling shivered with his deep sigh.

"Okay, Charley. Let me investigate this more." He surveyed the area. "Bad news. The ladder's broken."

"Can you fix it?"

"Sorry, it's beyond me. The hinge or whatever it is has pulled out from the frame. It's all metal."

"Yeah." Charley sighed. "Can't fix that. Do you have a ladder?"

"I'll check outside in the storage shed where Hector keeps the lawn mower."

When he didn't find one there, Adam came in through the office door instead of straight into the fellowship hall—no use worrying Charley about the lack of a ladder yet—and into the supply closet in the hall. There he found a short but sturdy ladder. He didn't think Charley could lower his feet to that, but they had to try. If that didn't work, he'd go to Hoover's Hardware and buy a longer one.

"Okay, Charley," Adam called as he entered the fellowship hall. "The good news is I found a ladder."

Charley didn't speak immediately. Finally he said, "Do I want to know the bad news?"

"It's six feet. Seems sturdy. Yours was— what?—eight or ten feet tall?"

"And reinforced all over. You know, Preacher, I'm not a lightweight."

Adam didn't say a word.

"Okay, see if you can wiggle me out a little."

After placing the ladder under Charley's legs, Adam flipped it open, steadied it, and set the supports. "I'm coming up. I'm going to grab your knees and see if I can break you loose."

But he couldn't. Charley had again managed to wedge himself in.

"I can't get the right angle," Adam explained. "I'm going to have to lift the ladder." Not that Adam had the slightest idea how to do that. He couldn't lift the ladder and still grab Charley.

"I'm going to have to run to Hoover's."

"Please don't, Preacher. They know I'm coming here. I had coffee with Dan and some of the guys when I picked up supplies this morning. If you buy a ladder there, they'll guess I'm in a mess again." He paused. "And they'll tell Rita Mae." His voice quivered.

The two studied the situation: Charley from above and Adam from below. Then Adam pulled the ladder away from Charley's position and climbed on it to ponder the problem. Didn't help at all. Merely pointed out how short the ladder was.

"A table?" Charley suggested. "Put the ladder on the table?"

"The tables aren't constructed for . . ." Adam couldn't think of a nice way to say this.

"For a fat guy to land on." After a few seconds, Charley started laughing and the ceiling shook. "I get in such predicaments when I'm around you, Adam." Then Charley noticed that the few remaining ceiling tiles had begun to shiver as well and he stopped.

"Let me think about this, okay?" Adam climbed down the ladder and walked around the fellowship hall until inspiration came.

"Here's what we're going to do, Charley. I'm going to break down several tables, put them flat, and stack them up. When the tables gets high enough, I'll put the ladder on them and see if I can reach you and get you loose. Then . . ." Adam stopped. He figured he'd fill Charley in on the rest of the plan if he got him loose. The last option was to dismantle the entire ceiling but he doubted Charley would go for that, would probably prefer to rot away up there instead of facing Rita Mae and a life of carrots for all meals.

Adam discovered eight flattened tables, which allowed him to lift the ladder almost to Charley's feet. He climbed up, reached forward to get a good hold, and said, "Okay, Charley, push."

It felt as if he were attempting to tickle a trout, the old poacher's method of fishing by finding a fish under a ledge and wrenching it out. He bet no one had tried it with a fish this big. Gently, he wiggled Charley's legs then tugged hard. With a loud *"Ooof"* from the plumber, Adam felt him come loose.

"Still holding on, Preacher, but I can move now."

"Keep holding, Charley." Adam jumped off the ladder. "Can you reach the ladder?"

Charley kicked his legs, searching for the top of the ladder.

Adam still worried. He had no idea how Charley could let go with his hands, balance on the top platform, and climb down. Charley was a great plumber, a nice guy, but not nimble.

"Okay, the rest of my plan is to get all the cushions from the sanctuary and the sofa in the parlor and put them all around the tables."

He ran off to do that and ignored Charley's shouts of "What? Why? What?" and "My arms are getting tired," which echoed through the building.

Adam gathered up as many cushions as he could fit beneath his arms, ran into the fellowship hall, and dropped them before he headed back for more. Satisfied with the amount, he spread them around the ladder and on the floor around the tables. "Finished," he said. "I put the cushions all around in case you fall."

Silence followed by a long sigh came from the ceiling. "Okay. Let's try it."

"Charley, I don't want you to get hurt. Are you sure about this? Maybe we should call EMS."

"I don't want to get hurt, either. Then I'd have to

explain to Rita Mae, and confessing what happened would be worse than breaking a leg."

"You'd still have to explain . . ."

"Please, Preacher."

Adam heard terror in Charley's voice, so he held the ladder. "We'll try this once. Put your feet down so I can see if the ladder's in the right place."

Charley swung his feet down, but they dangled a little in front of the ladder.

"Off a few inches," Adam said. He got off the tables and shoved the stack—pretty heavy by now—under Charley. Then he stepped back on the pile and steadied the ladder. "Try it now."

Charley dropped his feet slowly until they hit the ladder, but he put no weight on them.

"Lower yourself about a foot more. I'll guide you."

Charley let his body down, inch by inch, until his feet touched the next-to-the-top step.

"Good, Charley. Keep coming."

"I'm going to have to let go."

"Okay. I've got a good hold on the ladder." Adam could only hope he did.

Little by little, Charley descended until he let go of the vertical support and dangled by the diagonal one with his left hand.

"Almost there," Adam encouraged. "Keep coming."

At exactly the second Charley's feet landed

solidly on the next-to-the-top step, a voice from the hall screeched, "What's going on here?"

Charley attempted to balance himself but the ladder swayed and he fell, knocking over Adam, who ended up with the ladder and most of the plumber on top of him. As he lay there, unable to breathe and fearing a quick death, Adam looked into the shocked eyes of the church secretary standing over him.

"Maggie," he croaked.

"Get off." She flapped her hands at Charley. "You're killing him."

Immediately, most of the weight was lifted from Adam's chest. He took in a deep gasp of air.

"What's going on here?" Maggie demanded again.

"Sorry, Preacher." Charley stood and tugged the ladder off Adam. But when he reached out his hand, Charley disappeared before Adam could grasp it.

"Oh, dear." Maggie put her hands over her mouth.

Adam considered his body for a moment. Nothing seemed broken. He'd probably have a few bruises but, all in all, everything seemed intact.

"Pastor Adam, I think Charley's had a heart attack."

Adam leaped from the stack of tables and immediately fell over the large lump that was Charley and the lesser lumps of the pew cushions, ending up on his hands and knees on the fake-brick floor. Loud gurgles and wheezes came from the plumber.

"He's not dying. He's laughing." Adam reached out a hand before he immediately pulled it back. No way he could pull the big man up alone.

"Just a minute." Charley grunted as he attempted to push himself up. "If you could move some of the cushions, that would help."

When they'd cleared the pew pillows out of the way, Charley struggled like a Weeble to get up but he kept falling back.

"Come on, Pastor Adam." Maggie pulled him toward Charley. "If both of us try, we can pull him up."

In a scene reminiscent of a Three Stooges film, they tugged and Charley fell back. They tugged and Charley got to one foot and fell back.

"I have a suggestion," Charley said from where he lay. "Once you two get me to my feet, Maggie, you grab a cushion and stick it under me while Adam keeps me standing."

On the third try, the plumber finally came to both feet, steadied himself on the stack of tables, then grinned in the sweet way he had.

"Maggie, please don't tell Rita Mae. If you tell my wife, she'll put me on celery and water for the rest of my life."

"Charley, she loves you. She worries about you," Maggie said.

"Please. I promise I'll lose weight but I can't face forty years of salads and nutritious stuff. It would take the joy from my life."

She nodded. "All right. But I'm going to keep an eye on you." She shook her finger in front of him. "And I will tell her if I don't see a few pounds coming off."

"Thank you." Charley saluted her. "I'll be back tomorrow with my helpers to finish up but I have to call Rita Mae, tell her I'm fine." He pulled out his cell and hurried out.

"What happened?" Maggie asked.

After Adam told her, they both laughed so hard they had to sit on the cushions. Maggie said, "He could have called her from up there. He had his phone."

"No, if he'd tried to get the phone out, he would have fallen. Besides, if you were Charley, would you call Rita Mae and tell her you were stuck in the ceiling?"

"No, she's a sweet lady but she can get riled up with Charley and his weight. Let's get these cushions back to the sanctuary, Adam. Then I'm going home and have another good laugh. Wish I could share it with someone."

Chapter Fourteen

Gabe had worked all day and into the evening closing up the beds in the gym and moving some patients to the hospital. Others he drove home because they had no other transportation.

Not heavy work, but twelve hours of it wore him out. When had he become such a wimp? He'd have to start playing basketball with Adam more, maybe run with Hannah every morning.

He stepped out of the shower, pulled a towel around him, and glanced up at the clock. Nearly eight. He'd missed dinner and had no idea where to find Hannah. Finding her was his first priority.

After dressing, he wandered into the library. The food line was dark. But Hannah sat there, her head on the table, probably taking one of her speed naps. To her left sat a plate and drink. She'd thought of him. She'd saved him dinner. Hannah liked him—at least, she didn't want him to starve, which seemed like great progress.

"Hey." He put his hand on her shoulder.

She looked up at him, blinked, then smiled. Her expression showed every thought and emotion. She did like him.

"I saved you dinner." She stretched and pointed toward the plate. "Probably cold by now. Where've you been? Working?"

"Had to take a couple home way up north." He sat next to her and took a long drink. "Then helped them with the livestock for about an hour."

She tilted her head. "You know how to take care of livestock?"

"No." He picked up a limp french fry. "But the man was really good at telling me what to do."

"You know, you are a nice guy."

He looked down at the cold fish sticks, sawed off a piece with his fork, drenched it in ketchup, and ate it before he said, "You sound surprised."

"Guys like you . . ." She stopped and snapped her mouth shut. She watched him chew for a few minutes. "When are we leaving in the morning? I'm on call until eight."

"What do you mean, 'guys like me'?"

"You know, good-looking, athletic. I mean that in the best possible way. So, when are we leaving tomorrow?"

"Do you really believe I'm going to let you get away with telling me I'm good-looking but shallow?"

"I'm sorry. It didn't come out the way I meant."

"I see. You meant shallow in only the nicest way." He raised an eyebrow.

"Okay, it came out the way I meant but I didn't really mean that." She paused. "But there is a reason I said that. I . . . well . . . I've heard you were dating someone in Butternut Creek. Are you?"

"You think I'm a two-timing jerk as well? Wow!" He grinned. "But you meant that in only the nicest possible way, too."

"No, it's not that." She held her hand up. "Please help me. I'm not good at this men/women thing. I want to understand."

He shrugged. "All right. The Widows set Mattie and me up for breakfast. We went out once after that."

"Then what?"

"We didn't go out again."

"Why not?"

"You can't leave this alone? Allow me to retain a little self-esteem?"

She leaned forward. "I just want to understand."

"Yes, I know. Because you're a scientist." He took a deep breath. "She told me she didn't feel any attraction for me, no chemistry."

"She didn't feel a spark? No electricity?" She leaned back and considered his words. "How could she not feel attracted to you? I do and I usually don't even notice men."

"I know. Go figure." Gabe rubbed his neck. "Now that I've clarified that, I need you to do something for me. I worked hard today, I have a headache, and my neck hurts, too. Could you give me a massage?"

She looked at the palms of her hands, then turned them over before she glanced up at him. "I'm not good at this. I tried it with the children and they all screamed and told me to stop. One said I have hands of stone."

He placed a hand on the back of his neck and grimaced. Must have twisted it a little when he tossed that last bale of hay.

"Okay, I'll try. Lean forward and try to unwind. Yell if I hurt you and I'll stop."

She began at the level of his shoulder blades and worked toward his neck with a soft mashing motion. Slowly, but with pressure, she rammed her knuckles deep into his spine.

"Ouch," he shouted when she hit a sensitive area. "But keep going." Agonizing, but once the pain lessened to only light torture, he could feel the headache diminishing and—racking pain by racking pain—the tension in his neck released.

She pulled his shoulders back, then let go. "Better?" she asked.

He stretched and considered the aches. "Yes, it helped." He rotated his shoulders back. "It feels better. Thanks."

She didn't know how to accept gratitude. First she looked at her hands of stone, then at him before she said, "I'm glad."

Her hair stood up in the funny curly spikes, and she'd regained the dark circles under her eyes, but that went with the hours she'd worked and the stress. All in all, though, her uncertainty made him smile because she was so cute.

"I was afraid I'd cause grave injury."

"You really helped me. That was very nice of you. You know, as hard as you try to be tough and hard to get along with, you really are a nice person."

"Eat." She shoved the plate of cold food toward him. "You've got to fuel all those beautiful, bulging muscles."

Cute and smart but snarky when tired. "Okay, then talk to me."

She thought for a minute as if considering a topic. As he ate, she made a statement, then asked a question. What was his opinion? Hannah really could not be considered a chatty person. Talking with her seemed more like being interviewed on a Sunday-morning news program. Different, but he liked that. No talking about the latest music or film or gossip about movie stars; she discussed stuff that mattered.

He listened to her, nodding. When he'd finished as much of that horrible meal as he could, Gabe stood and bused the tray. "Let's walk outside." He took her hand. After they'd wandered across the lawn, he asked, "Do you miss Africa?"

She took a few more steps as she considered her answer. "Not when I left. I was so sick. The last month there, I felt so terrible. I only remembered the deaths. But now I can recall many of the good times, my friends and patients."

"Tell me about them."

She did, reminiscing about the medical volunteers from France and Sadiki and her family. "But I can't forget everything tragic." She paused and drew in a deep breath. "What do you know about AIDS in Africa?"

Not exactly the topic he'd have chosen for a romantic conversation under a sky sprinkled with stars and the moon shining low on the horizon. Didn't matter. After all, he'd asked, and he knew well that this was how she conversed.

He listened because he liked to hear her opinions. She made him think. Challenged him. That was the last thing he'd thought he'd find attractive in a woman. What a surprise to discover her brain was a turn-on.

However, maybe not this particular topic.

Adam clicked the phone off and put it on the kitchen counter. "Hector," he shouted. "Yvonne made brownies." He poured two glasses of milk and set them on the table with the plate. Janey had eaten her brownies before bed.

Hector clattered down the stairs and threw his body onto the chair. "Hey, Pops. Thanks." He picked up three brownies, ready to shoot the next one in his mouth when he finished the first, always willing to do his share in reducing the brownie population at the parsonage.

Adam sat across from him and put a brownie on a napkin. "We haven't talked in a while. What are you thinking about college?"

Hector chewed his second brownie and swallowed. "I really liked the players from San Pablo. They like the coach." He took a deep gulp of milk, then wiped his mouth. "Seems like a good fit and it's close to home, but I'd like to go back for a real visit."

They both chewed a few moments, silently sharing their love of basketball and dark chocolate.

"Pops, there's another thing I want to ask you." He took another bite and meditatively chewed. When he finally swallowed, he said, "This might not be a good subject. I don't know. Tell me if you don't want to talk about it."

Those words scared Adam. What did the kid want to talk about? Dropping out of school? No, not likely. Was Bree pregnant? Also not likely. Hector had said he'd never end up like his parents, he wanted a better life for himself and his eventual children. That future included an education and not starting a family before he finished college.

"What happens to Janey when I go off to school?"

"What do the two of you want? Gussie and I love her. You know that. We'd like her to still live here but don't want to interfere in your decision."

He let go of his breath. "Thanks, Pops. Staying here's best for her. I'd take her with me but, with classes and ball, I couldn't spend much time with her."

"You know you both always have a home here, don't you?"

Hector nodded.

"You know when you're married and have two or three kids, we want you and your wife to visit. Come back on Christmas and other holidays." Adam reached out. "You and Janey are our kids, our children. We love you."

Hector couldn't make eye contact. "Thanks, Pops," he said.

"I took my old car to Rex. He said it'll be ready for you in a few days. Hard to get parts, and he needs to sand it down and repaint it."

"Thanks. As ugly as the turtle is, I could use wheels." He leaned toward Adam. "There's one more thing. Coach and your sister." Hector looked serious. "I saw them Tuesday evening when I went with Howard to take a load to San Pablo. They didn't see me. What do you think about them?"

"Why? Did you notice something?"

"Man, when they were together, they . . . I don't know. They seemed interested in each other. At least, she didn't ignore him and he kind of leaned toward her."

"Yeah." Adam nodded. "I saw something like that, too. Something's going on. At least she doesn't hate him."

"It's okay with you?"

"Why wouldn't it be? Do you have a problem?"

"They're so different. Coach is great. He's smart and a good guy, but he's not as smart as your sister and she doesn't like basketball."

True, liking basketball seemed like an important consideration with Gabe. "She probably has other traits he finds attractive."

While finishing a couple more brownies, Hector considered that. "She's not a people person, Pops. Not like you. Not like Coach. She's more serious and focused."

"Maybe they complement each other."

"Yeah, could be." Hector nodded. "Besides, probably not important. She'll be going back to London or Africa or somewhere and Coach, well, he's here."

"Different worlds but, you know, it's not up to us. Could be a temporary attraction because they were thrown together. Maybe when they come home," he added, shrugging, "it'll disappear." He hoped not. He'd seen his sister open up more to Gabe, look happy, absorbed in something other than airborne pathogens, at least for that short time he'd observed them.

"Could be. Too bad Miss Birdie's had to cut back. With the broken bone and the wedding, I bet the Widows don't have time for matchmaking," Hector said. "We'll have to wait and see if your sister and Coach can work this out without the

Widows' pushing them along." He took another brownie, stood, and strode off, leaving a trail of crumbs behind him that Chewy quickly licked up. Not enough chocolate to hurt him.

Yeah, guess they would have to wait and see. Adam knew he didn't have any say in the outcome. What did they say in Texas? He didn't have a dog in the hunt or in the fight? Something like that. He'd ask Henry. He'd know.

Hannah imagined most women did not bring AIDS in Africa up when wandering alone in the moonlight with a gorgeous man toward whom she felt a mixture of positive but frightening emotions. However, she wanted to hear Gabe's views. She liked to talk to him about serious topics because he had opinions he'd thought about, considered, even researched.

"I know it's worse there," he said. "It affects more people."

"Much worse than it is here. There's almost no education about prevention. No one talks about it. The death toll is staggering, but it's the children . . ." For a moment, she couldn't speak. "The orphans," she said as she struggled to talk around the emotion clogging her throat.

He didn't say anything, only took her hand as they walked toward what she'd begun to call "their bench." She grasped his fingers tightly, using that connection to strengthen her.

A terrible idea. She'd always believed she didn't need a man to strengthen her, but at this moment holding hands seemed acceptable. Actually, it felt nice to have the support of another person, at least for a while. Besides, oddly, she found his brain almost as attractive as his body.

"Go on," he said when she didn't speak.

"What do you want to know? Numbers? Facts? This could be boring."

"Not," he said, "if you're the one talking."

"Thank you." Few people ever told her to keep talking. That was a very attractive quality in a man.

"Okay." She took a deep breath. "Nearly two million people live with HIV in Kenya. Over a million kids have been orphaned. The death rate has fallen because education has increased—although not nearly enough—and because so many have already died." She sighed. "Depressing to know part of the decrease in the AIDS population isn't because people get better but because they die."

He slipped his arm around her. "What happens to the orphans?"

"We try to find family but so many people have died that there's often no relative or friend to take them in. There are some orphanages, but not nearly enough for all the children." Hannah leaned into Gabe. "I'm sorry to talk about this with you on our last evening together."

"What do you mean, our last evening together? Are you leaving the country?" His hand tightened on her shoulder.

"Oh, no. I mean here." She gestured around her, at the sky and the schools and then the bench. "We won't be here, like this."

"There's a swing on the front porch of the parsonage. We could spend time together there."

"Oh, sure."

"You don't sound convinced. Why not?"

"Oh." She tilted her head and considered his words. Most women would know how to answer that question. Most women would know instinctively what to say, how to react, perhaps with a little toss of the hair. Her hair was way too short to toss.

A woman of the world would probably give a coy wink but she'd never learned to wink with only one eye and a blink would not attract a man. In movies, women had pouty lips, but *pouty* was not Hannah Jordan's style. And flirty? No one had ever used that word to describe her, and with good reason.

No, she'd always been a take-me-as-I-am sort of person and could hardly change now. And yet, she had no idea what came next, what to do when faced with a gorgeous man in the moonlight. "I need to know something. Why do you want to spend time with me? I'm not a girlie-girl."

For a moment, he studied her. His gaze roamed from her eyes to her mouth and stayed there.

She shivered a little.

He leaned close, then even closer until his lips were barely an inch from hers. Slowly, they descended, slowly enough that she could feel his warm breath against her cheek, until they moved against hers.

For a moment she worried about that cut on the side of his mouth. She didn't want to infect it and felt a little worry about . . . then she could think of nothing but his kiss and his arms and his warmth against her.

When he leaned away, still holding her against him, she said, "You are a great kisser."

So he showed her again.

That finished, she pushed away a little, only a very tiny space, and said, "Are you attracted to me?" She asked because she'd always thought the best way to discover information was to ask a question instead of wondering.

"Didn't I make that clear?" He shook his head. "Must be slipping. You should know that by now."

"Are you sexually attracted to me?"

"What do you think?" He lifted her chin and kissed her again, very thoroughly.

She could barely put together a rational, coherent thought. Where had her logical brain gone?

"Oh," she said. Scintillating replies had never

been her specialty. "Really? No other man has been."

"They weren't paying attention."

He kissed her again, which made any reply, much less a logical one, impossible.

"Wow," Hannah said when he sat back. She could feel her heart thumping wildly. "I know you're not going to like this question, but can you tell me in words why you are interested in me?"

"I always wanted to kiss an epidemiologist."

She put her hand against his chest. "No, really."

"Okay, I decided my life had been far too easy and I want to add a little turmoil."

Before she could reply, Hannah's beeper went off. She glanced at it.

"Have to go." She stood. "On call."

More than anything, she wanted to stay out here with Gabe, to savor the last evening of enchantment—had she *really* thought the word *enchantment?* Who had she become?

"I'll walk you back."

A knock on the door awakened Birdie.

She couldn't believe she'd fallen asleep. Blinking into the sunlight pouring through that west window, she stretched. Well, she'd started to stretch but she couldn't move her left arm.

She hadn't hurt that, too, had she? How could she possibly get back to work when she had one broken arm and she couldn't lift the other? Then

376

she heard a rumbling from her left arm and glanced over.

That stupid Carlos the Cat lay there, head pressing down on her arm so heavily it seemed to weigh twenty pounds. What kind of weak old woman couldn't lift a cat with one arm? And why did the creature insist on curling up next to her? The only attention he'd given her before the fall had been to bite her ankles. Ever since she got home after the surgery, he insisted on sleeping with her, following her around.

For a moment, she thought of that newspaper article she'd read about the cat in a nursing home that always entered the rooms of people he knew were dying and slept next to them. She glanced at the cat. Did Carlos know something?

Birdie shifted in the bed but the stupid cat still slept, didn't move an inch, and she couldn't shove him away with the other arm.

With a tremendous effort, she pulled her knees as close to her chest as an arthritic woman could, then flung them forward so her body followed her legs and she sat up. Carlos fled at her upward motion. Her physical therapist had told her that was a terrible way to sit up, that she could do a lot of damage to her back throwing herself around, but her physical therapist wasn't being held to the bed by a two-ton cat while someone continued to pound on the front door.

"Birdie? You in there?"

She recognized the voice. The old coot stood outside her door hammering on it. Wouldn't you know?

"Just a minute," she shouted. Must not have heard her because she could hear him in the side yard, crunching across the flagstone path toward the back and bellowing, "Birdie? Birdie?"

She tried to answer but, with all his shouting, Farley couldn't hear her.

"You didn't fall, did you?" he yelled when he passed her window.

"I'm fine," she said.

As she turned to sit on the edge of the bed, she heard Farley climb the steps to the back porch and shout, "I've got milk shakes."

She'd better let him in or he'd stand out there all day with that milk shake melting down his arm and onto the porch. "Coming," she said loudly as she left her bedroom, moved down the short hallway, and turned into the kitchen to open the back door.

"What are you doing back here?" she asked. "Give a person time to answer."

He smiled at her, undaunted by her harsh tone. "Let me in." He held up both hands. "I brought milk shakes."

"I'm not letting you in." Birdie started to fold her arms until she realized she couldn't do that, not while she still had a sling. "What would people say if I entertained a single man alone in my house?"

He raised and lowered his thick white eyebrows several times.

Old coot. She wanted to say, *Don't promise more than you can deliver,* but feared he'd take that as a challenge. Besides, that sounded ruder than she allowed herself to be with someone who'd brought her a milk shake.

"Birdie, nobody would care."

"Farley, you might think a man and a woman alone in the house is acceptable, but I don't. Now"—she pointed over her shoulder—"you to the front porch. I'll meet you there."

While he walked around the house, she ran into the bathroom and looked at herself in the mirror. After seventy years, she knew she could do little to improve the way she looked, but she *could* take care of that piece of hair that stuck up from the back of her head. One-handed wasn't easy but she wet the comb, pulled it through her hair, then flattened it with her hand.

Before she could head to the front door, Farley had begun to pound on it again. He smiled when she opened the door and came out on the porch.

"Which do you want?" He held out two cups. "I got chocolate and vanilla."

"Vanilla." She took the cup and waved toward the Adirondack chairs Elmer had made all those years earlier so they could sit on the porch and greet their neighbors. "Why don't we sit down for a spell?"

Once settled, Birdie said, "We'd get along a lot better, you and me, if you'd stop calling me old girl."

He laughed.

How nice it was to hear a man's laughter around the place.

Gussie should've been prepared. She'd cleared her schedule and left work at two to head to Butternut Creek, looking forward to seeing Adam and, of course, her parents. The idea had been to sit down with the family to discuss everyone's week. What had Hector decided about college? How did Janey feel about school being over and the long summer stretching out ahead? Had her parents made any decision about where they'd live now that she and Adam had set a date? Had Hannah survived nearly a week in San Pablo? And she and Adam needed to discuss where they'd live after the wedding.

When she pulled into a parking space in front of the parsonage, she could make out two people on the swing.

They looked like Widows.

She should have expected them. Planning a wedding with Adam wouldn't be satisfying for them and would be frustrating for Adam. She guessed they'd staked her out for those reasons.

As she walked across the lawn, she recognized

Blossom's lovely platinum-blond coif and Winnie's practically styled white hair.

"Hello, ladies." Gussie walked up the steps to the porch. "Did you come by to see Adam? Isn't he at the church?"

"No, dear, we came by to chat with you."

Exactly what she feared, but she smiled and said, "Do you want to come inside? I'm sure Mom has some tea in the refrigerator."

When Blossom stood, Gussie noticed a tote stuffed with, well, stuff. Gussie groaned silently. She'd hoped for a quick preliminary meeting to discuss colors and flowers but nothing more. Looked as if this might last for days.

Once inside, they settled at the dining room table. By the time Gussie returned with tea, Blossom had laid out six stacks across the surface and Winnie had her notepad open.

"We know you've set two dates." Pen in hand, Winnie looked. "Have you decided yet?"

"No, we're still checking with friends."

She wrote something on her pad. "Have you chosen your attendants?" Winnie continued.

"My friend Clare will be my matron of honor. Hannah and Willow will be bridesmaids."

"Will she be able to do that? Willow? With the baby?"

Gussie nodded. "We hope so."

Winnie checked an item and added the names. "And Adam's?"

"You'll have to ask him. He's talked to people but I don't know what they've said."

"I'll turn that over to Birdie to finish up," Winnie said with the executive tone she must have used to run the asphalt plant. "We're trying to take the pressure off her while she recovers, but she loves to make phone calls."

Nearly two hours later, Adam entered. Where had he been? She glared at him. His uncomfortable expression told her everything she needed to know. He'd been fully aware half of the wedding planners had staked out the parsonage. He'd stayed away.

"Dear," she said in a voice filled with syrupy affection, "why don't you sit down and tell us what you think about the color and length of the runner on the cake table?"

She could tell he had no idea what she was talking about but, like a good fiancé, he sat next to her and listened for the next fifteen minutes until he checked his watch. "Your mother expects us for dinner in ten minutes. Hector and Janey are al-ready there."

"Oh, my," Blossom said. "I didn't realize how long we'd gone on." She began to stuff her files back in the tote bag. "I'll get out of your way." With a dainty grab, she picked up the tote and drifted out with her usual graceful tiptoeing manner.

Gussie stood. Winnie slapped her notepad shut,

shoved it and her pen in her purse, nodded at the couple, and hurried after Blossom.

As they watched the screen door slam behind the two, Adam said, "Do you have the entire ceremony planned?"

"Haven't even started that yet. They'll expect you to be present. No, we discussed the rehearsal and the rehearsal dinner and the reception. Blossom keeps saying, 'Nothing fancy,' then pulls out pictures of orchids and a menu for the reception, a sit-down dinner with lobster and all sorts of things we can't afford and I don't want." She picked up her purse and took Adam's arm before she looked around. "Is Hannah already at Sam's old house?"

"No." He grinned at her as if he had a great secret.

"Well, what?"

"Hannah has a date with Gabe tonight. He's picking her up in a few minutes. She ordered me to be out of here before Gabe arrives."

Gussie fell onto a chair.

"A little overdone, don't you think?"

"Not nearly enough drama," she said before demanding, "Hannah and Gabe? That's an even more unbelievable couple than you and me."

He pulled himself to his full height. "I resent that."

"Okay, we're perfect together, made for each other, but Hannah and Gabe together?" She moved toward the staircase. "I'm going to see how she's doing before we leave."

Hannah scrutinized herself in the mirror over the tiny sink in her infinitesimal half-bath. She didn't look like Hannah. For her evening out—she couldn't bring herself to say "date," because that signified much more than she could fathom or accept—she wore a dress. This morning she'd made a special trip into Burnet to shop at the Bealls department store. What had gotten into her? Who had she become?

Fortunately, she hadn't bought the gorgeous gold sandals with four-inch heels and bone-crushing straps. No, she'd chosen a pair of flip-flops with a little bling on the straps.

She even bought mascara and lip gloss at the H-E-B. Later in the evening, she bet the mascara would drip down her cheeks and, in the heat, the lip gloss would probably melt and spread around her mouth. She imagined herself looking like the villain of a bad horror movie.

In the department store, she'd looked good. She'd studied herself in the full-length mirror, amazed that the dress made her look as if she had a shape. The color—emerald-green—flattered her skin. She'd felt almost pretty six hours earlier.

But now she felt so unlike herself she couldn't breathe.

Gussie tapped on the door of her attic sanctuary and called, "We're leaving, as ordered."

"No, come on up first," Hannah shouted. When Gussie stood behind her, Hannah turned around and slumped. "I am so incredibly uncomfortable," she confessed. "I don't want to do this."

Gussie took her by the shoulder and looked into Hannah's eyes. "Really? You don't want to go out with Gabe?"

Trust Gussie to call her on the problem without beating around the bush. "Oh, of course I do, but I'm scared." Hannah gulped. "I really like him but I'm not good around men and I'm not a people person and I don't feel a bit like myself." She waved her hand toward her dress and her hair and the makeup. "The only part of me I recognize is my feet. The rest is someone else."

"You look terrific but, if you're not comfortable, why did you decide to wear a dress?"

"I want to be the person, the woman, Gabe wants."

"Hannah, you already are or he wouldn't have asked you out."

"Logical." She nodded. "But I'm not me," she whined. When had she become a whiner? "I have to fix this. Help me, please. I can't see well enough in the mirror."

"What's first?"

"The makeup," Hannah said.

"The mascara looks good and it's impossible to

remove if you don't have eye-makeup remover. Do you?"

"I'll keep the mascara."

"The lip gloss looks subtle. I can't tell you're wearing anything. Your lips are only a little more coral than usual."

"Okay."

"Tell me about the dress."

"I'm not a dress person. I take big steps and if I try to walk like a girl, I look like an idiot. I'm so clumsy."

"Okay, what do you want to wear? What would make you feel comfortable?"

Hannah pulled something glittery from the bag on the top of the dresser and held up a coral knit shirt with beads around the neck. "I bought this today." Then she reached in a drawer and pulled out a pair of dark, skinny jeans. "I'd feel more comfortable in these."

"Hannah," Adam called from the second floor. "Gabe's here. Gussie, we need to go. Your folks are waiting."

"Be right there," Gussie answered.

In no time Hannah pulled off the dress, tossed it on the bed, and changed. Then she slipped the flip-flops back on. "And my hair?"

"Let me take care of that." Gussie put both hands on Hannah's head and messed her hair up. Finished, she took a step back. "That looks more like you, both curly and spiky. How do you feel now?"

"More like myself." She let out her breath. "Thank you."

While he drove toward Austin, Gabe began several conversations, but Hannah only answered with *yes* or *no* and an occasional silence.

Once seated in the restaurant, Gabe took her hand. "Hannah, are you all right?"

"I'm sorry," she said. "I'm very uncomfortable."

"Why?" He studied her face, which did look tense. "We've been together for a week. During that time, you were fine."

"Yes, but we were working together in what seemed like a completely different world. This is reality." She nodded as if to emphasize the difference. "Now we're out to dinner and acting like . . . like we like each other and are adults, dating."

"Hannah, I do like you. We are on a date and we are adults but we're also still Hannah and Gabe who kissed each other a lot in San Pablo. It's good we're together." He rubbed his thumb across her palm and she looked up at him, eyes wide and startled.

"I'm not good with people," she said.

"You're very good with me."

"And I'm not myself, not tonight." She waved toward her nice, glittery shirt. "I'm wearing a spangled top and makeup." She leaned forward so her face was only inches from him.

He nodded. "Very nice."

"But you didn't notice?"

"I do now that you've pointed it out. You look fine but I always think you do." He watched her, hoping they'd settled that and could return to the Hannah and Gabe of San Pablo, but he hadn't convinced her. "I like the shirt. It fits great, and the sparkly stuff." He waved toward it. "Nice."

"I was shooting for pretty."

While he tried to figure out what to say that would satisfy her, Hannah continued, "I spent a lot of time to look like this and all you can say is 'nice' and 'great.' I expected you to say beautiful or magnificent and even . . ." She paused to take a deep breath. "Even sexy."

"You look really great." He grimaced as he recognized that wasn't the word she was looking for, then he said, "Absolutely gorgeous and really smoking."

Better, he could tell by her expression.

"I think you are the most beautiful woman in the world. I've always thought that," he said sincerely. The words almost shut her up.

Actually, they did for nearly five seconds before she said, "Even when I'd been working for twelve hours in scrubs and my hair stuck up and my face was shiny?"

"Even then."

"Then why did I bother . . . ?"

"Thank you for the extra effort. You look gr . . . really pretty. I like the makeup. Thank you." He leaned over and kissed her quickly.

"Oh," she said when he leaned away. "Then that's okay." She picked up her menu and studied it.

After they ordered, Gabe said, "I have a proposal for you."

Her eyes opened wider than he'd thought they could. Probably *proposal* hadn't been the best choice of words.

He started over. "I have a proposition for you."

Her eyes opened even wider.

Still not the best choice of words. The way things were going, he wished he'd brought a thesaurus.

"I have a plan." Much better. "I have a plan I'd like to discuss with you."

She still didn't relax.

"A plan?"

"You told me there aren't enough orphanages in Kenya for all the orphans."

"That's right." She nodded as the waiter placed their drinks on the table.

"Well, what if I build one?"

She frowned. He could tell she was turning the idea over in her brain, studying it, attempting to think it through.

"All by yourself?"

"Depends on how much it costs." He shrugged. "Might have to ask some friends."

She blinked and this time did lean closer to him. "Let me get this straight. You and maybe some of your friends want to come to Kenya and build an orphanage yourselves? Like a Habitat for Humanity project?" She sat back. "Are your friends carpenters? Electricians? Plumbers?"

"I didn't mean we'd physically build it. I meant, we'd pay for it."

She still looked confused. "Who'd pay for it?"

"I would and some friends if necessary."

She took his hand and patted it. "That's a wonderful idea, but, Gabe, where would you get that kind of money? You're a high school basketball coach." She stopped for a second before she added, "Do they get paid really well in Texas?"

"Actually, I have some investments from my playing days."

"Oh." As the waiter placed their salads in front of them, she let go of his hand and watched Gabe.

He handed the bread basket to her. She pulled off a chunk, but he didn't think she was paying attention to food.

He could almost see her logical brain attempting to evaluate and quantify his proposal. He'd thought his idea would interest her, that perhaps she'd respond with a smile or a *Thank you,* maybe even a *Tell me more,* not a puzzled stare.

"Hannah?" he said when the waiter left the table after grinding pepper on the salads.

"Gabe." She leaned forward and gazed into his eyes with a sweet smile, an expression he'd never seen cross her face before. "Thank you. You know, you can't just build an orphanage, as generous as that sounds. Any gift would have to include money to sustain it, hire and pay staff, begin new programs."

Did she think he was stupid?

"You probably didn't think that far ahead, but . . ."

Gabe did something he never thought he would. He glared at her. "I'm not an idiot. I know that. Yesterday and today, I talked to my accountant and the guy in charge of my investments as well as several friends. The backing would include both the initial building and future support at the level of five million a year."

"Five million a year? How?" She shook her head. "How can you do this? You're a high school basketball coach."

"You know I played in the NBA, right? I made a lot of money."

She nodded. "But I figured you lost it or spent it all or you wouldn't be here." She waved around her. "In Central Texas in a small town coaching a 3A team."

"I coach here because I like it. I don't have to work. I choose to."

"Oh." She took the information in and considered it. Finally she said, "You really are a nice guy."

"Thank you," he said in a solemn voice with no inflection.

She blinked. "I insulted you, didn't I?"

Before he could say anything, she rushed on. "I'm so sorry. I have no people skills. I can explain viruses to a classroom but when I try to talk to a person, I don't know how to and that makes me feel like such an . . ."

"Hey, hey." He picked up her hand again and held it between his. "I threw this at you with no lead-in or explanation. No wonder you're confused. I'm sorry." He grinned at her. "You thought I was like the prodigal son and had spent all my money in riotous living?"

She took a sip of water before she answered, "Not exactly."

"If you're not after my money, you must love me for my personality?"

"I . . . I . . . no . . . I . . ."

Her mouth dropped open and she straightened up, ready to grab her hand away, but he didn't allow that.

"Shouldn't have said that. I embarrassed you." He let go of her hand, which she speedily dropped on her lap. She didn't look at all ready to even tease about feelings. Certainly not about love.

"Let's talk about the orphanage or we could talk about us. You and me," he said as if to make sure she understood.

"Let's talk about the orphanage." Her voice

definitely set boundaries as to the topic of further discussion. She pushed the salad away while the waiter approached with their dinners and set the fish in front of her and the steak in front of him. "I want to understand everything about your plan."

"A few years ago, I formed a charitable trust with several other players. We use it for projects all over the world and here in the United States. I talked with all of the partners. They agree this is a great project."

Hannah bombarded him with questions. Her grilling lasted through the entrée and nearly to the key lime pie she'd ordered for dessert.

When, at last, he convinced her he had the backing and would carry through, she asked one more question. "Why do you want to do this?"

"You said there was a need."

"I expect you to tell me the truth. Are you saying that my expressing a need was enough for you?"

"No, there's more." He struggled for the words to express how she'd convinced him. "When you talk, I see Kenya in your eyes," he said. "I see how much you care. When you told me about the need for orphanages for the children you love, that moved me. My friends and I can help. We want to make a difference and we can, even if only for a few hundred children."

She studied him carefully and with so much attention he felt sure there was salad dressing or steak sauce on his cheek. He picked up his napkin and wiped at his face but Hannah didn't even notice as she considered everything he'd said.

"Thank you for explaining," she said slowly. "Thank you for your offer." She paused and smiled. "I wish I'd worn the dress."

He had no idea what she meant, but he really didn't care when Hannah smiled at him.

Chapter Fifteen

"Yes, I'm worried about not working." Birdie rubbed the ears of Carlos the Cat, who sat on her lap. Foolish creature acted like he was her little nurse.

She looked around the people assembled in her small living room on Tuesday evening, two weeks after the surgery to screw her arm together: her granddaughters, the Widows, the preacher, Hector, and Bobby. "But I don't need an intervention."

"I brought you a lovely piece of apple pie my cook made. It has a sugary lattice crust on top." Blossom nodded toward the kitchen. "Let me know when you're hungry."

The flighty woman had arrived at noon and moved in to take care of her. She hovered. Blossom hovered sweetly and considerately but having her around nearly drove Birdie crazy. Blossom kept asking if she could fluff her pillow. Birdie had never been a fan of fluffy pillows. When Birdie fell asleep on the sofa, Blossom woke her to ask if she wanted to get into bed. When Birdie had told her she was fine, Blossom had draped a blanket over her. Eighty-five degrees in here and the woman worried she'd get cold.

Everyone was watching Birdie, waiting for her to answer. "Thank you, Blossom." They kept watching her but she wouldn't give them the pleasure of speaking. If they wanted to get this intervention going, they'd have to take control.

Winnie flipped open her notepad and started, "We need to talk to you about several things." Of course she began the topic. Bossiest woman Bird had ever met.

"Birdie," Mercedes said, "we know you can't work for six to eight weeks."

Inside, Birdie became hysterical. How would they survive if she couldn't work for that long? But she nodded coolly.

They all looked at her, every one of them afraid to bring up finances. Then Mac went to the front closet, pulled out a box, and brought it over to Birdie's lap. A shoe box. Not wrapped because Birdie thought pretty paper was a waste of money and the motion of wrapping a complete bother.

For that reason, the shape of the box and the letters stamped on the top, SHOES FOR THE WORKING WOMAN BY COMFORT FOOT, gave away the contents. Birdie sat back and studied the words. "We can't afford these."

"Grandma," Bree said. "We can't afford for you to fall again. We can't risk that."

She couldn't say a word. Just sat on the sofa, not moving and feeling so squishy inside she couldn't speak, didn't dare try. Instead she checked the end of the box. Exactly her size. Well, of course. The girls knew it.

Opening the box, she reached inside to push the tissue paper aside. There lay the shoes she'd craved for so long. She put her hand inside and felt the softness that would cradle her foot as well as the strong arch support. The sole was crepe but the expensive kind that slid a little, not the kind that got caught on everything and flipped the wearer. On top of that, the soles were all one piece so she didn't have to worry about their pulling apart in layers. Brilliant white with round toes and laces long enough to tie but not so long she'd trip over them.

Her first reaction was to put them in the box and shove the shoes away because she hated to feel needy. Her second was to accept them because she really needed them.

She looked up at Mercedes, her friend for her entire life, and could read her lips when she whispered, "Just accept and be grateful."

"Thank you, all of you." She shook her head in wonder at what caring people she knew. Maybe an intervention didn't count as a terrible thing.

However, she knew the event wasn't over because everyone looked at the preacher. She figured he'd get all mushy. Pushy as well.

"Are you the spokesman for this collection of busybodies?" she asked Adam.

"Guess so, Miss Birdie." He glanced around the group. "We've heard that you haven't accepted the help others have offered."

The pillar attempted to look confused, then

innocent. Neither expression suited her at all.

"We talked, you and I, about church people returning some of your care during the hard times of their lives."

"Exactly what I've done."

"But Father Joe tells me his cook brought you a chicken potpie and planned to help with chores but you grabbed the pie and ran inside, closed the door, and wouldn't let her in to help."

"Preacher, there's no way an old lady like me could run that much."

He glared at her. She played the old-lady card when it suited her.

"Pansy says the nurse showed her how to clean your arm but you won't let her," Mercedes said.

"I can do that. I don't need all these people around to do things I can do for myself."

"Hard to clean that wound and dress it with only one hand," Winnie stated, calling Miss Birdie's bluff.

"Howard brought you a casserole to show how much he appreciates all you do and has more plans to work around your house. A little fix-up and some repairs here and there." Mercedes added, "But you locked the back gate."

"And Mattie Patillo brought a nice corn pudding to tell you how much she misses you at the diner but you wouldn't let her come in to wash the dishes. She'd signed up for that time."

Birdie didn't bother to answer any of them.

They'd lecture her no matter what she said.

"All in all, we're hearing you aren't allowing anyone to do anything but cook for you," Adam said. "And the Ladies' Guild wanted to . . ."

"I don't need . . . ," Birdie began, but she knew that wasn't the way to start.

"Be quiet, Bird," Mercedes muttered.

The preacher went on as if neither woman had spoken. "First, I want to tell you how much I admire the way you've accepted food from the community so graciously."

"Thank you." She nodded but knew that wasn't all he meant to say. Those words were only to soften her up. "Had to accept it for the girls."

"Grandma, just listen," Bree said.

"This intervention is to ask you to welcome the people who care about you and allow them to help you," he continued, as she'd known he would. "As you know, we have a schedule of who will come in and fix your lunch and help you with whatever you need."

"I'm perfectly capable of fixing my own meals," she stated.

"Grandma, don't make me tell on you," Bree said.

Ungrateful child. Maybe this morning Birdie sloshed milk on the table when she attempted to pour it in the cereal bowl and had sprinkled her frosted flakes across the surface because she couldn't get the hang of eating with her left hand.

And she could forget being able to butter toast or make a sandwich. Couldn't do those with one hand.

"The girls can fix me something before they leave for school." There. That took care of that.

"I'll worry," Mac said.

"I'll worry," Mercedes chimed in. "With your bad shoulder and broken arm and aching feet, you could fall and not be able to get up."

"Hrrmph. Not like I'd die there on the floor. The girls do come home."

Her gaze met eight pairs of eyes, none of which showed agreement. "All right, all right. Set it up and leave me a schedule so people don't just drop in unexpectedly."

"Don't throw them out," Mercedes warned.

She nodded toward Hector and Bobby. "What are they doing here? They don't want to take care of an old lady."

"Miss Birdie," Bobby said, "Hector and I volunteered to help you with the outside of the house or any chores you need inside, like to change a lightbulb or look at a leaky faucet."

She opened her mouth to ask if they were plumbers now but knew those words would sound grumpy. Such nice young men. She couldn't insult them. She'd become soft in her old age. "Thank you." She looked around the group. "Thanks to all of you."

"You haven't heard the best part," Bree said.

"Once school is out, I'm going to take over your shift down at the diner."

"My shift? At the diner?"

"Isn't that great? Mac's going to cover weekends until school is out because I have softball. After that, I'll work breakfast and lunch during the week so you won't have to worry. We'll have some money coming in."

Birdie started to lean back in the sofa but that darned Blossom had grabbed the sofa cushion and was fluffing it. For heaven's sake. Sofa cushions didn't fluff.

"Tips will be down," Birdie stated as she sat forward to accommodate Blossom. "From my regulars."

"Oh, I think there will be plenty of people who'll leave a tip for a friendly waitress," Mercedes said.

"Are you saying I'm not a friendly waitress?" Birdie glared at her friend.

No one answered.

"Well, everyone, we're finished here," Birdie said. "Move along. Blossom says there's a piece of pie. I'm going to eat that, then go to bed."

"Let me help you stand up," Hector said.

As she pushed with her good arm, he put his arm around her back and pulled. Once on her feet, she headed toward the kitchen while the guests left through the front door.

Carlos the Cat followed her.

The next weekend, Hector, Adam, and Gabe headed back to San Pablo for a short visit on campus with the coach followed by an afternoon of clearing rubble.

Hannah, Janey, and Yvonne spent Saturday working in the garden while Henry stayed at Sam's old house and watched baseball. Actually, Gussie knew, he slept. Her father always said there was nothing better to sleep through than baseball unless it was golf.

All those desertions—even her own mother!—left Gussie alone with the Widows, representing both herself and Adam. Although after all her years of working she could afford a blowout, an expensive wedding would make him uncom-fortable and take away from the simple act of celebrating a future together blessed by God.

However, she knew she had a fight on her hands because the wedding planners were determined to put on a bash that would show off the church, the Widows' skills, and, way down on the list, the bride and groom.

Gussie entered the fellowship hall to find tables covered with—well, she didn't know with what, but bright colors spread across each. All four of the Widows sat at the central and only uncluttered table. Miss Birdie wore a lacy pink sling over her cast, which didn't look at all like her. She guessed it was a gift from Blossom, who adored that color on everyone.

"How are you doing, Miss Birdie?" Gussie asked. She hoped her question didn't suggest Miss Birdie was too fragile to be here.

"Fine, just fine, but that's not what we're here for."

Gussie should've known better than to mention her concern about the pillar's health. Quickly she turned and greeted the other three women.

"Don't mind Bird," Mercedes said. "She's feeling a little down because Bree took off to visit a college today and she realizes the nest is emptying out."

"Don't try to explain my moods," the pillar said. "And I'm not a bit grumpy." She glared at her friend. "Not . . . a . . . bit."

"Let me show you around everything." Blossom placed her hand on Gussie's elbow and gently pushed her toward one table. "You need to pick a theme for the wedding. I have a few suggestions."

Gussie knew very well that Blossom didn't mean that she, Gussie, actually got to pick the theme. In fact, the wedding planners had probably tossed any they felt unacceptable; here, on the table, sat the few they approved.

Blossom picked up a card and began to read a verse. " 'Love is the joy of the human heart . . .' "

"I notice," Gussie said when Blossom stopped reading, "that the main color here is pink. I'm really not a pink kind of woman. In fact"—she gazed across the table—"I'm not really into pastels."

"Oh?" Mercedes stood on the other side of the table. "Weddings are very often pastels."

Gussie nodded. "Of course they are, but I don't wear light blue or mint green. I never do." She stopped and looked at the Widows/wedding planners. "I have an idea. Because the wedding is close to the Fourth of July, we could use red, white, and blue. Something patriotic."

She never should have said that. She should have realized the wedding planners wouldn't realize she'd joke about the serious matter of *the wedding*. All four stared at her, eyes wide and mouths open.

"I'm sorry," Gussie apologized quickly before one of the women had a stroke. "That's not a good idea at all." She paused and allowed the Widows to recover. "Perhaps we could negotiate?"

"Negotiate?" Apprehension filled Winnie's voice.

"We don't do much negotiating," Miss Birdie added.

"We want to work with you. Of course we do," Mercedes said. "It is your wedding."

"I do like pink," Blossom whispered through her little pink mouth.

"Give it up, Blossom. She's not going with pink," Miss Birdie stated.

"Now, Bird, don't be so grumpy," Mercedes said.

The pillar glared at her but didn't say a word.

"I would not be opposed to a pale gold," Gussie stated objectively.

"Pale gold would be light yellow," stated Blossom, the one the other three looked to for color information, manners, and everything concerning entertaining,

"No, yellow has more green in it. I want a touch of brown."

"Brown?" Winnie frowned. "You want a brown wedding?"

"No, no," Blossom said. "Like this." She reached for a paint color chart on another table.

Why Blossom had a paint color chart handy, Gussie did not know. Did they plan to repaint the sanctuary to fit the theme? Oh, certainly not, but she didn't ask. Adam and the property committee could handle that.

Blossom flipped the chips open to the gold section and pointed at one.

"Too light," Gussie said. After searching through the colors together, Gussie pointed. "How 'bout that? Coral."

"Peach," Blossom said.

"Peach?" Gussie took the chip and headed toward the window to study it in natural light. "It's coral."

When Blossom nodded and smiled, Gussie gave in. "I can go with that. It's pastel enough for you and not too pastel for me."

"Wonderful," Blossom cooed. "We have a color. What about the theme? Peach baskets? Summer fruit?"

"Let's just have 'wedding' for the theme," Gussie suggested, but it was a suggestion made with a hard, uncompromising edge to her voice. She refused to have peaches tossed around or to carry a basket instead of a bouquet. "Coral flowers and coral dresses for the bridesmaids, and that's it."

"And lovely peach napkins and flowers for the reception," Blossom stated.

Gussie gave in. "Yes, peach for the reception," she said because it made life easier.

"We could have the reception at the country club in Austin or at my house overlooking the lake," Blossom said.

"We'd like to have it here in the fellowship hall," Gussie said.

The wedding planners looked at each other. They didn't say anything because this was, after all, part of the church, their church, but Gussie could read disappointment.

"We don't want a fancy reception," Gussie explained. "We want to celebrate here with our families and friends and not spend more than we can afford." As she saw Blossom open her mouth to offer to help financially or in any other way, Gussie repeated, "We don't want to spend more than we can afford."

"A good idea." Winnie scribbled onto her

notepad. "With the reception in the fellowship hall, people won't have to drive."

Miss Birdie nodded her agreement.

"But that means no champagne fountain," Blossom said.

"Yes, Blossom, it does," Gussie said.

"All right, let's talk about the dresses for your attendants." Blossom accepted the loss of the fountain and moved on.

"We'll take care of that. We're meeting in town Saturday," Gussie said to warn away further suggestions.

Hannah wouldn't join the trip, but no need for the Widows to know that. Adam had told Gussie his sister would find shopping with three women absolute torture, but she had her future sister-in-law's dress size and promised to find something Hannah wouldn't hate.

"Who are the preacher's attendants?" Winnie asked, ready to write their names in her little book.

"Sam is best man," Birdie said. "I called the preacher to find out. Hector and Gabe will stand up with him."

"And Janey's going to sing," Gussie said.

"Oh, lovely." Blossom clapped her soft little hands.

"Reverend Patillo will perform the ceremony?" Miss Birdie shook her head. "A woman?"

Gussie felt the underlying concern was conflict of interests, not gender. Mattie had been the first woman the Widows had attempted to set Adam up with, back in the glory days of their match-making careers. Perhaps they feared Adam would look up at Mattie and decide to run off with her, leaving Gussie at the altar. Gussie didn't. "Yes, Mattie will preside."

"She'll do a lovely job, Bird. You know that. No one even notices she's a woman anymore," Mercedes said.

With that, they moved on.

"Invitations are next." Blossom led Gussie to another table. "We've already missed the deadline for the save-the-date cards."

"Don't worry. I already addressed them and will drop them in the mail next week."

"Adam's parents will be flying from London," Winnie read from her notes. "Where will they stay? With the preacher?"

"No, they're going to rent a car and stay in a bed-and-breakfast in Horseshoe Bay."

"Not here?" Winnie spoke as if her town had been insulted.

"Other than that Starlight Motel out east on the highway, we don't have many lodgings," Gussie said.

"That's right," Winnie said.

"We don't," Mercedes agreed.

"And the riffraff that stays at the Starlight." Miss Birdie sniffed. "A bed-and-breakfast elsewhere makes sense."

They discussed a few more details. Blossom had set a date to meet the florist. The choice of a baker was easy with Butch the only baker in town.

"I have three o'clock Wednesday of next week set for you to try a few samples," Blossom said.

"I can't be there. I'll be working in Austin, but I'm sure Adam will go with you."

All four wedding planners gasped.

"But . . ." Blossom's voice quivered. "He's the groom."

"And he loves to eat. I assure you that whatever the two of you choose will be wonderful."

"That's how things are these day," Mercedes said. "Couples doing things together. Bridal showers aren't just for women anymore, and the groom gets to make a few decisions."

"Surely not the important ones," Blossom said.

"That's not the way we used to do it," Miss Birdie said.

"We have to keep up with the times, Bird," Mercedes said. "Besides, I'm sure even the preacher couldn't mess up choosing a wedding cake."

"And Blossom will be there to guide him," Winnie added.

Gussie bit her lips to keep from laughing. Did they fear Adam might go rogue and decide on pistachio with fig frosting? "Would you ladies help him with that? Perhaps bring him a few samples? He could try each and, with your guidance, make a decision."

"That's probably best," Winnie said. "Blossom, you check with Butch." She made a note of that.

In only a few more minutes, the five ended the two-hour planning meeting. Then the Widows waved Gussie away because, as Blossom explained, "We need to talk."

The words paired with Miss Birdie's tone and body language made Gussie hesitant. Oh, not that she wanted to stay, but her color choice had already been changed from coral to peach; who could predict what they might decide in this private session?

Then she stopped worrying because, after all, she was marrying Adam and it didn't matter if the wedding planners had planted an orchard in the sanctuary or expected her to shimmy down the aisle in a pale pink dress with fringe to the accompaniment of a rockabilly band. She'd marry the man she'd love forever.

Less than two weeks later, Gussie studied herself in the mirror at the wedding dress department. The dress was gorgeous: white with a high waist. Strapless, showing off her nice shoulders. She took a step. The skirt walked with her, stiff and motionless. She spun. The dress spun with her, as if it were a cone attached to her waist.

"What do you think?" she asked Clare and Willow.

"Do you like it?" Willow asked.

"It's not you, Gus," Clare said with the honesty of a longtime friend.

"It's gorgeous," Willow added. "But it's not you. I don't think of you as a traditional bride."

"I'd like a soft dress that would twirl around me, that would billow out when I turned," Gussie said. "In this dress, I feel stiff and self-conscious."

Clare nodded. "It's not you."

"The wedding's at two o'clock, right?" Willow asked. "Isn't this a little formal for an afternoon wedding? I'm not sure the fabric or length is right." Willow stood and fingered the satin. "You're right. It's not you."

Dress after dress, even the ivory knee-length gown, received the same reaction from Willow and Clare. "You look marvelous but you don't look like you."

"May I suggest something?" the saleswoman said. "We do have a line of bridesmaid's dresses. Perhaps you could find something you'd like with one of those."

When the salesclerk returned with several dresses, Gussie's eyes fell on the exactly right one. Light and floating ivory cotton, it was sleeveless and with an empire waist and round neckline. Full-length and perfectly plain. No lace, no ruffles, no ruching.

"Perfect," Clare said when Gussie came from the dressing room.

"Lovely. Not what Miss Birdie expected." Willow studied her. "The Widows are going to regret they allowed you out of town without them," Willow said. "But this looks perfect."

May flew by so quickly Adam didn't remember much about it. A vignette here, a comment there, and a great deal of being with Gussie.

And two new babies.

"You are a beautiful girl," Adam said to one-week-old Lucy Rose Kowalski when he stopped in for a visit to his neighbors. Because the baby seemed so fragile, so tiny, and he feared he'd hurt her, he held her against him gently and attempted to stop himself from saying terrible baby-cutie sounds. Might work for a next-door neighbor to act gaga but it sounded unprofessional for a minister to say, *Bootiful, bootiful.*

Despite his best efforts, the words popped from his mouth. "Is Lucy-wucie a pwetty, pwetty wittle sweetie?" Before he could embarrass himself further, he handed her back to Ouida and turned to Carol and Gretchen. "What do you big sisters think about Lucy Rose?"

"She's okay," Carol said, obviously not impressed with another little sister.

"She cries a lot," Gretchen said. "But she's sort of cute."

Adam pondered the idea of asking George how he felt with another daughter. After all, his plan for the future had included a son, and George liked conformity to his schedule.

Before he could, the father of three daughters lifted Lucy Rose from Ouida's arms. "Come here, sweetheart." He rocked her and smiled down at his youngest. "Since I've started working at home more, I get to spend time with her."

"He's even changed diapers," Ouida added.

"Yuck," Carol said and both girls giggled.

"A beautiful, healthy daughter is a blessing," he said, beaming at the baby. "She's wonderful."

They chatted about a date to have Lucy Rose dedicated in the church, then Adam left and headed toward the parsonage. As he walked, he reveled in the Kowalskis' happiness, at least until his cell rang. Although it was only eight o'clock on a warm Tuesday evening in May, a call after office hours always worried him. Had a member of the congregation died? Been in an accident? Fallen? He flipped the phone open. "Hello?"

"Come quickly," a man—he thought it might be Sam—shouted.

"What's the matter?"

"Baby! Hospital!"

With those words, the line went dead. Adam

attempted to return the call but it went to voice mail.

He glanced toward the house. Janey was spending the night with a little friend. Not something he allowed on school nights but now that she'd taken the TTYA—the Texas Test of Yearly Accountability that she'd spent all year preparing for—many school days consisted of a visit to Schlitterbahn and field trips and field days and picnics.

He left a message on Hector's cell to explain he wouldn't be home, then got in his SUV and drove to the hospital where he parked by the emergency entrance. From Sam's call, Adam felt it must be an emergency. At the desk he asked for Willow Peterson.

"Good evening, Brother Jordan," the receptionist said. "She's in delivery. Take the hall toward the front, second right." As he left, she added, "You'd better hurry."

He stopped and turned back. "Are there problems with the delivery?"

"Oh, not with Willow, but the father's about to have either a stroke or a breakdown."

When he reached the waiting area, Sam strode back and forth on one end of the room. The other expectant fathers and families crowded together on the other end of the space, away from Sam.

"Thank goodness you're here," one of the huddled group said.

"Sam?" Adam said, but his friend didn't reply. He strode over and put a hand on Sam's shoulder.

Sam leaped into the air and executed an ungainly pirouette. Not that Adam would tease him about that now, but he would, later. After all, Sam had been a marine, had fought in Afghanistan, had faced enemy fire—but now he looked terrified.

"She's having a baby." Sam gasped and fell into a chair.

Adam sat next to him. "Why aren't you with her?"

"She kicked me out." He leaned forward, hands clasped, head down. "I was driving her crazy."

Adam could understand that.

"Adam." He looked up, eyes wide with fear.

This was not funny, Adam repeated to himself. He and Sam would talk and laugh about this later but now Sam needed support. Adam listened.

"I've never had a baby before," Sam groaned.

"Well, technically . . ."

"I know. I'm not literally having the baby, but how 'bout a little understanding here?" Sam snapped. "I could use a little comfort, Preacher. A little support."

"How is she doing? Are there any problems?"

"The nurses say she's fine. The obstetrician has checked on her. Everyone says she's fine."

Adam didn't say a word. He felt his comments would further aggravate his friend.

"But Adam, that's my wife in there and she's having my baby."

"Where are the boys?" he asked in an effort to distract Sam.

"They're with my dad and Winnie. I'm supposed to call them when we know anything." He leaned back in the chair, closed his eyes, and put his folded arms against his forehead.

"Should I go in and check on her?" Adam asked.

"Yes, find out what's happening and maybe a prayer."

Adam stood.

"No, a prayer now," Sam said as he sprang to his feet.

"You and me and Willow?"

"No, Adam," he said, his voice filled with frustration because his friend couldn't understand the simplest request. "With me."

Adam placed a hand on Sam's shoulder. "Dear Lord, we pray for peace for Sam. Let him know that You watch over him, that You have his wife and child in Your care. We rejoice in the coming of this new life—"

Before he could complete the sentence, a nurse came into the area and said with a smile, "Mr. Peterson, your wife—"

Sam ran down the hall and passed the nurse in seconds.

"Amen," Adam finished.

When Sam disappeared, Adam called Gussie to tell her the news, then phoned Sam's dad to give him an update. After that, he found a magazine that wasn't too old, sat, and read for an hour. When he'd finished reading an article about . . . well, he didn't know the subject of the article because he'd begun to worry. What was taking so long?

He stood and headed toward the nurses' desk when Sam sauntered into the waiting room with a smile as broad as the entire state. "It's a girl," he said.

Adam knew they expected a girl. Sam had known that. He even knew they'd chosen the name Sarah Elizabeth for her. Still, Adam said, "Congratulations." He grabbed his friend's hand and pumped it. "How's Willow?"

"She's fine. Sarah is beautiful and so tiny." Sam held his hands about five inches apart.

"Did you call your father and the boys?"

"A minute ago. They're on their way over." Sam took a few steps toward a chair and dropped down, placing his head in his hands. "Do you know how lucky I am?" He gazed up at Adam. "Do you remember what I was like when we first met? I was angry, drank too much, and hated everyone."

"I remember." Adam sat across from him.

"I give thanks every day that Leo and Nick

417

broke my sliding door and that you broke my swing. Those kids saved my life. I met their mother, fell in love, stopped drinking, made friends, and now we have a baby, a little girl." He shook his head. "Life is a miracle." He grinned at Adam. "Thank you, my friend."

Chapter Sixteen

On Friday morning, the Widows kicked Adam out of the parsonage at six. After swearing Hector and Janey to a vow of silence, they allowed the kids to stay and get ready for school. They'd told Gussie to come to town by two so she'd scheduled her day around that. Adam had told her they were decorating the master bedroom and bath as a wedding present, which worried her a little. However, Blossom did have a way with decorating. She could only hope Blossom was in charge.

When she got to the church, Adam had his head on the desk. When she opened the door, he lifted his head.

"I wasn't sleeping," Adam said, only half awake.

"That was Chewy snoring?"

He stretched. "Okay, that was me. I stayed with Sam at the hospital until after midnight and got up at five this morning." He glanced up at the clock. "Guess we'd better get over there for the big reveal. I've watched cars and trucks pull into the parking lot all morning, and women have been bustling in and out of the parsonage."

"You can't see the parsonage from here."

"No, Ouida told me when she brought lunch."

After they left the church and headed toward

the parsonage, Gussie could see all the activity. "How sweet of the ladies to do this," Gussie said.

"Wait till you see what they've done before you decide that."

"You can't believe how many women are in there," Ouida called from the Kowalski porch. "They kept coming and coming. Not quite enough to qualify as a multitude and I wouldn't dare call them a herd, but they've been tramping in and out all day."

As they ascended the porch steps, Blossom opened the screen door and beckoned them inside.

Women filled the front hall. Gussie attempted to count: the three Widows and Pansy—who often joined their projects but was, sadly, a happily married woman and couldn't become a Widow—and six or seven other women quivered with anticipation in the hallway while a few more lined the staircase. Too bad Birdie couldn't be there. Farley had to drive her to a doctor's appointment or X-ray or physical therapy. Gussie couldn't remember the conflict.

The women swelled with pride because this counted as a special occasion. They'd come together and donated items and ideas to redecorate both the nuptial bedroom and bathroom.

Adam hadn't wanted that. He'd said he was perfectly happy with his two sets of towels from his seminary days. He didn't need curtains because the blinds did fine for privacy and darkness. A nice bedspread would be ruined by Chewy's huge body. However, beating off a determined group of Widows and the women who'd joined them seldom worked. Certainly hadn't done so this time.

Gussie agreed with the women. She'd never seen the second-floor bedrooms but she could only guess what the living area of a single man would look like. Spartan. And a set of towels from seminary? If the Widows and friends hadn't provided them, she would have.

"Let us show you around," Blossom fluttered.

When all the women nodded, Gussie felt as if she were surrounded by a dozen blue- and gray-haired bobbleheads.

"Let's go," she said gamely because, after all, they could not get out of this and it should be if not fun at least interesting. She grabbed Adam's arm tightly as he attempted to sneak out the front door. "You're not going to abandon me," she whispered and kept a strong hold on his hand.

Most of the women crowded up the stairs in front of them although, perhaps having noted Adam's attempt to break free, Winnie and Mercedes stood behind them, arms folded at the foot of the steps. Both smiled and glared, a mingled expression only a Widow could carry off.

Without a word, Gussie and her soon-to-be husband headed upstairs. On each side of the hallway stood grinning women.

"Here's the bathroom. You just go inside and tell us what you think," Blossom said.

When she entered, Gussie bit her bottom lip. The decor struck her as incredibly funny, but she refused to insult these nice ladies by laughing.

The color choice was subtle, almost ministerial. Willowy flowers in a dark maroon—perhaps chosen by a Texas A&M fan—covered a beige shower curtain. On the floor lay a matching bath mat. Thick bath towels in beige with maroon washcloths and hand towels hung from two towel bars. A maroon toilet-seat cover completed the ensemble. Gussie had never understood the need for a toilet-seat cover. After all, everyone knew what lay hidden there—and why did one need to dress up that utilitarian object? However, because the women had donated it all, she nodded and grinned in delight.

"We chose this dark maroon color because we know Gussie doesn't like pastels," Mercedes said.

Heaven forbid Gussie should wash up in a pastel bathroom.

"And because we wanted a more masculine color for you, Preacher."

But it was the art that tickled Gussie so much. They'd hung several calligraphy Bible verses, each in a maroon font and a gold frame. Very elegant. Very pious.

They made the bathroom look like a prayer chapel.

"Very holy," Adam said in the voice Gussie recognized as the one he used to cover his mirth.

"Lovely." Gussie studied the walls.

Behind her, she could hear their words of praise—very holy and lovely—being passed down to the women at the end of the hall.

"Thank you," she said. She felt deep gratitude that they had not put a picture of Jesus in here or she'd have to shower fully clothed.

"Go on into the bedroom." Blossom waved toward the other door.

When Adam opened the door into the chamber, they saw that the women had all hurried from the hallway and now stood against the walls of the bedroom.

In the middle of the bed, taking up almost every inch, lay Chewy. He lifted his massive head to look around at the invaders, then dropped it back on the bed and fell back asleep.

"Off the bed," Adam whispered to the creature. When the dog didn't move, he snapped his fingers. Chewy let out a snore.

"If that dog's going to be there, where are you going to sleep?" Gussie whispered. She spoke softly because she feared the fact she and Adam would be sleeping together in the same bed might embarrass the women.

"Now, if you could see it under the dog," Blossom said, "you could tell how lovely the pattern is. The bedspread picks up the same motif as the shower curtains."

When Gussie looked at the small section of the bed that was not covered by long, canine legs and his huge body, she could see the pattern. "How lovely," Gussie said.

"Chewy, move." Adam shoved until he exasperated the dog so much, the creature rolled off the bed.

"Yes." Gussie rubbed her fingers over the texture. "Beautiful."

Photographs—really lovely ones—hung around the walls. A view of the Capitol from Sixth Street hung over the bed. The picture on the wall next to the closet showed an old barn surrounded by bluebonnets; a third was a framed old map of Texas.

"These are pretty," Adam said.

Gussie fingered the taupe drapes that matched the walls. "Silk," she said. Had these lovely curtains come from a guest room at Blossom's or had they been donated to the thrift shop? She hoped they hadn't bought them, because they must have cost a great deal.

"Ladies," Gussie said filled with deep gratitude. "Thank you so much. I have no idea how this looked before . . ."

"Very masculine, not a bit feminine or fancy," Winnie said.

"Plain," Blossom added.

"Now this is a lovely room," Gussie finished. "It is beautifully decorated. Thank you."

Adam took the hand of each woman and squeezed it as he thanked them. "You have always taken such good care of me," he said. "You furnished the parsonage when I arrived. You got furniture for Hector and Janey." He waved his hand around the room. "And you've made this look like a real bedroom for my bride and me. Thank you."

As they ushered the ladies downstairs, Gussie looked back to see that Chewy had jumped back onto the bed.

The last night of her conference in Galveston, Hannah sat on the balcony and absorbed the beauty of the scene. Now she could see the separation of water of the Gulf and the dark skies but, little by little, as the sky darkened, they became one. No longer divided. She knew there was a metaphor in that but wasn't sure what.

Could be it had to do with her and Gabe, and that terrified her.

If she admitted she loved him, if she married him—not that he'd asked, nor did she know if he would and he hadn't admitted undying love for her—she was afraid she'd lose herself in him. Her feelings for Gabe so overwhelmed her. Would she forget who she was and what she did? Would she turn away from the dream she'd spent years preparing for? She couldn't live in Butternut Creek and, at the same time, go all over the world to eradicate disease.

Her cell rang. Gabe's ringtone. She didn't move. When the call went to voice mail, she listened to the message immediately.

"Sorry I missed you. Guess you're not back from the meetings. Maybe you went out with friends?"

His voice spooled from the phone, wrapped itself around her, and filled her with such deep yearning it almost hurt. No, it did hurt.

"I miss you," he said, and his voice dropped to a loving, intimate tone. "See you Sunday." Then he clicked the phone off.

She stared at the invisible horizon where sky met water. "You idiot," she scolded herself. "You love him." How could she love him after such a short time? After only five or six dates? Idiot. She'd loved him since they'd worked together in San Pablo.

Okay, so she loved him. But if she gave up her goal, who would she be? If she married Gabe, would she end up fat—well, probably not fat because she'd never been able to gain weight—with a bunch of children? Doomed to live the rest of her life in Butternut Creek?

Not that Butternut Creek wasn't a lovely little town, but it would drive Hannah crazy. Probably the use of the word *doomed* gave that away.

If she forgot her dreams and married Gabe, she might act like a sweet, adoring wife for a year or two until she got angry about giving up on her goals. Her frustration would drive them apart, because she did not suffer aggravation quietly. She knew herself very well.

"Dear God, please help me. What do I do?"

She kept her eyes on the moon reflected in the water and she knew exactly what she had to do. But maybe she didn't have to do that yet. Maybe she could stay happy and in love for a little longer.

Hannah had spent a week at a conference in Galveston about something Adam would never understand but fascinated her. She'd caught up with friends from Kenya, learned a bunch of stuff, lugged home several new books and journals. She and Gabe were dating. Okay, if not dating, at least going out together from time to time. Looked as if things were going well with them, but he never knew with Hannah.

But since she'd come back, she never combed her hair. He thought she'd hacked at it because the length was uneven, here spikes and there curls. When he'd taken the trash out, he noticed that her tube of mascara and lip gloss were on the top. Even more worrisome, she hadn't returned Gabe's calls.

"So," Adam said to Hannah from the sofa

where he and Gussie had been watching the news. "How are you and Gabe doing?"

Hannah, her head buried in a journal, mumbled something.

"Did she say fine?" he asked Gussie.

"I didn't understand. I don't speak 'Hannah.'"

"It's a rare and seldom translated language," Adam agreed.

"I'd think that, because she's your sister, you would be able to communicate with her."

Hannah lifted her eyes from the page. "Very funny and none of your business."

"Gabe seems to be a good guy," Gussie said to Adam because she knew the impracticality of carrying on this conversation with Hannah. "How long did he play in the NBA?"

"He played for five years," Adam added to the odd dialogue being pursued because Hannah refused to join. "Then Gabe decided he wanted to work with kids."

"Really?" Gussie feigned interest. "Was he injured? Did he have other choices?"

"He had lots of other options and was perfectly healthy." Adam had begun to feel this was a bad movie with all the backstory told in a stilted conversation, but it was sort of fun and he bet it drove his sister crazy. That in itself was reason enough to continue. "He could have played for the Lakers at double the salary but quit."

"Sounds like a really great guy," Gussie repeated. "What do you think, Hannah?"

Hannah tossed the journal on the floor. "What I mumbled before but you didn't understand was 'none of your business,' but in a much less polite way." She stood and stretched before she wandered out, tossing "Leave me alone" over her shoulder.

"Oh," Gussie said. "Maybe it's just as well we didn't know what she said."

"I'm worried," Adam said. "I asked her where she's going after this, what she's going to do, but she won't answer. I know she doesn't want to stay in Butternut Creek. There's not a lot for an epidemiologist to do here."

"Which also brings up a question about Gabe. Would she stay here because of him?"

Adam shrugged. "I don't know. She won't talk to me. I don't even know what she's thinking. Could be she's perfectly fine, has a plan for the rest of her life, and I'm worrying for nothing." When Gussie didn't respond, he asked, "What do you think?"

"Have you watched her when she looks as if she's reading her journals? She isn't. She goes several minutes staring at the page. Her eyes never move. I think she's trying to figure her life out."

"At least she's started to do that here surrounded by family instead of shutting herself up in the attic." He shook his head. "Then I had to run her off. What a terrible brother I am."

"Give yourself a break. No one understands Hannah. We try our best."

"I know." He put his arm about Gussie. "Let's change the subject to one we can figure out. How are we going to figure out the living situation?"

"I've thought and thought and looked at it in different ways." She leaned against Adam. "I want to be with you here in Butternut Creek all the time but I have that expensive business in Austin."

"A very successful business."

"I love photography but not as much as I love and want to be with you. I don't want to be away from you Monday through Friday."

"Could you work your schedule around? Be in town for only two or three days? Or maybe we could move closer to town, so you could drive."

Gussie rolled her eyes. "Oh, sure. We'll move out of the parsonage and spend money on a house. What do you think Miss Birdie would think of that?" She held her hand up. "I know you're going to say you don't care what she says."

"No." He shook his head. "Actually, I wasn't. I was going to say I appreciate her opinion but I want to be close to you." He put his cheek on Gussie's head and held her. "I want to spend evenings cuddled with you. Could you find any jobs up here to fill in? Maybe your school pictures?"

"I've thought about that, even put out a few feelers to schools around Creek County and checked with friends around Llano. I've also considered not renewing the lease on the studio and moving up north, closer to Highway 29, maybe only keep hours a few days a week. It's not a long drive from here to Leander or Liberty Hill." With a sigh, she stood and pulled Adam to his feet. "Come on. Walk me home. It's getting late."

"So we've decided?" he said as they strolled. "We've made the decision to think about this another time."

"It'll work out," she said.

He knew it would.

The next afternoon, as Hannah sat in the window seat in her top-floor room and looked out at the street through the huge trees, she pondered her future. She had no more idea what she was going to do than her brother did. Besides not communicating with him, she'd been rude. Although Gussie and Gabe had helped her a lot with her people skills, she still scored far below average.

Yes, Gabe had helped her a lot, and she had no idea what to do about the man. With him, she felt treasured and cared for but she'd never considered herself a woman who needed to be cared for.

She'd enjoyed being with him—oh, she had to stop lying to herself: She loved being with Gabe. Every second spent with him felt like a moment outside of time and completely beyond her normal world.

Why can't Hannah Jordan have a fling? her inner voice of frivolity suggested. *Why can't she stay in town for a few months and have a very moral and proper fling, but a fling nonetheless?*

You're not exactly the kind of woman who has a fling, the voice of reason spoke up. She did not want to hear it.

What was she going to do?

"Hi, Hannah." Janey appeared at the top of the steps. "Yvonne left part of a pecan pie. Do you want a piece?"

Pe-can, stress on the first syllable. The Southern pronunciation.

"I knocked but I didn't hear anything. Are you okay?"

"I'm sorry. Must have been thinking."

"Do you want a piece of pie?" Janey repeated as she settled onto the window seat next to Hannah.

"Did my brother send you?" She shouldn't have said that. Hannah didn't doubt her brother might be underhanded in finding out information about her, but he wouldn't use Janey. If she hadn't known that, Janey's confused expression would have told her. "Sorry. I'm grumpy today."

"When are you going to leave here?"

After Hannah looked into Janey's face, she put her arm around the girl. "I don't know."

"Maybe you'll stay in town and live up here forever?"

Hannah shuddered. As much as she'd grown to love Janey, thought of her as a strong link to the rest of humanity, the idea of living up here for years, the maiden aunt to Adam's future children, the old maid in the attic who spent her entire life reading journals, gardening, and running from life, terrified her. It frightened her almost as much as the thought of admitting she loved Gabe and wanted to be with him.

"For what I do, the kind of doctor I am, I have to be in a big city."

"You could be a doctor here. We have to go all the way to Marble Falls or Austin to see a doctor. And you could marry Coach and have children and be my friend forever."

"Janey, I'll be your friend forever wherever I am." She felt the warmth of Janey snuggled into her side and closed her eyes. She wished more than anything she could stay here, be happy with Janey as her best friend and loving Gabe and having his children.

But she couldn't. At the seminar she'd realized Kenya still called her, that she still had work to do there. She'd learned so much in that week that could help people. As much as she'd attempted to deny the call, those few days at the conference had clarified her duty.

How hard it was to be torn between two countries, between what she loved and . . . well, another thing she loved.

At one forty on a Thursday afternoon, Adam stood in the church kitchen, looking at the ceiling to make sure all the tiles matched up. He knew they would. Charley expected perfection from his workers. With the new air-conditioning system, the entire building felt cool and the church treasurer mentioned that the utility bill had dropped.

"Hello, Preacher. I need to ask you something," Blossom said. The other Widows flocked in behind her, each with a tote.

Adam had learned to hate the phrase *I need to ask you something,* because it concerned something he hadn't done yet or didn't plan to do. However, he had no choice but to smile as the wedding planners filed in. He might as well forget returning to his study to do . . . oh, one ministerial task or another. No, with no escape route open to him he had to face the inevitable.

The women sat in chairs around the kitchen table as designated by seniority, and Adam joined them.

"We've measured the fellowship hall," Miss Birdie said. She handed him several pieces of stiff paper with diagrams on them.

"Here are some suggestions for the setup." Blossom moved next to him to point and explain. Each design had been carefully drawn with tiny figures representing guests scattered around, every line to scale. In detail, she clarified each design and the Widows expounded further on its positive and negatives points.

Finally, after carefully studying them all, Adam wanted to do nothing more than say, *The only important part of the day is marrying Gussie. We can all stand on our heads at the reception for all I care.*

But he couldn't. "I like this one." He handed Blossom one.

"Really?" Blossom said. "You don't want a gift table?"

"Lots of people bring their gifts to the church," Mercedes pointed out.

"Which do you ladies like?" He attempted to hand the diagrams back to Blossom.

"No, no, no. This is your wedding. You choose." Blossom refused to take the sheets.

For a moment he thought about holding them up one by one and discussing them as he did with a children's sermon. Instead, he studied each again. On the third of the five plans, all the Widows perked up and nodded.

"I choose this one," he said.

"Excellent choice," Blossom said.

Not really a choice. If he hadn't picked that one, they'd end up with it anyway.

"Now, tell us which napkin is your favorite," Blossom said.

He chose one but knew it didn't really matter what he liked.

Then Mercedes opened the box she'd brought in. "You need to make a final decision on the cake." She took out a round container, took the top off, and handed it to him with fork and napkin. All four Widows watched him as if he were judging their entries in the Pillsbury Bake-Off.

He jammed his fork into the mound, came up with a hunk of cake, and placed it on his tongue. He chewed slowly before he swallowed. "Delicious," he said as he closed the box. "What's next?"

"Next?" Mercedes echoed, her voice colored with confusion. "There isn't anything else."

He hid a grin. This one cake constituted the only option he had. "Great choice."

"We have some swatches we need to go over with you." Winnie set her notebook and pen down and handed him an envelope.

What, exactly, was a swatch? "I think swatches are a Gussie decision."

"We have some sketches and suggestions for the flowers," Blossom said.

436

"I know Gussie wants you to decorate the sanctuary." Actually he knew no such thing. Did it show a lack of love and commitment to toss his bride to the Widows? "But she'd want to choose the bouquets for her flowers and the bridesmaids."

"Of course," Blossom said.

"This is, after all, her wedding," Mercedes added.

On Friday evening, Adam walked outside to check out the turtle and hand Hector the keys.

"Took a little longer than Rex hoped," he started before he realized Hector hadn't heard a word of what he'd said. No, the young man was walking around the car and touching it.

Rex had done a great job. He sanded and undented the body and painted it a brilliant orange with black racing stripes. He'd replaced the bumper that had fallen off a year earlier with one that was centered and shiny.

After scrutinizing every inch of the exterior, Hector opened the door and slid inside. "No spring sticking through the seat," he said. Then he put the window down and back up, checked the clock, and turned on the radio, which now also had a slot for a CD.

Hector didn't comment on the new tires and had no idea what Rex had done to the engine but Adam felt great relief that he shouldn't have a flat or break down on the highway between San Pablo and here.

Rex had also said he might as well get a new car for all this one would cost to fix up, and it would still be an old car. But that hadn't been the deal his father had come up with.

Hector got out of the car, strode toward Adam, and threw his arms around him. "Thanks, Pops. This is great."

"Write my dad. He funded it."

"Going to pick up Bobby and Bree." Hector got back in the car and drove off.

For a moment, Adam felt a bit nostalgic. Things were changing. Hector would leave for college, the turtle ran, and life would be different. Different but good, because he and Gussie would spend their lives together and watch more of their children grow up and head for college.

With a wave at the turtle, he turned back toward the parsonage and into the kitchen, where Gussie handed him a basket of ripening tomatoes she'd picked.

"Too bad we couldn't use tomatoes for the wedding instead of flowers or in place of the cake," she said. "Might could hand them out as favors."

"Even Hector begged for a moratorium on BLT sandwiches," he said. "I never thought he'd turn down food of any kind."

The parsonage garden had yielded tomatoes,

beautifully red and delicious but far more than everyone could eat.

"Have you seen the shelves in the basement? They're filled with vegetables Mom canned."

"I stay out of the basement and the kitchen. There's so much going on, I do my wash after your mother leaves. Otherwise, I get in her way or she tries to feed me."

He looked out the window to the backyard, where Hannah was digging in her corner. He noticed her shoulders slumped. "I'm going to go out and talk to her," he said to Gussie and headed out to the yard.

When Hannah looked up, Adam stifled a gasp, because Hannah really hated people to gasp when they saw her face. She didn't look as terrible as she had when she arrived, but the glow she had around Gabe had disappeared. How could he have missed that? Oh, he knew. Gussie and the wedding distracted him greatly, but he should have noticed. He now realized he hadn't heard her laugh since she got back.

She looked back down at the soil, carefully pulling out weeds. He stooped next to her and reached out toward a plant. He drew his hand back when she slapped it. "That's not a weed."

"Sorry." He watched as she pulled a few more clumps that, to him, looked exactly like what he'd attempted to remove. "What's wrong, Sis?"

"Wrong," she said in a bright little voice, or at

least what she thought might sound like a bright voice. "Nothing. Happy as a lark."

"Sis." He knew her well enough to say nothing more.

"Why . . . ," she began. She swallowed. "I . . ."

This must be serious. Hannah was seldom at a loss for words.

"Okay, Preacher," she said. "I need to ask you something."

He nodded.

"About faith."

He'd guessed that when she called him preacher. "Go on."

"I have to go back to Africa," she said.

"But . . ."

Before he could say more, she held her hand up. "Let me finish. Now I feel God wants me to return to Kenya. I'm as surprised about this as you are. I thought I'd lost my faith, but little by little it's come back."

"Wow." He considered her words. "That makes it tough. You love Gabe but you think God is calling you to return to Kenya."

"Good job of summing that up, brother. Yes, that's it."

"It's good that you've found your faith."

"Yeah. Not that mine was nearly as strong as yours, and the horror of those years in Kenya about destroyed it. At least, that's what I thought."

"Then?" he urged her.

"Then, at the conference, I listened to the lectures and realized how much I know and how much I care for the people in Kenya, for all those I can help. I realized God gave me this brain and filled me with knowledge and I can heal a bunch of God's children." She shook her head. "Odd. I rediscovered my faith during a Power-Point presentation on updated nomenclature for H5N1 avian influenza and I don't understand what happened."

He waited.

"That's it," she said when she realized he wasn't going to say anything. "I do not understand."

"Go on. What don't you understand?"

"You know I like facts, I deal with data. I like the world to be logical, but faith is not logical." She closed her eyes and sighed. "Faith is not rational. It's not scientific but I feel it. Faith fills me but I can't quantify it. I can't explain it but I know it's there. Do you feel that way? That there's this inexplicable force pulling at you?"

"That's why I'm a minister."

"But I'm a scientist, Adam. How can I, how can anyone, explain faith in a logical or scientific way?"

"No one can. That's why it's called faith, not certainty."

Gabe studied himself in the car mirror and straightened the collar of his shirt. He'd dressed up a little but stopped short of putting on a tie. He tousled his hair a bit, then patted it down.

Why was he primping like a girl getting ready for the prom?

Because he had an idea the date with Hannah wouldn't go well.

Oh, all day he'd gone around grinning and whistling because he was in deep denial. When she'd gone to Galveston, she hadn't returned his calls. After she got back in town, she had excuse after excuse for why they couldn't go out. Each one filled him with deep foreboding.

He'd never been filled with foreboding of any kind—deep, shallow, narrow, or wide—before. No other woman had ever turned him down. Sounded conceited, but no other woman *had* turned him down for a date ever, until this week. Hannah couldn't find time for him, not an hour here or an evening there or lunch or a coffee break. Nothing until she finally called him and set this up.

Maybe he cared about her more than she cared about him. He wanted to see her every day, all day, if she'd agree. Finally, tonight, he'd see her again.

He waited for ten minutes before she came downstairs. Not that he minded. He could always talk to Gussie and Adam, although the two of them were so much in love and so excited about the wedding they weren't good company. They spent most of the time making goo-goo eyes at each other or talking about flowers or napkins.

When Hannah finally came down the back stairs and through the kitchen, he watched her expression at the moment she saw him. For a second, not even that long, he could read her face. For that tiny moment, he saw joy in her eyes and a smile quickly curved her lips before she replaced them and displayed no emotion whatsoever.

No, Gabe didn't have a good feeling about the evening.

He walked toward her and took both her hands before he leaned down to kiss her. Again, for a fleeting moment, she leaned against him and returned the kiss before she tugged her hands away and stepped back.

"Hello," she said levelly.

He couldn't allow her to get away with indifference. As she walked past him, Gabe put his arm around her shoulders. Oh, she could pull away, but she had allowed his touch. She looked up at him, her gaze caressing his lips and the curve of his chin before she twisted away.

"Bye." Hannah waved at her brother and Gussie before she headed to the door, leaving Gabe to stare after her.

But he knew, although she attempted to hide it

in her quick stride and the confidence of her movements, that she cared about him very much. She just couldn't or wouldn't or didn't want to admit it.

Why not?

Chapter Seventeen

Life had closed in on Hannah.

For a moment, she'd allowed herself to relax against Gabe. To kiss him. To drink in his beauty, knowing that within that gorgeous exterior was a great guy who helped others and who cared about her. As Hannah and Adam had said, this was a nice man and—for reasons she'd never understand—he seemed to be attracted to her.

"Where do you want to go for dinner?" he asked after he'd held the car door open for her and steadied her as she climbed up to the seat.

He made her feel loved and protected but she was a woman who didn't need to be protected. However, she'd discovered she did want to be loved.

Once in the driver's seat, he stuck the key in the ignition. "I thought we could drive to Fredericksburg. Feel like German food tonight?"

She nodded because, suddenly, her throat had closed up and she couldn't force words out.

After they'd driven for a few miles in silence, Gabe said, "How was your conference?"

A safe topic. She cleared her throat and babbled on about stuff no one outside of her field would understand, but he listened. That was the amazing thing about Gabe. He listened to her and didn't mind asking her questions—ooh, elementary questions like, "What is a spirochete bacterium?" He focused on her words politely as if he were interested. Not even she thought leptospirosis was interesting, but Gabe listened.

Then he turned and smiled. She couldn't speak anymore. He reached across the seat and took her hand. It felt so good, she couldn't pull away for a few seconds. Then she finally did.

Bringing every iota of her willpower together and reaching inside to remind herself who she was and where her future lay and who Gabe was and what God had said, she forced the words out. "I can't see you anymore."

The truck swerved a little. Gabe brought it back into the lane. He didn't say anything until they reached a wide shoulder, where he pulled off the road and stopped the truck.

"What do you mean?"

"Just that."

"You don't want to go out with me anymore?"

"I can't see you anymore," she repeated because she couldn't lie. She *wanted* to see him but she couldn't.

He sat back in the seat and looked out the windshield at a field of prickly pear cactus. A few weeks ago the deep reddish orange flowers had covered the area, but no longer. Now there was little to look at other than the spiny pads, but he kept staring at them and she couldn't read his expression.

"Why not?" he asked.

"We're very different people. We have nothing in common," she explained logically.

"Hannah." He turned toward her and tried to pull her toward him.

When she didn't allow that, he put his fingers on her chin. She could hardly pull away, not without hitting her head on something, although, looking in his face and at the pain in his eyes, she thought a bump on the head would hurt less.

"I love you," he said. "Did I misread this so badly?" He shook his head. "I thought you felt something for me."

He ran his eyes across her features. She attempted to keep them passive, uninterested.

"I know you do," he said. "You love me, too. Why won't you admit it?"

She had admitted that, at least to herself. The fact only made this so much more difficult. "I'm very attracted to you. What woman wouldn't be?" She attempted a light laugh.

"I'm not talking about any woman." His voice was serious, and his eyes still studied her face. "I'm talking about you, the woman I love. What's wrong?"

"We're very different. We both have our own lives and our own futures and plans that are"—she hardened her voice—"incompatible."

He dropped her chin. "I've never asked you to give up or change your plans," he said.

No, he hadn't, and that made this more difficult. But she knew how she felt. She knew what she could do and what she couldn't and still respect herself.

"I love you," he repeated. "And you love me. Why can't we discuss it?"

"Because we're very different people."

With that, he turned in the seat and pounded his fist on the steering wheel. "That's it? No more explanation? May I ask you one more question?" He kept his gaze on the highway before he turned to scrutinize her expression. "Do you love me? At all?"

"You're very attractive," she said. "Manly, charming, handsome, and rich. Everything a woman would want."

"But not you?"

She nodded because she knew she couldn't speak without her voice giving her away.

"Hannah Jordan, you are a coward," he said. He put the truck in gear and looked over his shoulder before he made a wide U-turn on the highway and headed back to Butternut Creek.

"That's another reason," she said. "If I married you, my name would be Hannah Jordan Borden." After the words were out, she wished she could suck them back in again. Her hiding place had always been snark and sarcasm, not humor. Adam often told her she wasn't funny. Besides, the words hadn't come out as amusing and sophisticated as she'd meant and were a huge mistake because her voice had quavered.

"I never asked you to marry me."

Oh, that hurt. The words stung but the cold, sharp edge to his voice tore her up inside. She looked at his set profile and his hard chin and bet his eyes were flinty too if she could see them.

What had she done?

"I couldn't look at another doily or napkin or tablecloth or nut cup." Adam pushed the swing on the porch of Sam's old house and covered his face.

"Suck it up," Gussie said without a bit of sympathy. "You got away easy."

He put his arm around her shoulders and massaged her arms, enjoying the peace of a Sunday evening. "Can you believe it? We're going to be married in a week. I figure the Widows have run out of questions."

"Adam, you are such an innocent. The Widows will have questions and changes all the way to the moment I walk down the aisle." She closed her eyes and leaned against his arm. "They'll probably follow me asking about some detail of the reception like the setup on the tables or placement of flowers or where we're going on our honeymoon."

"Two days in Austin, then back to work." He hugged her. "Sorry it couldn't be more romantic."

"What could be better than being with you?"

Adam watched her in repose, an expression he seldom saw with Gussie, and swept a curl from her forehead with a light touch. "You're exhausted," he said. "Go in to bed. I'll see you tomorrow."

Gussie opened her eyes and yawned. "Hate to cut our time together short but I'm going to fall asleep." She pulled him close for a kiss before they stood.

When Adam reached the parsonage a few minutes later, Hannah still sat in her chair reading. Hadn't moved for hours, he thought. Then he glanced at the clock. Nearly eleven.

"You're up late," he said.

She looked up from her book with eyes devoid of joy and vitality.

"Did you get any sleep last night?" he asked.

"Thanks, brother, for mentioning how bad I look." She stood, put her book down, and moved to the sofa. "Sit with me?"

The woman next to him didn't act like his sister at all, but whoever she was she needed comfort— or at least companionship. He put his arm around her. She leaned against him but said nothing. His arm got numb after a few minutes but he wiggled his fingers and didn't move away because a moment like this with Hannah was rare.

When she didn't say anything, he asked, "What's the matter, champ?" using his mother's childhood name for her.

Her answer was an odd groan mixed with a mirthless chuckle. "Champ. Yeah, I'm a real champ."

"Hannah?" he encouraged after a long silence.

"I took another look at my life. I decided I do not want to be Miss Birdie, alone and with children afraid of me and dogs running in the opposite direction. Of course she does good works and she's not alone and she did have a husband so, other than the grumpiness, we really aren't a bit alike."

Then she began to cry. He knew she'd cried for sick children who suffered from malnutrition, for adults slipping slowly away from AIDS, for young people riddled with bullets who'd died before they'd ever lived, and for the homeless marine who died on the street alone, but this was only the second time he'd seen her cry for herself. Her sobs broke his heart.

All he could do was pat her shoulder. That's what he did. He patted and held her, and waited and passed her the box of tissues.

"I really messed up."

He couldn't contradict her. She'd told him what she felt she had to do. Since then neither Hannah nor Gabe would talk to him about the breakup. With Hannah, silence was her preferred method of communication. With Gabe, Adam didn't want to hurt his friend, so he kept quiet. Or maybe Gabe didn't want to talk about it at all, wouldn't even if Adam asked. Whatever the reason, Adam had no idea *exactly* what had happened, but he did know both of them were miserable.

"Do you want to talk?"

Hannah wiped her eyes and shook her head but almost immediately she said, "I miss Gabe. I really love him."

"Then why did you break up with him? I know Gabe isn't stupid enough to break up with the woman he loves."

She nodded. "I didn't ask you to judge me, only to love me, to comfort me."

So he'd failed as a brother.

"Part of this is your fault, you know."

"Oh, I don't accept any blame."

"You helped me find my faith." She looked up at Adam. "Living with you and watching your faith in action, I realized I had a call, too."

"Okay, you have to go back. I understand that."

"Thanks." She gave him a wavering smile.

"I understand that you have to go back to Kenya. What did Gabe say about it when you told him?"

"I didn't."

"Don't you think it would help if you did?"

She shook her head slowly, as if she hadn't considered the possibility. "It's irrelevant," she said at last, sadly.

Hannah the stoic who thought she had to

sacrifice everything—her health, her future, and her happiness.

"Do you think he'd . . ." She turned back toward Adam.

"I think you owe it to him, and yourself, to explain. Maybe it will work out."

"I really messed up. It's already too late."

"How're the wedding plans?" Gabe asked as he and Adam played HORSE at the hoop on the church parking lot.

Adam put in a long jumper and tossed the ball back to Gabe. "Fine. I'm not interfering in any way. I stay out of discussions and run when I see the Widows."

"Good groom." Gabe bounced the ball a couple of times and shot. It hit the rim and bounced off.

So far, Gabe had H, O, R, and S. Adam had never beaten Gabe.

"You don't seem to be on today, Coach."

Gabe didn't respond.

Adam dribbled to the basket for a layup. If Gabe couldn't get that, the man had real problems. Of course, Adam already knew that.

When the ball popped from Gabe's hands on his approach to the basket, he said, "Okay, you win."

"How're you sleeping?" Adam asked.

"Fine." He shrugged. "Why?" He picked up the ball, tossed it to Adam, and headed toward his truck. He hadn't come to the parsonage in days. Didn't refuse. Just didn't call or show up.

"Hannah isn't sleeping at all well."

Gabe froze in place, then turned. "Why would you tell me that?"

"She seems unhappy," Adam stated.

His eyes wary, Gabe studied his friend. "And?"

"She said she'd made a big mistake. Said she really messed up."

"She did?" The first slightly positive expression Adam had seen in days covered his face.

"What are you going to do about that?" Adam turned and missed a ten-foot jumper.

Gabe picked up the ball on the long rebound and held it. "Go on."

"You going to be at the rehearsal dinner?"

"Don't I have to be?"

"You need to let her know who's boss."

The men looked at each other, then both laughed.

"That's exactly the way to treat her," Gabe said. "If I want to make sure that she runs off to Kenya and I stay here."

"Women fall all over you. You've dated thousands of women."

"Hardly that many."

"Why can't you figure out my sister?"

He bounced the ball. "That may be why I care about her. She's herself. She doesn't change to attract me. She's honest and caring. She doesn't give up on her beliefs to accommodate me. In fact, she's probably the most unaccommodating woman I know."

"And you find that attractive?"

"Go figure." Gabe shrugged. "I have no idea why I want to be with your sister. She's not easy to get along with. She's hardheaded and outspoken and opinionated and sometimes I don't even think she likes me."

Adam didn't even bother to contradict that.

"Okay, I know she loves me. Now I have to convince her that she likes and trusts me. That I want to be with her forever." With those words, he tossed up a shot from across the parking lot.

Swish. Nothing but net. "Think I'll head home." He dribbled the basketball as he walked off, and Adam headed back toward the parsonage. He grinned. In his efforts to get Gabe and Hannah back together, was he becoming a fifth Widow?

"Hey."

Adam turned to see a low and expensive sports car drive into the parking lot.

"Anyone know where the parsonage is?" his mother called out the window.

"Good to see you! Park here and we can walk over."

His father opened the door and leaped out. Tall, and lean—but no longer skinny—with thinning gray hair, Dad played tennis every day and liked to show off that vigor and flexibility.

"Your father rented the sports car in an effort

to regain his lost youth," Mom said. "But I can't get out of the thing."

He reached for his mother's hand and helped her from the car. She was also tall but rounded, with carefully arranged salt-and-pepper hair and blue eyes.

"Let's go inside and find Gussie, and you can meet her parents." As they walked, he said, "So you're staying in Horseshoe Bay?"

"Yes, it sounds like a nice place," Mom said.

"Great. That's not far away." He led them onto the porch and opened the door. "Hannah, our folks are here."

Then the reality of their presence hit him: His parents had come for his wedding. This was going to happen.

Miss Birdie shifted her arm in an effort to find a comfortable position. She'd stopped wearing the sling a few days earlier and would start back to work in a month when Bree had to get ready for school. Hated to admit it but she'd enjoyed being off, really loved being taken care of.

Now, on the eve of the wedding, Birdie stood in the church kitchen with Mercedes, Winnie, and Blossom as they made final preparations for the rehearsal dinner.

"Ladies, this is the proudest moment of my matchmaking life," she said.

All the Widows wore expressions of smug pride

and confidence. They had succeeded. The skinny, awkward—both socially and physically—minister they'd welcomed to Butternut Creek two years before, the young man they'd matched with numerous women until they found Gussie, the perfect match—well, that young man was getting married. They stood here together, successful matchmakers and wedding planners looking forward to tomorrow, to the culmination of their efforts.

"Blossom, you've done a wonderful job with decorations," Mercedes said.

"Yes, you have," Birdie agreed.

Peach tablecloths from Blossom's enormous collection of linens covered the tables, each with a circle of white lace in the middle. Peach-colored candles cast a soft glow from inside hurricane lamps, and white china—also from Blossom's collection—sat at each place.

Gussie's parents had insisted on catering the dinner. "Don't want to wear the church ladies out," Yvonne had said immediately after the date was chosen. "Not when you're in charge of the reception."

The caterers had placed chafing dishes and warming pans on the counter between the kitchen and the fellowship hall. Three servers stood behind the counter with serving spoons.

The Widows had nothing left to do except eat and gloat.

At a little before six, the guests began to arrive. First came Sam and Willow, one of the matchmakers' most spectacular successes.

"They left the baby with the Kowalskis," Winnie said.

Then Gabe and Hector entered with Gussie's friend Clare and her husband followed by Mattie—Reverend Patillo. Finally, the group from the parsonage appeared. Everyone looked happy and excited. Well, except for Hannah. Her hair looked nice and the slacks and shirt complemented her dark prettiness, but she looked tired. Birdie couldn't quite read her expression. Certainly she couldn't be sad the eve of her brother's wedding, could she?

As she watched, Birdie saw Hannah looking around until her gaze fell on Gabe. Then Gabe looked at her. A crackle of electricity passed between them, then each looked away quickly and ignored the other in the most obvious way.

Birdie blinked. How had she—as chief matchmaker—missed that? Gabe and the preacher's sister were in love. Must have happened in San Pablo, and clearly things weren't going well between them now. What should she do? She was fairly busy this weekend but could set aside a moment or two for matchmaking.

Then she grinned. When the two finally worked things out—and she assumed they would, because the heat in that glance promised a future—the

Widows could and would take credit. Even though at the time they'd thought their match-making efforts had been not only a failure but an embarrassment, they *had* been the first to shove these two together.

She punched Mercedes with her elbow. "Did you see that?"

Adam had rounded up the entire family to walk over to the rehearsal dinner because, right now, he couldn't take on the Widows by himself, bless their hearts. This close to getting their minister married, they were so insufferably full of themselves that everyone in town ran off whenever they saw any of the ladies.

He took Gussie's hand. In front of them walked the Miltons and his parents. He'd decided they could run interference. Then he glanced at Hannah. Janey, who seemed to have the magic touch with his bristly sister, had forced her to curl her hair and had chosen a sparkly red shirt for her to wear with tailored slacks and a pair of gold sandals Janey had purchased for her at the Dollar Tree. Janey held her hand and pulled her along.

Despite looking terrific in her outfit and with the circles under her eyes concealed by makeup Gussie had forced on her, Hannah looked terrified.

Served her right.

"Isn't this beautiful," Gussie said as she entered the fellowship hall.

But Adam didn't answer because Hannah had grabbed his arm and pointed toward Gabe's truck. "What should I do?" she whispered.

Adam patted her hand. "As you often tell me, you're a grown-up. Take control of your life."

Oh, sure. As if taking control of her life in an area so far outside her experience would be easy. Attracting men and apologizing or admitting error had never counted as her strong points. In fact, if she were a gymnast and if relationships were the balance beam, she'd receive a minus score on that apparatus after having spent most of her time falling off.

Then she saw him, gorgeous in a crisp white shirt that stretched over broad shoulders. Of course, everything Gabe wore stretched over broad shoulders. Not unexpectedly, the sight of him made her breathless, which showed how stupidly she behaved around him.

For a moment, their eyes caught, and emotion stretched out between them like a lit fuse. She looked at her sandals.

Coward.

From the corner of her eye she could tell he'd started toward them. Well, of course. He had to greet the bridal couple and their families.

"Gussie." He nodded toward her nearly sister-in-law. "Yvonne"—he took her hand and kissed her cheek—"nice to see you." He gave Janey a hug, waved at Adam and Hector, and shook her parents' hands before he turned toward her. In the low voice that turned her brain to scrambled eggs, he said, "Hannah." One word, only two syllables, and she wanted to throw herself at him.

She was weak. She said, "I don't know who I am."

Had she really said that, out loud? She didn't think so because no one had turned toward her, but Gabe still watched her. Maybe he'd heard the words. She smiled at him. One normal action.

Then he took her hand. Startled, she pulled it back. Good heavens, she'd acted like a frightened virgin—which was, of course, exactly what she was. However, she'd hoped to look a little more poised.

"Hey," she said, because she spoke so eloquently around him. Logic told her that becoming either a babbling idiot or a silent jerk didn't show her best side.

But she didn't care. She felt that, if they ever managed to be together—fat chance—if he ever kissed her again, everything would be fine. She'd be able to talk to him in words that made sense and sentences with all the necessary parts of speech.

Mercedes was doing something with the little cards on two of the round tables. Finished, she nodded at Miss Birdie, who then waved everyone toward the tables as she said, "We have place cards at the tables."

Only when she reached her chair did she realize what had happened. Mercedes had switched the place cards; she was sitting next to Gabe. For a moment, she considered changing the seats around, putting herself at another table or between . . .

Too late. Gabe arrived at his place and was greeting the others.

Hannah guessed the food tasted great because everyone commented on the lettuce wedges and the sirloin tips, but she didn't know because Gabe sat next to her. To her left were Sam and Willow who'd been married for over a year and adored each other.

"Isn't she gorgeous?" Sam asked the entire table. "She just had a baby and is more beautiful than ever."

"Oh, Sam." A blush covered Willow's cheeks.

"Wonderful to see such a happy couple," Gabe said before he glanced at the table where Gussie and Adam sat. "Isn't love wonderful?"

Rounding out the table were the organist and his wife, a very quiet couple who said little even as the Petersons and Gabe attempted to chat with them. Gamely the three kept up a conversation. Hannah listened and thought of comments long after the topic had changed.

When the meal was over—finally!—everyone headed toward the sanctuary for the rehearsal.

The only catch came at the beginning, when Mattie said, "Where are you, father of the bride? You need to give—"

Gussie interrupted to say, "I don't want my father to give me away."

The Widows—who, Hannah thought, really had nothing to do with the service but seemed determined to control it—all gasped from the middle of the center aisle, which they'd claimed.

Miss Birdie hurried toward the back of the church where Gussie stood. "You don't want your father to give you away? It's tradition."

"I know," Gussie attempted to explain. "But I'm over thirty and the idea of my father, as much as I love him, handing me over to another man seems absurd."

"If I know anything about her, Birdie," Henry said, "I know she's independent and stubborn and can take care of herself."

"Preacher . . ." Miss Birdie turned toward where Adam stood in the front.

"Whatever Gussie wants is fine with me," Adam said.

"Yes, Birdie," Mercedes said with an edge to her voice. "This is, after all, Gussie's wedding."

"Her wedding," Blossom added while Winnie nodded.

With that insurrection, Miss Birdie moved

toward a pew to sit and the rehearsal began anew.

"Let's start over," Mattie said. "We need the groomsmen and the groom to go back in the hall."

The short time spent in practicing hadn't been all that uncomfortable, not until the end when Gabe escorted Hannah back to the narthex. Knowing how her resolve weakened around him, she'd pulled her arm from his and hurried away to hide behind Gussie. Inconsiderately, the bride kept moving around to greet and thank everyone.

When everything had been discussed and agreed to and everyone began to say good-bye, Hannah left the wandering protection of Gussie's presence and headed out the door.

As she began to stride toward the parsonage, thinking she was safe, Gabe said, "Wait up, Hannah." She hadn't noticed how close he was. Usually so aware of where he was, how could she not have realized that? He'd sneaked up on her. She should have been more aware of her surroundings.

"I'll walk Hannah home," Gabe announced to Adam, who stood at the door to the sanctuary.

Adam nodded. "Take your time."

Take your time? Hannah glanced between Gabe and her brother and bridled. They'd set her up.

She became even more aware of the treachery as everyone rushed from the church and flowed quickly around and past the two of them, leaving her alone with Gabe and the sound of triumphant laughter from the Widows.

"Your brother tells me there's a little garden on the side of the building. Why don't we sit there and chat?"

"I . . . I . . ." While she fumbled for words, Gabe took her hand and gently led her around the church.

A light outside the church shone on the small wrought-iron table and a couple of chairs. A streetlight farther away added a bit more illumination, enough that she could see his face and his square chin and broad shoulders and great shirt. She sat down and turned to study the bushes around the tiny slab and wondered what they were because she could not look at Gabe.

For a few minutes he didn't say anything, only sat on the other spindly chair and held her hand. She refused to embarrass herself by pulling it away again so she concentrated instead on keeping her heart rate and breathing steady. As a doctor, she could recognize elevated respiration. As a woman, she had no idea how to regulate it.

"You know," Gabe said. "I'm a scientist."

"No, you're not," Hannah blurted and lifted her eyes to his face. A mistake. Looking at him always interfered with her thought process.

He ignored her statement. "I like to know *why* people do things."

"Wait." She held up a hand. "That's what *I* say."

"I know," he agreed agreeably. "But what you said makes a lot of sense. Why don't you tell me—because I'm deeply interested in the scientific method—why don't you tell me why you broke up with me?"

She opened her mouth to explain before she realized she couldn't.

After nearly a minute of silence as he watched her expressions, she knew he saw her complete inability to explain flitter across her face. He said, "Do you love me? I'm counting on you to tell the truth."

"Not fair. You can't use my words against me."

"Sure I can," he said.

His complete disregard for her rules took the wind out of her sails.

Then he put his hand on her cheek and looked in her eyes. "Do you love me?"

His touch and the sincerity in his voice left her floundering in still water. She nodded.

"You know, I like to know reasons. I'd like to know why you love me."

He wasn't going to make this easy for her. "I love you because you're smart and a really nice person and, most important, I don't scare you. And . . ." She gulped in air. "And I know this is shallow but you're gorgeous. When you smile, I can't breathe."

So, of course, he smiled and she thought she'd pass out.

"I don't know why I'm telling you this. I never tell people how I feel. I don't communicate." The words tumbled out and she had to clench her teeth from giving away even more.

"Okay, you love me. Then would you please tell me why you broke up with me?" he asked.

She'd prefer to walk away, to not have to explain this because she loved Gabe so much and hated, hated, to hurt him. She'd heard pain in his voice, seen it in his eyes, which was strange because she was usually clueless about other people's emotions.

This was no time for cowardice. She cleared her throat and said, "Because I have to return to Kenya."

"And?"

"Did you hear me? I have to go back to Kenya. I believe God called me to return."

"Okay." He paused. "And?"

"And what?"

"Did God tell you to go alone?"

"No." She shook her head. "But who would want to go with me?" When he continued to study her, she added, "You wouldn't want to."

"Did you ask me?"

"No. Why would you want to go to a refugee camp when you have everything here?"

"I wouldn't have you," he said simply and so sincerely, Hannah could feel her heart beating wildly.

"I'm not the right woman for you. I'm hard to get along with and push myself to succeed and shove others away and . . ."

"That's what I told your brother."

"You told my brother I'm hard to get along with?"

"I also told him you may not be the most perfect woman in the world but you happen to be the woman I love. You're the perfect woman for me."

"Oh," she said, feeling a little awed but needing to understand the whole thing. "But I don't need a man to take care of me if that's what you think."

"Why would anyone who knows you think you do? I don't want to take care of you." He paused and glanced across the lawn. "I don't know how to say this." He turned back. "I see how much you care and how much pressure you put on yourself. I want to be with you, to take your mind off of the horror you see. I want to love you and hold you and support you. I want to be with you and serve, too, in whatever way I can. What's wrong with that?"

When she didn't answer, he said, "Okay, let's make this simple: If you're going to Kenya, that's where I want to be. Does that make sense?" he asked, his lips hovering over hers.

It did.

● ● ●

On Saturday afternoon, three of the Widows stood together in the fellowship hall and looked around.

"This will be the biggest social event in Butternut Creek for years," Blossom said.

"We won't have enough room for everyone," Mercedes added. "Some of the guests are going to have to stand outside."

"Don't forget, it's also a religious event," Birdie reminded them. "This is a wedding."

"The biggest wedding in years," Blossom said, completely missing Birdie's point.

"Here I am," Winnie called as she hurried in, her new granddaughter, Sam and Willow's baby girl, in her arms. "It certainly looks lovely in here," she said.

Bree and Mac had taken the peach tablecloths home and washed them. Now one covered the table graced with the four-tier wedding cake, white frosting with peach-colored flowers sprinkled across it. Chairs had been spread out in front of the cake table, and the gift table was exactly where they'd planned to put it. Some of the men had placed folding chairs outside under trees on the narrow strip of grass and the edge of the parking lot for the overflow as well as opening the gates into the backyard of the parsonage to accommodate even more.

"What's next for us?" Blossom asked, her

little pink mouth turned down. "Haven't we accomplished everything we set out to do?"

"This isn't the end," Miss Birdie said. "The preacher and Gussie are going to have children. We'll have to teach Sunday school."

"And we'll need to find them someone to marry when they grow up," Mercedes said.

"I'm not ready to give up yet," Winnie said. "There's still Mattie Patillo. We have to find her a husband."

"If we don't do that soon, she's going to lose all that sweet prettiness, won't be able to attract a man," Mercedes said.

"On top of that, she's getting too old to reproduce," Birdie added.

"But we've tried everyone." Winnie bounced the baby up and down. "Where will we find a single man?"

"We can't give up," Blossom said. "I've had so much fun."

"Then we'll have to get busy, look farther away, maybe even go into Austin," Mercedes said.

How four elderly woman would find a single man in Austin, Birdie didn't know. None of them had the slightest idea of how to pick up a man at a bar, and no man would be lured by four old ladies walking down the street.

Still, she wouldn't correct her. They'd celebrate today and work on Reverend Patillo tomorrow.

• • •

At one forty, Adam looked out the bedroom window toward the church. The parking lot was full. He recognized Charley's truck and Farley's car and Father Joe's among many he didn't recognize.

He straightened his tie, one Blossom had given him, shrugged on his jacket, and glanced in the mirror over the dresser. He smiled. Actually, if it didn't sound so un-macho, he gleamed with happiness. Today he'd marry Gussie.

"Hector?" He pounded on the door then moved down the hall and knocked on the next door. "Janey?"

Both stepped into the hall, Hector in the suit Adam's parents had purchased for him and Janey in a dress of pink cotton Ouida had made for her.

He hugged each before he turned toward the attic steps. "Hannah, are you ready?" he shouted up to the attic.

When she started down the steps, Adam smiled again. "You look beautiful."

The persimmon cotton swirled around her legs and made her look like a flame. When she arrived downstairs, he gave her his arm and the four of them went downstairs and headed toward the church.

"Look at all the cars, Pops. Twenty minutes before the ceremony and the parking lot's full, with cars lining both sides of the street."

Adam waved at his friends who covered the sidewalk in front of the parsonage and the church and grinned. Today he was marrying Gussie.

Gussie looked at herself in the mirror in a classroom that had been turned into a bride's room by the Widows. The dress looked wonderful, like her. When they heard the music begin from the organ, she lined the three attendants up. Clare wore peach, Willow wore deep coral, and the persimmon was wonderful on Hannah.

Then Yvonne looked out into the hall. They had to head out the side door and over to the entrance of the church. Not the handiest way for a bride to get to the sanctuary, but knowing Adam would be waiting for her made everything wonderful.

"Here are your bouquets." Yvonne handed one to each attendant and the lovely cascade of coral and peach roses to Gussie.

Thank you, most loving and generous God, for this moment, for Adam and our lives together.

"Are we ready, ladies?" Gussie asked. With their nods, they headed toward the entrance to the sanctuary.

"Do you have the ring, Sam?"

"Calm down," Adam's best man said. "I've had it the last twenty times you've asked." He held out his hand to show the tiny ring box.

472

When they heard a chord from the organ, Adam led the men from his office, across the hall, and into the sanctuary. He looked toward the chancel area where Mattie stood in her white robe, holding her worship manual. She looked very ministerial until she winked at him.

Then the music began and his father escorted his mother into a pew. After a few chords from the organ, Hannah came from the narthex and walked toward them, glowing with happiness. Willow came next, followed by Clare. After her, Henry escorted Yvonne down the aisle and they settled into a pew.

Impatiently, Adam looked toward the narthex but couldn't see Gussie. He turned toward Janey when she stood on the other side of the chancel. In her lovely, clear voice, she sang "Whither Thou Goest." As she sang, gratitude filled Adam. The young man he considered his son stood only a foot away. His daughter sang in front of the church. He stood with his two best friends. In a few minutes, Mattie would join him and Gussie in marriage.

All of that was terrific, but he wanted to see Gussie.

As Janey sang, he studied the congregation. The Widows sat in the back, ready to leap up before the end of the service because they were, after all, in charge of the reception. The Kowalskis must have come early because they sat immediately behind his parents with Carol and Gretchen fighting for the aisle seat and Lucy in her father's arms. Sam's father, the general, kept an eye on Leo and Nick. His minister friends were sprinkled throughout the congregation, as were Gussie's friends from Roundville and camp and area churches. There were chairs in the side aisles. People stood against the back wall and the deacons had placed chairs on one side of the center aisle, leaving a narrow passage for the bridesmaids and Gussie to come through. Still, there must be people outside.

When Janey finished singing, the chords of the wedding march began and the congregation stood. Adam looked to the door where he knew from the rehearsal Gussie was supposed to be, but he couldn't see her over everyone's heads. So he took a step and then another until he stood at the head of the aisle and looked down at her standing in the doorway. She smiled at him, that wonderful, loving Gussie smile he adored, and walked toward him. His life clicked into place and stretched out ahead of him with Gussie next to him. They'd have children—maybe not the number the Widows hoped for but enough to fill the parsonage with laughter and life. They'd serve the community and go to camp and respond to emergencies and live happily and joyfully, blessed by God and surrounded by family and the people of Butternut Creek. This moment was the beginning of that promise and those adventures.

When she reached him, Adam took Gussie's hand. Together they turned toward Mattie.

"Friends and family," the minister said. "Those of us who love Gussie and Adam have gathered here to celebrate their love, to witness the joining of their lives before God . . ."

Reading Group Guide

Discussion Questions

1. Gussie has put off choosing a date for the wedding. Why do you think this is? Why did she suddenly decide to set it? Have you ever made a choice during a difficult or frightening time? Did you feel as if God was leading you in that direction?

2. Bree and Hector are heading off to college. How does Adam feel about Hector's leaving? Why is Janey worried? Do you believe Miss Birdie has accepted Bree's leaving? How have you handled the departure of someone you love?

3. Why does Adam dread counseling others? This happened in *The Welcome Committee of Butternut Creek* when Sam came in for a talk. Have you ever felt that way when a friend or family member comes to you with a problem—or if you need to approach them? Why does Adam go ahead and counsel his sister? Does he talk to her as a brother or minister or both? For Adam, are those two roles hard to distinguish? What did you think of his

way of reaching Hannah when she didn't want to hear him?

4. Hannah believes her goals and dreams have vanished. Has that happened to you? If so, how did you handle that? Did you pray or talk to someone you trusted? Did that help? If so, how?

5. How would you deal with a friend or family member who feels as if his or her dreams have been dashed? What would you say? How would you respond to their depression?

6. Gabe is very good-looking and talented. He seems to have lived a charmed life. Have you ever envied someone whose life seems perfect? How did that feel? Does anyone have a perfect life?

7. How did the following people help Hannah when she returned to the United States?
   a. Adam
   b. Janey
   c. Gabe

8. When Hector first came to live in the parsonage, he didn't have a high opinion of churches. How has that changed? How does Hector show his appreciation of the church

and the congregation? In what ways do you attempt to reflect the nature and goals of a church or of groups you belong to?

9. Contrast Adam and his father. How do you think Adam became the man he is? How did Hannah react to her father's expectations?

10. Adam feels guilty about his love of several possessions. Did this make sense to you? Why or why not? Why do you think Adam felt that way? Do you believe a Christian's having nice possessions is all right or is it wrong? Why?

11. From working in the refugee camp, Hannah believed she'd lost her faith and wondered where God was in the midst of suffering. Where can we find meaning in the midst of tragedy and loss? Does God cause suffering? Why do you believe this?

12. Where have you found strength during times of sorrow and crisis? Do you have a favorite Bible verse that helps you at these times? Psalm Twenty-Three speaks to many people about God's steadfast love and eternal care. Does it lead you? If so, what lines or passages are particularly helpful?

13. How do people you know handle difficult times? Have any turned away from God? Did you find a way to support friends who hurt? How? Were you able to speak a word of healing or show how God worked through you for their recovery? If so, what did you say or do?

Center Point Large Print
600 Brooks Road / PO Box 1
Thorndike ME 04986-0001 USA

(207) 568-3717

US & Canada:
1 800 929-9108
www.centerpointlargeprint.com